CITY OF DUST

Joe Topliffe

CITY OF DUST

Copyright © 2017 by Joe Topliffe

The following is a work of fiction. The story, characters, setting and events are the product of the author's imagination. Any resemblance to real persons, living or dead, events or locations is completely coincidental.

ISBN-13: 978-1974587278

ISBN-10: 1974587274

No part of this book may be photocopied, reproduced or distributed (electronically or otherwise) without the prior written permission of the author.

To my beautiful wife, Hollie.

Thank you for sacrificing so much quality time so I could fulfil this crazy ambition.

CHAPTER ONE

Quiet. Everything had been quiet for hours now. Darkness had consumed the city, but for the luminous circle of the full moon and gentle twinkling of the stars. Cyrus took a moment to count the ones he could see from his restricted viewpoint. He didn't have the clearest angle to recite all the constellations, but with the lack of cloud cover that cold night he imagined they would all be out shining bright.

He began to ponder the situation he was in. How long had he been down here? It was definitely daytime when he climbed into the hole, and it was now well into the night. Cyrus rubbed his arms to keep warm. The thin t-shirt he was wearing had been just right for the warm temperature during the day, however at night it seemed to drop what felt like twenty degrees. His exposed arms had goose bumps all over, and his ripped cargo pants offered minimal protection from the chill. He felt his hand brush against something cold on his wrist. It felt heavy and steel-like. He tapped it twice and suddenly remembered it was the watch he had salvaged from a pile of old junk that same day. It had been so long since he had last worn a watch, he wasn't yet used to the feel of it against his skin. He looked down at his wrist and tilted the watch to catch the light of the moon through a gap in the rubble. He caught a flash of the analogue display and exhaled a short sigh of relief. It still worked.

Half nine. I've been here quite a while.

He began to re-evaluate his surroundings.

The place was dark, empty, lifeless. It made Cyrus feel lonely and helpless. But despite all its gloom, the quiet meant it was safe, for now.

A piercing light entered the hole, beneath the rubble Cyrus had been hiding in. The light flickered and danced in his vision. Cyrus squinted and tried to focus on where it was coming from. Another light appeared and seemed to fix on his position. He could feel his heart beginning to race, and a cold feeling grasped his whole body. Were they back? Had they found him?

Cyrus sunk slowly into the hole and closed his eyes. Maybe they hadn't seen him. Maybe they'd give up and move on. Fear began to take hold and he could feel his hands shaking as he caught sight of something shimmering around his neck. It was the crystal necklace his father had once given him. He wrapped both hands around it to cover it up. He knew it would reflect the light and give away his position. He started to whisper to himself, praying that he would be kept safe.

A few moments later, a sound echoed some way away from him. Cyrus couldn't make out what it was. Was it human? His eyes widened as he focused on where it had come from.

The sound came again, this time a little closer.

'Helloooo?' The sound was muffled through the rubble. It was definitely human, but it wasn't clear enough to know who it was coming from.

'Helloooo?' The sound came again, much closer this time.

Cyrus could almost recognise who the voice belonged to. He knew this was no foe, perhaps his companions had made it out alive after all.

'Cyrus, are you there?' Cyrus sat bolt upright. He knew this voice. A wave of calm cascaded down from his head to his toes as he knew he was safe.

'Rowley, over here!' he yelped. His voice was hoarse and stifled as he hadn't spoken in a while. He suddenly realised how thirsty he was. His water bottle had dried up sometime that morning.

'Cyrus?' the voice replied, somewhat in shock. 'Guys, he's over here!' He could feel footsteps running towards him, echoing around the rubble like a stampede. Cyrus squinted again as more lights shone over him. He put his hands out in front of him to shield his eyes. At last a hand swooped in and pulled him out of the hole.

'Boy are we glad to see you!' Rowley exclaimed. 'We've been looking all over for you. How long have you been in here?' Cyrus looked at his surroundings and winced at the torchlights blinding him. 'Stop pointing those at him!' Rowley barked, and one by one the lights started to move down towards the floor around them. Cyrus tried to remember back to when he had lost contact with his friends.

'A... I... I thin...' he began to cough and splutter as he spoke. Rowley reached into his pocket and fumbled around.

'Damn, I'm out too. Can someone give him some water please?' He fired a glance at the three other companions that had gathered around.

'I have some left,' one piped up, as she reached for her belt and produced a half-filled water bottle. Rowley grasped it with both hands and passed it to Cyrus. Cyrus began to sip the

3

water, the sensation of the cool liquid trickling down his throat being the one simple pleasure he'd had all day. The more he drank, the more he wanted. His instincts took over and he started to glug.

'Careful Cyrus, that's all we have left,' warned Jennifer, rather sheepishly. Cyrus could sense the sympathy in her voice, despite her caution. Despite her generosity, Jennifer had always been one of the more resourceful members of the group. He twisted the cap back on the bottle and stretched out his arm to give it back to her.

'Thanks, Jennifer.' Cyrus wiped his mouth and cleared his throat. Rowley beamed at his reunited friend.

'So, how long?' he pursued.

'Since the attack. When the mechs ambushed us, I got separated.'

A shadowy figure stood behind Rowley chipped in.

'Yeah dude, I saw that. One of those things almost had you for dinner.' There was a shared sense of uneasiness around the group. Cyrus looked at the figure and raised his eyebrows. Making jokes was Zion's way of dealing with just about anything, but maybe this wasn't the best time for it.

'Yeah, something like that,' Cyrus continued. 'I got cut off as everyone made their way into cover. One of those panthers clocked me and started to chase. I knew I wouldn't make it to you, there was just too much open ground. So I headed for a building to my right and tried to lose it.'

'And we ended up losing *you*,' joked Zion. Rowley scowled and waved for Cyrus to continue.

'And that's pretty much it, I think,' said Cyrus. 'Luckily the building was so run down that bits of it had collapsed everywhere. It made it impossible for the mech to get in after me. After I lost it I found this hole. Looked as good a place as any to wait it out.'

'God I hate those panthers,' Jennifer sighed. 'Why do they have to be so damn fast? I guess whoever made them didn't think two legs were enough?'

'They were built for recon, weren't they?' suggested Zion. 'They would need to be fast for that. Now there's no war and no handlers I guess they have nothing better to do than hunt around in packs and scare the living crap out of us.'

'You can say that again.'

'Anyway, glad you're safe, Cyrus. Let's get you home.' Rowley offered a hand to help Cyrus walk. His legs had gotten pretty stiff so he needed to lean on a friend, at least for the first few yards.

As they started making their way back, Cyrus realised there was one more companion who hadn't spoken a word since their reunion. Guy was usually quiet, but he seemed particularly reserved this evening. He had joined the colony a few weeks ago, lost and alone with nowhere else to turn. He didn't speak much of where he came from, just that he was glad to be in a safer place now. It must have been hard for him; a fifteen year old boy wandering the streets of Novasburgh by himself. Today was his first time out hunting for salvage. Some of the group thought it might be too soon for him at his age, but he wanted to help, and they really needed it. The general feeling was that if you were strong enough to hold a plasma rifle, you were ready enough for a salvage run. He'd been through a lot, as they all had. He probably had a lot of things going through his head right now. The mech attack obviously didn't help.

'How you holding up, Guy?' Zion chirped. His ability to keep things light-hearted was astounding.

'Yeah, I'm fine,' Guy mumbled dismissively. Zion cast an eye back to Cyrus.

'He's been pretty quiet since the attack. Understandable, first timer an' all.'

**

They'd been walking back home for what felt like hours, but as Cyrus glanced at his watch he could see it'd only been twenty minutes. He shook his wrist and wondered whether the device had given up on him. Then, not a second later, he noticed the minute counter change. Cyrus shrugged and looked up at the starry sky. He used to spend hours looking up to the sky as a kid, daydreaming about space travel and otherworldly adventures. He imagined that there were other species out there, and one day he would meet them. Those were happier times, thinking about the future and what might be, but lately all he could think about was the past.

He'd heard stories about how the world had heated up over generations, to a point where the daytime became unbearably hot, and the nights, though cold, became almost a welcome reprieve. He hadn't travelled much around the country, let alone abroad, so he didn't know to what extent that was true for the rest of the world.

It had been nearly seven months since the ten-year long war ended, after which the city of Novasburgh was left in tatters; a prime example of the fallout of the conflict that destroyed society as Cyrus once knew it. Artificial intelligence robots were created by the government, dubbed as the 'Future of Policing'. The government claimed that weaponsing these robots, officially named *mechs*, would provide a more efficient means of keeping the people safe.

An organisation called *The Mech Initiative Resistance*, or *MIRE*, opposed the mechs, believing they were a disaster waiting to happen. They campaigned across the world against the program, protesting peacefully at first before realising that the only way to stop the mechs was to take them down by force. This led to ten years of fighting, by which time the reason for conflict in the first place became sketchy to everyone involved. All Cyrus knew was that the government fought MIRE, utilising their mechs to do so. Both sides were entangled in war, each reacting to the next assault from the other side, until everything was torn apart. Those that survived the war were left to live in a barren world where half-destroyed skyscrapers lined the skyline, and the laws of society hung from a thread.

The mechs were the most terrifying things Cyrus had ever seen; robotic monstrosities of metal and teeth. Or were the teeth made of metal? Cyrus hadn't had the misfortune of getting close enough to find out. They were stationed in every major city to eliminate any threat caused by MIRE, and the result was devastating. Now, in the aftermath of the war, mechs patrolled the streets, hunting anyone they could find, regardless of allegiance. They didn't need to eat, they didn't need anything. They were built for war and killing is all they were programmed to do. With the mech handlers gone, killed during the conflict, the mechs now roamed free. Cyrus had never met anybody who knew how to destroy them; he'd never met anyone who even knew how to so much as weaken them.

The government had focused so much effort on getting these robotic soldiers out into the world that the process was rushed and the technology that went into them was flawed. It seemed that there was nobody left with the knowledge of how to shut them down. The lack of a fail-safe was astonishing.

'We're here!' Cyrus's daydreaming was suddenly broken by Rowley's enthusiastic voice. 'Home sweet home.'

The outline of a shopping mall appeared in the distance. Cyrus and his friends had called it home since the end of the war, when the mechs ran free and society fell apart. Although ransacked, the place had so far remained safe from mech and bandit attacks. Cyrus was glad to be home, but he couldn't shake the thought of having to go back out in the wilderness of the city another day.

CHAPTER TWO

On arrival at the shopping mall, the group were greeted by several friendly faces. Jennifer's younger sister April was the first to reach them.

'You're back!' she exclaimed. 'You'd been gone so long, we were all worried.'

'We ran into some trouble and we lost Cyrus for a while, but we're fine now. It's good to be home,' replied Jennifer, as she hugged her sister. Accompanying April were Doug, Gabriel and Jane, a group of survivors who had recently joined the colony. Doug was in his late twenties, but he had the appearance of a teenager. He was short and slim in build, which gave him a juvenile likeness of sorts, not to mention the spots on his face and shaggy blond locks of hair that sprawled out of his trucker hat. His appearance was in stark contrast to that of Gabriel, who was a giant of a man with a large dark beard that matched the dark pigment of his skin. He had been a soldier in the war, but deserted his fleet when he lost faith in the cause.

He stepped in to take a heavy bag from Rowley, while his companions helped share the rest of the load. Cyrus breathed a sigh of relief as others rushed over to help him inside. The group then started to make their way into the shopping mall to set down their backpacks and weapons.

'We ran into some mechs the day before we reached this place,' said the deep, gruff voice of Gabriel. 'We didn't think there would be anybody anywhere near here.'

'But we're glad we found y'all when we did,' Jane added enthusiastically. Her southern drawl was unmistakable; a telling sign of her upbringing. Proud of the small farm town she came from, she had often referred to herself as a cowboy, if only to ward off similar jokes from others. She was tall and stick thin, the bottoms of her trousers barely touching her ankles. She had a fair complexion, bordering on pale, which was dotted with small clusters of freckles on her cheeks. She always wore her ginger hair in a ponytail.

'Just about how many mechs we talking?' asked Rowley inquisitively.

'About half a dozen I'd say. Quick ones too.'

'Yeah, that could have been the same pack we just had the pleasure of meeting,' replied Cyrus. 'Those quick ones, we call them *panthers*.'

'Huh,' Doug chuckled. 'Sounds about right.'

Jane spotted that Guy seemed unusually quiet as they walked through the entrance of the mall. She weaved in and out of the group so she could walk alongside him.

'Hey, are you alright?' she asked plainly. 'You seem a little quieter than your usual self. Now I know I haven't known you that long, but I find that I'm pretty good at picking up stuff like this.'

'I'm fine, don't worry about me,' Guy replied coldly. Jane's face contorted as she frowned at his response.

'Well alrighty then,' she chirped, trying to maintain her positivity. 'You know where to find me if you wanna talk.' She knew there was something bothering Guy. Her intuition and ability to read other people was discovered in the underground poker clubs she frequented in her early twenties. Some of the other players would accuse her of cheating, and claimed she must have looked at their cards when they went to the bathroom. Her friends joked that she had mind reading powers, like some sort of superhero.

Jane always had a fascination with human behaviour, and during the war she'd dreamt of going to university and studying psychology. For some reason it never really panned out, and by the end of the war any hopes of that were dashed. She was a warm person with wisdom beyond her thirty-three years, and most importantly she had an incredible temperament that allowed her to keep cool in the face of plain rudeness.

Zion tapped her on the shoulder. 'Don't worry about him, he's been cranky ever since the mech attack.' He lowered his voice to a whisper so as not to alert Guy. 'I figured he was just scared or something. The kid's never been in that kind of situation before. It's his first time out with a salvage team.'

Jane nodded in acceptance and they followed the group into the mall.

**

The corridors leading into the mall were dark and narrow. There were a number of worn posters on the walls advertising various products that were once sold there. Cyrus glanced at one of a small boy playing with a model space rocket, which reminded him of his childhood. Before the war started, humanity was making great steps towards space travel, but they hadn't quite perfected it for commercial flights. Maybe if the world were to get back on its feet they'd find a way.

As they moved further into the complex the corridor slowly became wider, until it merged into a large opening. Cyrus could suddenly hear a mass of voices from a crowd of people dispersed around the place. He looked up at the high glass ceiling in the centre of the mall, and the floors above where they were standing. Shops lined the edges of all three floors; the display windows of which were mostly smashed. The power to this place had long been cut, leaving the inside in darkness, but for a few small exposed areas the light could find through the broken glass ceiling. He tried to envision the whole place completely full of people, like it once was; a bustling inner city.

This home that he'd known for the last few months had remained safe this long, it didn't seem like an altogether out of this world idea for it to become a safe haven for humans for a long time to come. But for now only the ground floor was occupied, with a few sleeping tents set up on the first floor. Cyrus wondered how many people could live here. There were about fifty of them, and it definitely had room for more.

He noticed the dim light of a fire burning out of an old metal barrel to his right. The smoke drifted up from the flames and rose high towards the glass ceiling, where the smashed panels of the skylight allowed it to escape. They passed a few more familiar faces, who briefly stopped their chatter to give a quick thumbs up to their arrival, before continuing their conversations again. As the group walked further into the centre he could make out more fires and even more people laughing and conversing around them. It was as if the people had completely forgotten, even just momentarily, of the dangers outside.

'Hey, Cyrus!' A figure came running towards him. The light from the fire illuminated them, and Cyrus could see who it was. Her wavy caramel hair bounced around her shoulders as she raced to him. Cyrus caught a glimpse of her bright smile, which warmed his heart. She leapt into his arms, knocking him off his weary feet and flat on his back.

'What happened to you?' asked a concerned Mia. 'You said you'd be right back, but you've been gone all day. We were all really worried.' Cyrus slowly got back to his feet, a little dazed as he rubbed his head.

'I know, it was supposed to be a normal food run but we got ambushed by a pack of panthers.'

'I heard there were mechs nearby. They're getting closer to home now.'

'Luckily it looks like it's the same pack that Doug, Gabriel and Jane ran into before they found the mall.'

'Well let's hope so,' sighed Mia. 'I'd hate to think there are any more out there, particularly since I'm supposed to be going on a salvage run tomorrow. Anyway, let's get you some water, you must be thirsty.' She gestured to the empty bottle strapped to his belt.

**

The group settled down and began to cook what little food they had managed to find from their day. Surprisingly there were still a few tins of food left to keep in the storage area for the following morning. Rowley offered a blanket to Cyrus and Mia, who were sat together. He was met with another of Mia's beaming smiles, and then proceeded to warm his hands by the fire.

'Such a messed up world we live in, isn't it?' he said, matter of fact. 'I mean, it's unbearably hot during the day, and as soon as night comes it's time to get the blankets out. How exactly does that make sense?' There was a short pause as nobody responded, and his comment was met only with tired looks.

'I hear that!' called a voice from across the room. Jennifer walked up to Rowley and kissed him on the cheek. 'But please warn me if you're going to rant on like that all night, because I actually want to get some sleep.' She ushered him away, leaving Cyrus and Mia to talk.

'How's your hand doing?' Cyrus asked, turning his attention to Mia and the bandage around her wrist. 'You said you're going on a salvage run tomorrow?'

He remembered back to a few days before, when Mia had hurt her hand after falling badly on the way back from a salvage run. Her group had stumbled across a lone mech, and in the process of trying to bring it down her plasma rifle had backfired, throwing her into the air. There were a few temperamental weapons the group had salvaged on their outings, but it wasn't clear which ones were faulty until they were fired. Mia had drawn the short straw in this case.

'It's OK I suppose,' she replied, unwrapping the bandage for Cyrus to see. The skin looked blue with bruising and she winced as he gently touched it.

'Still looks pretty swollen if you ask me,' he offered. 'I don't think you should be going back out there so soon.'

'We all have our part to play Cyrus. Everybody's tired, everybody's hungry. Everybody has an injury of some sort, we just have to put on a brave face. Besides, if I don't go someone will have to go in my place. It's not fair on them, and what if something were to happen to them? I can't face that guilt.' Mia's compassion was one of his favourite things about her. Her stubbornness on the other hand was not.

There was a protective part of Cyrus that wanted to keep her inside and out of danger for as long as possible.

'I understand,' he managed to say at last. 'But if you can't handle a gun, not even a proton pistol, then you shouldn't be allowed to go out there. It isn't safe. Please wait until your hand is better.'

Mia smiled and nodded, then rested her head on Cyrus's shoulder. She placed her hand over the crystal hanging from his neck, and as she did so it started to shine a pale blue colour.

'We will find them, you know?' she said softly.

'I hope so, Mia. I hope so.'

CHAPTER THREE

Darkness entered the shopping mall and a howling wind whistled through Cyrus's tent. A shadowy figure appeared just outside in the flicker of the light still burning from a nearby fire. Cyrus stirred, his vision blurry. He couldn't make out any of the figure's features and began to feel uneasy as it moved slowly towards him.

The sudden high-pitched scream of a girl made him sit bolt upright. The figure changed its course and darted towards the sound. Cyrus clambered out of his tent and began to chase the figure down the broken escalator and into the main opening of the mall. He caught a glimpse of more shadowy figures heading for the exit, dragging behind them what looked like two women. Cyrus found it odd that despite the distance between him and them, he could clearly see the women's features, yet the shadowy figure who'd been little over three feet away from him seemed to be no more than a silhouette. The women called out to Cyrus for help, as they were dragged out of the building. Cyrus instantly recognised who they were.

'Mum! Izzy!' he tried to scream, but the words didn't come out. He watched with an outstretched hand as his mother and sister were dragged away out of sight. He tried to give chase but his legs wouldn't move. It was like they had been set in concrete. There was nothing he could do. He tried to call out again, but still, nothing. The room around him started spinning, and at last he heard a voice echoing around his head. It was calling his name.

'Cyrus!' The voice became louder. 'CYRUS!'

Cyrus suddenly woke, to find he was back in his tent. Rowley was looking over him with a concerned expression.

'Cyrus! Are you OK?'

'Uhhh, yeah I think so,' Cyrus stirred, slowly realising that he must have been dreaming.

'Still having that nightmare?' inquired Rowley, still staring intently at him. 'You were calling their names again.'

'The same one,' sighed Cyrus, as he began to sit up and wipe his eyes. He took a look around him and got his bearings. He saw the light streaming into the gap in the tent behind Rowley. It was morning.

'What time is it?' he asked groggily.

'You tell me, hot shot,' replied Rowley with a smirk on his face, tapping Cyrus's wrist. Cyrus looked down to find the watch coiled around his wrist. He kept forgetting he had it on.

'Oh, right,' he replied, feeling a little silly. 'I'm not used to it yet.'

'So I see,' Rowley turned around and ducked his head as he exited the tent. He glanced back at Cyrus as he left. 'Breakfast?'

'Right behind you,' Cyrus replied, forcing a half-smile. As Rowley walked away, Cyrus began to ponder the events of his dream. Ever since his family went missing, he'd been having the same nightmare frequently. He prayed that his mother and sister were safe. He started making his way out of the tent and caught the eye of a figure walking past. The bleach blonde hair gave her away.

'You look rough,' Jennifer teased, one eyebrow raised.

'Um, thanks,' Cyrus replied, a little taken aback.

'I'm kidding!' she insisted. 'You just look like you slept funny, that's all. Rowley's worried about you, you know?'

'I know, he doesn't need to be. I'm fine,' he dismissed. Jennifer got the message and relaxed her tone a little.

'You've got a lot on your mind. I get it.' She decided to change the subject. 'So, what do you reckon we've got for breakfast today? Cold beans or cold soup?'

They walked together down the stationary escalator. Cyrus thought about what it was like when there was power in this place. The small comforts people were so used to, like not having to walk up and down stairs, suddenly taken away when the electricity finally gave out.

He looked on at the foray of people gathered in the centre of the mall, chatting amongst themselves and eating from tins of baked beans. Cyrus sighed.

Beans again.

The living situation was pretty dire and he knew he should feel happy to have food at all, but he would have given his right arm to eat something other than baked beans or soup, just this once. He looked up as they reached the bottom and tried to spot Rowley. His friend always saved a tin for him.

'Cyrus, over here!' Cyrus looked to his left to see Rowley waving at him. There was a smile on his face. Cyrus had become more and more uneasy with Rowley's smile as the days went on. They had been best friends since he could remember, but the war had changed everyone. Now the war was over, and what felt like the world with it, it was affecting people in different ways. It seemed to affect Rowley through his smile. He didn't show any signs of weakness or sadness, other than in that smile. That damn creepy smile. Cyrus studied Rowley for those brief few seconds. It wasn't just the way his mouth appeared wider than it should, it was his eyes. His eyes were wider than he'd ever seen, as though the size of his pupils were attempting to cover up the deep and unsettling pain behind them.

He's losing it.

Jennifer sat down next to Rowley as Cyrus sheepishly sat on the other side of him. Rowley put a big arm around him and produced an open tin of beans with a spoon sticking out of it.

'Breakfast is served,' he announced with an air of panache. Cyrus took the tin and began to eat quietly.

Zion was sitting opposite the three of them. He was reading an old magazine from before the war. Cyrus couldn't make out what it was about, but it had a picture of the solar system on the front cover so he assumed something to do with science. Zion didn't seem like the astronomy type though. Perhaps he was trying to look intelligent in front of his friends? Cyrus shook off the idea. He had been so pessimistic recently. Reading material was hard to come by these days, so anything you could get your hands on was a welcome blessing, and who was he to judge another man's motivation for reading a science magazine?

As he stared at the picture, Zion peered over the top of the magazine with a perplexed look.

'You OK buddy? You look like you've never seen an atom before,' he remarked. Cyrus squinted at the image on the cover.

Shit.

Zion looked very assured of himself reading that magazine, and Cyrus couldn't even correctly identify what picture was on the front cover. He thought it was maybe best if he didn't reveal what he thought it was. He simply laughed and stared deep into his tin of beans.

'So what's the plan for today?' asked Jennifer. Zion looked up from his reading.

'I'm guessing nothing much, given that salvage group two are out today.'

Jennifer nodded. 'What time did they leave?'

'About half an hour ago I think,' Zion replied, looking at his watch. His watch was in much better condition than Cyrus's. Zion had found it in an abandoned store soon after the war ended, and somehow it had managed to survive this long. Its silver frame shined as it sat wrapped around the dark skin of Zion's wrist. It was clear that Zion took good care of his possessions.

'Who went out this time then?' Jennifer continued.

'The usual group I think. Gabriel, Doug, Jane, Mia, some of the guys from—' Zion was interrupted as Cyrus choked on his food. Rowley offered to help but he pushed him away.

'Mia?!' he spluttered. 'Mia went too?'

'Yeah dude, she's in group two,' Zion offered bluntly, as if nothing was wrong.

'Her hand isn't better,' Cyrus argued. 'She can't go out there when she can barely handle a weapon. It's not safe!' Cyrus's crystal began to glow a dim red colour. Jennifer took note of this and stepped in.

'Chill out Cyrus, I'm sure she'll be fine. She's with good company, they'll look after her.'

Cyrus could feel a rage building up inside him. He wasn't usually the overprotective type, but the war changed people. His family had gone without a trace, and now Mia was putting her life in danger. He grasped the crystal hanging over his chest, which was now a bright crimson, and closed his eyes.

His friends looked on in discomfort. This wasn't like him, he never got this angry. Cyrus had always been a calming influence over the rest of the group. He never got this emotional. They stared at this alien friend they didn't recognise and wondered if he was going to snap. What would happen when he did? They just didn't know.

At last, Cyrus stood up abruptly and rushed towards the other side of the room. Rowley clocked what he was doing.

'Cyrus, no!' he yelled. 'There's nothing you can do, you just have to wait for them to get back.' Cyrus ignored his protests and marched on. He was heading towards the array of guns resting against the wall at the far side of the room. He pushed through a small crowd of people eating their breakfast, knocking a tin out of the hands of a small girl. It bounced noisily on the floor, spilling beans everywhere. She yelped and started to cry as others rushed to help her. Cyrus hardly flinched as he pushed on.

He soon found himself in front of a plasma rifle, which he grabbed as he swivelled towards the south-east corridor. However, his exit was cut off as Rowley caught up with him and slammed him against the wall. Jennifer winced as she saw two of her closest friends confronting each other in a way she'd never seen before.

'You're not thinking straight. What's gotten into you?' Rowley tried to get through to him, but Cyrus simply looked up at his best friend with a cold stare. A few seconds went by with the two just staring at each other, until Rowley loosened his grip on Cyrus's arm. Cyrus looked over at Jennifer and Rowley followed his gaze. As they were both looking in her direction, Cyrus began to speak quietly.

'If it were her out there, you know you'd do the same.' Rowley's eyes widened and after a moment he took his hand away from Cyrus's arm completely. He let out a sharp exhale as he watched Jennifer's shocked expression from across the room. His head then moved back towards Cyrus, his eyes fixed on his.

'I'm coming with you,' he replied.

**

The streets outside were swept up in a dust storm as Cyrus and Rowley ventured forth. The city looked deserted as always, but the sound of the wind howled as a combination of sand and dust were blown into their faces. Rowley grabbed Cyrus's shoulder as he tried hard to keep up with his eager friend. They headed for shelter in the remains of a building on the corner of the street. There was a corner where two walls met, providing temporary relief from the storm. The two had geared up with the usual weapons and supplies, and had fashioned scarves as partial balaclavas to keep their faces protected from the sand and dust particles. In the heat of the day the scarves made their heads sweat, however in conditions like these they had no choice but to wear them.

Cyrus pulled his scarf down from over his mouth. 'Where do you think the group went to?' he shouted into the wind. Rowley reached into his pocket and produced a tattered map.

'I don't think they went far,' he replied as he located a specific part of the map with his finger. 'They were scheduled to investigate this area first,' he continued, pointing at the old market square. 'And then move on to where we were yesterday. If we hurry we might be able to catch up to them.' Cyrus nodded as Rowley folded the map back up and tucked it into his back pocket.

'Stay close.'

**

As the dust storm began to lift, Cyrus could see the old market square, where the hub of this part of the city used to be. There was a giant open space in the centre where a water fountain had once trickled in the sunshine. Shops lined the outside of the square, although like the shopping mall they had been long since abandoned. The centre was at one time used for temporary market stalls on a busy Saturday, bustling with people buying and selling goods and going about their daily lives. Cyrus took a moment to reflect on the state the area was in now and tried to remember what it was like before everything fell apart. He could barely remember what a normal world looked like. The desolate feel to the place was in sinister contrast to what was intended for it, but was in keeping with the rest of the landscape.

The pair walked to the middle of the square and began to look around for a trace of the salvage group. There was a breeze blowing through the open space; the remnants of the storm that was passing through. They split up to check nearly buildings.

Cyrus stood outside a run-down tech store and observed the broken glass littering the floor of the entrance. He spotted a piece of torn clothing by the window and bent down for a closer inspection. He wondered if it belonged to one of the salvage group. Maybe they'd gotten into trouble?

A faint rustling grabbed his attention. It was coming from within the shop. He peered in through the broken window, but it was too dark inside to see. Cyrus produced a torch from his belt and clicked it on. He slung his rifle onto his back and took out his proton pistol, before slowly making his way into the shop. The shop was small, with just a couple of aisles. He could shine his torch into all four corners of the room from where he was standing. There was no sign of anybody.

Must have been the wind.

He holstered his pistol and prepared to step back outside, when suddenly a huge explosion came from a shop across the square. Cyrus jumped out of his skin and fumbled around to ready his rifle. He darted outside to see where it had come from, to find a large plume of smoke emanating from the bank on the north side of the square.

Another explosion followed, this time from the bakery. A cloud of dust appeared from its cracking walls, as though something had been thrown against it hard. Cyrus flinched and pointed his weapon towards the building the sound had originated.

Where the hell is Rowley?

In that moment Rowley appeared from the bakery, sprinting back to Cyrus's position with his rifle in his arms. He kept glancing back at the shop as he ran. Cyrus could see a look of terror in his eyes. Seconds later, there was a loud bang and a smash as a panther jumped through the bakery window, shattering the fragments of glass from its broken frame. The shards flew through the air in a shower, almost in slow motion as Cyrus watched the sudden appearance of the mech leap out onto the dusty ground of the courtyard.

As it began to chase Rowley, another mech appeared from the bank and started to follow suit. This one was different to the first. Unlike the panthers, this mech stood on two legs and appeared very human-like. It was roughly the same size as the panther; about twice the size of an actual human. They were known as *golems*; their most notable and terrifying feature being their right arm, which were mouldered into the shape of a gun. Its gun arm raised, it began to fire after Rowley.

'RUUUUUUUN!' Rowley shouted as he got closer to Cyrus.

Cyrus froze in panic and didn't know what to do. He could see the mechs gaining on Rowley and he wasn't sure if his friend would make it to him in time. He looked swiftly around for inspiration, desperate for any ideas. Eventually he tightened his grip on his rifle and aimed it at the panther, which was gaining on Rowley fast. A few seconds went by as the sound of Cyrus's pounding heart matched that of the panther's galloping footsteps. Just as the mech was almost on Rowley, Cyrus fired. The plasma shot cannoned off the metal plate of the panther's shoulder and ricocheted onto its leg, causing it to trip and skid into the dusty ground.

Rowley caught up to Cyrus and looked back at the mechs that had been chasing him. The panther looked disorientated from the plasma shot and was slowly getting back to its feet. The other mech was still firing at the pair as it ran towards them.

'In here!' Rowley yelled as he raced past Cyrus into the tech store. Cyrus fired off another couple of rounds in the general direction of the mechs before following Rowley into the store.

'What's the plan?' Cyrus was wide eyed, desperately hoping Rowley hadn't just cornered them for their certain doom.

'It's dark in here,' he replied, matter of fact. 'They'll struggle to see us.'

It was true that some of the less well-developed mechs, such as panthers, did not have the ability to see in the dark. However some of the more advanced ones that carried weapons, such as the human-like golems, did.

'There's a golem out there too!' Cyrus exclaimed.

'Oh shit, where did he come from?' Rowley looked worried now. His plan didn't account for a golem. It would just take a few seconds for its targeting system to find them in the dark.

'There's no way we're getting out of this. We can't destroy these things.' Cyrus started to panic.

'Shoot them in the head,' Rowley replied. 'It'll buy us some time to escape while they're down.'

'Oh sure, I'll just shoot them in their one small weak spot in the split second I have before their tear my heart from my chest!' Cyrus countered. They both knew it was easier said than done.

Silence fell on the tech store as they both aimed their rifles at the entrance. What felt like an age passed, and there was no sign of the mechs. Then suddenly, a shot fired right through the front of the shop and hit the wall next to Cyrus's head.

The golem entered the building and started searching for them with its targeting system. The stomping of its metal feet echoed in the space as Cyrus felt his stomach turn.

It scanned the premises and located the pair, but just before it could fully lock onto Cyrus, Rowley fired a perfectly placed round straight into its head. The mech collapsed and began to malfunction. Immediately after, the panther leapt into the shop and began to tear the place apart, blindly swiping at the dark. Cyrus recovered his poise and fired a series of plasma rounds in its direction, screaming in terror as he did so. One round hit the panther's eye, causing it to fall over, its circuits whirring and crackling as it lay in a heap on the floor.

'That's it, let's go!' shouted Rowley, and the pair escaped out of the shop, vanishing into a side-street around the corner of the square.

CHAPTER FOUR

Back at the shopping mall, Zion had finished reading his magazine and walked over to sit by Jennifer. She had become ghostly pale after the earlier events and was sitting looking at a photo of the group, which was taken on an old Polaroid camera they'd found after they started living in the mall.

'They've never fought before,' she started. 'They've hardly ever disagreed about anything.'

Zion took the photo and smiled.

'I like this photo. Despite everything that's been going on, we still found time to smile about something.' He looked at Jennifer and tried to think of anything he could say that would comfort her. She looked back at him with wide eyes.

'I want to know that they're safe, that's all. But we can't all go out there one by one trying to make sure we're all OK.'

'Cyrus shouldn't have gone out there, we all know that,' Zion offered. 'I think even Cyrus knows that. Rowley did what he thought was right; he stuck by his friend. Cyrus was pretty set on going out, so Rowley's just going to cover his back. You don't need to worry about either of them, they're smart guys and they watch out for each other.'

Jennifer smiled and the worry lines across her face seemed to relax somewhat. This was the first time she could remember Zion saying something that wasn't intended to make people laugh.

'Thank you, Zion.' She looked up from where they were sat and saw Guy walking up one of the escalators towards the sleeping tents. He hadn't spoken to anyone since the previous day.

'Maybe I should go check up on Guy,' she suggested. 'He's been acting funny since yesterday.'

Zion nodded. 'Go ahead and try your luck. You might just be able to get something out of him.'

She got up and followed Guy up to the first floor.

'Guy, wait up,' Jennifer ran up the escalator steps two at a time to catch up with him. Guy turned his head as he reached the top and scowled at her arrival.

'Do you wanna talk?' she asked.

'I'm fine, really,' he replied coldly. 'I don't know why everyone thinks I'm some kind of charity case. I'm fifteen, I'm not scared. I'm not a baby.'

His words pierced right through her. She closed her eyes and took in a deep breath. Perhaps this would be more work than she thought. She wondered why he was so insular, why he continued to push people away. But she composed herself and chose to press on.

'I know you're not a baby, Guy,' she reassured. 'We all think you did a great job on the salvage hunt yesterday.' She smiled at him, hoping to get one in return, but instead she was met with another cold stare.

'I'm just as capable as all the others,' he insisted.

'Yes, I know you are. You're fifteen, you're just as much a part of the salvage group as everyone else. We think you're more than capable.' Jennifer forced the words through her lips, despite not believing a single one of them. Guy was acting like a complete baby, and he wasn't just as much a part of the salvage team as the others. Everyone knew he was a liability waiting to happen; he was young and scared. There was a lot he needed to learn about the world.

'OK.' Guy seemed to let his guard down a little.

'What are you doing today?' Jennifer asked. 'Zion and I were just sitting around talking, do you want to join us?' She maintained her artificial smile as she spoke.

'No thanks, I have some stuff I want to do.' Guy stopped outside his tent and turned to Jennifer. His body language told her that he wasn't in the mood for talking. He probably needed a little more time by himself. He was holding onto a camera stick, which had become a very popular piece of tech in recent years. They were small cameras contained inside a piece of plastic, about the size of a lighter. The images the user took could be cycled through from a holographic display that emanated from the device. Jennifer looked at the camera in his hands and then back to his face.

'OK, I'll leave you to it then,' she conceded. 'But you know where to find us.' She turned around and walked away, returning to Zion who had started re-reading his science magazine.

**

It had been twenty minutes since Cyrus and Rowley had lost the mechs and continued their journey to the second site the salvage group were scheduled to visit. This part of town was once a particularly good area to search for useful supplies, as the city hospital once stood here. The building itself had crumbled halfway through the war; a safe haven for wounded troops that was the target of enemy airstrikes. Nowadays, the colony's salvage teams would occasionally find medical supplies dotted around here. Anything from bandages to the odd pair of surgical scissors among the debris. However as the days went on there was less and less to find, and the high concentration of people roaming these parts meant mech attacks were becoming more frequent. This was the same place the group had been the day before, when they were ambushed by panthers. Cyrus could see the crumbling building he had hidden inside.

'I can't believe we're back here so soon,' said Rowley. 'Let's find the group ASAP because I don't like it out here.'

'They should be here already, I wonder what took them so long,' Cyrus replied disconcertingly. He looked up at the sky. It was completely clear. The sandstorm of that morning felt like a lifetime ago now, such was the state of the ever-changing weather of the new world. What used to be sunny days in summer and rainy days in winter had now become extreme storms one minute and clear spells the next. The strong winds from the west also seemed to bring with it the sand from the desert regions miles away, which often led to the sandstorms they'd witnessed today.

The pair stayed hidden in an area of rich rubble and waited for the salvage group to show up. Rowley took off his backpack and sat down. He opened the zip of the front pocket and retrieved an old looking baseball card. The picture was in black and white and appeared worn. He showed it to Cyrus proudly.

'Your prized possession,' joked Cyrus. Rowley had shown him this card many times over the years, and each time he did Cyrus could never work out whether Rowley thought he was showing it to him for the first time. Maybe he just *really* liked showing it to people.

'Jackie Robinson. It was my father's,' said Rowley, as he ran a finger over it. 'It's been passed down our family for generations.'

'So you've told me.' Cyrus felt himself starting to show his tiredness at the conversation he knew he'd had a million times before.

'You know this guy was the first—'

'First African American to play Major League Baseball. I know,' Cyrus interrupted Rowley and finished his sentence for him. Rowley frowned, as his story was cut short.

'This is a really old card Cyrus. You'll be hard pressed to find another one like it anywhere.'

Cyrus looked sceptical.

'I've seen a bunch of baseball cards before. What makes *that* one so special?'

'Cyrus, it's really old!' he replied, shocked that Cyrus couldn't understand its significance. Rowley stopped himself and sighed. 'You don't get it.'

The pair began to hear heavy footsteps coming from down the street. Rowley popped the card back in his rucksack and zipped it up. He wandered over to the edge of the rubble and peered around the corner.

Moments later, Cyrus darted back to his friend with a concerned look on his face. He crouched down and put his finger to his lips.

'What?' Rowley mouthed to him, unaware of what his friend had just seen.

'Mech,' Cyrus mouthed back. 'Panther.'

A few moments passed as the sound of footsteps got louder and louder, echoing around the rubble. Cyrus suddenly got a sense of déjà vu of yesterday's exploits. He wondered how long he'd be able to keep going, doing this every day.

Where would it end? There was no real goal other than to keep scouring the city for food and supplies, against the danger of mech attacks and probable death. Was this it? Was this the life humanity was destined for?

The sound got closer, until Cyrus could hear the clanking of the mech's metal bones and its artificial grunting as it moved. He readied his plasma rifle and prepared to fire. Rowley lowered his body into a crouched position and did the same. The mech would surely see them when it came around the corner. There was no way it would miss them. The sunlight was shining right on the pair, but they couldn't move now or the noise would give them away.

The mech's head appeared first, and it stopped to survey its surroundings mere yards away from them. Cyrus held his breath as his heart raced. His heartbeat was drumming in his head so loud he thought the mech would surely hear. The beast started to stalk slowly around the corner. Suddenly, there was a flash of light in the distance. The mech turned its head and let out a piercing metallic screech, which forced both Cyrus and Rowley to cover their ears. The light appeared to shine in the panther's eyes and flickered about. Cyrus and Rowley both looked at each other in confusion. What was going on?

A rock banged against a sheet of metal in the distance, as if thrown by someone, and caught the mech's attention. With a final screech, it raced off towards the source of the noise, leaving Cyrus and Rowley to breathe a temporary sigh of relief. They knew the mech wouldn't be gone for long, but they needed to stay where they were to catch up with the salvage group.

Moments after the mechanical beast had rushed off, the pair heard a loud bang, followed by two short pops. They heard the mech cry out.

'Someone's shot it!' exclaimed Rowley. They couldn't believe their luck. Seconds later, a group of people emerged from around the corner and started hurrying over to them. Cyrus recognised them, it was the salvage group, led by Gabriel's mammoth figure.

'What the hell are you two doing out here?' the big man asked.

'Looking for you,' Cyrus replied, astonished to see them. 'Where's Mia, is she OK?'

'I'm fine, Cyrus.' Mia's soothing voice came from behind Gabriel. She walked into plain view and Cyrus's eyes lit up. His heartbeat raced even more than before, yet he felt an overwhelming sense of calm. It was a strange feeling.

The mech screeched again from around the corner. Rowley interjected.

'Guys, it's not going to stay down for long, we need to get out of here.'

'Agreed,' Gabriel nodded and the group moved on to the safety of a nearby building.

**

The nearest building happened to be the old town hall. It was a grand place with pillars both outside and in, and huge paintings hanging off the wall. This was one of the few buildings that had remained intact during the war. However, it had long been abandoned as there had been little reason for a mayor in a city as damaged as this.

The end of the war was signalled more as a necessity than a real truce. There was so much fighting and killing that there were very few people left. No order had been established after the end, but it would have been impossible to bring order or normality to a place dominated by killer metal creations with artificial intelligence.

The group set down their bags and weapons and took a break. It appeared as though the group had managed to find a little food on their outing, but not nearly as much as Cyrus's group had found by the same time the previous day.

'Resources are becoming scarcer by the day,' he acknowledged. 'We might have to start thinking about moving further afield to get them.'

Jane chimed in. 'That's what I've been sayin' all this time.'

'Yeah, but going further out, that's going to be more dangerous,' added Doug. 'Jane, we just found these people, we can't ask them to just up an' leave their home and risk everything to look for a new one.'

'I know, Doug, but that's where the food is gonna be at, so it just makes sense, doesn't it?'

There was a long silence where no one said anything. Jane folded her arms uncomfortably and looked at her shoes. Finally Gabriel spoke up.

'I think the heat's getting to us all a little. You're right, Jane, we're running out of supplies and we need to find somewhere with more food. But Doug's also right, we only just met these people. We can't ask them to leave right away. We should ask them what they want to do.' Both Doug and Jane nodded in appreciation.

Across the room, Cyrus was desperate to talk to Mia, and used the temporary silence as his opportunity.

'I'm so glad you're safe.'

Mia smiled at him. 'You didn't need to worry. I can't believe you came all this way for me. That was really—' she paused for a moment. 'Dumb,' she finished, teasing him.

'I think it's romantic,' Jane interjected, firing a cheeky wink at Cyrus.

'That's one way of looking at it,' Mia replied.

Cyrus got straight to the point, assessing Mia's arm. 'Is your hand feeling better?'

'Not especially, but I can still carry a bag, so I'm not completely useless,' Mia smirked. She reached up to her hair, which was tied into a small ponytail, and removed her bobble. Cyrus watched intently as her silky caramel hair waved as she set it free. He wondered how in a world like this it had managed to stay looking so shiny. Perhaps it hadn't at all, and it was all in his head. However if that was true, he was more than happy to be blissfully ignorant.

Cyrus was about to speak again, but Mia got there first.

'I know you said you didn't want me to go if my hand wasn't better, but I felt too guilty. And then Guy said he'd go if I didn't want to, which made me feel even worse.'

'Guy said that?' inquired Cyrus, bemused not only at Guy's offer but at the fact that Guy had actually *spoken* to someone since yesterday's events.

'Yes, he seemed very keen,' Mia replied. Their conversation was abruptly interrupted as Gabriel made his way over.

'OK, let's make a move. We've still got a few more places I want to check out before we call it a day.'

**

The group spent a couple more hours scouring nearby buildings for supplies. Cyrus yawned and checked his watch. He could see the weariness in the rest of the group, and that only meant that they were more vulnerable to mech attacks. The watch's hands read ten past one. It was only lunchtime, but a salvage run usually only lasted a few hours anyway because of the daytime heat. He decided to call it.

'Guys, let's head home,' he suggested. 'Not much more we can do today.'

'But our bags are only half full,' Jane replied, perplexed at Cyrus's suggestion.

'We've scoured this area and there's nothing left. Let's regroup at home and figure out where to go from there.'

Jane seemed content with this idea. She thought it might be a good time to bring up moving to a new home. The group turned around and started to make their way back to the mall. The sun was bright and shining down over the whole city, without a cloud in the sky. The dust storm of that morning felt like a lifetime ago. Mia caught Cyrus's eye and beamed at him, as she so often had done.

'I'm really glad you came after me,' she said. Cyrus smiled and felt his heart skip a beat.

'Me too.' He gazed into her bright green eyes, but was woken from his trance by Doug's voice.

'Hey, what's that?' Doug called, signalling to an alleyway to their right. Everyone stopped in their tracks and tried to see what Doug was pointing out.

'I don't see it,' said Rowley. Cyrus was the furthest away, and struggled to see into the dark alley. As he moved in closer he could make out the outline of a large metallic figure.

The group had now all moved into the alleyway, and could see the object more clearly. They all shared the same confusion by what they saw. It was a mech. A panther, lying on the ground. It appeared to be completely lifeless, as if it had run out of power. The group sheepishly examined it closer, afraid it may reanimate at any moment.

'I've never seen anything like it,' gasped Rowley. He readied his weapon as Doug prodded the mech with the end of his rifle.

The mech didn't move, it remained completely motionless. The lights in its eyes had gone out, as if someone had flicked a switch.

'Who did this?' Cyrus wondered out loud.

'I think you mean, who *could do* this?' Gabriel interjected. 'What kind of weaponry must there be out there that can take down a mech, and kill it?' There was a shared feeling of discontent creeping into the group.

A hundred yards further down the road Mia stumbled on a small piece of parchment folded up two ways. She bent over and picked it up. As she unfolded it to see what was within she began to shake her head. 'No, no, no, this can't be.' She presented the parchment to the rest of the group. It was a map of the city, with a large building circled in red. Arrows were drawn on, pointing to the building from all sides. Jane gasped as she realised what it was. Rowley and Gabriel looked at each other; they had the same idea.

'Bandits,' they said in unison.

'Do you think they're the ones that destroyed the mech?' Doug asked.

'I don't know,' Gabriel scratched the back of his neck. 'But one thing's for sure.' He pointed to the building that had been circled on the map. 'They're heading right for the mall.'

CHAPTER FIVE

April was pacing around the mall with a worried look on her face. Like everyone else, she was still a little shaken up at how Cyrus had reacted to Mia accompanying group two on their hunt. She needed something to take her mind off it. She had been chatting to a few of the other survivors in the camp, but she had never really connected with anyone. She was just sixteen and felt in a place of limbo between child and adult. The twenty-somethings of the group protected her like they would a child; especially her older sister, Jennifer. The only person who really understood how she felt was Guy.

She'd grown quite fond of Guy in their short time together within the confines of the building. She'd had crushes before, but with Guy it felt different. Guy was mysterious, which intrigued her. She wasn't sure if he felt the same way about her, but she knew he was going through the same struggles, which gave them a common theme of conversation. April wondered what Guy was up to now. He carried a camera stick around with him, but he wouldn't share his photos with anyone. She thought he must have been one of those tortured artist types, and she longed for him to trust her enough to share his work with her.

She couldn't see Guy around the camp. Looking up to the first floor, she decided he must have been there. Perhaps he was looking through his photos.

I bet they're amazing.

She left the group of people she had been conversing with and made her way towards the escalator. As she reached the top, she felt goose bumps develop all over her skin. She stood outside Guy's tent and could see his silhouette lit up by a torch inside. She decided to make a joke.

'You know we're not supposed to use the torches unless we really need them.' She pulled a funny face in hopes that the right tone would come across.

'Yeah, I know. I'm trying to see something,' he dismissed. He *was* looking through his photos. She got butterflies in her stomach and she could feel her next words trying desperately to get out of her mouth.

'That's OK,' she said. 'Are you looking at your photos?'

'Yeah,' came the abrupt reply.

'But surely you don't need the torch on to see them,' April remembered. 'The hologram is lit up by itself.'

The torch suddenly clicked off. The tent went from a bright yellow to the dim blue colour of the hologram. April couldn't see the photos through the gap in the entrance of the tent. Guy must have been sitting with his back to her.

'Happy now?' Guy's voice stung the air with a sarcastic tone. April felt a cold dagger travel right through her chest. Guy could be so rude sometimes. She tried to remain unfazed and pressed on.

'Um, Guy?' she caught herself starting to say. Was she going to do it? Could she really ask him? How would he react? She couldn't take another day not knowing, so she drew a deep breath and said it.

'Can I see the photos too?'

There was a silence that seemed to last an age. Finally April heard the short blip sound from the camera, and the whole tent fell into darkness.

'I don't like sharing my photos,' Guy said, matter of fact as he climbed out of the tent. 'They're not that good anyway.'

'Oh I'm sure they're brilliant,' April replied excitedly.

'Just let it go. Please?'

April's eyes dropped to the floor. She knew he'd say no, but she had hoped today would be different. But maybe today *could* be different. A wild determination came alive within her. Maybe he was playing hard to get?

Without thinking, she touched Guy's arm as he walked past. He froze dead in his tracks and looked down at her hand gripping his bicep. April realised she was practically squeezing it, and relaxed to a more gentle hold. Guy looked up from his arm and into April's eyes. For a moment April thought she might explode, her heart was racing more than ever. What should she do? Should she kiss him? Is that what he wanted? Her eyes began to water.

'Please, Guy,' she whispered softly. 'Please let me in.'

Guy's eyebrows arched into a defensive stance, and April started to feel scared. She braced herself for the reaction.

'No. I told you no,' he said, in almost a mumble. April felt desperate. She was losing him, but she had to try one last time.

'Guy,' she started, reaching her other hand out slowly to his.

'NO!' he bellowed, yanking his arm away from her and knocking her to the ground. 'I told you no!' Guy stormed away, clutching the camera in his left hand. April was left shocked and speechless on the floor. She felt like her whole world had been shattered. This encounter had been a rude awakening for her. Guy wasn't a tortured artist at all. He wasn't looking for approval of his work. He was just a jerk with a camera. She felt stupid for being so blind.

Zion and Jennifer came running up the escalator after her. They'd obviously heard the commotion.

'Are you OK?' Jennifer asked, concerned for the safety of her sister. April's eyebrows arched aggressively, as Guy's had done moments earlier. In those last few moments, her feelings for him had been completely transformed from infatuation to infuriation.

**

Gabriel pushed open the doors of the shopping mall as the salvage group returned home. He had the parchment they'd found by the destroyed mech in his hand as he marched through the narrow corridors of the south-west entrance. The loud bang as the door opened alerted a few members of the colony. They rushed over to see what the commotion was and caught a glimpse of Gabriel's giant figure storming towards them. He had a look in his eye of a man possessed as he came nearer. The small crowd carved a path between them for Gabriel to slip through. He made his way through to the opening in the middle of the mall and stopped dead at the centre. The rest of the group followed behind him, trudging along at a slightly slower rate.

Gabriel took a long look around at his fellow people and lifted the parchment in the air with one hand. The whole colony was looking right at him, their gaze fixed on his outstretched hand.

'People,' Gabriel bellowed. 'We are being watched.'

His words echoed around the mall as the onlookers stood in complete silence, their eyes fixed on Gabriel's towering presence. He carried on. 'We found this today on our hunt.' He waved the parchment in his hand. 'A map, circling this very shopping mall.' An uneasy feeling set in among everyone. Gabriel's words hung in the air, and the group waiting in anticipation for some sort of context. Finally an elderly man appeared from the back and spoke up.

'What does it mean?' he asked, his voice croaky and soft. There were a few murmurs from the rest of the gathering as they pondered the answer to his question. Gabriel paused for a moment as he looked upon the old man. He'd marched into the mall with the exuberant confidence of a born leader, but as he stared at the helpless face of this frail old man he suddenly felt a strange sensation sweep through his body, as if someone had dropped a ton of weight onto his shoulders. He suddenly realised how doomed they all were. He couldn't save these people, he was no leader. In all of his experience as a military man, he'd only ever given orders to hardened soldiers like himself, and he'd even failed them when he fled the war. Now he was faced with the sobering reality that these civilians, these weary, scared survivors were soon to be robbed of their possessions and left to die, if not killed at the scene. He took a deep breath as his palms began to sweat.

'It means that someone is heading this way. Most likely bandits.' Gabriel's voice had lost all of its volume and he was now speaking in a much softer tone, as if he had admitted defeat. 'I've seen it before; they come in numbers and steal your food and supplies. It's the reason we had to leave our last home.' He looked at Jane and Doug as he spoke. 'We were out looking for food at the time. By the time we returned there was nobody left.'

The old man's face drooped and his bottom lip began to tremble. Gabriel felt a sinking feeling in his stomach. He was way out of his depth, he needed help. Nobody spoke for a few seconds as the sombre atmosphere of the room appeared to make the temperature drop ten degrees. Rowley waved his arms at Gabriel to catch his attention. As Gabriel turned in his direction, his arm still raised with the parchment in his grasp, Rowley lifted his right hand and made a fist. He nodded to Gabriel and gently patted his chest with the fist, right above his heart. Rowley's father had been in the military, and had once taught a ten year old Rowley this same sign. It was a signal of stability and strength, of togetherness and hope, used throughout the army to fire up the troops.

Gabriel clenched his own right hand and replicated the sign. He felt an ounce of hope rekindle within him; Rowley had given him the confidence he needed to muster his next sentence.

'Take heed of this warning, but please do not panic,' Gabriel continued, his voice sounding a little more assured now. He looked around the room at the sea of faces watching him. 'We will be ready for them, and we will not let them hurt us.'

Gabriel's hand remained firmly rested over heart.

Zion, Jennifer and April were watching from the first floor, and caught his attention. They all copied the sign, as others in the crowd did, until everyone was doing it, looking up at Gabriel with hope in their eyes.

Gabriel smiled, lowered his arms and began to tell the colony about the fallen mech and the bandits that had attacked his previous colony. The group was encouraged by the prospect of a weapon that could wipe out the mechs, but the map they had retrieved posed questions that remained fixed in everyone's mind. Had the bandits marked them as an easy target? And how did they know they were here?

CHAPTER SIX

Half an hour had passed since Gabriel's speech and the colony were making preparations in anticipation of the suspected bandit attack. Gabriel was using his experience to guide the plans.

'We need to be ready for anything,' he started. 'If bandits *do* attack, we need to see them coming. The last thing we want is to be caught napping when they storm in here.' A few people nodded in agreement. Doug was among them and he stepped in to make a suggestion.

'We should have someone stationed on the roof. We can get a good view of the surrounding area from there. We'll have to take it in shifts if we're waiting a while. I can take the first watch,' he offered.

'That's a good idea,' encouraged Gabriel. 'The sun will be on the roof all day too, so it'll be too hot for one person to stay up there long.' He quickly scanned the room around him. 'Does anybody have a pair of binoculars?'

Everybody looked at each other and shrugged. It was surprising the number of unnecessary items people held onto while they were living this way, but it seemed that binoculars were not one of those items.

'How about rifle scopes? Do we have any of those?' he added, trying to cover all bases.

'No, none of our rifles have scopes on them,' Doug replied.

'Damn. OK, well let's all keep an eye out for anything useful. There may be something else we find that could help us out.'

Another member of the colony spoke up. 'Gabriel, just how long do you think it'll take for the bandits to get here? I mean, do we actually have any idea *if* they are even coming?'

Gabriel's reply was candid. 'To be honest, there's no way of knowing for sure. If the same thing happens to us as with the last group we were with, they *will* be coming, and in great numbers. Could be anytime in the next few hours, or the next few days, and if they're smart they'll attack at night.'

The man looked sceptical at his response. He was hoping for a more accurate time-frame.

'One thing we do know about bandits is that once they've marked out where their next target is, they don't hang around too long,' Doug interjected. 'But don't worry, Gabriel knows what he's doing. He'll make sure we're ready for them.'

Gabriel smiled at Doug and decided to leave the group to catch up with Cyrus, who was sitting alone on the far side of the room. Cyrus caught a glimpse of Gabriel's hulking frame walking towards him in the corner of his eye and perked his head up welcomingly.

'How you holding up?' Gabriel asked. Cyrus let out a long sigh and smiled back at his friend.

'As well as anyone else, I guess. I was just thinking about our water supply, it's getting pretty low.' Cyrus motioned towards the lone gallon of water that was sitting by the food supplies. 'I mean, there's around fifty us of here, Gabriel. It's not going to last that long.' Gabriel did some quick maths in his head as he looked around the room at the rest of the survivors.

'I think you're right, we need to find some more,' he decided. 'But where exactly will we find some? We've been all over this part of town. There's nothing left.'

'And going too far from the mall is a bad idea,' Cyrus added. 'It's way too dangerous with all those mechs running around.' The two looked at the ceiling as they pondered the situation. Gabriel rubbed his beard as he thought. At one point he raised a finger and seemed to have an idea, but as Cyrus looked at him hopefully he shook his head and went back to playing with his beard.

'I'll see what the others can come up with,' Cyrus said at last, as he went off in search of inspiration.

**

A small group were sitting in the doorway of a women's clothing store. The clothes had long been looted, as with everything else in the mall. Mia was leaning against the glass of the display window, playing with the bandage on her wrist. Zion was sitting next to her with another magazine he'd found; this time a woman's magazine. Mia giggled as she realised what it was.

'A little different to what you usually read, isn't it?' she quipped. Zion chuckled.

'I figured I'd see what all the fuss was about. My girlfriend used to read them all the time. Always seemed like total bullshit to me, but she practically lived her life by these things.' He went back to reading an article. Mia was unsure of how to respond next. Zion had never mentioned a girlfriend before. Should she ask about her, or was it a sore subject?

Zion had never revealed anything that personal to her. She decided to delve in.

'What was her name?'

'Carina. Swedish name, think it means *pure*.'

'That's pretty,' Mia beamed. 'I like finding out those sorts of things. I think mine means *beloved*.'

'I think mine is *smooth criminal*,' Zion said, deadpan.

'What? No way.' Mia started giggling again.

Zion smiled as he continued to look at the article. Mia couldn't help but carry on quizzing him.

'What happened to her?' she asked, rather forward. 'I mean, if you don't mind me asking?' Zion didn't seem too fazed.

'Same thing that happened to a lot of people in the war. She died.'

'Oh Zion, I'm so sorry.'

'It's OK, it was a long time ago,' he reassured. 'It is what it is.' Mia decided to leave her questions there. She looked for a way to change the subject.

'I feel a bit guilty for not helping out with the preparations,' she admitted. Zion put down his magazine and faced her.

'The way I see it,' he started. 'There really isn't that much preparation we can do. Let's think about it. We're ready for the bandits, the bandits show up, we know they're here, they try to take our stuff. The only thing that can change is whether or not we see them before they storm in here. Doesn't take fifty people to organise that.'

'I guess,' Mia replied, a little unsure.

'Don't get me wrong, Gabriel's a great guy. I'm really happy he's found his mojo here, organising people and being the inspiration they need at a time like this. He's found his purpose. But that doesn't change the fact that there really isn't that much we can do until these bandits show up. If they even *do* show up.' He went back to reading his magazine. Mia nodded in understanding.

'So are there any good bits in there?' She pointing towards the magazine. 'They usually have some funny personality quizzes and stuff.'

'Actually yeah,' Zion perked up. 'They had one a few pages back. Let's have a go.'

**

Cyrus called after Jane as she started to make her way up the escalator to the first floor. She turned around to wait for him.

'What's up?'

'Gabriel and I were just talking. We need to find more water, we're running pretty low.' Jane looked over at the food stash as she listened to Cyrus. She anticipated his next words, but let him speak. 'Earlier on you mentioned that you thought we should move home, somewhere closer to supplies.'

'Yeah, I think it makes sense. This part of the city is bone dry.'

'Well my question was, what makes you think there are any supplies further out? What if other people have already taken them? Bandits for example. There may have been plenty of supermarkets with water just sitting there waiting to be taken before the end of the war, but do you really think it'll still be there now?'

Jane felt like she was being tested, like Cyrus was trying to point out what a terrible idea she had. She was only trying to help, and as far as she was concerned moving the colony could have turned out to be the best idea anyone had in months. By staying here all they were doing was running out of time and options. Her head began to spin. She paused for a moment and focused on Cyrus, trying to prepare her defence for his next words. But something caused her to pause momentarily and recalculate. Cyrus's tone wasn't sarcastic, she could spot that kind of thing a mile away. And his face wasn't contorted into a smug grin. He looked intrigued, almost desperate. Maybe he was genuinely asking for her opinion.

'I don't think we really have much choice,' she replied. 'It's either we go and look for a new home, which may or may not be near a new source of supplies, or we stay here and run out of food and water. With the threat of bandits coming this way I think there's only one thing we can do.'

Cyrus knew she was right, it was the best thing for the colony. But he hated putting those he loved in danger. The mall had remained safe this long, but for how much longer? He needed some answers first.

'I'm going to go to the other side of the city,' he declared. 'Gabriel can help keep everyone safe until I return, but I need to know what's out there before we ask everyone to uproot and move.'

'Are you sure? Cyrus, it could be real dangerous. We know there's mechs out there for sure, but what if you run into those bandits as well?'

'Like you said, we don't have any other choice,' Cyrus forced a half-smile. 'Do you have any idea of where to start?'

'Actually yes. There's a Super Save, a big one, out on the east side of the bascule bridge. If there's any water around there, I'll wager it's there.'

Cyrus nodded and took note of the instructions. He was dreading going back out in the heat again, but he knew it had to be done; the colony were depending on him. But he knew he couldn't go alone, he'd need someone to watch his back.

'Please tell me you're taking someone with you,' Jane continued, as if she had read his mind.

'Of course. Rowley made it very clear earlier that he won't let me go out there by myself.' They parted ways as Jane climbed a second escalator to meet Doug on the roof. He leaned over the balcony, looking out over the ground floor, and saw a group of people sitting and laughing. Rowley was among them, with Jennifer leaning her head on his shoulder. As he watched them together, he regretted having to drag his friend away again into the wilderness of the city.

Something caught his eye briefly from the other side of the mall, up on the second floor. A sharp flash of light that faded as quickly as it had appeared. He squinted at the origin of the light, but his attention was distracted as he heard the infectious laugh of Mia a few yards away. He looked to his right to see her sitting with Zion. Of course it was Zion. Cyrus had always been a little jealous of Zion's sense of humour. No matter who he was with, he always seemed to find a way to make them laugh; a trait he wished he possessed.

Mia laughed as she pointing to a page of the magazine. 'No way are you the 'quiet, sensible one'.'

'Like I said, it's all bullshit,' Zion quipped.

'Hey guys, what's so funny?' Cyrus attempted to join in.

'We're taking a personality quiz. Oh Cyrus, it's your turn!' Mia excitedly passed the magazine to him as he sat beside them.

Cyrus glanced at the page. 'Twenty questions?' he grumbled. 'Maybe later, I need to leave soon.'

'Leave?' Mia looked concerned. 'But, why? We just got back.'

'We're running out of water, and we need to explore another part of the city to check if it's safer than here.'

'Cyrus, please. Let someone else go,' Mia protested. She hated how hypocritical he was being. Why would he risk his life to come after her if he was then going to leave her and go back out without giving it a second thought?

'Come on man, at least wait a little while,' Zion pleaded, backing Mia up.

'Guys, I wish I didn't have to, but we really need the water.' Cyrus stood up to signal his intent. Zion copied him.

'At least let me go with you.'

Cyrus paused. He appreciated Zion's offer and was very keen on taking it up, but he didn't want to make him go.

'No, it's OK. I want you to stay with Mia. If the bandits arrive while I'm away, I want to know she's in good hands.'

Mia butted in. 'You know I'm right here, don't you? Cyrus, I'm not a child, I don't need a babysitter.' Cyrus looked stunned at her outburst. 'Zion, I want you to go with him,' she declared. 'No doubt Rowley will want to go with you too, so if you are going to be so stupid as go out there in this heat without proper rest, I want to know there's at least two people with half a brain looking after you.'

There was a short silence as Cyrus was lost for words.

'Right, I think that's our cue to leave,' Zion said at last. As the two of them headed towards the escalator, Mia rushed over to Cyrus and hugged him, kissing him on the cheek.

'Come back in one peace, you dumb hero,' she whispered in his ear. Cyrus's heart raced and a fire started within him. If he hadn't known it before, he knew in that moment that he loved her. He knew he'd be counting every minute he spent away from her, praying that she stayed safe, despite his own peril. He didn't care about the risks, he wasn't concerned for his own safety. Whether brave, ignorant or just plain blind, he hadn't even thought about the dangers that lay ahead of him. Mechs, bandits, worse? Nothing. All that went through his head was a steely determination that he had to make it back to Mia.

Cyrus and Zion walked down the escalator and towards the array of weapons stacked against one of the walls. Rowley was waiting for them, with a rifle on his back and a smile on his face.

'Gabriel told me about the water. I'm coming with you.'

'Wouldn't have it any other way,' Cyrus replied cheerily.

Zion slapped a playful hand on each of their backs and proceeded to pick up a rifle. 'Come on, lovebirds. Let's go. The sooner we go, the sooner we get back.'

CHAPTER SEVEN

The sun shone brightly over the trio as they stepped out into the street. Cyrus squinted and shielded his eyes with one hand as he tried to get his bearings. He'd known this heat for a long time, but it always seemed to take him by surprise when he made that first step out into it. As he looked up to the sky he attempted to identify a notable landmark. A lone skyscraper towards the east of the city caught his eye.

'You see that skyscraper over there?' Cyrus pointed to the building. 'We only have one map with us, so if we get separated head over there.' Zion and Rowley followed his finger and nodded in acknowledgement. Cyrus continued. 'The Super Save Jane was talking about is just beyond that building, over the bascule bridge. With any luck the bridge will be down so we can get across.'

'And if it isn't?' Zion asked.

'Well, er, let's hope it is,' Cyrus bumbled. 'Look, I hadn't really thought it through. There should be other bridges but it'll mean a longer journey and a detour, which we really could do without right now.'

'Two trips out here in one day is bad enough, let's pray it's a short trip,' Rowley chirped. He took the map from his back pocket and unfolded it. As he glazed over it he tried to get a sense of how long it would take. He located the supermarket on the other side of the bridge. 'We're lucky it's just over the bridge,' he said with a sigh of relief. 'Shouldn't take us much more than thirty minutes each way.'

'Best thing I've heard all day.' Zion marched off with a slight skip in his step. Cyrus and Rowley shared a perplexed glance at each other before following.

**

Half an hour later and by a stroke of luck, the three companions had reached the skyscraper without any sign of mechs or bandits. Cyrus knew their luck had to turn at some point. The last couple of days had been particularly eventful and they had been rather unlucky to have as many mech encounters as they'd had. He peeked around the corner of the towering building to check the coast was clear. There appeared to be nothing but a couple of burnt out cars and a few lowly bits of litter blowing about in the breeze.

'Looks clear,' he declared. 'I can hear the river.' The three of them made their way around the corner to see the bridge a couple of hundred yards in front of them. The strong current of the river forced water to lap up into the foundations of the bridge, like gentle waves bouncing off a sea wall. The sound of the water teased their thirst, but they knew they couldn't drink from it. A few months ago they had learnt that the river had been polluted by unknown means, meaning the water was contaminated with all manner of filth and disease. Only the rats would dare drink from it now. As they drew nearer to the river, they could clearly see that the bridge was in its lowered position. They each let out a relieved sigh. The light breeze blew some dust into their eyes as they were almost at the bridge, forcing them to stop for a moment to look at the ground and blink repeatedly. Finally Cyrus looked up to the far side of the bridge for signs of the supermarket.

'Over there. It's exactly where the map said it would be!' he exclaimed. Rowley looked at Zion with a raised eyebrow and smirked.

'Well, yeah. Maps are generally pretty good at letting you know where things are, Cyrus,' he replied smugly.

'And he *does* have a sense of humour!' Zion retorted, throwing him arms in the air. Rowley's grin was quickly wiped off.

'Come on Zion, I'm not that bad am I?'

'I have to say buddy, you've been pretty dry recently. It's good to hear you crack wise. I was beginning to think you'd lost it completely.' Zion fired a wink at Rowley. He was right, Rowley used to make jokes all the time. But as with many things, his sense of humour was lost somewhat in the aftermath of the war, but for the odd flash here and there. Rowley turned to Cyrus, who was still looking out over the bridge.

'Cyrus, you don't think I've lost my—' he stopped mid-sentence as he realised what Cyrus was looking at. 'Oh shit.'

The three of them were now looking out over the bridge in front of them. Whilst it was in the right position to walk over, it had been substantially eroded in places, leaving a particularly large gap in the middle where the concrete had broken away. Crossing would be extremely difficult, if not impossible. The three continued to stare at the gap as their hopes were dashed.

'We'll never make it across there,' Rowley said at last. 'Let's try and find another way around.' He began to turn, but Cyrus put a firm hand on his shoulder, holding him by his sweaty t-shirt.

'No, we're not giving up.'

'Cyrus, look at that void right there. There's no way we can make it across. I don't fancy falling to my death today, thank you very much. Have you seen how strong that current is?' Rowley pointed to the river below.

'We have to at least try,' Cyrus challenged. He scoured the area with his eyes wide, searching for inspiration. A rush of adrenaline took over his body as he desperately looked for an idea. He caught sight of a large upturned lorry on the near side of the bridge. The cab was still attached to the container, however the front was resting on the edge of the gap, partially leaning over it. 'Look, there,' he pointed enthusiastically. 'We'll climb on top of that and jump from there. Easy!'

Zion and Rowley looked at each other in bemusement. It was clear to them that Cyrus had completely lost his head. He was so desperate to get to the other side he was coming up with ludicrous plans that would surely lead to their doom. They needed to stop him, somehow. But before they knew it, Cyrus was marching towards the back of the lorry.

'Come on guys, boost me up.'

'You're out of your mind,' Rowley called after him through cupped hands. Zion looked at Rowley and shrugged. It was obvious that Cyrus wasn't going to take no for an answer. He was an idiot, but without their help he may soon be a dead idiot. Zion had a flashback to the look on Mia's face before they left the camp. That sweet, smiley face of hers had so quickly turned into something much darker and unpredictable. That told him everything he needed to know; she wasn't to be messed with. He didn't want to find out what she'd do if she found out they'd left Cyrus to jump off a bridge. Unfortunately it looked as though Cyrus was set on jumping off bridges today, so the least they could do, for all their sakes, was help him avoid plunging to his death. Zion rushed to his aid.

'Hold on buddy, we're coming!'

Rowley couldn't believe his eyes. Zion was just as daft as Cyrus. Now they were both going to fall into the river, and there was no coming back from that. He'd have to explain to everyone at the mall how he watched two of his closest friends jump to their death while he stood and watched. He saw Zion boost Cyrus up onto the container of the upturned lorry and decided enough was enough.

'Cyrus, wait,' he yelled after his best friend. 'Wait for me to get up there. I'll help stabilise the cab as you jump.'

Cyrus beamed and waited patiently at the top. Zion boosted Rowley, who in turn pulled him up. All three were now crouched on top of the container and began to slowly creep forward. The container rattled and creaked beneath them.

'I'm starting to get a bad feeling about this,' Zion remarked. The wind started to pick up and a strong gust came out of nowhere, nearly knocking them off. Cyrus was getting close to the front of the container and could see the cab half exposed over the edge of the gap. He took a deep breath and planted a timid foot down onto it, holding on to the edge of the container for support. After a moment he let go and slumped his full weight onto the cab. As he looked down he could see he was standing right over the door, where he could see into the truck's cabin. There was nothing of note inside, apart from a pair of lucky dice hanging from the sideways tilted rear-view mirror.

Here's hoping.

A loud screech came unexpectedly from the street behind them. The three companions turned around simultaneously in horror; they knew this sound well. Low and behold, a panther had emerged from around the corner of the skyscraper and spotted Rowley and Zion on top of the lorry. Cyrus was slightly lower down on the cab and couldn't see past the top of the container.

'What's going on?' Cyrus looked back at his petrified friends. Rowley turned to him as he gave his shaky reply.

'OK Cyrus, you need to jump now,' The pounding sound of heavy galloping footsteps began to echo in Cyrus's ears. He got the picture.

Shit, shit, shit.

Cyrus trembled as he threw his heavy plasma rifle over to the other side of the bridge, giving him a little extra spring as he prepared his jump. He looked down into the rapids that was the river and gulped.

'NOW, CYRUS!' Rowley screamed. Cyrus took a small step back and attempted a running jump. As he sprung off the front of the lorry and into the air he seemed to fly for a short while, almost in slow motion. In that brief moment, everything went quiet. The noise from the river, the galloping footsteps; everything seemed to stop. Cyrus wondered if he'd suddenly gone deaf. Then a moment later all his senses came rushing back as he landed clean on the other side of the bridge. He rolled on the concrete and felt a sharp tug on the back of his neck as the thread of his necklace got caught under him. Luckily the crystal didn't come off and remained hanging over his chest. He picked up his rifle and turned back to his companions. Soon after, Rowley got ready to repeat Cyrus's procedure, chucking his rifle to the other side before preparing to hurl himself over the gap. The cab gave a little more height to their jump, allowing them to make it, just.

Rowley's landing wasn't as clean as Cyrus's. Whilst Cyrus had a rather skinny physique, Rowley carried a little extra weight. The lack of food over the last few months had trimmed him down a bit, but he was still a little on the heavy side. He had always said he was 'big boned'. Cyrus watched painfully as Rowley's left foot hit the concrete of the bridge, followed by almost every other part of his body as he rolled a few feet before finally coming to a rest next to him. Rowley let out a pained groan and slowly tried to get back to his feet.

Back on the other side of the bridge, Zion was waiting on top of the truck's cab. His heart raced and his breathing grew heavy and panicked. He glanced back at the panther that had almost made it to the other end of the lorry. It was looking right at him with its soulless robotic eyes. He looked back at the void in front of him and caught a glimpse of Cyrus beckoning him to jump. He drew in a final deep breath as he pushed off and raced a few steps forward. On reaching the end of the cab he took off on one foot like an Olympic triple jumper, but his trailing leg scraped against a chunk of loose metal, once the lorry's wing mirror. Zion let out a cry as his jump was cut short, his leg cut from the impact. Cyrus rushed to the edge of the gap from the other side, holding his hand out for Zion to grab. Zion threw both arms into the air and grasped Cyrus's hand with his. Cyrus struggled under the weight of his friend and tried desperately to cling onto him as he stared into the rushing waters below.

As Zion dangled over the river, the panther had now reached the lorry and shaped up to pounce across the full extent of the gap. Cyrus looked over at the mech as it started to leap instinctively over, mouth open in their direction. Cyrus closed his eyes as he anticipated his and Zion's certain doom.

Suddenly a loud bang caught Cyrus by surprise, forcing him to open his eyes. He just managed to catch sight of the panther as it smashed against the edge the bridge, its circuits popping and fizzing. It then slumped down into the river, completely lifeless as it was washed away by the strong current.

Rowley threw down his rifle and hurried over to help pull Zion up. With one big heave they managed to get their friend back to the safety of the flat concrete surface. Zion started to laugh uncontrollably in his sheer state of shock. Cyrus lay flat on his back as he tried to catch his breath. All of his strength had been completely drained clinging onto the dangling Zion.

'Everyone alright?' Rowley asked, relieved. Zion and Cyrus were too exhausted to respond.

After a few moments Cyrus sat up and looked back at the side of the bridge they'd just come from. There was something standing in the distance, at the far end of the bridge. He strained as his weary eyes struggled to see through the waves of hot air wobbling in his vision. It was another mech, a golem, standing completely stationary. Cyrus was confused as to why it wasn't chasing them like the panther had. Had it not seen them? It seemed to be looking right at him. Suddenly he could see another one emerge from behind it. And another after that. All three companions were now looking in the direction of the mechs. In that moment, they started to hear a faint rumbling sound coming from the skyscraper. It came in waves, like the footsteps of something much larger than a regular panther or golem. Then they saw it; a gigantic monstrosity of metal parts. This was at least three times the size of a golem and something none of them had ever seen before. They looked at each other in bewilderment and then back at the enormous mech that was bearing down, albeit slowly, on the bridge. Like the panthers, it walked on four legs, however it was different in nature. Cyrus thought it vaguely represented the look and movement of a tortoise as it grew closer. It had four chunky legs and a large shield-like barrier over its back, almost like a shell. It appeared to have no head, but rather one large robotic eye protruding from the front. Finally, as it reached the other end of the bridge alongside the three golems, it stopped. Cyrus was mesmerised by the thing. He had no knowledge of this mech, nothing whatsoever. But he was about to learn a lot about it very quickly.

The giant mech's back seemed to arch slightly, revealing a colossal canon that pointed right in their direction. Zion, who had long stopped laughing, squinted at the weapon for a second and then proceeded to scamper in the other direction.

'RUN!' he called. Neither Rowley nor Cyrus needed a second invitation. As they darted towards the other end of the bridge there was an almighty boom from the mech as it let out a shot from its canon. The round hit the spot where the companions had been standing moments before, and a ten-metre radius of concrete exploded, sending fragments everywhere. Another shot was fired soon after, this time completely obliterating the middle of the bridge, creating an even bigger gap between the two sides and sending the lorry tumbling into the river with a loud screech and a thump as it hit the water.

**

Back at the shopping mall, Gabriel was pacing around tirelessly from one corner to the next. He felt fired up as he anticipated the possible arrival of bandits. The scare he'd given the rest of the camp in alerting them to the news had resulted in the colony now looking to him for inspiration and instruction. As much as he was worried for their safety, it had given him a sense of purpose, for which he was secretly glad. He marched over to the food stock and inspected the contents. There were a few tins of various long-lasting food, mostly beans and soup as usual, and the water had all but been depleted, save for a half-filled gallon bottle.

He stroked his long beard. The bottle was full when he had spoken with Cyrus earlier. They didn't normally go through that much so quickly. Gabriel looked down at the ground around the bottle to see if someone had spilt the water. That seemed like a logical explanation. But there was nothing, the area was bone dry. He glanced around his immediate location to see if he could spot anybody drinking water. April was nearby, talking with her sister, Jennifer.

'Have either of you had any water recently?' he asked, rather accusatory. They both looked up, a little startled.

'How recently?' Jennifer replied. 'Do you mean in the last couple of hours or since this morning? Because judging by my headache I think you can tell which.'

Gabriel started to get irritable. 'I mean *very* recently. Half a gallon's gone in the last hour or so.'

Jennifer pulled a confused look and looked at her sister. April shook her head. 'I haven't had any for at least two hours, and I didn't see anyone gulp down half a gallon. I think I would have noticed that.'

Gabriel started to get worried. Someone must have been tampering with the water supply when everyone was busy planning the defence of the mall.

'But you agree that half a gallon is a lot in such a short time-frame?'

The girls both nodded simultaneously. Gabriel started to panic. Why would someone waste so much water when they had so little to spare? Was someone sick? Nobody had mentioned anything about having a fever.

In that moment he caught something in the corner of his eye. Someone went into the restroom on the other side of the ground floor. Of course this was a very normal sight. Despite the lack of running water in the mall, people still did their business in the privacy of the restrooms. However instead of using the toilet stalls or urinals, they filled up buckets to dispose of outside in a nearby sewage grate. It seemed to be a short-term solution through the chaos until the world got back to normal again. If it ever did get back to normal again. Gabriel couldn't make out who it was, and completely without hesitation stormed over to the over side of the room and followed them in. April and Jennifer looked at each other, completely bemused.

Gabriel had no idea why he was following this person, but he was desperate and needed answers. Perhaps this person was using their precious water supply to clean up a mess? It was probably nothing, but at this stage Gabriel wasn't thinking straight at all. He had literally gone for the first person he'd seen, and they happened to be going to the toilet. As he pushed open the door of the restroom, he found himself looking at two doors; one with the standard male toilet logo, and another with the female logo. Ordinarily the next decision wasn't a difficult one, unless you were visually impaired or extremely drunk. But Gabriel wasn't looking for the toilet he needed to use, he was looking for a clue.

He heard a gentle cough come from inside the women's restroom. Gabriel rolled his eyes; he was hoping for a different outcome. He placed his hand on the door, but hesitated a moment. Could he really just walk into the women's restroom? What would they think? He'd look like a pervert. He needed to come up with an excuse. He softly opened the door just a crack to peer inside. He could see three sinks, each with their own mirror on the wall in front of them. However there was no sign of anyone. He started to open the door more fully, however one of the cubicle doors suddenly swung open and Mia appeared. She walked up to one of the mirrors and studied the reflection of her own face. Gabriel bolted backwards to escape in time and instinctively hid in the men's restroom.

He slapped his face to shake himself out of whatever it was he was going through. Moments later, as he stood by one of the sinks in the men's restroom, the door swung open. Gabriel half-expected to see an enraged Mia, who would then question his motive for going into the women's restroom. However it was just Guy, and Gabriel breathed a sigh of relief as he walked into the room. He smiled as Guy walked past him and stood over by one of the urinals. Gabriel looked into the mirror and pretended to check his beard, still recovering from the events that had just taken place. Had he really just tried to follow Mia into the restroom? He could hear the trickling of Guy urinating coming from behind him. He looked into his own eyes through the mirror to try and focus and block out the sound.

Get a grip, Gabriel.

Finally he composed himself and started to move back towards the door to leave. As he opened the door, something caught his attention. It was that sound, the trickling sound from moments before. It was still there, and had been for a fair amount of time. Guy must have really needed to go, almost as if he'd drunk a gallon of—

Gabriel froze where he stood. He couldn't believe it, he'd cracked it! By following Mia and subsequently hiding in the men's restroom he'd inadvertently found the culprit. With one swift movement he swivelled on the ball of his foot and practically launched himself against the urinal next to Guy. Guy didn't appear fazed, and barely looked up as Gabriel pretended to unzip his fly next to him. Gabriel cautiously waited a couple of seconds as he noticed the pool of liquid being collected as it funnelled down the urinal drain and into the bucket below. He took a quick glance at Guy's stream to take note of the colouring. It was completely clear and could easily have been pure water. Gabriel felt a rage building up inside him and could feel his eye twitching. What was Guy playing at? How could he be *that* thirsty? He needed answers.

Guy finally finished and zipped his fly back up. As he turned around to walk towards the exit, Gabriel grabbed him with both hands and slammed him against the door of one of the nearby cubicles, staring down at Guy's face as he towered above him.

'What do you think you're doing?' he yelled. 'You silly little boy. Do you know that water's for everyone?'

Guy was taken completely by surprise and looked shocked at Gabriel's aggression.

'What do you mean?' he replied, timidly.

'You know EXACTLY what I mean! You've been drinking far too much water and leaving none for anyone else. Do you realise how little water the colony has?'

Guy started to shake and cowered in a slump. 'I've had an awful headache, I, I, thought the water would help ease it. Besides, I figured Cyrus and the others would bring back more soon so it wouldn't matter.' He was really testing Gabriel's patience now.

'You idiot!' he shouted. 'Everyone has a headache, it's a part of living in this heat with such little water. But you don't see anyone else chugging it all down, do you? I mean half a gallon, Guy? That's a hell of a lot of water.'

'Half a gallon?' Guy protested. 'Why would I drink that much? Is it even possible to drink that much? Everyone's been drinking from that bottle.'

A few other members of the colony had heard the kerfuffle from outside the restroom and decided to step in to see what was going on. Nathaniel, a middle-aged man who had lost a leg in the war slowly entered the room first with the aid of his crutches. Gabriel eased his grip on Guy's shoulders and relaxed slightly.

'Gabriel, Guy, what's going on here?' Nathaniel asked concernedly. Gabriel started to panic and his eyes darted around the room at the new faces that had entered after Nathaniel. What should he say? He was going to look like a fool in front of the rest of the colony. Accusing a teenage boy of drinking too much water? They'd surely lose faith in him as a leader. He looked back at Guy, who had a tear running down his face. Maybe he was jumping to conclusions? Everything had escalated so quickly, he hadn't really thought this through. He was so jumped up about the bandits he had started attacking everything and everyone he saw.

'I... Guy...' he began to say. Guy interjected to save face.

'Gabriel's worried about the water supply, and rightly so. I had a headache so I drank more than my share to try and get rid of it. I'm sorry.' He bowed his head in shame and fell silent.

Gabriel took a deep breath and sighed as he exhaled. Nathaniel looked at the pair and shook his head.

'Gabriel, I know it's frustrating, but Cyrus, Rowley and Zion volunteered to help us with the water situation. You should probably focus your energy on preparing us for the bandits.' He looked disapprovingly at him, before leaving the room with those that had followed him. Guy slowly stood up and wiped his face.

'I'm sorry Gabriel. What I did was wrong,' he said remorsefully. 'I'll go up to the roof to see if Jane or Doug want to swap shifts on look-out.'

Gabriel was still a bit stunned by the previous events, and just stared down at his hands. Those giant hands that had nearly throttled a fifteen year old boy. Yes, what Guy had done was wrong, and he had been acting a bit strange recently, but he was just a boy. Only the other day he'd been attacked by mechs, and everyone seemed to be using him as a scapegoat to cover up the real issue of how doomed they all were. It was only a matter of time before the bandits came and then none of it would matter.

CHAPTER EIGHT

As they ran from the bridge, Cyrus could feel the rumbling vibrations of the explosions behind them. Adrenaline had kicked in as he rushed away from danger, but now his body was starting to remember how tired he was. He desperately needed water and rest. Cyrus could feel his head pounding from the sticky heat and dehydration. He longed to be at the supermarket, and as his legs tired he began to imagine what he'd see when he finally arrived. Perhaps the power was still on and he'd be greeted by a large chilled bottle of water? He prayed that the freezers were still working; he'd have given anything for an ice cold drink. Although right now he needed wheels on his shoes, as he was slowing down and they weren't out of the woods yet.

Cyrus heard the echo of another boom from the bridge, followed by a loud creak and a crash as the lorry toppled into the river. The three of them glanced back over their shoulders as they ran.

'Looks like we'll need to find another way back,' Zion quipped.

'No shit,' Cyrus replied sarcastically. He gradually slowed down to a jog as he looked back down the street they just came from. The bridge was well out of view now, tucked away behind the buildings they'd passed. He motioned to Rowley and Zion to stop.

'I think we're safe here,' he started. 'From the sounds of it, they've blown up most of the bridge so they won't be following us in a hurry.'

'Yeah,' Rowley agreed. 'That panther barely made it across and I doubt the golems and whatever the hell THAT thing was could make the jump either.'

'Not with half the bridge in the river,' Zion added.

'I've never seen a mech like that before,' Cyrus remarked. 'It was huge.'

'Gargantuan,' added Rowley. 'Let's just hope that's the last we've seen of it.'

'Gargantuan,' Zion repeated. 'Good word.'

The companions headed for a small pocket of shade in a nearby alleyway. There was a large industrial bin at the far corner and the light breeze that had picked up near the river had sent a small pile of old newspapers into a miniature whirlwind a foot or so from the floor. Cyrus took a knee and retrieved his map while Rowley and Zion investigated the contents of the bin.

As he studied the map, Cyrus was quickly able to locate their position. They were close to the supermarket, but in their panic as they escaped the bridge they had taken a detour and ended up in Peltaville. This place was once a notoriously dangerous part of Novasburgh and had been a hub of criminal activity. Just across the bridge from the financial district, this was a hotspot for muggings and pickpocketing as wealthy businessmen ventured through here on their way home from work. The main street was lined with dubious shops selling knock-off electronics and jewellery, and even the odd strip club. Of course in the wake of the war nothing much was left, but the area still maintained its stigma as the survivors of the stubborn gangs that once ruled it remained, lurking in the shadows.

'Guys,' Cyrus called after his friends. Zion was holding up the lid of the bin with one hand as a light flickered from inside. He looked back at Cyrus and accidentally let his hand slip, letting go of the lid which slammed shut with a bang. A cry came from inside and Zion hurriedly opened it again. Rowley's head popped up and he swung an arm out of the edge, sheepishly holding the other above his head towards the lid. Zion offered an apologetic smile as he put two firm hands on the bottom side of it for safety.

Cyrus rolled his eyes. 'Find anything?' Rowley shook his head as he hauled himself out.

'It's been picked clean,' he replied. As the days went on this was becoming the standard response.

Cyrus decided they should get back on track soon. The sooner they got to the supermarket, and away from this place, the better.

'We've stumbled into Peltaville. We should stay alert.'

Rowley looked around cautiously and picked up his rifle from the floor next to the bin. Zion closed the lid as quietly as he could and crept over to Cyrus.

'If there's anyone out there, I'm pretty sure they already know we're here, Zion,' Cyrus remarked with an eyebrow raised.

'Well, let's start as we mean to go on,' Zion replied, upbeat as always.

'We started with you slamming that lid over there.'

'OK guys, that's enough.' Rowley took charge. 'Cyrus, where's the supermarket?' Cyrus showed him the map and pointed to their location, then dragged his finger across the page to the Super Save a short walk away. As Rowley followed his finger, a shadow briefly covered the map and then left as quickly as it had arrived, as if the sun had been temporarily blocked by a small cloud. Rowley and Cyrus simultaneously leaned away, as if they had accidentally created the shadow themselves, and looked up to the sky. Not a cloud in sight. A strange uneasiness fell on the pair as they suddenly got the feeling they were being watched.

'Zion, did you see anything?' Rowley was getting nervous.

'No, chief, nothing. Why?'

'I don't like this. We need to get out of here.'

**

No more than fifteen minutes had passed before the group found themselves in front of the Super Save supermarket. The three of them stared at the large building from a distance and marvelled at it. They each shared the same thought and prayed that there was still food and water inside. As they made their way towards the front of the store, they noticed something wasn't quite right.

'Uh oh,' Zion said, deflated. Cyrus and Rowley soon saw it too.

'Arrrgh, damn it!' That was the final straw for Rowley. He marched over to a lone shopping trolley and kicked it over onto its side. Cyrus and Zion carried on looking at the entrance, and specifically at the huge metal shutters covering it. They were locked tight and looked to be electronically sealed. A red light flashed on and off in the top corner of the doorway. The alarm must have still been on.

'Well, at least we know there's power,' Zion chirped, optimistically. Rowley was still taking his anger out on the trolley.

'Yeah, that's a point,' Cyrus replied, wiping a bead of sweat from his brow. 'But we'd need the password, or fingerprint, or retina or whatever to get through, right?' There was a long pause as Cyrus tried to weigh up their options. He looked up at the bright blue sky and squinted under the light of the sun. Surely this wasn't it? There had to be a way. All the heat, the exhaustion, coming inches from death. It couldn't all be for nothing.

'Or, we could just hack it?' Zion offered, playfully. Cyrus reeled at the idea and directed a confused expression at his friend.

'What did you say?'

'We could hack it. I could hack it.'

Cyrus paused as he tried to process what he'd just heard.

'*You* can hack it?'

Zion smiled and winked cheekily. 'Yup.' He turned back to the entrance and studied the shutters. Cyrus didn't move, his face frozen in a perplexed state as the words bounced around the walls of his mind. He still wasn't sure if he'd heard right. He considered the possibility that he'd gone crazy, that he was hallucinating. He was lost of all hope and Zion's words were his oasis. He snapped out of his gaze and looked back at the shutters, and then at Zion studying them. Maybe he wasn't crazy at all. Maybe it was Zion. How could he have been so blasé about this? He must have gone mad. There's no way he could just 'hack' this thing. Cyrus decided that Zion had lost his marbles and got stuck in another mindset where he thought he was some kind of super spy. He watched as Zion started running his hand down the side of one of the walls, as though he knew what he was doing.

Meanwhile, Rowley appeared to have calmed down and was panting as he leant over, one hand on his stomach and the other resting on the handle of the trolley. Cyrus wondered whether he had calmed down, or if he was just unfit. Either way, he'd stopped shouting and kicking stuff.

'Wha—' Rowley tried to catch his breath. 'What... are we... gonna... do?'

Cyrus turned to him and stared for a while. What should he say? That Zion's gone insane and thinks he's a secret agent? That they weren't getting in here any time soon and they should consider plan B? What even was plan B? There was no plan B. He could have said any number of things, but the words that came out of Cyrus's mouth were simple and matter of fact.

'Zion's going to hack it,' he said, with a half-smile on his face. He watched as Rowley's face mimicked the exact expression he'd pulled moments before. Rowley threw a hand up in the air and shook his head in bemusement.

'Oh, right, OK then. Sure, Zion's going to hack it.'

Cyrus turned back to the entrance as Rowley continued. 'Just one question. What the hell?'

Zion was looking up at a wire at the top of the supermarket doorway as Cyrus interrupted his concentration.

'Zion, buddy,' he started, calmly, as if he was trying to talk him down from jumping off a building. 'Can you actually, you know, hack it?'

Zion looked offended by the question. 'Well, yeah.'

'Why haven't you mentioned this before?'

'Nobody ever asked. The power to the mall can't be restored, so the situation never really came up before.' He carried on looking at the wire, tracing its path with his finger in the air. Cyrus turned to Rowley and shrugged. Zion's casual attitude had completely thrown him, and now he wasn't sure what to believe. He started to reach out to touch the cold metal shutters. If he wasn't getting near a freezer anytime soon, he may at least get a moment of shameless gratification from the cool steel of the barriers. As his outstretched hand was an inch or so away from the shutters, Zion quickly batted it away.

'Don't!' he snapped. 'We don't know what kind of condition it's in. If it's sensitive it could set off the alarm and then we'd really be screwed. It'd be a beacon for every mech in a quarter-mile radius.'

Cyrus stepped back cautiously, holding his wrist in his other hand. 'Oh. Right. OK.' It was only then that it occurred to him that the metal barriers would conduct the sun's heat, and would actually have been hot to the touch.

You're an idiot.

Rowley decided to press on with the questioning. Zion was starting to annoy him with this mysterious vibe he was sending out.

'Seriously dude, what the hell? I get that everybody had a life before all this happened. I worked in construction, Cyrus worked in the gift shop at the observatory—'

Cyrus frowned. It was always a crushing dose of realism when someone else mentioned his former job. He enjoyed working at the observatory, but he and everyone else knew he would have stagnated in that job forever. Classic underachiever.

'But I thought you were in the military?'

'I *was* in the military,' Zion replied candidly.

'Then how come you know so much about, well...' he flapped his arms at the barrier. 'This?'

'Rowley, we don't even know for sure that he does,' Cyrus cut in. 'The heat's doing crazy things to our heads.'

Zion stopped looking at the wire and turned his attention fully to his companions.

'Yes, I was in the military,' he started with a sigh. 'But I wasn't always in the military. After finishing school I wanted to become a scientist. And not like the boring kind who spends their time lecturing half-interested students. I wanted to be in a lab, creating stuff. The government were offering a few scholarships for an engineering programme at the Academy, and I got a place. I loved it there, it was exactly what I wanted. I learned a ton and I got to build robots. Every kid's dream right?'

Cyrus and Rowley exchanged approving nods as Zion continued.

'Anyway, the final year involved a practical where we had to come up with something our own. A test of innovation before they offered us a full time gig among the scientists. They were working on new prototypes of robots. I'd overheard some of the senior researchers saying that they were having problems keeping them mobile, as they used up so much power they could only be used in short bursts—'

'Wait a second,' Rowley interjected, aggressively. 'Are you telling me you were around the scientists who worked on the mechs?' His eyes widened as his blood boiled. 'These Godforsaken mechs that tear us apart every day. YOU were in league with the people that created them?'

'Rowley, cool it,' Cyrus intervened. 'He's on our side. Let the man speak.' Zion seemed apprehensive of Rowley's building anger, but nodded appreciatively at Cyrus as he finished his story.

'My project was to find a way of storing the power in the robots. The mechs,' he corrected. 'With the days as hot as they are I figured the sun was the best form of renewable energy we had. The wind came and went and the wind farms to the north drove electricity in bursts throughout the year. Sometimes they'd generate energy, sometimes they wouldn't. Sunlight was the most reliable source, so I tried to find a way to harness that in an element small enough to fit inside the head of the robots.'

'The mechs,' Rowley corrected through gritted teeth.

Zion sighed. 'Right. They needed to be small, but also powerful enough to power them through a night of complete darkness. And it worked.'

Rowley lunged towards Zion, but Cyrus had anticipated it and attempted to restrain him.

'Rowley, stop! He's one of us, remember?' Cyrus pleaded as he struggled under the strength of his friend. The crystal started to glow a pale red as it swung to and fro around his neck. Rowley ignored his protest, temporarily deaf with rage, and overpowered him. With a clenched fist he reached over and smacked Zion hard in the cheek, causing him to fall to the floor with a thump. Rowley turned away, shaking off his hand as he retreated and slumped down next to the wall at the corner of the entranceway.

After a few moments, Zion sat up, clutching his face which had been cut over the cheekbone. Blood dripped onto the floor next to him. 'I'm sorry, Rowley,' he said softly. 'I didn't know what they were building. They weren't mechs when I worked on the prototypes. They were harmless robots. If I had any idea of what the world would turn into, what the government would use them for, I would have quit long before I did what I did.'

Rowley refused to look at him and stared intently between his legs at the floor in front of him.

'I'm ashamed of it. All of it,' Zion said. 'I was so desperate to follow my dream that I was blind to what was really going on.'

Cyrus tried to persevere with the peacekeeping, while getting answers from Zion.

'The government were a bunch of snakes. It's not your fault.' He paused for a moment as he pondered the mech issue. 'So the mechs have a way to be powered continually, as long as the sun exists?'

'Not exactly,' Zion said. 'The sunlight powers their chips, keeps them going. Without sunlight they'd simply power down into a sort of sleep state. But I think there's something else that activates them. Whatever it is should be able to deactivate them too, make them immobile. I wasn't involved in that part. I guess it was classified.'

'Then how can we deactivate them?' Cyrus demanded.

'Honestly, I don't know. There must be something in the facility, like an off switch somewhere.' Zion thought for a moment while he rubbed his pained cheek.

'So let's go to the facility,' Cyrus insisted.

'No chance. I heard that it had been blown up by MIRE.'

'So that's it?' Cyrus felt sick inside. 'What are we going to do?'

Zion looked up at him and said nothing. He had the look of a broken man, with nothing left in the world. Cyrus felt a sudden pain as his headache got worse. He winced as he rubbed his forehead. The stress of the situation wasn't doing him any favours. He'd almost forgotten the reason they were here. The colony were waiting on them, they needed to get into the supermarket and bring back water. He looked over at Rowley, and then back at Zion. Rowley had at least seemed to calm down, for good this time. Cyrus let out a long sigh.

'Well, let's start by getting into this place. How exactly can we 'hack' into here, Zion?'

Zion pointed to a wire at the top of the door, which ran across the wall and around the corner of the building. 'We follow that wire.'

CHAPTER NINE

As the three companions made their way around the corner of the Super Save, they simultaneously looked up to track the wire's journey around the building. As it clung to the wall in a thin black line around eight feet from the ground, they could see it continue its path around another corner.

'Looks like it's around the back,' Cyrus declared.

'There must be a fuse box around there,' Zion added. 'If there isn't, we're screwed.'

As they reached the far end of the building and turned the corner, all three let out a short burst of profanity under their breath. Sure enough, there was no fuse box. Instead, the wire simply disappeared into the wall. The fuse box must have been in a security room inside. Cyrus kicked the brickwork in frustration, and instantly regretted it as his toe seared with pain.

'Great. Now what?'

Rowley shrugged his shoulders and hunched over in a defeatist stance. After a moment, the beginnings of a wry smile appeared on Zion's face.

'We could just climb through the window?' he said. Cyrus and Rowley looked at him in disbelief, as if he'd just offered the worst contribution to any conversation ever. With a quick motion with his eyes, Zion guided their attention towards a window a bit further along the wall, which was open just a crack. He could see his friends' eyes light up as they realised what they'd seen, followed by a scramble to get to it.

'Looks like we hit the jackpot. How lucky can you get?' Rowley chirped. The events of a few minutes ago seemed to have been temporarily forgotten. 'We should check it's safe before we go in.'

The panel itself was so dirty and smeared that it was almost impossible to get a clear view in. Zion rubbed the glass in an attempt to clean it, but it made no difference.

'We'll have to chance it,' he said.

'Can you open it more?' Cyrus was adamant to go in first. He had positioned himself by the side of the window, ready to hop in. The window opened from the bottom, causing the top half of the frame to move further into the room on its hinge. Rowley put two hands on the bottom part of the panel, wrapping his fingers around the edge and pushed gently upwards. The window started to give way, albeit with a creak.

'How's that?' Rowley asked.

'Keep going.' He added a little more force, causing the window to squeak louder as it opened. 'Almost there…' The window reached a forty-five degree angle and stopped. Rowley tried to put more strength behind it, but it wasn't going to budge without coming clean off its hinges. 'OK, that should be enough.' Cyrus stooped down and placed his rifle inside, before climbing in himself. The top of his arm scratched against the frame, which was badly worn and jagged. 'Arrgh.' He looked across to see a white scratch line on his skin, but no blood.

'Stop being a baby and just climb in already,' Rowley joked.

Cyrus picked himself up and dusted himself down. He took a quick look around the dark room before him, which was littered with cardboard boxes. 'Coast is clear, we're in a storage room.'

Zion climbed through the window next, and then Rowley, who caught his arm in the same place Cyrus had and let out a muffled cry. Cyrus rolled his eyes at him.

'Stay alert, we don't know if there's anyone here,' warned Cyrus. 'Let's move through to the security room and disable the shutters. Then we'll explore the shop floor and see what's there.' He crossed his fingers at that last bit. With rifles at the ready, the three of them moved towards a door to their left.

'OK, stack up,' Rowley whispered as they got near.

'What?' Cyrus whispered back.

'It's something they say in the military. When someone says 'stack up' you adopt a certain formation to prepare to enter a room,' Zion explained. 'Rowley must have seen it in a film.' He raised an eyebrow at Rowley.

'Oh, right. OK sure, let's 'stack up',' Cyrus mocked as he proceeded to open the door without much care. The room inside was empty and dark, but for the dim glow of a computer monitor. Zion quickly spotted the fuse box on the outside wall and marched over to investigate it while Cyrus and Rowley studied the computer screen.

'Well, the power is definitely on,' said Rowley.

'Of course it's definitely on. The shutters were down and that blinky little red light was on,' Cyrus replied coldly. Rowley rubbed his head sheepishly, embarrassed and a little offended by his response.

'Well, if there is someone here then they definitely know we're here too.' Rowley declared.

'How do you know?' Zion asked from the other side of the room.

'Because of this.' Rowley tapped the bottom corner of the monitor where there was a live video feed of the entrance.

'Let's keep on our toes then.' Zion opened the metal door of the fuse box and was greeted by a multitude of coloured wires. Cyrus had walked over to take a look and gasped at the sheer number of different cables sprouting out from inside. 'This might take a while,' Zion sighed.

Cyrus decided to take a look around the room for anything useful. The room was mostly empty, but for the desk the computer was sat on, the office chair that was currently occupied by Rowley, and a filing cabinet in the far corner. Cyrus walked over to the cabinet and tried in vain to open the drawers.

'Locked,' he muttered to himself, noticing a keyhole on the top drawer. 'Rowley, see if there's a key somewhere in that desk.'

'Sure thing, boss.' Rowley started rifling through the drawers of the desk. He pulled out a stack of paper, along with a hundred or so receipts, and various stationery items. Finally he produced a key and held it up high.

'Voila,' he said proudly. Cyrus took the key and slotted it into the cabinet. It clicked as he turned it, allowing the drawers to slide. As he looked inside each drawer he found nothing but more paper, until he reached the bottom of the cabinet.

'Bingo.' He produced a chocolate bar from underneath a few pieces of crumpled loose paper.

A sharp pop and flash of light came from the fuse box and the lights in the room flickered. Zion recoiled, shaking his hand in pain. 'I... I think I've almost got it.'

'You better had, for your sake,' Cyrus added sarcastically, as he tried to break the chocolate bar into three even pieces. Meanwhile, Rowley was tapping away on the monitor.

'Zion, hang on a second. Before you electrocute yourself to death, do you actually need to hack the system from there? We're inside now and we can access this computer. Can't we just shut it down from here?' He tapped on the monitor again as he looked over in Zion's direction. Zion stopped to look back at Rowley, and didn't say anything for a few moments. Rowley suddenly clocked onto what he was thinking.

'Oh my God. Are you really that stubborn? You'd risk electrocution just to prove a point? That you can actually do it? You really are crazy.'

Zion's eyes dropped to the floor. It was clear that his past was affecting him and his earlier confession had been a big weight off his chest. He'd hoped his friends would react differently, that they'd understand. Maybe if they'd been in his shoes they'd understand. He was ashamed of his contribution to this hellish life, and a punch in the face was probably justified. The short silence prompted Cyrus to pipe up, in an attempt to hurry things along.

'Guys, this has to stop, now. Rowley, I know you hate Zion for what he did, but that's in the past now. You have to let it go. He's trying to help and if you hadn't noticed, he's been helping the colony survive as long as you or I have.'

Rowley let out a long exhale and slumped into his chair. Cyrus swivelled on his heel as he turned his attention to the deflated Zion.

'And Zion, what the hell is wrong with you? Look, I'm sorry we didn't believe you. Your hacking knowledge is still news to us and it took us by surprise. But you don't need to prove it to us. Right now we need to speed things up, because in case you'd both forgotten, we're not here for the fun of it. We're here to fetch water for our friends, because without it they'll die.'

There was a moment of complete silence as the last few words hung in the air, bringing Zion and Rowley back down to earth. The excitement of recent events had given them an escape from the life they were living, and they had been cruelly dragged back into it. As he looked over to Zion, Rowley offered a small olive branch.

'Do you want to do the honours?' he asked, gesturing to the computer screen. 'You'll probably be quicker than me.'

Zion smiled and closed the fuse box. 'My pleasure.'

Rowley vacated his seat for Zion to settle into his workspace. He watched as his friend stretched his fingers before pulling up a holographic display of a keyboard and rapidly typing away on it. He opened various windows and command boxes, and a few taps later a second holographic screen emitted from the monitor, extending out over the top and to the side, producing various displays for Zion to choose from. He studied each one carefully before swiping at them, shuffling through the options that were presented to him. Eventually he found what he was looking for and pinched the screen with his thumb and index finger, enlarging it to fill the whole area.

'Gotcha.'

The three of them watched the video feed of the entrance intently as Zion hit enter on the keyboard. With a loud screech that could be heard all around the building, the rusted shutters slowly began to lift. The red flashing light in the corner of the screen turned off, signalling the deactivation of the alarm.

'Piece of cake,' Zion said as he cracked his fingers and nonchalantly headed towards the door. 'Let's go find some water.'

**

The colony were starting to get restless. After Gabriel's announcement of the potential bandit attack, the mall had turned into a frenzy of people running about trying to help prepare for the imminent invasion. Now it had been a few hours, and people were beginning to doubt Gabriel's prediction. After looking to him for inspiration, the cracks were starting to show and a few of the survivors wondered whether he'd lost his mind. The floundering about had been replaced by many by sitting in a circle, chatting away as if it was just another day.

Nathaniel was leading the talk and seemed to be riled up about something.

'I mean, the kid was just, you know, doing his business. And then Gabriel comes over and starts attacking him, accusing him of drinking all the water.'

Doug joined the discussion, relieved of his duties taking watch on the roof. He took off his trucker hat and wiped a line of sweat from his forehead with his arm.

'I dunno guys, Gabriel's a good man. We've been together through a lot, and he's never once shown signs of losing it. He's a rock.' He looked around the group for support, but was met only with unimpressed looks.

'What makes you so sure? I think your loyalty to him has blinded you,' Nathaniel continued. A few others nodded in agreement. 'Let me ask you something, Doug. In your last group, with Gabriel and Jane, who was in charge?'

Doug sensed a trap, but decided to oblige as he didn't really have much alternative.

'Gabriel.'

'Interesting.' Nathaniel grimaced as Doug's words played right into his hands. 'So Gabriel likes to be leader.' He looked around the group in an attempt to maintain their attention. 'I have a theory. Do you think it's not entirely outlandish to suggest that Gabriel made it up? He's found a new group that has no clear leader, no human embodiment of hope to guide them through the end days.'

'The end days?' Doug questioned, confused by what he was suggesting. Nathaniel ignored him and continued.

'He's missing that feeling of being important, special. He wants to be the one people look to when things go bad, the one to protect them from the monsters outside.'

'This is outrageous! You're twisting this whole thing.' Doug was getting worried. Nathaniel was clearly set on a path to stir up trouble in the camp, and disagreement within the colony was the last thing they needed right now. He trusted Gabriel and knew he just wanted to protect those he cared about, so regardless of whether he was right or wrong the colony needed to support him for their own safety.

'Admit it, you know it makes sense.' Nathaniel was getting impatient now. 'He made the whole thing up. The bandits, the so called 'weapon' that can destroy the mechs. It's all bullshit. He just wants people to depend on him so he can get an ego boost for whatever complex he's built up from his time in the military.'

Doug felt something snap inside his head. It was like a restraining bolt had suddenly come away from the rest of his brain. 'You know nothing about him!' He raised his voice in protest. 'Gabriel is a good person. He's a fine leader and you can bet your ass he provides hope for us all, because when it comes to it he will put his life on the line for the people he cares about. You say he's a liar, but I think you're the one with the poisonous words, old man.' He stood up and put his cap back on. Nathaniel looked angered by the confrontation and continued with his argument.

'You can't admit it, but you know it's true. He's lying to us all. He shouldn't be the one leading us.' The rest of the group looked worried. Nathaniel seemed to be getting more unstable as the argument went on. The logic behind his disapproval towards Gabriel was becoming less clear, and came over more like a personal vendetta now. A woman shushed him as she spotted Jennifer making her way over to them.

'What the hell is going on?' Jennifer demanded. 'We can hear you shouting from the first floor.'

Nathaniel relaxed his tone. 'My dear, we were simply having a little debate about leadership.'

Jennifer sighed and rubbed her forehead with her hand. 'Not this again. Nathaniel, if I have to listen to one more of your rants about how things were better in *your* day, I don't know what I'd do.'

'So *this* is what it's about,' said Doug in a moment of realisation. 'You want to be the leader of this place, don't you?' He stared accusingly into Nathaniel's eyes.

'I have the most experience, it should be me,' he replied. 'Just because I'm older and have a stump for a right leg. That doesn't mean I can't do it.'

'Nobody is talking about your leg, or your age, Nathaniel,' Jennifer pointed out. 'The truth is, we don't need a leader. We were fine working as a group until now, but Gabriel isn't doing any harm. He thinks there might be bad people out there who want to rob us, and maybe even kill us. So if he thinks it necessary to prepare us for that then I'm more than happy to let him guide us through it.'

'We've seen it before,' Doug added. 'It's how our last group went. Or did you think that was a lie too?'

Nathaniel chewed his lip, thinking about his rebuttal. But he decided against it, instead picking up his crutches and moving away, leaving behind a rather sombre atmosphere.

Jennifer addressed the rest of the group as Nathaniel hobbled away. 'Please don't give up on Gabriel, he needs your help. We're all in this awful situation together, so show some support and lend a hand when it's needed. The last thing we need is everyone turning on each other.' With that, she left to head back to the first floor. The group muttered to each other for a while, before dispersing around the camp.

**

As they left the office and headed back through the storage room, Cyrus reflected on the day. Today had been a monster of a day, and he was exhausted. There were no uneventful days anymore, as every day brought with it peril of some variety. But this day had exceeded those in recent memory. For a moment Cyrus almost wished to be back in the days of the war. At least then the streets weren't crawling with uncontrollable mechs and people actually had normal lives, as far as normal stretched. Homes, families, jobs; everybody had a purpose, and despite the interspersed fighting between the government and MIRE life felt like it was moving forward.

The last few years of the war brought devastation as mech development grew to an advanced state, and soon both government and rebel troops were depleted in numbers, to the extent where those who fought were no longer interested in politics. After ten years the cause no longer seemed to matter, and what was left of humanity was forced to make a fresh start. It would take years to develop a renewed infrastructure, and while the mechs were still around it wouldn't happen at all.

Cyrus wondered whether MIRE had actually won in the end.

'Cyrus, are you coming?'

His daydreaming was broken by Rowley, who was looking at him strangely.

'You OK buddy? You look liked you zonked out there again.'

'Zonked out?' he replied.

'Yeah, that's what I'm calling it. When you go off into dreamland. Don't think I don't see you do it. It's weird, like you're playing the statue game or something, but with your face like this—' Rowley pulled a gormless, motionless expression.

'Like a zombie,' Zion added.

Cyrus rolled his eyes and tried to ignore them. As he moved forwards he felt something dig into his leg through his pocket.

'Oh, guys, I almost forgot,' he said, placing his hand into the pocket and retrieving three squashed pieces of chocolate. He handed a piece each to Rowley and Zion and ate one himself. 'That should keep us going for a little while. You know, in case there's nothing here and we have to go back empty handed.' The other two nodded as they enjoyed the heavenly taste of the chocolate in their mouths.

'Oh man, this is so much better than beans and soup,' Zion declared. 'And is that honeycomb? It's getting stuck in my teeth; I'm gonna be savouring this for the rest of the day.'

Cyrus pulled a disgusted face, but he secretly agreed with every word. The soft caramel centre of the bar swirled slowly around his mouth, the texture contrasting perfectly with the hard outer chocolate shell. A few moments went by where no sound could be heard, but for the chewing and smacking of lips. Cyrus couldn't recall ever taking this long to eat one third of a chocolate bar.

'You know,' Zion said, pulling a strange face as he struggled to pick bits of chocolate from his teeth with his tongue. 'I've been thinking about that giant mech, the one that blew up the bridge.'

'Oh yeah?'

'We haven't given it a name yet. Rowley, I think you got it spot on earlier. 'Gargantuans'.'

Rowley shrugged. 'Are you giving me credit, Zion?'

'No. You can bet your ass I'll claim I came up with it later. But good job,' Zion joked.

'OK, let's check out the shop floor,' Cyrus said at last, after swallowing the last remnants of chocolate. 'It doesn't matter what we call those things, they're all monstrosities to me and the less I think about them the better.'

'Ooo, 'monstrosities',' Zion repeated.

'We're not calling them that,' said Rowley. 'You already gave me naming rights.'

They readied their weapons and moved slowly into position by the door. As they were about to open it, Cyrus could see Rowley was desperate to say something. 'What?' he asked with a sigh.

'Look guys, we're stacking up,' he whispered with a big smile on his face. Cyrus shook his head in disbelief.

CHAPTER TEN

As they entered the shop floor, the three of them stopped in their tracks, mesmerised by what they saw. The whole place was completely intact, and the shelves of the aisle closest to them were stacked full with tins of food. Zion's jaw dropped.

'Well, looks like someone else likes stacking too, Rowley.'

'Holy smokes that's a lot of food!' Rowley couldn't contain himself. He rushed over to the nearest aisle and started scanning the labels on the tins. 'Green beans, carrots, lentils, rice pudding. Cyrus, they've got rice pud—'

A loud bang erupted through the supermarket and a tin next to Rowley exploded, splattering tomato soup over him. He instinctively dropped to the floor, disorientated. A few moments went by as the sound echoed in his ears. He finally got his bearings and wiped the soup from his face. He took a quick glance back towards the door, but his friends were nowhere to be seen. His heart raced as he briefly considered that they'd run and left him there. The storage room was much darker than the shop floor, so Rowley struggled to see if his friends were still inside. Even with the door wide open it was difficult to make out. He squinted to try and focus on the storage room, but was distracted by another loud bang. Another tin near the first exploded and more food fell onto his face.

'AHHHH!' he screamed out, helpless. Still no sign of his friends.

A voice came over the tannoy system. 'Drop your weapons and get out of the building. If you do not comply, I will shoot you.' The voice belonged to a man, but his accent didn't sound native to the city.

Rowley remained on edge and completely isolated on the floor. However, he was half relieved that it at least wasn't a mech.

'We don't want any trouble,' Cyrus' voice came from inside the storage room at last. Rowley breathed a huge sigh of relief. They hadn't deserted him.

Another shot fired, this time towards the storage room door, followed by the voice over the tannoy again.

'You brought trouble the moment you set foot in here. Leave now with your weapons on the ground, or I will shoot you.' The voice sounded more annoyed this time.

'Put the guns down,' Rowley pleaded. 'We can talk it out with him.'

'I don't trust him,' Cyrus insisted.

A fourth bang came, this time a lot closer to Rowley.

'Put the plasma rifles down on the ground, NOW! Or next time I won't miss.'

There was a short pause that to Rowley seemed to last a lifetime. Then two rifles appeared from the storage room, skidding along the waxed floor of the supermarket. Rowley pushed his away from him and spread his arms on the floor.

'That's better. Now the pistols.' The man behind the tannoy clearly wasn't stupid. Moments later three proton pistols followed and formed a small pile next to the rifles. The tension in the air was as tight as the string of a drawn bow. The three of them were now completely unarmed, their lives hinging on the uncertain temperament of this stranger.

'We just wanna talk,' Cyrus called out.

'Then come out and talk,' came the reply. Rowley looked over towards the dark doorway of the storage room. He couldn't see his friends, but he knew exactly what they were thinking; there was no way in hell they were going to just walk out in plain sight. Who knew what this guy would do? He didn't sound very friendly to say the least. After a few moments a voice came from the storage room, this time Zion's.

'Not going to happen, man. How do we know we can trust you?'

The voice behind the tannoy was starting to lose patience. 'Trust me? All I see are three armed bandits waltzing into *my* home looking to steal *my* food, and you want to know if you can trust *me*?'

'Bandits? We're not bandits,' Rowley protested. 'We're just looking for some water for our—'

Another shot fired. Rowley ducked as he heard the plasma round ricochet off of the shelf next to him. He looked up to the tins of food, but nothing had moved. Either the shot missed its target or the man had stopped aiming for it. He thought it was probably for the best, they couldn't afford to keep wasting this food with pointless shows of aggression.

'Enough! Here's what's going to happen,' the voice boomed. 'All three of you are going to walk out here VERY slowly with your hands in the air.' The man's voice paused, then calmed slightly as he continued. 'I'm going to keep my gun on you, but we're going to talk. You're going to tell me exactly why you're here and how you managed to break your way into this place.'

Cyrus had one hand on the wall as he leant against it, listening to the words being spoken. His other hand rubbed his pounding head. He didn't like what he was hearing, but it seemed as though he didn't have much other choice. Turning back wasn't an option, they'd come too far. Could he really take a leap of faith and place his life, and those of his friends in the hands of an unknown? A total stranger who was holding them at gunpoint. He began to wrestle with his thoughts. Perhaps this man was scared too? He tried to put himself in his shoes. He was probably right to do this. It must have looked sinister, the three of them coming into his home, armed with rifles. Cyrus decided that he would have done the same in his position.

'Don't shoot, I'll come out!' Without warning, Rowley stood up in the aisle and threw his hands behind his head. His face was white with terror as he walked slowly out into the open. 'Just stop blowing up all the food and let my friends go, OK?'

Cyrus and Zion were completely taken aback. Rowley was risking his life to buy them time to escape. A brave gesture, but a futile one at that; they weren't going anywhere.

'Rowley, don't be stupid.' Zion called after him. 'We're not leaving you.' He followed his friend out to the shop floor and put his hands in the air. 'OK, I'm coming out.'

Cyrus was left alone in the storage room, pondering his options. Perhaps he could find a way around to where the man was, and from there disarm him? He shook his head at the thought, it was too dangerous. Plus he didn't want to hurt anyone, or worse get his friends hurt. They were going to have to trust the stranger.

'Me too,' he called, following suit.

Moments later, all three companions were standing in plain view on the supermarket floor, hands either in the air or behind their head. They looked up towards an office on the level above them, which had a clear view of their location. There was a man sitting by the window with a rifle rested against the glass. The window panel had been slid open just enough for the barrel of the gun to rest against and for the man's head to look out. They could just about make out the man's features. He was bald, with a straggly beard. It was difficult to make out as he was sitting, but he appeared to have quite a skinny build. If Cyrus was to hazard a guess at his age, he would have said anywhere between forty-five and fifty. With one hand on the barrel, the man lifted his other hand away from the trigger and towards a button at the console next to him. The speaker system let out a quick burst of feedback, which pierced their ears. The man's voice quickly followed once more.

'OK, tell me who you are and why you've come here.'

Cyrus stepped forward and spoke up. 'My name is Cyrus. These are my friends, Rowley and Zion.' The other two gave a quick smile and half a wave. 'We're from a group of survivors across the river. Our group is in danger of bandit attack and we're running very low on supplies. We desperately need water if we're going to make it. Someone told us this place might still have some.' He glanced over towards an aisle about twenty feet away and caught sight of a large water bottle; the sort that would ordinarily be served in a dispenser.

'Well you've been informed correctly, I've got plenty of water here,' the man said, candidly. 'Trouble is, I've kept myself nice and safe in here the last few months. Last thing I need is you robbing me blind so I starve to death.' He looked at Cyrus intently, watching him with a heightened sense of intrigue. Cyrus started to feel uncomfortable. His stare was penetrating, as though even from this distance he was staring right into his soul. Cyrus could see the sudden change in the man's face. A glint of recognition appeared in his eyes as he watched him.

'You. Cyrus.' He pointed at him and cocked his head slightly. 'Your face is familiar. I know you from somewhere, do I not?'

A long silence followed before Cyrus replied. He racked his brain for a time in which he would have met him. He would have remembered meeting a man like this. That unsettling stare, those piercing eyes. He must have been mistaken.

'I don't think so, friend,' he replied at last, being careful to maintain a friendly demeanour towards the man pointing a gun at him.

Rowley thought he should try and help. 'Do you have any family? Friends? Are you alone here?' he asked. The man paused for a while, before finally responding.

'No, it's just me.' He voice was less commanding now, and they could feel him starting to let his guard down.

'There are people who need this food, this water,' Rowley continued. 'By the look of things, you've done well to keep this place safe. It could make a great safe haven for our friends.' They waited in hope for his response, but the man changed the subject.

'So you said there's trouble at your place?'

'Yes, it's chaos out there. Those mechs from the war are tearing the city apart, and what little supplies we've been able to get hold of are under threat of being taken by bandits.'

'Bandits? Did you just say bandits?' This seemed to strike a nerve with the man. He had now completely taken his hands away from the rifle, the butt of which was now resting on the ground, propped up against the window. He rushed out of the office and onto the balcony alongside it, in plain view of the companions. Cyrus could see the full extent of the man's skinny physique. For a man living with the luxury of so much food, he certainly didn't look any better for it.

'The Crimson Crows!' the man exclaimed. 'Sometimes I hear them, at night. They bang on the front gate and set off the security alarm. When the mechs come to the noise they scatter and move on, but they always come back.'

'We can help you,' Zion offered. 'We have people. Strong people, with military experience. We'll have safety in numbers if you let us in.'

The man continued, completely disinterested in what Zion had said, as if his words had completely evaded him. He was looking towards the supermarket entrance, as though he was distracted by something.

'I can hear them. They shout and make threats. How did they find me?'

Zion shared a look with Cyrus. Something was wrong here. If this man really was alone as he said he was, it wasn't doing any favours for his sanity. And that worried them. For now at least he was away from his gun. Despite the man's ramblings, there had been at least some level of subconscious trust formed between the two parties for him to move away from his weapon. None of the companions had moved towards theirs either, which must have registered. Rowley turned to whisper to his friends.

'We have to help him. This place is a godsend. If he's going to let us stay here we have to find a way to help him.' He turned his attention to the man and called up to him.

'You didn't give us your name. You asked us who we were, but you never told us your name.' The man's trance-like state was broken as he looked down at Rowley. His eyes were wide and his face pale, as if he'd just seen a ghost. It sent a cold and uneasy feeling through Rowley's bones.

'Isaac. They call my name. 'Isaac! We're coming for you.' They always come back, they always find me.' Isaac was struggling with his thoughts, caught up in the paranoia that was consuming him. Rowley knew he needed to get through to him, but he also knew doing so would involve a tough balancing act to avoid aggravating him. Rowley tried to compose himself and planned his next words carefully.

'Isaac, we can help you. The Crimson Crows won't bother you anymore. Our people can keep you safe. They won't get in here.'

'Well, disabling the security system probably made it easier for them,' Zion joked under his breath. Cyrus scowled and slapped him in the chest with the back of his hand to shut him up. Isaac reached behind his back and produced a small handgun that had been tucked into his ragged trousers. He pointed it at Rowley, his hand shaking as he did so.

'You're one of them!' he screamed. Rowley's hands went up again in a plea of surrender, followed quickly by Cyrus's and Zion's. 'I'm not going to fall for your tricks. You just want my supplies, you're not interested in helping me!'

Rowley slowly inched closer, until he was half-way between his friends and Isaac. 'Isaac, listen to me,' he started, calmly. 'We're not here to rob you, and we're not here to cause any problems. We're not like them, we won't hurt you.

We have a common interest here, Isaac; we both hate The Crimson Crows. Our friends are in danger, just like you are. If you let us take some water back to them, we will come back and make sure those people don't get to you. What do you say?'

Cyrus and Zion looked on in amazement at his composure during this situation. Isaac's lip trembled, and after a moment he broke eye contact with Rowley and looked at his gun. He watched as his hand shook on the spot, and after a few moments lowered it and relaxed.

'OK, yeah,' he breathed. 'We got a deal.'

**

'I hate having a permanent headache. It's just there ALL THE TIME.' Jennifer accentuated the last three words with aggression as she lowered her head and held it in her hands. April played with her sister's hair in an attempt to comfort her.

'I hope the boys come back soon. They've been gone for ages.' April looked over towards Mia, who was helping a group of people allocate food rations for the evening. 'She's still pretty mad at Cyrus.'

'Well that makes two of us,' Jennifer added. 'Why are guys so stupid?' April let out a loud snort and proceeded to giggle at the comment, drawing the attention of a few passers-by.

'That's the million dollar question!' she exclaimed.

'Rowley's no better. I mean, he's a really sweet guy, but damn is he dumb sometimes. The way he follows Cyrus around, I might start getting jealous.' Jennifer sat back against the shop window, leaning her head against the glass as she stared up at the ceiling. The shop they were sitting outside was one of the few in the mall that had remained in surprisingly good condition, to say the whole place had at one point been completely ransacked. The display window to the left of the double doors had been smashed in one place; probably the result of a stray stone or brick during the looting. The shop was a relatively small one compared to the rest, so it might not have been a prime target for looters. That was one explanation for its condition; the other being that one of the double doors was missing.

April could see that her sister was worried about Rowley, more so than usual. Jennifer had always been the tough, headstrong one of the family. Nothing seemed to phase her and she wore her thick-skinned attitude like a bulletproof vest. When she was young, April thought her big sister was secretly a superhero, like the ones she used to read about in comic books. Jennifer always protected her from bullies at school. But things were different now. In this new hellish world, even the strongest showed signs of reaching breaking point.

Their mother had died when April was very young, meaning Jennifer had to take over the nurturing role while their father worked his hands to the bone on the farm. He was a good man and did everything he could for his family, however that often meant working long hours and barely seeing them. Two years into the war, the military came to their farm in search of new recruits. Their father was drafted, and that was the last time they saw him.

A tear ran down April's cheek as she reflected on the past. She wiped her face and sniffed loudly. As she looked over to her sister it was like looking into the mirror. Jennifer rarely cried, and April had almost forgotten that she was able to. She shuffled over and wrapped her arms around her, hugging her tight.

'Thanks sis, I needed that.' Jennifer wiped her eyes and gave April a half smile, which she reciprocated.

'They're going to be OK. I can feel it,' April encouraged. 'They might be idiots, but they're together. They always seem to make it through when they're together. It's like they're each other's lucky charm. Plus they have Zion with them, and he actually knows a few things.' Jennifer giggled as April stuck her tongue out in jest.

Mia, who had finished handing out food tins, began walking over to join the pair.

'They're still not back.' She sounded annoyed, as April had predicted. They both smiled at the fact, before turning their attention to Mia.

'They'll be back soon, they probably just got way-laid or something,' Jennifer offered. 'You know how stupid they are, they probably took a wrong turn.'

'God, they *are* stupid.' Mia reiterated. She plonked herself down beside Jennifer and turned her head to glance into the shop, looking for something to take her mind off things for a short while. She read the sign on the front of the store. '*M's Comics.*'

'No way!' April jumped up in excitement. 'I love comics.' She too turned her head to peer inside. 'I don't remember this store being here, it must be fairly new.' The store inside looked pretty bare, and she couldn't make out anything left on the shelves. 'It's a shame they all got stolen. I mean, who loots a shopping mall and takes comics? Is reading material really at the top of your priorities?'

Mia shrugged. 'People are weird, that's all I know.' April thought about the comics she used to read, and remembered the time Zion had revealed how much he loved them too. He was into different characters to her, but she didn't mind. It was the best conversation she'd had since living in the mall.

'Who was your favourite? Superhero I mean.'

Mia scrunched her nose up slightly. 'Oh, I'm not really into them. I mean, they're OK I suppose, but I think they're a bit predictable.' Jennifer nodded in agreement. 'Who was yours?'

April thought about it for a second. She had so many to choose from. She looked at Jennifer and beamed. 'Hmm, I think I'm gonna have to go with *Big Sis*.'

Mia drew a blank. 'I haven't heard of that one before.' Jennifer clocked on and beamed back at her sister.

'So what happened with you and Guy?' Mia questioned, changing the subject again. 'I mean, you liked him right?'

'*Liked* being the operative word,' April snubbed. 'I thought he was nice, interesting even. But it turns out he's a jerk just like all the guys at school.'

'But you did only hang out with the popular guys. The jocks,' Jennifer teased. 'I think nerdy is more your type.'

'Well that's just it,' April retorted. 'That's what I thought, and that's why Guy seemed different. He's not loud or obnoxious. Well, he was a bit loud when he yelled in my face.'

Mia chuckled, her infectious laugh causing the other two to join in. 'His loss,' she said at last. A few moments went by as the laughing slowly died down and the girls looked for something else to talk about.

'I wonder what Cyrus and Rowley were like at school,' said April. 'Zion's an easy one, he was probably top of the class; teacher's pet. But then he'd surprise everyone by scoring three touchdowns at the football game.'

'Yeah, that actually sounds about right,' Mia agreed. Jennifer fired a warning glance over at her little sister; she knew exactly what she was thinking.

'Don't even go there, he's way too old for you.' She stuck her tongue out to dampen her words, but the point still came across.

'How old is he?' Mia asked. 'Like, we've never really asked him. I think he looks younger than he is.'

'Well, he's older than me, and that's too old for April.'

'OK, what about Cyrus and Rowley then?' asked April.

'Cyrus and Rowley were best friends at school, as they always have been,' Mia started. 'I went to the same school, in the year below them. It's funny, Cyrus and I never really spoke. We were, err, in different circles.'

April arched one eyebrow. 'What circle were *you* in?'

Mia shuffled about on the spot uncomfortably. 'Oh, you know. I hung around with one set of friends, Cyrus and Rowley were sort of in another clique.'

'That didn't answer my—'

'Cheerleader,' Jennifer interjected. 'It's obvious. With a figure like that, you had to have been a cheerleader, right?'

'Erm, yeah. Thanks?'

'Me too.' April was excited by this new found common interest. 'Although I found that the girls on the team could be quite mean.'

Mia looked even more uncomfortable as she continued to shuffle about where she sat. 'Yeah, girls can be really mean.' She turned to Jennifer. 'So, you must have been on the team too then?'

Jennifer laughed in response, and April winced in anticipation of the flurry she expected to follow. 'I wasn't pretty enough for the team,' Jennifer replied plainly.

Mia's jaw hit the floor. 'Are you serious? You're gorgeous!' Jennifer eyes widened at the compliment and she swept her hair behind her ear. 'Thanks, but let's just say I was a bit of a late bloomer. I looked quite different at fifteen.'

Mia nodded in understanding. 'Well, it wasn't all that great anyway. Being popular at school means diddly squat once you graduate.'

Jennifer appreciate what she was trying to do, but she didn't need reassuring of her past school life. She tried to turn their attention back to the original question.

'So, Cyrus and Rowley; massive geeks?'

Mia laughed. 'Not exactly, although they were both in the astronomy club. Rowley always seemed like a nice guy, but like I said I didn't know him very well. All I did know was that he didn't seem much good at sports. Cyrus however, was on the, erm, gymnastics team.'

Jennifer and April burst into laughter.

'Don't get me wrong,' Mia continued. 'Gymnastics is really difficult, and it takes a lot of balance and skill. But you know how people are. The guys on the team weren't exactly the 'cool kids'.' She emphasised the loose nature of the phrase with air quotes as she rolled her eyes.

'Well, you never know, those skills could come in handy,' said Jennifer. 'I bet he's really flexible…'

Mia blushed as a wave of embarrassment swept over her. April put her hands over her ears. 'That's gross.'

'Just putting it out there,' Jennifer replied innocently. The three of them sat in the strange atmosphere she'd created between them and a couple of minutes went by where nobody said anything.

As she sat there, April had been wondering if she should ask Mia more questions about Cyrus. She found it odd that Mia and Cyrus had ended up together when they were in such different circles at school. It sounded like a horrible thing to think, but she wondered whether they were only together because of the situation they were in. The two of them didn't exactly have a lot in common, but Mia didn't have an awful lot of people to choose from now.

'So, Mia, how long have you and Cyrus been together?' she asked. A fair question, she thought. There's no obvious agenda with a generic question like that.

'Oh, I don't know, what month is it now? September? I guess nearly two years.'

Two years. That meant way before the war ended. April's doubts were very much short-lived. She figured that to be together for this long, it was likely that their relationship was built on something sturdier than convenience.

'So, how did you guys meet?' she found herself asking, almost involuntarily. 'You said you didn't know each other very well at school.' April couldn't believe what she was hearing. The words were coming tumbling out of her mouth without her really anticipating saying them. She started to get worried that her questioning was moving past inquisitive and bordering on rude. She waited anxiously for Mia's response.

'We actually met at a party, as cliché as it sounds,' Mia said with a smile. 'Of course this was long after school, we both had jobs in the city.' April and Jennifer sat quietly, listening intently to her. 'We got talking and after we realised we'd been to school together we starting reminiscing about that. All the good stuff, the bad stuff.' She paused briefly as she closed her eyes and smiled. 'We laughed a lot. All the cliques, the 'cool kids'; none of it mattered anymore. It was just two people who played different parts in the same story. We kissed that night, and then, well, that was it.' Mia finished talking and felt an overwhelming sense of embarrassment as April and Jennifer sat there, looking at her.

'Sorry, too soppy?'

'I like it,' April reassured. 'It's the kind of thing I want.' April's feelings towards Cyrus and Mia's relationship had been turned on its head, to the point where she felt slightly jealous of their happiness. She was still curious to learn more about them, and how a real relationship differed to the brief ones she'd had at school. But she didn't want to appear nosey, so she decided she'd just ask one more question for now. But before she could speak, Jennifer asked one of her own.

'I've been meaning to ask, do you know what that necklace is all about? The one Cyrus wears. The crystal changed colour when he got angry this morning.'

'Was it only this morning?' April interjected. 'That feels like a lifetime ago now.'

'Angry? That doesn't sound like Cyrus,' replied a perplexed Mia.

'When he found out you'd gone on a salvage run. Things got pretty intense,' Jennifer added.

'Oh, right. I wish he wouldn't worry,' said Mia. 'Oh and I think the crystal is a mood stone. It changes colour depending on how he feels. Don't ask me how it works, because I couldn't tell you, but it's very special to him. His father gave it to him when he was young.'

Jennifer smiled. 'It's nice for people to have things to remember family by. I wish I had something to remember Dad. A picture would be nice; I've started to forget what he looked like.' April put her arm round her sister.

The trio were distracted by a flash emanating from the balcony above them. April squinted as her eyes adjusted to the flash and sudden darkness. She thought she'd caught sight of a figure, but it had disappeared as quickly as the flash that preceded it.

'What was that?' Mia asked. She hadn't seen where it came from. Without saying a word, April stood up and marched purposefully in the direction of the flash's origin. When she got to within ten feet away of the other side of the room, she looked back up at the balcony, to the left and then the right, searching for a trace of the figure. She cursed under her breath as the person was nowhere to be found.

'That slimy little pervert.'

'Who?' Mia needed some more clarification, but before she could get it April had raced off in search of the figure.

CHAPTER ELEVEN

As the sun beat down on his warm head, Aiden sat slumped against an old lamppost; one of the charming historic features still left in the old town. The lightbulb itself was smashed, but the well-crafted curves of the post remained relatively intact, save for the paint that had been worn off in places from the sandstorms. He ran his hands through his hair, causing a mixture of sweat and dust to sweep off into the air behind him. There was a light breeze whistling through the courtyard where he sat, which was very much welcomed by the rest of his group who had decided to take a break from their scavenging to recuperate.

How much longer can we keep going like this?

Michelle had been ordering them about like slaves, marching through the heat like soldiers going to war in search of food and water. But these people weren't soldiers. Hell, they were barely human anymore. He opened the zip of the near-empty rucksack he'd been lugging around and retrieved a plastic water bottle. He looked closely at the pen markings he'd made on the side; thick lines of black ink that at one time marked the water level within the bottle. Each line had a small word scribbled next to it. The first read *hope*, appearing near the top of the bottle. The second, *worry*, was written about half-way down. The third, around three quarters of the way down, read *familiar*. Aiden raised the bottle to eye-height to study the current water level. It barely reached the third line. A bead of sweat dripped from his thick black hair to his forehead, and then sped up as it ran down his face to the end of his nose. He wiped it off with a finger and contemplated tasting it, but instead decided on flicking the droplet into the air.

'OK, listen up,' Michelle barked at her weary looking companions. 'I make that about five minutes. Time to move out.' There were a few groans around the group as everybody slowly picked themselves up. Aiden slung his rifle over his shoulder and picked up his rucksack, placing the bottle back inside.

Michelle was a stubborn soul, and didn't like waiting around. Somewhere along the way this group of survivors had recognised her as their leader; or more likely she had appointed herself as such. In the week Aiden had spent with them he'd learned many things, but this fact had taken mere seconds for him to register. She had a particular presence about her, almost drill-sergeant-esque in her attitude, with a 'don't mess with me' looked etched across her face.

Aiden had always tried to avoid such unsavoury characters in his twenty-seven years: bullies, bosses, girlfriends. Blind stubbornness was a tiring trait, and one he could never respect. But it served Michelle's purpose for now, as nobody seemed to challenge her so called 'authority'. A day into joining the group, Aiden had asked her in passing if she had ever considered moving at someone else's pace, instead of the full steam ahead approach that seemed to be wired into her brain. The response he got was venomous, and he'd since decided to keep his head down.

The group were all now back on their feet, and began to move off towards the northern exit of the courtyard. However one straggler was yet to follow, still adjusting the straps on their rucksack. They struggled with their plasma rifle, which was far too heavy for them to carry, especially in their exhausted state. Michelle glanced back from the front of the pack and spotted the weak link in her ranks. She let out a loud sigh and stopped to face their direction.

'Cameron!' she snapped. 'You're slowing us down. You've already lost the map I entrusted you with. Don't keep me waiting as well.' The boy looked at her with wide, terrified eyes. The sort of look a dog gives his master after being caught with his head in the grocery bag. Aiden didn't know his age, but the poor lad could have been no older than eight. Certainly not old enough to be carrying heavy, not to mention dangerous, equipment. Aiden hung back as the rest of the group trudged on ahead. He looked over at Michelle, who was still staring in their direction. Her eyes turned to his and for a few seconds they were locked in a staring contest.

'Don't help him,' she said finally. 'He needs to learn to be strong on his own.'

Aiden's eyes squinted in disbelief. Cameron was just a child, he couldn't manage on his own. He was far too young to be carrying a rifle, let alone be trusted with one. He thought Michelle would have been harsh saying that to *him*, given the circumstances. But a boy? Aiden said nothing, and began walking back to help Cameron.

'Let me take that,' he smiled, taking the rifle from him. Cameron smiled back sheepishly, before looking past him towards Michelle.

'Are you thirsty?' Aiden asked, distracting him. As the boy looked up at him, he realised what a stupid question that was.

Everyone was thirsty. Aiden reached into his bag and presented the water bottle to him. 'This should keep you going until we get there.'

The two started to make their way back towards the group. Cameron stared purposely at the floor as he walked passed Michelle, who was chewing her lip as if she was fighting back some more harsh words. Aiden attempted to follow the boy's example as he reached her, but Michelle grabbed his arm.

'He needs to learn,' she said in a hushed tone, so as not to draw attention. She moved in closer to whisper into Aiden's ear. 'If he doesn't learn to cope by himself, he will die out here. The sooner you realise that, the better chance he will have.'

Aiden's eyes widened, and he was left speechless. Michelle released his arm from her grip, and walked on ahead. 'I hope you hadn't been saving that water,' she said with a wry smile. She retrieved a bottle from her own bag and took a swig as Aiden looked on with a dry mouth.

**

An hour or so later, the group settled down for another short break in a spot of shade underneath an overpass. Aiden was getting more and more tired with each step and practically fell to the floor, his rucksack still on his back. A woman from the group walked over to check in on him.

'How you holding up?' she asked. Her shoulder length auburn hair shimmered as the sun briefly illuminated her face, before she entered the shade of the overpass.

'How do I look?' Aiden replied. She pulled a concerned face, which made him laugh. 'That bad, huh? I guess that's about right.'

'We'll be there soon. Michelle knows this city like the back of her hand, and she reckons the mall is about another hour north of here.'

Aiden started to remove the bag from his back, shuffling about as he wriggled his arms out of the straps. 'Why are we going there? Has anyone even asked her?'

The woman looked offended. 'She knows what she's doing.'

'Are you sure?' Aiden pressed. He was starting to lose patience. 'From what I've seen, everyone just seems to be following her about without question. What's her deal anyway?'

'What?'

'What's her deal?' Aiden repeated. 'Come on, Caitlin. You know what I mean. Why is she so uptight all the time? Sounds like she's ex-marine or something.'

Caitlin raised her eyebrows. 'No, it's not like that at all. The shopping mall, that's where she worked before everything fell apart. She owned a small comic book shop; it was her pride and joy. Not sure what she did before that though, we didn't talk all that much.'

'Oh, so you knew her before?' Aiden asked.

'Yeah, I worked in a clothes shop next door. Every Friday she'd close up an hour early and bring cupcakes in for us. It was sweet, but I think she just got a bit lonely.'

Aiden was surprised to hear this. 'Are you sure we're talking about the same person?' He couldn't imagine Michelle got many customers with an attitude like hers.

'I know, it's hard to believe but she was very different back then.'

He was still struggling with the idea; it just didn't add up. The last few months had felt like a long time, but was it really enough time to change someone's character completely? The end of the world as they knew it must have awakened something inside Michelle; something perhaps even she didn't know existed. Maybe this desperate world was where she thrived.

'Hey. Mister, erm, Aiden.' Cameron came rushing over to the pair with a concerned look on his face. He had Aiden's water bottle in his hand. As he got closer, they could see that there was still some water left. 'I thought you might be thirsty, so I saved some for you.' He handed the bottle to Aiden, who gulped down what was left.

'Thanks,' he replied.

'That was very nice of you, sweetie,' Caitlin encouraged. Cameron beamed and wandered back to where he'd left his bag.

Aiden was puzzled. He looked at Caitlin and then at Cameron. She looked too young to have an eight year old son.

'Sweetie?' he asked. 'So Cameron, is he—'

'My son?' she finished, with a smile on her face. 'Yeah, he's mine all right.' She recognised the perplexed look on Aiden's face; she'd seen it a hundred times before. 'I was young.'

'Why do you let Michelle treat him like dirt?'

Caitlin looked at Aiden like he was stupid. 'She knows what she's doing. Michelle knows how to make people strong. She's hard on Cameron, but she needs to be if he's going to survive. I'm very grateful that she's kept us alive this long.'

A loud scream came very suddenly from further up the road. Bursts of gunfire followed, and then a booming sound erupted, causing the pair to jump. Caitlin, who had been kneeling next to Aiden, fell right on top of him, before awkwardly climbing off again to search for Cameron. Aiden reached for his rifle and quickly surveyed the road ahead and behind them. A figure emerged from further down the road, running back towards the group. Two of Michelle's closest followers, Connor and Finn, had been sent to scout ahead to check if the way was clear. They could now assume that it was not.

'What happened?' Michelle demanded, as Connor reached the group.

'They got Finn!' he screamed. 'He's dead.' He broke down in tears. But Michelle wasn't prepared to give him time to grieve just yet.

'Did they follow you?'

'I don't know,' Connor started. 'It all happened so fast. I saw him die, Michelle. They tore him apart right in front of me.' He fell to the floor and yelled in frustration.

'Connor, did they follow—' Michelle was interrupted by the screeching sound of a mech, which couldn't have been more than a hundred yards away. She recoiled in fear and looked up towards the overpass. She got the answer she was looking for.

'Everybody, under the bridge, now!' she commanded, and grabbed Connor by the back of his shirt, pulling him into the shade under the overpass.

The group waited in complete silence while the stomping of mech footsteps echoed around them. Soon after, a golem appeared on the top of the overpass, making the concrete above them quake with every stomp. As it reached the middle, the stomping stopped, and the whole group held its breath. The screeching sound came again, and quicker footsteps could be heard, growing nearer and nearer. Finally three panthers appeared alongside the golem, and began peering over the edge of the bridge, seemingly looking for their escaped prey. The group below huddled as close to the middle as they could to avoid being detected. Aiden could hear the snarling of the beasts' artificial voice mechanisms, which sent shivers down his spine. He held his rifle close to his chest and readied his finger on the trigger. All it would take was one panther to jump down to investigate and all twenty or so of them would be in real trouble. A single sound could alert them to their presence. Aiden glanced over towards Caitlin and Cameron, the latter of which was pale with fright. Paralysed with fear was the best Aiden could have hoped for from the youngest member of the group, as it meant he was keeping quiet, for now.

After a few moments, the panthers gave out one last screech and cantered off down the road. The golem followed suit, albeit much slower. When the pounding footsteps had gotten almost too faint to hear, the group breathed a sigh of relief and began to mutter amongst themselves. Aiden turned to Caitlin and Cameron.

'Are you OK?' he asked, looking at the little boy. He was still white with fear, but managed a shaky nod.

'We'll be much better once we get to the mall,' Caitlin admitted.

Aiden couldn't help feeling like there was something he was missing. Everyone he'd spoken to in the last week had been going on about the shopping mall, like it was some kind of paradise. He searched for Michelle before she could order them all back on the road again.

'Michelle, I need to speak with you,' he said with a tone of authority that surprised even him. Michelle looked annoyed at the inconvenience.

'Yes, yes, go on then,' she hurried. 'We need to get moving if we're going to make it there before those mechs come back.'

'That's what I wanted to ask you. Why is it we're going there exactly?'

Michelle paused for a moment and sighed. 'Aiden, there are some things in this world that you are yet to learn. People are not always what they seem. Did I tell you about what happened to me and my shop as the war was coming to an end? When there was nobody left to protect us?' Aiden shook his head. 'Looters, Aiden. MIRE. The government's guards were depleted, they couldn't protect us anymore. Those damn rebels cut through the city, and came into our mall, with their rocks and their bats. They took everything. They destroyed everything. We didn't do anything to them, we were innocent in all this. The mall is a good place to stay, a good place to find supplies and make a home in this wicked world. They knew that, and they drove me and everyone you see here out onto the street.'

Aiden suddenly felt uncomfortable. He felt sympathetic towards Michelle, which he'd never thought was possible. But he was also unsure of where she was going with this.

'They're bad people, Aiden,' she continued, her voice getting angrier with each sentence. 'They're going to pay for what they did to us.' A few others started nodding their heads in agreement.

'What, so this is vengeance?' Aiden asked. 'You're planning on killing them?'

Michelle said nothing and started to walk off. 'Time to go, people.'

Aiden chased after her and cut off her path. 'Are you seriously saying we're going there to kill people? We don't even know if they're still there.'

'I have it on good authority that they are,' she replied, bluntly. 'And I know just when to hit them.'

'But what if they're not the looters? They could be innocent people. Good people.'

'They are NOT good people!' Michelle snapped, drawing attention from the rest of the group, who stopped to watch the argument. 'You're getting too big for your boots, Aiden. You had nothing. Nobody. And we took you in, accepted you as one of our own. You should learn your place and be grateful that you're alive. There are people in this world who will exploit you and do whatever it takes to survive. If we don't stand up to them, you can bet your ass they won't show mercy on us.'

As twenty pairs of eyes fixed on him, Aiden suddenly realised how alone he was. Michelle intimidated him, but the overwhelming fear stemmed from the mass of people standing behind her. He couldn't make out whether they genuinely supported her extremist views, or were too afraid to say anything otherwise. Regardless, they seemed prepared to go along with her plan.

'There's no way you can be sure these people did it, Michelle. They could be innocent. Can you not understand?'

Michelle gave a wry smile and looked down at the ground, before looking back up at Aiden, her head tilted slightly to the side. Her pose was more relaxed now, as if she was talking to a friend. There was a swagger to her attitude, displaying the confidence that oozed out of her. This unnerved Aiden even more.

'I never said we were going to kill them.'

'What?' Aiden's eyes squinted as his confusion was plain to see.

'I'm not a monster, Aiden. I want these people gone, but I don't want to kill them, if I can avoid it. Those people can pay for their wrongdoings another way.'

A cold shiver ran down his spine as he pondered what possible misfortune Michelle could have planned for these people. He looked desperately around at the rest of the group for some kind of context. Not one person appeared interested in intervening. He was beginning to regret ever joining them. Their true colours were coming out and he didn't like the picture they painted. He locked eyes with Caitlin, who seemed to be the only other person who shared the same panicked expression that was etched on his face.

'We need to look after our own,' Michelle continued, distracting Aiden as she turned to address her supporters. 'We can have food, water, shelter. We can be safe. But nobody will give it to us. If we want to survive—' she looked at Cameron, who was standing in front of his mother, her arms around him. 'If we *all* want to survive, we have to take it for ourselves.' She turned back in Aiden's direction and slung her rifle over her shoulder. The rest of the group followed suit, until only Aiden was left. He stared at Caitlin as she walked behind the group with Cameron, silently pleading to her for something. Anything. She stared back despairingly and shook her head, almost apologetically before walking on.

'Pick up the pace people,' Michelle's voice boomed from up front. 'We should be there within the hour.'

CHAPTER TWELVE

April fumed as she stormed up the escalator to the first floor. She mumbled under her breath, glancing back occasionally over her shoulder in the direction of the balcony. There was still no sign of the figure, but she wasn't giving up easy.

Mia and Jennifer followed suit, the former of which was still trying to figure out what had riled April up so much.

'April, what's going on?' Her plea fell on deaf ears.

On reaching the balcony, April scanned the surrounded area as she panted like a hungry wolf stalking its prey. She stood there for a few seconds, just long enough for Mia and Jennifer to catch up.

'What is it, April?' Mia asked again. Again the response went missing. Jennifer placed her hand carefully on her sister's arm, to gently catch her attention. As she made contact, April grabbed her wrist and pointed it in the direction of the far end of the mall.

'There,' she said through a whispered tone, almost as if she was hushing them. The flicker of a light came and went very suddenly, briefly illuminating a figure climbing through a broken shop window. 'That pervert,' April hissed.

The three girls hurried over to the shop the figure had entered, taking care to tread as lightly as they could. As they reached the broken window, they could see the back of a person's head leaning against it. His jet black hair and skinny physique gave him away instantly. April grabbed Guy with both hands, the adrenaline rushing through her, giving her the strength to haul him up and back out through the gap in the window frame. He yelped in surprise, and looked up to find the three women staring at him, one with fury written over her face.

'What, so you're spying on me now?' April questioned. Guy opened his mouth but nothing more than a few helpless gasps came out. 'You're sick, you know that?' she continued her interrogation. Jennifer and Mia looked on, still not really sure what was going on. 'To think I even liked you,' April laughed to herself. 'You're nothing but a little pervert.'

Jennifer thought it was about time she was on the same page. 'April, what's this about?'

'I'll tell you what this is about,' April's voice grew more aggressive. 'This little creep has been taking photos of me.' Her eyes stared deep into Guy's, and she saw the same terror he had made her feel earlier that day. It pleased her to see the roles shifting between them, and she could feel the power being sucked right out of him.

'I don't know what you're talking about,' Guy protested. 'I haven't done anything wrong, I swear!'

'You know what, tell it to Gabriel,' April dismissed. 'You can explain it to him.' She knew that would scare him.

**

A few minutes later, Guy found himself in front of the giant leader of the colony. The commotion had caused a crowd to gather, with the majority of the colony absorbed in what was going on. Gabriel had the tiny camera in his oversized hand, which made a blip sound as he pushed one the buttons. The holographic display appeared, revealing the first photo on the machine. It was a scenic landscape shot from the roof of the building, taken at sunset. It was a beautiful image, showcasing the city's crumbling skyscrapers against the orange background of the sky, with the sun setting behind a much smaller building.

'You're quite the artist,' Gabriel remarked, slightly surprised by what he saw. He fired a concerned glance towards April, who was stood behind Guy with her arms folded. She knew what that look meant, but she was sure she hadn't made a mistake. Gabriel looked back at the display, and Guy winced as he started to swipe through the photos. The next photo was another sunset, very similar to the first. Two or three more swipes, still more landscapes, this time during the day. A bead of sweat ran down from April's forehead. She was starting to feel tense. The adrenaline had worn off and the sense of power she had felt moments earlier was beginning to waver.

A few more swipes went by, and Gabriel let out a large exhale. Then, his eyes widened as he stumbled on the next image. He frantically swiped through the next few, and then moved back through them, studying each one carefully. He didn't explain what he found, but it was clear that it had disturbed him.

'Thank you for bringing this to my attention, April,' he said at last. 'I think there's something we need to address here. Guy, you need to explain yourself now. Taking photos of a girl without her knowledge, it's not right.' Guy hanged his head as he felt the judgement of the entire colony bearing down on him.

'See, I told you he was taking photos of me. It's disgusting!' April exclaimed.

Gabriel hesitated as he looked back at the display. 'Well, that's the thing, April.' He walked over and passed the camera to her. With a confused narrowing of her eyebrows, she took it and gasped as she saw the images before her. The photos were not of her, but of someone else. She hurriedly flicked through the images, which become more unsettling as she went on, before turning worriedly to Mia.

'They're all of you,' she remarked, her tone matching the pale colour her face had become. Mia was completely taken aback, but needed to see it for herself. She took the camera from April's outstretched hand and perused hesitantly through the images. April was right, they were all of her. But why?

The first few frames were of her sitting with her friends, some of her smiling, others where she wasn't. The lens had been zoomed in to focus on her face. She continued to swipe. Another photo, this time of just her, sitting alone by one of the stores. And then another one with Cyrus. She was sitting with him, leaning her head on his shoulder. But for some reason Cyrus's face had been blurred out. Her heart began to race and a rush of anxiety flooded over her as she realised what was going on. She continued to scroll through the many photos of her. Just her. As she started to reach the end of the album, a few people stood around her gasped. A photo of her asleep, again focused on her face. The sides of the inside of her tent were visible in the background. She dropped the camera in a panic and it fell to the floor with a smack and turned off. She leered at Guy, who, like everyone else in the room, was looking at her with a pained expression. It was as if they were waiting for her reaction. Mia fought back a tear and marched right up to Guy, until she was merely a foot away from him.

'You sick bastard,' she said, with deathly calm, before walking away. Guy winced at the words, knowing that any blind hope he had for his infatuation had crumbled.

Jennifer picked the camera up from the floor and turned it on again. Fortunately it hadn't broken. The same blip sound came, before the last photo taken showed up on the holographic display that emanated from it. It was the one that had been taken a few minutes earlier, of Mia, April and her. The camera then made another blip sound and a menu opened up. Jennifer studied her grip on the device, thinking she'd accidentally pressed a button. But then something caught her eye. There were two available albums to view. One titled *Album 1* and the other *Album 2*. She tapped her finger on the hologram next to the *Album 2* option, and a whole new collection of photos popped up, similarly to the first. As she swiped through the album, there appeared to be a number of photos, all of the shopping mall.

'Gabriel, you might want to see this,' she suggested, gesturing for Gabriel to come over. The pair of them looked through the images. The south-west entrance doorway, the north-east entrance, the long corridors, the roof, the weapons lined up against the wall, even the food stash. Everything in the mall had been documented in this album, with numbers edited in next to each picture. The final image was a photo of the map in the centre of the mall, which labelled the shops and key features with numbers. The numbers in the map corresponded to those edited into each photo.

'What's this album for?' Jennifer asked, rather accusatory. Given the events that had unfolded, it seemed everything would be thrown Guy's way with an air of suspicion moving forward.

Guy lifted his head and muttered.

'Speak up, boy,' Gabriel bellowed. Guy kept his head up, but was still facing away from the pair. He chewed his lip before repeating himself.

'I wanted to record the way things are now, so people can see how we had to live during this time. You know, after civilisation gets back to normal again.'

Jennifer eyed Guy carefully, before powering down the camera and planting it in Gabriel's hands.

'I'm done with this. We should get back to our posts and remember what dangers we have to—'

Jennifer was interrupted by the crashing sound of the doors springing open in the north-east entrance of the mall. She swivelled around to face that direction, her gaze shared by the whole colony.

Footsteps were heard as the door slammed shut with just as great a force as it had opened. The steps were quick, hurried. The colony grew uneasy as they waited in nervous anticipation of the new arrivals. Mia, who had made her way half-way across the room, had now stopped in her tracks and turned on a pivot in the direction of the north-east corridor opening.

The centre of the mall had become so quiet you could almost hear the quickening heartbeats of the people. The footsteps echoed louder and louder down the corridor, emulating those of the very monstrosities they feared outside.

Finally, two exhausted looking figures emerged, one tall and slim and the other shorter and round. Rowley fell to his knees as he reached the group, like a marathon runner collapsing after crossing the finishing line. Jennifer raced over to catch him, embracing him and kissing his forehead in relief.

Zion slowed his pace and bent over to catch his breath, before giving a timid wave to the many pairs of eyes staring at him.

'H, hello,' he panted awkwardly.

'What news?' Gabriel asked hastily. 'Did you find water?' He looked at the two weary travellers and then back at the dark corridor from which they came. 'Where is Cyrus?' he asked. Mia's face turned pale and she felt a sickening feeling in her stomach. A second later, she heard a thud from the corridor. And then a loud groan.

'Can someone help me with this please?' a plea came from the dark. It was Cyrus's voice.

Mia's heart skipped a beat as the colour quickly returned to her cheeks. She yelped in delight and sprinted over to the far north-east side and into the corridor. There sat a dishevelled Cyrus, next to a heavy looking plastic barrel, which was completely full of water.

Jennifer fired a disapproving glance in Zion's direction.

'We took it in turns,' he shrugged.

Gabriel marched over to assist Cyrus, throwing the barrel over his shoulder without much effort, before making his way back to the centre of the room.

'Someone will need to help me distribute this water. Where's Doug?' He quickly scoured the group, turning full circle. Doug was nowhere to be seen.

'He might be on watch,' a woman offered.

Gabriel shook his head and scratched his beard. 'No, his shift ended a while ago. Jane took over from him. Speaking of which.' He swivelled to face the woman. 'Could you please fetch her? Sitting on the roof with the sun on your back is thirsty work.' The woman nodded and rushed off towards the escalator. 'I'll cover the next shift,' he called after her.

His mind focused back on the task at hand. People from all sides of the mall were moving in quickly on Gabriel's position, waving empty water bottles in his direction. He unscrewed the top of the barrel, and grabbed it with both hands as he poured the glistening liquid into the first empty bottle. One by one he began to decant the water into the small bottles. As the minutes went by he wondered what was taking Doug so long.

The north-east door of the mall bashed open once more with a loud smash, startling the colony. Gabriel twisted his head in that direction, knocking over the bottle he'd just filled. He felt a sickening feeling in his stomach as he listened to the pitter patter of footsteps coming slowly down the corridor. It couldn't have been Doug, there were far too many steps and they were out of sync with each other.

The footsteps got gradually louder, and started to echo through the opening to the centre where they stood. Gabriel glanced at the weapons stash, hoping he'd have time to rush over and distribute plasma rifles. To his horror, and for the first time since he'd been living at the mall, the weapons were nowhere to be seen. They had simply vanished without a trace. His head started to spin and his blood chilled. They weren't ready.

Cyrus, Rowley and Zion were the only ones still armed, and they stood in a line facing the opening, their rifles drawn. A few moments went by as the tension in the air grew thick. Everybody held their breath as the slow footsteps clipped and clopped all around them. The spilt water trickled out of the bottle over the floor, running underneath Gabriel's boot.

Nobody had stopped to pick the bottle up. Everyone was transfixed on the dark entranceway.

A shadow began to emerge slowly from the corridor. It was Doug. Cyrus began to lower his weapon.

Doug continued moving forward, his hands behind his head as a large group of armed strangers emerged from the shadows, pointing their guns in the direction of the colony. A woman walked right behind Doug, digging her proton pistol into his back, with a hand on his shoulder to dictate his moves.

'That's far enough,' Cyrus called to her, quickly raising his rifle again once he saw that Doug wasn't alone. Michelle stopped walking and put pressure on Doug's shoulder to make him do the same.

'You should learn to tighten up your security,' she replied with a wry smile. 'You never know what's out there.'

Doug pulled an apologetic expression towards Gabriel, whose hulking frame was still clearly visible through the crowd of people around him. Doug knew he wasn't supposed to go outside alone, and it had come back to haunt him.

'Your time here is over,' Michelle continued, getting straight to the point. 'If you put your weapons down and leave right now, I might spare your lives. But first,' she waved her hand to the men to her left, who starting moving in on the colony. Cyrus and Rowley intercepted them, standing in their way with their rifles trained on them, as Zion maintained his fix on Michelle.

'Back away!' Rowley shouted.

Michelle let out a loud exaggerated sigh. 'I'm trying to make this easy for you. You cannot win this fight, you're vastly outgunned.' She turned her head towards Gabriel as that same smile returned to her face. 'For a colony of, say, fifty people.' She did a quick estimated mental headcount. 'You don't have an awful lot of firepower.' She raised one eyebrow, mocking him.

Gabriel's fist clenched and his blood went from chilled to boiling point in a matter of seconds.

'Another outburst like that.' She turned her attention back to Cyrus and Rowley, switching her gaze between them and Zion. 'And your friend here gets a proton round in the back of his head.' Doug closed his eyes in fear as Michelle went on. 'I won't ask you again.' The gun in her right hand moved up from Doug's back to the back of his head. She pressed the barrel against the gap in the back of his trucker hat. 'Put. Them. Down.'

Cyrus looked desperately over to Zion, who after a moment's hesitation nodded and proceeded to place his rifle slowly on the floor. Rowley quickly followed suit, as Cyrus's head began to spin.

Think, Cyrus, think.

Cyrus watched Doug's terrified face, and suddenly began to feel his friend's life hanging by a thread, completely dependent on his next move. He dropped the rifle and took a step back.

'Good boy. Now we can talk.' She looked across the room to the other side of the mall. 'Ah, hello dear. You've done a sterling job.' The whole colony swivelled around to see the smug grin written on Guy's face as Michelle addressed him. 'I see you've met my nephew,' she continued, focusing purposefully on Gabriel's enraged face.

'Son of a—' Gabriel whispered under his breath, leering at Guy as he walked right past him.

'He's figured it out,' said Michelle. 'I'll elaborate for those of you who haven't quite caught up. Guy is my nephew. He used to help me run my shop here. He loves comics does Guy, don't you dear?' Guy nodded. 'This is my mall. When the war ended, you savages took it from me, and everyone else who worked here.'

'What? No, that wasn't us,' April protested. 'This place got looted long before we took shelter here. It was deserted when we arrived.'

'Like hell it was!' Michelle pursued. 'You took it from us, and now we've come to reclaim what's rightfully ours. I sent Guy to join this group and learn more about you. I didn't want to risk bringing my people here to get slaughtered. An innocent boy lost in the wilderness? You wouldn't send him away. Guy has been sending me updates, showing me exactly the best place, and time to strike.'

More crashes were heard as a small group of armed strangers moved quickly into the mall from the entrances of each of the other corners of the building. The colony was completely surrounded. Jane and the woman who had been sent to fetch her appeared by the escalator, but froze in their tracks when they saw a number of rifles lock onto their position.

Michelle motioned to the men to her left to carry on with their task. They waded through the crowd and plucked a young boy, his mother and two other women. They dragging them, kicking and screaming, back to Michelle.

'What are you doing?' Cyrus demanded. 'You said if we left no one would get hurt.'

Michelle laughed maniacally. 'My boy, I said I'd spare your lives. And so far I've kept that promise pretty well, wouldn't you say?'

'This is madness!' Cyrus cried. 'They've done nothing wrong, you don't need them.'

Michelle grimaced. 'No, you're quite right. I don't need them. But there's someone who does.'

'What are you talking about?' Cyrus questioned. But Michelle neglected to answer.

'Enough talk,' she announced. 'It's time for you to leave.'

The large room was silent, and the people looked at Gabriel for advice. He had the look of a madman, seconds away from exploding into a rampage, but inside he was completely broken. He was faced with a tough decision: let them win and capture their friends for who knows what, or launch a futile attack that would surely lead to their deaths. He struggled through his anger and despair, whilst Michelle spoke again, buying him some more time.

'Not her though,' she said, pointing at Mia, who had backed into the crowd around Gabriel. 'We need one more.' The man to her left moved back in to pluck her from the crowd, dragging her back to Michelle. Cyrus's heart raced and his mind flashed back to the dream that had been haunting him since his mother and sister disappeared. His vision this time was of Mia calling his name as she was dragged away, and now it was very real.

'Well aren't you a pretty one?' Michelle said snidely. 'The Jackal will like you.'

The crystal around Cyrus's neck was glowing redder than ever, and it started to grow hot against his skin as if its fiery aura was spitting out into the air around it.

Before Cyrus could protest, Guy intervened, stepping between his aunt and Mia.

'Wait, you can't take her,' he pleaded. Michelle loosened her grip on Doug's shoulder, pushing him out of the way. Rowley rushed over to help him up as he stumbled onto the floor.

'And why not?' Michelle questioned with suspicion. Guy panicked as he looked around at the faces of those he'd betrayed, including Mia's.

'Because, I, I—'

'What, you like her?'

Guy fell silent.

'Enough of this nonsense, Guy. Step aside.'

'No!' he shouted, much to everyone's surprise. 'I won't let you take her.'

Michelle pointed her pistol at Guy in an act to scare him. 'I won't tell you again, we're taking her to The Jackal. He wanted five people, that was the deal.' She addressed the rest of the colony. 'Everybody else, leave NOW!'

But Guy wasn't giving in. Without thinking, he grabbed Michelle's gun and the pair grappled over it for a few seconds.

'Guy, let go!' she yelled.

A loud bang quickly followed, causing Michelle to recoil. Almost in slow motion, she saw her nephew fall to the ground, her eyes wide as she realised what she'd done. She went temporarily deaf from the shot, her head filled with white noise. Meanwhile, Zion pulled his sidearm from his makeshift holster and chucked it behind him in the direction of Gabriel, who had anticipated the moment perfectly as he rushed forward through the crowd to catch it. It was perfectly choreographed, as if they had practised it a million times before.

Michelle fell to her knees as she watched the blood pour from Guy's lifeless body. Still in a daze, she heard the loud click of a pistol whistle through the white noise right by her ear, before the cold metal of the end of the barrel nestled into her temple, catching her off guard. She drew in a deep breath and closed her eyes as her blood ran cold. The gun fired with a loud bang which rumbled through the whole mall, silencing everyone.

Caitlin's hand trembled as she held the gun, still fixed at the same angle she'd fired from. A tear dropped from her face and ran down her outstretched arm. Aiden slowly approached her, taking the gun gently out of her hand and lowering it to the floor. She stood there, still trembling as she looked at Michelle, lying motionless on the ground. Aiden hugged her and she buried her face into his chest as she cried.

Michelle's followers were completely stunned, now with the four guns of Gabriel, Cyrus, Rowley and Zion all trained on them. One by one they started to drop their weapons and rush back to the door they'd arrived from. But one still remained. Connor had been Michelle's most faithful follower, risking his life on many occasions for the group. He looked down at his dead leader and then back at the four men locked onto him with malice. A moment went by where Cyrus wasn't sure if he was going to lose it and shoot at them, like a wounded beast clinging onto the last shred of hope of life.

Connor wanted to fire, and it took all of his strength to stop him pulling the trigger on all of them there. He knew he wouldn't make it out alive, but he wanted revenge. He saw Caitlin and Aiden embracing, which sent him over the edge. Thinking desperately for a way to level the score and avenge the woman who had been betrayed by one of their own, he spotted Cameron hiding behind a pillar merely yards away. With one quick movement he pulled the boy out from his hiding place. Cameron yelped as the man dragged him out. Connor pointed his rifle to the back of the boy's skull and looked into Caitlin's despairing eyes as he reached for the trigger.

Caitlin pushed herself away from Aiden into Cameron's direction, but she knew it was too late. She screamed out as two shots were fired in quick succession. Again the echo of the blasts rumbled through the mall, startling the whole colony.

Cameron opened his eyes as he heard the thud of Connor hitting the floor behind him. A shivering mess, his little face looked up towards the origin of the blast. Gabriel was still training his gun in their direction, ensuring his mark stayed down. The proton rounds had gone straight through Connor's chest and shoulder blade, leaving a splatter of blood on the wall behind.

With that, the last few remaining stragglers of the invading group across the other side of the mall rushed back out the way they came, the entrance doors swinging open with a bang as they escaped.

**

Caitlin embraced Cameron, crying tears of relief as Gabriel walked slowly across the room towards the fallen Connor. The man lay on the floor, coughing and spluttering from his wounds. On reaching him, his pistol still trained on him, Gabriel kicked Connor's rifle away, sending it skidding across the floor. He wasn't taking any chances.

'Our people. Why did you want to take them?' His tone and presence was that of a seasoned interrogator.

'Why would I tell you?' Connor spluttered. 'I'm dead anyway.'

Gabriel stuck the end of his pistol firmly into the wound in his shoulder, causing searing pain to coarse through Connor's body. He screamed out in agony. 'Because these people are innocent,' Gabriel replied, taking his gun away again. 'I might be a killer, but this colony is a group of decent people who have done nothing to hurt anybody.'

Connor looked confused. 'So you weren't the ones who drove her from her shop? The looters?'

Gabriel shook his head.

'There's another colony,' Connor continued. He started to cough heavily, which broke up his speech. 'They're not like you. They're not like anyone. But they're powerful, and somehow through all this shit they've found themselves in a position of wealth. As if anyone could benefit from this life.'

'What do they want with our people?' Gabriel pressed.

'We made a trade. They give us food, water, weapons, and we can take the mall back. In return, we give them gifts. People, for their colony. I don't know what they want with them, they didn't say.'

'Slaves?' Gabriel recoiled. 'That's slavery you're taking about.'

Cyrus caught up with Gabriel to ask his own questions. He remembered back to the fallen mech they'd discovered earlier that day. 'We found a mech in an alleyway,' he started. 'Those weapons they gave you, did they include one that could disable them permanently?'

Connor chuckled through his coughing. 'If only it were that simple. If such a thing existed, we wouldn't need to hide ourselves away.' Cyrus felt a little stupid to have asked. 'The mechs operate on solar power. They get low on power towards the end of the night, until the sun comes and they're back to full health. But what happens if one's distracted before the dawn?'

The answer came to Cyrus like a smack to the head. 'They're not smart enough to realise when their energy is low,' he replied.

'Yes. It gets caught in a dark spot, and shuts down like it's taken a sleeping pill. For as long as the darkness surrounds it, it cannot get back up.'

The answer seemed so simple, yet it offered no real solution to their mech troubles. They just simply couldn't rely on trapping every mech they come across into a dark alleyway and wait for it to run out of power.

'Now you have your answers,' Connor continued, spluttering more and more. 'Finish it.'

Cyrus turned away as Gabriel lifted his pistol up in the direction of Connor's head. A few long seconds went by as Connor braced himself for the shot, but it didn't come. Gabriel's eyebrows arched as he thought deeply. Shortly after, Connor could see his pupils dilate, like he'd come to some sudden realisation.

'This isn't your first rodeo, it is?' Gabriel asked, calmly.

'Wha—' Connor wheezed through his pain. 'What do you mean?'

'This isn't the first time you've done this. Threaten a group of innocent people with your so called 'wealth of arms'.' Connor knew he was being tested, and a crooked smile etched across his face as he realised what Gabriel was referring to.

'You were too late,' he mocked. 'You couldn't save them.'

Gabriel gritted his teeth as his index finger twitched around the delicate trigger. Connor started to laugh maniacally, his chest hurting with each movement. 'They'll be back you know,' he warned through short breaths. 'The Jackal will want his payment, and this time—' he coughed and spluttered. 'He won't be so merciful.'

Gabriel's grip tightened as he started to squeeze the trigger.

'You son of a—'

The bang of his proton pistol rippled through the mall, before silence fell on the colony.

CHAPTER THIRTEEN

As the morning light streamed into the crack in the opening of his tent, Cyrus stirred and groaned as he slowly gained consciousness. He'd been asleep for what seemed like an age, and he could really feel the benefit as he stretched and yawned aloud. He wondered if the events of the previous night could have been a dream. Yesterday had been the longest day he'd ever experienced, and it had drained him physically and mentally. He had almost lost Mia, his friends, not to mention his own life. Had things gone differently, had Guy not intervened, he might not have been in the privileged position he found himself in now.

A few minutes went by as Cyrus lay there, staring up at the roof of the tent and listening to the muffled sound of voices conversing on the floor below him. This morning was a nice change of pace, and he felt something he hadn't felt in so long. Peace. Almost tranquillity. This was the closest he'd come to it in such a long time.

He cast his mind back to a time when he had felt so content. He instantly thought of his first date with Mia. He had taken her to the observatory where he worked, after hours when it was quiet. He'd shown her the stars through the large old telescope that had been there for a hundred years. It was an old piece of technology, built long before they started to incorporate digital schematics to highlight the constellations as you peered through the lens. He liked the old fashioned ways; viewing the stars, the planets, worlds outside the world, in their most natural form. Artificial imagery as visual aids ruined their beauty. Sure, it served an educational purpose, but it added something that took away the purity of its true form.

Something caught Cyrus's attention, causing his daydream to dissipate. The fold of the opening of the tent was rippling. Cyrus sat up and watched it move, like what he was seeing was completely novel. It was almost as if the material was alive, dancing playfully from side to side. He crawled slowly on all fours towards the opening, stretching a hand out to touch it. As his fingertips were merely an inch away from the material, he felt a strange sensation. It was cool, like a small invisible presence blowing gently on his skin. His eyes widened as he studied the individual hairs on his arm, which were now standing on end. He edged closer to the opening and peered outside. The light breeze tickled the tip of his nose, sending cool air through his nostrils and into his lungs. He breathed deeply and closed his eyes, savouring the moment. He couldn't remember the last time he'd felt a breeze in this city. Sure, dust and sandstorms were a plenty, but they were characterised by howling gales and bits of dirt and dust peppering your eyelids. The weather moved from one extreme to the other, and if it wasn't sandstorms outside, it was a sticky heat that made your clothes cling like cellophane to your skin.

The voices were much clearer from just outside the tent. Cyrus pulled on his torn t-shirt and made his way towards the origin of the conversation. The girls spotted him rubbing his eyes from a distance, and stopped their conversation briefly to acknowledge him.

'Good morning, sleepy head,' said Jennifer. Cyrus rolled his eyes, but couldn't contain a smile.

'Lord knows I needed that. What time is it?'

Jennifer put her hands on her hips and arched an eyebrow at him. Mia followed suit.

'Come on Cyrus, are you serious right now?'

Cyrus look perplexed for a moment, before suddenly realising. 'Oh, yeah.' He looked down at his wrist, and the watch still wrapped around it. The time read ten thirty-five. 'Wow, I *really* needed that.'

'I figured,' Mia replied. 'I was going to wake you up when I did, but you looked so peaceful I thought I'd sneak out and leave you to rest.'

'That's creepy.' Jennifer remarked. 'You watch him sleep?'

'Not in a weird way,' Mia retorted.

'Sounds weird to me.' Jennifer took her opportunity to head down the broken escalator, leaving Mia and Cyrus alone.

Cyrus took advantage of the moment instantly, and leant in to kiss Mia. But before his lips met hers, she turned away. Cyrus's eyebrows raised involuntarily and his forehead wrinkled as he was taken aback by what had just happened. He struggled to comprehend why she had purposefully avoided his affection. This was very uncharacteristic of her.

Of course, in the time they'd been together there had been times when Mia had openly shown her frustration at Cyrus. But he had always known where he stood, and her emotions were always transparent. This time it was different, like she was hiding her real emotions behind a mask. It was as if for the first time he couldn't read his girlfriend, like the book of her life had suddenly changed to a language he didn't understand.

'What's wrong?' he asked, touching her hand with his. Mia held his hand briefly, before letting go again.

'Nothing,' she replied, smiling at him for a second. 'I'm fine.'

Cyrus knew she wasn't fine. He knew her well enough to know when she was OK. That smile was a dead giveaway. When Mia smiled, her whole face lit up and it kindled a small fire in his heart. But that wasn't a smile, more a token gesture. Cyrus's instinct told him to question the response, but something stopped the connection from his brain to his mouth, causing him to just gape at her while his mind started playing tricks on him. Did he know her well enough? She'd caught him completely off guard just now. Perhaps he didn't know her at all. He started to wonder if this wasn't the first time she'd masked her real feelings in front of him. The very idea cut through him like a sharpened blade, leaving behind an overwhelming feeling of instability.

'OK,' he replied sheepishly. 'Let's get some breakfast. The guys and I brought something a little different back with us.'

He thought it best to change the subject and not press the issue. Yesterday had been a rollercoaster of emotions, and Cyrus could understand her needing some space.

Mia nodded and led the way hastily down the escalator to the main forum. Following her down, Cyrus couldn't help but wonder what was troubling her. He had always feared that one day she'd wake up and not feel the same way about him anymore. He tried to shake off the poisonous doubts that were clouding his mind and put it all down to shock. She had just almost been kidnapped. She'd talk to him when she was ready.

A large group of people were dotted around the centre of the mall having breakfast and conversing. The mood around the camp seemed surprisingly not too somber, given the trauma of the previous day. Rowley spotted Cyrus immediately and beamed at his arrival. He had a tin of soup in each hand.

'Cyrus! Guess what?' he said, rather too enthusiastically for Cyrus's liking.

'What?' he humoured.

'Not beans!' Rowley replied, stretching his left hand out for Cyrus to take the tin. The smile was still painted wide across his face.

Cyrus wasn't in the mood for jokes this morning. His mind was still racing through the events of a few moments ago and he couldn't face anything else. But as he glanced over to Mia, who was walking away from them towards another group, he decided he'd try a bit of patience. He'd been taking his best friend for granted recently. But, being the loyal companion that he was, Rowley had waited for him every morning with breakfast and a smile. A damn creepy smile by Cyrus's account, but a genuine one at that.

'So, what's the plan today?' Cyrus asked, between sips of soup. He was so hungry he hadn't bothered looking for a spoon. Sometimes he even ate beans that way. He winced at the liquid's cool temperature; the tomato flavouring not quite feeling right as it sunk into his stomach. 'We couldn't have heated them up first?' he asked.

Rowley looked a little offended. 'I think it tastes just fine,' he replied defensively. He proceeded to slurp his down noisily. The sound was reminiscent of a child stubbornly drinking through the straw of a fizzy drink, despite it being empty. It really grated on Cyrus.

'Do you have to?' he pleaded, with a little more than a slight air of passive aggression. Rowley ignored him and continued to drink his soup. He barely took a breath before emptying the tin, and finished with a loud exhale of satisfaction. Cyrus tried hard to compose himself. This patience thing wasn't going to last long.

'So,' Cyrus started over. 'What's the plan today?'

Rowley shrugged his shoulders. 'I dunno.' He looked around at the others having breakfast. 'I mean, we've got food and water now, but this isn't going to last.'

'We should head to the supermarket,' Cyrus suggested. 'That crazy guy there said he'd let us all stay if we protected him from The Crimson Crows.'

'Isaac. His name is Isaac,' Rowley corrected. 'And he's not crazy.'

'Seemed crazy to me,' said Cyrus frankly. 'I mean, he tried to shoot you, remember?'

'I think he was just trying to scare us. Come on, think about it. If you'd been cooped up on your own for so long, and then three armed strangers waltz into your home, what would you do?'

Cyrus pursed his lips and looked in the corner of his vision as he thought about it for a moment. He then nodded his head in agreement. 'Yeah, I guess you're right.'

'Exactly.' Rowley looked pleased with himself. It was a rare occasion when he could prove a point to Cyrus.

As he finished the last of his cold soup, Cyrus looked to the far side of the mall, where Aiden, Caitlin and Cameron were sat. They were slumped in a triangular shape, each facing outwards as their hands were bound together behind their backs. After the madness of the previous night, cruel truths had been learned. Aiden had pleaded with Gabriel, explaining how the companions they had arrived with had shown their true colours, and weren't the people they thought they were.

He expressed his desire for the three of them to stay with the colony for their safety. Of course Gabriel, being the cautious man that he was, particularly in light of the events that unfolded that night, had insisted that they be kept under what he called 'probation' until they could earn his trust. A harsh response, Cyrus thought, but it made sense. It certainly kept the rest of the colony at ease while they slept. Gabriel was now sitting next to the newcomers, taking his turn to keep an eye on them.

At least they've been given breakfast.

Gabriel caught his eye and ushered him over. When he arrived, Gabriel took a quick look to check the new arrivals were still securely tied up, and brought Cyrus to one side, slightly out of earshot.

'I don't know about this,' he whispered. Gabriel looked as worried as always. It was clear to see that something was still affecting him, even after the attack. He'd been constantly on edge ever since they saw that lifeless mech, which felt like an age ago now.

'They look like good people,' Cyrus replied, trying to reassure him.

'How can you be sure? We don't know them, they could be anybody. This could all be another plan, like with Guy.' He paused and gritted his teeth as he remembered his dislike of Guy, and how much anger had built up inside him when he realised what he'd done to them. Cyrus put his hand sheepishly on his shoulder, to try and bring him around. It was a bold move, as an enraged Gabriel could easily break it by simply brushing it off. Luckily, it did the trick.

'I want them to join the group, Cyrus. I just don't trust them. You saw the people they were with. They were brutal.'

'They're good,' Cyrus insisted. 'I can feel it.'

Gabriel seemed to take note of this, and it looked like it was exactly what he'd been hoping to hear. He let out a loud exhale, as if a small amount of the strain he'd been carrying had been released.

'I still don't like this. I can't just forgive them.'

'Forgive them? They did nothing wrong.' Cyrus was perplexed by this, and when Gabriel realised, his expression quickly altered to one of surprise.

'You really don't get it, do you?'

'Get what? Gabriel, they haven't done anything wrong. They helped us—'

'They murdered our old group,' Gabriel interrupted bluntly. His tone was still of a whisper, but the volume was loud enough to be heard by Aiden and Caitlin, who looked up in panic. Cyrus was completely caught off guard, and his head started to spin as he tried to take it in. He glanced at the trio, and then back at Gabriel. He refused to believe it was true.

'Impossible. They look so harmless.'

'Not just them, you idiot. The whole lot of them, the ones who were here. That's the group that killed my friends. Jane's friends, Doug's friends.'

'You're sure?'

'I'm sure.'

Cyrus thought back to last night. The man that Gabriel killed, who'd threatened to murder that little boy. It looked like the two knew each other, like there was some kind of history between them. The man appeared to mock Gabriel, but Cyrus hadn't heard exactly what he'd said. He slowly pieced it together.

No wonder he shot him after that.

A timid voice piped up behind Gabriel. 'It wasn't us!'

Gabriel turned quickly around to face them. Aiden and Caitlin were sat bolt upright, staring at him with panicked expressions. Cameron looked nervous, and was leaning on his mother. He couldn't turn around to see what was going on from where he was sat, not that he wanted to. Gabriel terrified him.

'Don't play games with me,' Gabriel retorted. Without thinking, Cyrus darted in front of him and put his hand on Gabriel's chest in an attempt to get him to back down. Again, much to his surprise, it worked in his favour.

'Who *did* do it then?' he probed, offering the trio a lifeline.

'Gabriel, I'm so sorry for what happened to your friends, I truly am. Those people are...' she paused for a second, '*Were* pure evil. But you have to know, we weren't involved.'

'Just tell us what happened,' Gabriel replied impatiently.

Caitlin winced, and then turned to Aiden. He, like Cyrus and Gabriel, was staring back at her, waiting for her to explain. He nodded to encourage her to start. She took in a deep breath before recounting the events of a day she'd repressed to the deepest parts of her soul.

'It was a little over a month ago,' she began. 'Aiden hadn't joined our group yet.' She gestured to Aiden, in an attempt to clear his name from the off. 'We had no place to stay, we were running out of food and water. Michelle was always tough on us, but she kept us going and she kept us alive. She sent Connor away on an errand of some sort. She told us he was going to make a trade with another colony to get us the food and water we so desperately needed. When Connor returned, he had a huge bag full of weapons. The deal was that we get our supplies, and in return we had to offer the colony something they wanted.'

'Slaves,' Gabriel interjected. 'But that's not how it went down. You didn't kidnap anyone, you murdered them all.'

Caitlin ignored his comment and continued. 'We found a small group of survivors, much like ourselves. They were camped out in a building near the ruins of the old hospital. We surveyed the place for hours, making sure they were unarmed. And then, when the morning came and the more able bodied went out in search of food, Michelle told us to attack. I pleaded with Michelle for her not to go through with it, but she brushed me aside and marched in. I grabbed Cameron and hid in the rubble of the hospital. We didn't come out until it was over.'

Gabriel wasn't satisfied by her story. 'Are you kidding me? So because you hid while my friends were slaughtered like animals, you expect me to just forgive you?'

'This doesn't explain why you stayed with them after that,' Cyrus added. 'You knew what they were capable of, so why did you stay?'

'I had no choice. I have a child. What chance do we have alone against those, those, *things* out there?' A tear ran down her cheek and her bottom lip started to tremble. 'I'm so sorry.'

The air grew thick around them as everyone waited for Gabriel's response. Aiden struggled with the bindings on his hands. He wanted nothing more at that moment than to hold Caitlin and wipe away her tears. He leaned his body to one side to touch her fingers with his.

Gabriel let this new information stew inside him as he wrestled with his feelings. During his short time as a leader figure in this colony, he'd been rather hot-headed and quick to pounce on anything or anyone he wasn't comfortable with. He thought about his friends who'd lost their lives so cruelly. He'd failed them, even if it hadn't been him that dropped the axe on their lives. But something inside him clutched to him, making it impossible to ignore. A feeling that he'd almost forgotten existed. Compassion. He couldn't blame Caitlin for what happened, nor could he continue to blame himself. He realised that he needed to do everything he could to keep hope within the colony; the hope that there might be a way out of this, a light at the end of the tunnel to rebuild mankind. And that needed to start with him embracing those that wanted to be part of it, uniting against those who exploited the innocent.

'Alright,' he said under his breath. 'I believe you.'

Still trembling, Caitlin looked up at him with tears sparkling in her eyes. 'Can you forgive me?'

'No,' he replied softly. Everyone watched as for the first time in what seemed like forever, a smile appeared on Gabriel's face, like the rising sun of dawn that follows the longest night. 'Because there's nothing to forgive.'

CHAPTER FOURTEEN

Cyrus glanced down at his watch and tapped it twice, more out of habit than anything else. The hands were at twelve fifteen. The whole colony had gathered in the centre of the mall, all eager to discuss what was next for them. The events of the previous day had created tension in the camp, with some people wanting to leave the mall and others wanting to stay. Safety couldn't be guaranteed either way, but they had to play the odds and roll the dice. The people muttered amongst themselves, voicing their opinions on the matter. Gabriel was stood in the centre of the gathering, surveying the crowd and conducting a mental headcount to ensure everyone was present.

Towards the back of the mass, Caitlin stood quietly with Cameron. She nursed her sore hands, turning them over as she studied the rope marks on her wrists. The tight bindings had left a red imprint; a temporary reminder of the insecurity she was feeling. She felt very alien here, considerably lacking any sense of belonging.

In the early stages of the war she had family, friends, a job, a husband-to-be. It was everything she needed, and despite human nature she didn't feel the need to pursue anything more than that. Her cup was always half full, and she was happy. Even when she had Cameron things felt right. She always said a war was no place for a child. But in the early stages the fighting was so far away, so disconnected from her life and the lives of those she cared about that it almost didn't feel real, or like it really made any difference. But then MIRE started causing havoc in Novasburgh, and everything changed. The place was torn to bits, buildings crumbling and the sound of gunfire replacing the chirping of birdsong in the mornings.

After her fiancé left her and her son, the war had suddenly felt very real, and all security Caitlin had once held onto was gone in a puff of smoke. As she moved from colony to colony in the wake of the war, taking refuge among fellow lost souls, she had never regained that sense of belonging. And now, as she looked down at the red marks on her tender wrists, it was as absent as ever. She was still breathing, her heart still beating, but she was far from alive.

'OK, OK.' Gabriel cleared his throat as he addressed the crowd surrounding him. His hulking frame was difficult to miss, even from the back of the gathering. Caitlin raised her head to see what was going on. One by one the anxious survivors stopped their murmuring and fixed their eyes on their leader. This was a shift in culture to that of just a few days ago, where there had been no leader figure in the colony, no sense of hierarchy whatsoever. Now the whole group looked to Gabriel as if they were gazing upon an idol. It was a scary thought, and one that put them all in a vulnerable position. A lesser man may have exploited this power, but Gabriel understood the responsibility that rested on his shoulders. The fair nature of his leadership seemed to bring more hope to the colony than the equality it took away. For now it was exactly what they needed.

The crowd awaited Gabriel's next words as a moment's silence went by just a little too long.

'Is everyone here?' Gabriel asked, surveying the area.

'Yes, we're all here, just get on with it,' a voice heckled from near the front. Gabriel recognised it instantly and turned to face Nathaniel, his teeth gritted.

'I'm just making sure. This meeting requires everyone's attendance.'

'Look, I said we're all here, so we're all here. Now get a move on will ya?'

Nathaniel was testing Gabriel's patience, but his subtlety required some work. Gabriel relaxed a little and regained control of the situation.

'OK, so I wanted to set up a meeting to—'

'Sorry, sorry! We're here now.' The panting sound of Mia's voice came from the escalator, which she was running down with April. 'Sorry everybody, I was on the roof. I didn't get the message until now.'

Gabriel nodded and smiled at the two girls, before raising an eyebrow at Nathaniel. As the girls joined the group, he took a final quick look around.

'It was just you up there?' he asked.

'Yes, just me,' Mia replied softly. She caught Cyrus's eye a few feet away, before quickly sweeping her hair back behind her ear and looking sheepishly at the ground.

'OK, so if that's everyone, we'll begin,' Gabriel announced at last, ignoring the loud sigh from Nathaniel that followed. His mind raced a million miles an hour as he weighed up the different approaches he could go with in this situation. He wanted everybody to realise the harsh truth of the situation they were all in. Staying where they were was prolonging the inevitable; they'd run out of food and water. However moving on meant the probable danger of being attacked and picked off by mechs as they crossed the city. He needed to unite the whole group towards one decision, which was going to be tricky.

'We are a colony, a community,' he began. 'Our best chance of survival in this cruel world is to stick together.' A few people nodded their heads in agreement. 'We all know what little difference it made to which side you supported in the war. That war is over, and nobody here is responsible for the terror and destruction it created. We are good people, innocent people. We must fight together if we're going to survive this.' Gabriel looked over towards Caitlin, Cameron and Aiden. 'The newcomers to our group, they are *not* our enemy. They're innocent people, just like you and me. They're one of us now. Those people they arrived with yesterday, they're not like them. They were monsters. They wanted to rob us and sell us into slavery.' A few gasps emanated from the group, and people started to mutter to each other in panic.

'Hey! Listen to me.' Gabriel waved his arms about to draw the attention back on him. He couldn't lose them now. He'd scared them, now he needed to give them hope. Sure enough, the colony simmered down for him to continue.

'We have two choices. We can stay here, or we can move on and find a new home. Cyrus, Rowley and Zion travelled to a supermarket across the river yesterday. I hope you've all taken the chance to thank them for their bravery.'

Mia took her eyes away from the ground and glanced in Cyrus's direction. A brief smile appeared on her face, her eyes sparkling like the light of the stars in the night of summer.

'They brought back a small sample of the supplies that await us there,' Gabriel went on.

Zion stood forward to chip in. 'The man who lives there said he'd be happy for us to take shelter there on the condition that we offer him protection. There's plenty of food for everyone.'

'Protection from what? We can't stop the mechs,' a man's voice shouted out from the gathering.

'Not just mechs,' Zion continued. 'There are others out there, like the ones that came here yesterday. We don't know the full story, but this man is worried for his safety.'

'His name is Isaac,' Rowley shouted from the back of the mass.

'Seems like a gamble,' Nathaniel added with scepticism. 'How can you be sure we'll be safe there?' More muttering commenced as everyone weighed up the options with the people next to them. Cyrus had barely spoken since his conversation with Gabriel earlier that morning. He shuffled about on the spot, before plucking up the courage to weigh in with his opinion.

'The way I see it is we don't really have a choice.' He was met with perplexed expressions around him. 'I mean, think about it,' he started. 'We have two options; stay here and starve in a few days, or take a chance and move across the river. Either way we're in a vulnerable position and people know where we are; whether it's the people who were here yesterday or the ones Isaac is worried about. At least if we go to the supermarket we'll have food and water.'

A few moments went by as everyone digested his suggestion.

'A still don't like it,' Nathaniel grumbled. 'We're not all as able as you younger ones.' He tapped his leg with his crutch. 'We'll be completely exposed if we leave here, even before we reach this supermarket place. How does a guy like me stand a chance against one of those mechs?'

Cyrus didn't know how to respond. He knew the answer; he didn't stand a chance at all. None of them did. But he couldn't say it in front of everyone. In the end he didn't need to.

'You don't,' Gabriel replied candidly. 'Hell, none of us stand a chance against those things. They're killing machines, that's all they do. That's all they're programmed for. If we get caught by them between here and there, we won't all make it out. But we'll only have a chance of making it if we try. We stay here, and we die anyway.'

Nathaniel's face went pale and his stomach turned. He knew he wasn't going to win this one. Gabriel gave the colony a few minutes to think about what they wanted to do. After that they would vote.

**

'OK, let's have a show of hands. Remember, we're a community. We all go with the majority. If you think we should stay here, please raise your hand now.'

The atmosphere in the mall suddenly become thick. The tension hung in the air like a bad smell. At first, nobody raised their hand. After a second, Nathaniel's arm proudly reached the sky, his other hand clutching his crutch for support. He looked around at the rest of the colony, his bottom lip trembling. Two more hands went up, and then a few more sheepishly followed. Gabriel gave it a few seconds before doing a quick count with his finger in the air.

'OK, thank you. You can put your hands down now. Please raise your hand if you think we should try for the supermarket across the—'

Before he could finish his sentence, more than forty hands raised simultaneously into the air. Even Cameron's went up early, although Gabriel couldn't see it behind all the people. It took him by surprise, and he knew he didn't need to start counting to know the outcome.

Nathaniel's heart sank as the reality of the situation became clear. There was no getting around it, he was going to have to follow the rest of the colony across the city. But he couldn't bear to think about it, being exposed, out there in the wilderness. Gabriel was right, they didn't stand a chance against the mechs out there, and if they got caught there would be guaranteed casualties. As he looked down at his crutch he knew what that meant for him.

'This is bullshit,' he cursed, his fist clenched and his face screwed up. 'I'm not going anywhere. Anyone who wants to stay with me is welcome to do so.'

The tension grew even more palpable as the rest of the colony looked on silently. Even those that had voted to stay seemed to have had a change of heart, or at least were refusing to speak up. Cyrus offered an olive branch to soothe the atmosphere.

'Nathaniel, we're all in this together. Sure, between here and across the river it's a dangerous road. We went down that path just yesterday and barely made it through the skin of our teeth. But we'll be smart about it.' He moved towards the centre of the gathering and stood alongside Gabriel. 'If we go in small groups we have a better chance of making it. As one mass we'll be spotted and picked off easily. Nathaniel, I'll go with you myself and make sure we get you and everyone else safely to the other side. We stay here and we die anyway.'

He caught Mia's wide eyes staring at him through the crowd as he spoke. Her face was expressionless, as though she was completely absent of emotion. But her eyes still appeared to glisten as they always did.

After he finished talking, Cyrus remained standing in front of the colony, waiting for Nathaniel's response. He received it in the form of a reluctant nod of approval.

'OK people, it's settled,' Gabriel announced, cutting to the chase. 'Let's get everything packed away and once we're ready we'll organise everyone into groups.' He continued to bark out instructions as the gathering dispersed into different directions, murmuring away to each other. 'Every group will be assigned two rifles for safety, and will reconvene here for briefing on the location of the supermarket and the best route to get there.'

**

An hour later, a small group of people sat chatting amongst themselves in the centre of the mall, where they had previously met to discuss the colony's new home.

'And then she said, 'why can't you fix it? I thought you said we were good with a screwdriver?' And the man replied 'no, miss, I'm not a mechanic, I'm a bartender!''

The group erupted with a simultaneous guffaw. Cyrus rolled his eyes as he chuckled quietly, more out of politeness than anything. He'd heard that screwdriver joke a hundred times before. It was one of Zion's favourites, and he loved to tell it as part of his repertoire. He was pretty sure everyone else in the group had heard it before too, but for some reason this retelling seemed to be particularly funny. Cyrus glanced around the mall to check on the progress of the other survivors. Most of the place was packed up, with all the tents at least partially dismantled. But they were the first few to be sitting among their packed up tents and belongings, ready to go.

'Alright, gentlemen.' Gabriel approached the group with a rifle in each hand. Cyrus couldn't help noticing what a tremendously cool spectacle it made; Gabriel walking slowly towards them dual-wielding plasma rifles, his muscles bulging out of his arms as the fabric of his shirt was torn at the shoulders. It was like a scene from the action movies he used to watch as a kid where the hero emerges from an explosion to finish the fight. He exchanged glances with Rowley, who seemed to be thinking exactly the same thing.

'I'm going to have to split you guys up, I'm afraid,' Gabriel continued. 'Cyrus, Rowley and Zion, you're the only ones who've been to the supermarket recently, so you know the best route to get there. We'll need each of you to guide a group there, and keep everyone safe. Once you've made it there with your groups, we'll need several volunteers to come back and guide the remaining people. I'll wait here for your return, and take a group of my own based on your instructions. That sound OK?'

The three of them nodded sheepishly. It sounded far from OK, but it was the best option they had.

'Alright then.' He handed a rifle each to Rowley and Zion. 'There's twelve people ready and waiting to go.' He pointed to the escalator, where they were sitting with their belongings. 'Some of them will need help carrying everything, but I think there's enough of you to share the load.'

Zion quickly surveyed the amount of luggage and the rough physicality of the people, before nodding in agreement.

'You guys split into two groups of seven and head off. Try and keep a couple of minutes behind each other, to stop us bunching up. Smaller groups are more difficult to spot, and you know how good those mechs are.'

'Understood,' Rowley nodded. He put his arm on Cyrus's shoulder and looked him dead in the eye. 'See you on the other side, buddy.' He gave an encouraging smile before heading over with Zion to their new groups.

'OK, Cyrus, I've found some more people who are ready to go.' Gabriel ushered over a small group towards them. Cyrus turned around to see who they were, and his heart skipped a beat as he saw Mia walking among them. Gabriel winked at him and tapped his bear-like hands on his shoulder, like a proud father. However the warm feeling that was bubbling up inside his chest quickly faded to a chill when he saw another companion in the group. Nathaniel hobbled over slowly, trailing behind the rest. Cyrus gulped as he remembered the promise he'd made to him. He knew this trip was going to be particularly difficult for them.

'Right, let's get this over with,' said Nathaniel with a rather pessimistic tone. 'Obviously someone will have to carry my things for me.'

CHAPTER FIFTEEN

The light of day broke suddenly on the group as Cyrus opened the door to the outside. He shielded his eyes with his arm, giving himself time to adjust. He could already feel the heat of the sun warming his skin. As his vision started to become clearer, he noticed Rowley's group rounding the corner ahead. He counted to five Mississippi, and when they were completely out of sight he turned to his own companions.

'The good news is the weather's holding up,' he started, in an attempt to set the tone off positively. 'There's no sign of sandstorm for now. The bad news is, I forgot my sunscreen.'

Given the situation, he wasn't expecting much of a response from that. But Mia let out a muffled snort, before quickly trying to compose herself after she realised she was the only one laughing. Cyrus smiled at her as she looked to the ground in embarrassment.

'So how far is this supermarket of yours, Cyrus?' Nathaniel asked.

'It's a fair trek,' he replied. 'Hard to say how long it'll take us. It depends how quiet our journey is.'

Cyrus turned back to face the way Rowley's group had disappeared moments earlier. With Nathaniel in their company they wouldn't need to give as much room between the two groups as he first thought. It was time to head out.

**

Walking a few yards ahead of the group, Cyrus turned his attention away from the road ahead to check on his friends. The luggage strapped to his back began to feel cumbersome, trapping heat from the back of his neck to his pelvis. He could feel the sweat collecting in a damp cluster under his shirt, sticking the material to him. His companions were faring no better, their foreheads shimmering with beads of sweat that ran down from their wet fringes. Nathaniel was lagging behind a little as he hobbled on his crutches.

Cyrus looked at his watch. They'd only been walking for twenty minutes. Ordinarily he'd insist on marching on to make good time and get out of the open as quickly as possible, but something told him he'd be better off giving them a break to rest and recuperate. If they carried on and got spotted by mechs down the road, they'd be screwed.

He held his arm in the air to catch their attention without making unnecessary noise, then gestured to a nearby building. It looked as good as any in this residential part of town. The doors and windows were missing, and it was surrounded by rubble, but its roof was intact, offering them shelter from the sun. He kept watch on the road while his companions entered the building one by one. Mia was the last to enter, and as she got to the doorframe she spun around to face Cyrus, who was busy surveying the road ahead, his rifle poised for action. She watched him take one final slow turn, before he lowered the gun and entered after her.

A few minutes went by as everyone sat down and took a few swigs of water, happy to relieve themselves of the heavy luggage. Cyrus sat down by the doorway, just out of sight to keep watch. Mia had sat across the other end of the room, almost as if she was purposely avoiding him. It frustrated Cyrus, as he thought there were signs earlier of her coming around to the Mia he knew again. It felt like he was back at square one, as he'd felt that morning outside the tents.

He tried thinking about something else to take his mind off it. He looked down at the crystal hanging around his neck, and thought of his family. The events of the previous night had posed a lot of questions, and Cyrus was desperate to find the answers. Who were these slavers people were talking about? How many people had they captured and imprisoned already? Every night he'd dreamt of his mother and sister being taken away, and he'd thought about them every day, praying they were still alive. They had disappeared one day after going out to buy groceries, just before a bombing raid from MIRE hit the city. Nobody else seemed to share his hope; even Mia seemed resigned to never finding them again. But yesterday had felt like déjà vu when Mia was so nearly taken too. It was almost as though Cyrus had seen it coming. It had to be connected.

Someone sneezed loudly, snapping Cyrus out of his thoughts. He decided to check in on his group.

'How's everyone doing?' he whispered. 'You ready to head back ou—'

Everyone jumped as a loud screech interrupted Cyrus. A cold shiver went down his spine; he knew what that was. Still sat down, he leant across to his right to grab the rifle he'd propped up against the wall. He fumbled with it a little as he panicked, before clutching it against his chest. Mia drew a proton pistol from her belt, gripping it in her non-favoured left hand and cushioning it with her injured right palm.

Cyrus leaned slowly to his left and poked the rifle outside the doorway. He looked carefully through the sights to catch a glimpse of the road. He waited a while, scouting the area. Nothing to be seen. Every silent second that went by added to the tension. It was a mech alright, but Cyrus had no idea where it had come from, or worse where it had gone.

Everyone in the room exchanged nervous glances as they watched Cyrus. He waved the rifle back and forth in an oscillating fashion, surveying every stretch of road within his vision, but still nothing.

Another screech pierced the air, followed by another shortly after. Cyrus jolted on the spot, almost firing the gun accidentally.

Come on Cyrus, get a grip.

A loud bang erupted behind a collection of buildings just beyond where they were, and Cyrus started to hear the faint sound of voices shouting. Without thinking, he leapt to his feet and moved into the entranceway to get a better view. Adrenaline ran through his body as his finger twitched over the trigger. He wondered who the sound had come from and started to narrow down the options in his head, like a calculator crunching complex numerical sums. It had to be Rowley or Zion's group, unless there were others out there in trouble. The bandits from last night? The people Isaac talked about? Maybe they were one and the same.

A loud booming sound came, this time nearer, and following it the bangs of plasma rounds being fired. Suddenly a figure emerged from a small alleyway between the buildings opposite. They looked in a hurry, as if they were being chased.

Soon after, five more figures hurried through and out into the road where Cyrus was now stood.

'In here!' Cyrus shouted, ushering them over to the building he stood outside. He recognised the group to be Rowley's, but their guide was nowhere in sight.

'Where's Rowley?' he questioned as the people flocked inside. Nobody replied, they seemed to still be in shock from their escape.

'WHERE?' Cyrus tried again, getting impatient fast. A man looked back at him with fear in his eyes.

'He just told us to run and find somewhere to hide,' he replied. 'We don't know where he is.'

Cyrus let out an angry cry of frustration, before rushing back out the door. Someone called after him, but he was already gone.

**

'OK folks, listen up.' Gabriel addressed the people still waiting at the mall. Twenty minutes had passed since the first three groups went out, and the rest of the colony were starting to feel anxious for their friends' safety, not to mention the thought of having to follow suit when their time came to venture out into the wilderness of the city streets.

'We're going to make this as easy as possible,' Gabriel started. 'Cyrus, Rowley and Zion know the way, and they know what's out there. I have no doubt that they'll get their groups safely to the other side, and when they do they'll come back for us.' His attempt to create a sense of calm among the place was futile, evidenced by the bleak expressions of every face he turned to. But it was worth a try, and it was his responsibility to do at least that. Sometimes that was all that was needed; someone who was trying. That effort might not have made the slightest bit of difference to the fear the colony held towards the dangers outside, but it was comforting to know that at least one person knew, or appeared to know what they were doing. Gabriel could be unwittingly sending them all out to their deaths, like lambs to the slaughter, but he at least *believed* they'd be OK. Blind courage was courage all the same, and it provided a glimmer of hope for them to cling to.

Aiden cut away from the main pack to help Caitlin, who was struggling with the zip on her bag.

'How are your hands?'

Caitlin stopped to show him her palms, the marks from the rope burn still an inflamed red.

'I'm sorry,' he sighed.

'Don't be, this is nothing of your doing,' she replied candidly. 'And before you ask, I'm not holding anything against Gabriel either. I don't blame him for treating us how they did last night. Connor and Michelle were ruthless, vicious. We were tarred with the same brush, but can you blame him?'

'No, but Caitlin—'

'They took everything from him, and it's not completely outlandish for him to assume we're murderous psychopaths too.'

Aiden took a step back to give her some more personal space. 'But we're not.'

'No, we're not. But they don't know that, not really. We might not be tied up right now, but I'm not stupid, Aiden. They don't trust us, and it's going to take time for them to do so. They've been burned already with Guy, and that wound is still pretty fresh for Gabriel.'

Aiden reeled as his mind raced back to the events of the previous night. He hadn't really given the whole Guy thing much thought. When he joined Michelle's group, Guy hadn't been there. Yesterday was the first and last time he'd encountered her nephew. He struggled to comprehend what he'd learned about Michelle and what she was prepared to do, to sacrifice, to get her way. Planting her own nephew amongst a group of strangers to learn their weaknesses and plot the perfect time to attack? It was incredibly clever and foolish in equal measure. Caitlin was right, she was ruthless.

Although he was facing away, Aiden could feel several pairs of eyes burning through his back. He turned his head in their direction briefly to let them know he was aware of them, and then fixed back on Caitlin.

'So that's it? We just go on being the outcasts forever?'

'Don't be melodramatic,' Caitlin retorted. 'It'll take time, but we're just going to have to grin and bear it while it lasts. Let's be patient, OK?'

Aiden nodded as he acknowledged the power firmly placed within Caitlin. This was a strange feeling, given the nature of the history, albeit extremely brief history, of their plutonic relationship up to that point. This was the first time since they'd met that Caitlin had seemed more in control of a situation than him. Instead of acting like the protective guardian figure he instinctively adopted when around her and Cameron, the balance was shifting the other way. It was surprisingly refreshing, bordering on sexy. He liked this side of Caitlin.

'Aiden.'

'Huh?' Aiden suddenly realised he'd been staring right at her for quite some time.

'You alright?'

'Uh, yeah yeah, fine.' He went red with embarrassment as he looked to the ground and cleared his throat.

'OK good, because if you're not OK, I'm not OK. And if I'm not OK, Cameron's not OK. And I need him to be OK, OK?'

Aiden was a little confused, but he thought he got the point. He nodded again sheepishly.

'I'm going to ask Gabriel that the three of us stay together when we head out. I need you.'

A warm sensation flushed around Aiden's chest as he heard the words. As he looked upon her beautiful face, he started to imagine their life together in a distant place, away from all this chaos.

'Aiden, are you listening to me?'

'Uh, what?'

'I said I need you to help us with the luggage. We don't have a lot, but there will be others who need help carrying theirs. Is that OK?'

'Oh, yeah, of course.' He knew at that point that he needed to stop with all this daydreaming.

**

'ROWLEY!' Cyrus shouted as he charged out of the building, leaving behind both his entire group and Rowley's. He barely heard Mia's plea for him to stay, as if he'd gone temporarily deaf. His senses numbed as he ran, his arms swinging to and fro under the weight of the plasma rifle. He felt his heartbeat thumping through his chest as it echoed in his head. Dust kicked up from the cracked concrete as he ran, looking for the quickest route to reach his friend. He raced down an alleyway, throwing the rifle to his back as he freed up his hand to vault the fence blocking his path. As he leapt for it, the gun's strap pulled around his neck, catching his Adam's apple. He wheezed as he hauled himself over to the other side, landing with a thud on the hard ground. He caught his breath quickly, before taking off once more.

The sound of more gunshots rippled through the air. It sounded a lot closer now, behind another row of buildings. Cyrus bolted towards the origin of the sound. As he reached the road, an explosion of bricks and glass caught him off guard, stopping him dead in his tracks. A panther leapt out from the building directly in front of him, cutting off his route.

The mechanical beast snorted through its artificial voice system, and poised itself to strike. As it leapt at Cyrus, it let out a loud screech which shook him to the core. In the nick of time, Cyrus managed to pull enough guile together to roll to the side, out of the way.

The mech landed exactly where Cyrus had been not a second earlier. Cyrus had focused so hard on getting out of the way that he'd not thought about where he was going to roll to. He found himself in a small crater in the road, his rifle flung from him to the other side. He felt a searing pain where the concrete had scraped his side. Desperately trying to get his bearings, he scrambled around to see where the mech was. In that moment, a flash of light reflected off the metal body of the beast, blinding him for a split second. Again he instinctively rolled to the side, narrowly missing the panther's second leap in his direction.

As he rolled, Cyrus reached for his belt and drew his proton pistol. But before he could set his sights on his target, the mech swiped a giant paw at him, knocking the gun clean out of his hands. The mech snarled and bared down on him slowly, as he lay helpless on his back. Terrified, Cyrus tried to keep himself moving and not freeze in shock. The adrenaline pumping through his body was the only thing preventing him from fixating on the thought that this was probably the end for him.

His arms flailed about as he urgently tried to grab something to shield himself from the mech's next attack. His fingers touched something hard on the ground next to him. As he looked to his hand, the world appeared to be turned on its side. He lifting his head slightly to see a piece of lead piping lying beside his outstretched hand. It must have been blown out of the building when the mech came crashing through it. As the mech got slowly closer, Cyrus's sweaty hand attempted to grip the pipe, but it kept slipping away, just out of reach.

The beast was now towering right above him, ready for the kill. The sunlight disappeared immediately as the mech consumed his vision, and for the first time Cyrus got a close up view of the panther's jaws. Its teeth were indeed made of metal, and were about to take a huge chunk out of him. With one final cry as he stretched him arm out as far as it would go, Cyrus grabbed the pipe and held it out horizontally in front of him, just as the mech launched its head towards him. Its jaws snapped onto the pipe as Cyrus clung to it for dear life, holding it up with a hand at either end with all his might. After a short struggle, the mech let go of the pipe and reared its head back for another strike. Cyrus quickly pointed the pipe into a vertical position and yanked it upwards as the jaws came back down. The end of the pipe got wedged straight into the roof of the mech's mouth. Cyrus thought it must have hit an important part of its circuitry as he watched the mech jolt back and fall to the floor alongside him. As the mech floundered about in a daze, Cyrus jumped to his feet and set off around the back of the nearest building, scooping up his rifle as he ran.

**

As he reached the far side of the building, Cyrus vaulted the fence as quickly as he could to get out of sight of the mech. He could hear it screeching from the road behind him.

'Where are you, Rowley?' he whispered to himself with a sense of urgency as he focused back on the task at hand. He could barely believe he had escaped that encounter; the odds of surviving that must have been a million to one. He felt a twinge in his left arm and looked down to find a large gash running the full length of the outside of his bicep. Then the pain started to seer through his arm, as if someone had just flicked a switch. The adrenaline must have been wearing off. As he watched the trail of blood drip out onto the ground, Cyrus contemplated stopping to try and patch it up. Instead he carried on in search of Rowley.

Another gunshot went off, this time very close. It came from just around the corner, where the street hit a T-junction. From what Cyrus could hear, the sound seemed to be coming from the right side. As he reached the junction he leant against the wall of the building on the edge of the street, partly to keep out of sight, but mostly because his arm was hurting so much he needed to rest. He took a quick swig of water from his bottle and poured a little onto the open wound through gritted teeth.

Peering around the corner through the sights of his rifle, Cyrus got a good view of what was going on. There was a second mech, but he couldn't spot Rowley. He could however make an educated guess as to where he was, as the panther seemed to be extremely interested in a battered old car. So interested in fact that it was trying very hard to get in through the window, teeth first. Another gunshot fired from inside the car, hitting the panther in the face and ricocheting away. Cyrus took three deep breaths and then, without any real plan, raced around the corner making a lot of noise. As he screamed towards the mech, firing at it to get its attention, he realised how frequently he had been doing things without thinking them through lately. And it almost always seemed to end badly.

The small plan he did have seemed to be working, as the panther turned its attention away from the car and onto the crazed Cyrus who was still running in its direction. A couple more plasma rounds hit its armoured body before it decided to race towards him with purpose.

I was in that moment Cyrus realised what a truly horrible idea this was. He had had a lucky escape with the last mech, and he knew he couldn't possibly be so lucky this time. Watching the panther gallop in his direction was like seeing a countdown to his death. He continued to fire at it, determined to at least try and hit a weak spot before being torn apart limb from limb. As the mech was almost on him, Cyrus crouched to get ready to try and evade the beast's leap. There was no guarantee it'd do any good, he was too far in the open to get away from it. He'd just be prolonging the inevitable.

Sure enough, the panther pounced towards him, jaws wide. Cyrus stopped firing and closed his eyes as he began to dive to his left. Next thing he knew, there was a loud clanging sound of metal clashing together. As he hit the floor, Cyrus looked back to his attacker, and to his bemusement saw two stunned looking panthers lying just away from each other on the road. One seemed to have been hit pretty hard, its circuits whizzing and popping. The other was struggling to get back on its feet, looking straight at Cyrus as it stumbled. The mech Cyrus had encountered minutes earlier must have followed the gunshots there. It had to have been through sheer luck that the two had attempted to pounce on him from opposing angles at the same time, colliding in mid-air.

Cyrus lifted his rifle and attempted to shoot the mech that was quickly regaining its composure. But the gun didn't fire. He started to panic and glanced frustratingly down at the weapon. It looked like it was overheating, and an error message was flashing up on the ammo counter display.

'You gotta be kidding me!' he cursed, as the mech was now back on all fours. Still lying on his side, he grabbed his sidearm and let off a couple of blasts towards it. The first ricocheted off the beast's metal shoulder plate, the second hitting it straight in the eye, causing it to imitate its malfunctioning twin lying a few feet away. Cyrus leapt to his feet and dashed over to the car.

'Rowley! Rowley!'

His friend popped his head up to the window to greet him, and a relieved expression washed over his face.

'Oh buddy, am I glad to see you. My group, I haven't seen them since—'

'They're fine, Rowley. They're safe,' Cyrus reassured. 'Now come on, we need to hustle.' Rowley passed his rifle to him as he hauled himself out of the broken window with a heavy groan. The mechs were still incapacitated on the ground, but there was no telling how long it would stay that way. A mech could malfunction for anything from a few seconds to almost a minute. It was just pot luck which it would be this time. All Cyrus knew was that it was best to get out of there as quickly as possible.

CHAPTER SIXTEEN

Cyrus and Rowley ran as fast as they could, staying away from the roads where possible to stay out of sight of mech patrols. Cyrus was desperate to be reunited with his group. He had a responsibility to uphold and although it could be said that he'd kept them safe and out of sight while he went in search of his friend, some would argue that he'd left them exposed with one less weapon to defend themselves with. Cyrus tried hard to tread lightly as he ran, but with the speed in which they were travelling it was a luxury they couldn't afford. The thought didn't seem to have crossed Rowley's mind, who seemed to be stomping extra loudly, kicking stones this way and that as they darted from one building to another.

As they reached the rest of their group they were greeted by an animated Mia, who had been standing guard in the doorway waiting for them. The relieved look on her face was plain to see, and Cyrus waited for the stern telling off that was no doubt about to follow as they slumped against the wall by the door.

'So glad you're OK,' Mia smiled at them, before sitting down on the other side of the room. 'Were they following you?'

Cyrus was taken aback by her reaction. The old Mia would have torn him to shreds for putting himself in danger. Her reaction was a lot less passionate than anticipated. He wasn't sure how to take it.

'Cyrus?' Mia was looking straight at him, waiting for an answer. Cyrus looked to Rowley, who was still wheezing from their running.

'Uh, I dunno,' he replied with a gormless expression on his face. 'It was all a blur. I, err, I don't think so.'

'We need to get out of here. It's only a matter of time before they find us,' a woman offered urgently. Her suggestion was met with a round of nods and murmurs of agreement. Nathaniel looked very uncomfortable at this.

'If we go now, they'll be expecting us. They'll tear us to pieces. These guys are quicker than most of us, and they barely made it through the skin of their teeth.'

'What are you suggesting?' the woman responded.

'I say we wait it out. If we keep quiet, those mechs will glide right past and move on to another part of town.'

The woman rolled her eyes. 'They won't just go away, Nathaniel. We need to take our chance now. You're just scared because you know you'll be the one that gets left behind if they find us. You're the slowest one in the group.'

Her words cut right to Nathaniel's core and made his blood boil in anger. A red mist began to descend over him, like a wounded beast trapped in a corner.

'WE'RE NOT LEAVING!' he yelled, his eyes mad with a mixture of rage and fear. The place fell silent as the tension grew thick. Alarm bells starting ringing in Cyrus's head; they needed to shut up before the mechs heard them. He needed to simmer things down somehow, but with two polar opposites going head to head in a heated debate, it wasn't going to be easy. He waved to the pair with flailing arms to get their attention for a moment. It seemed to work, albeit temporarily.

'You're going to get us all killed,' Nathaniel snapped, directing his attention immediately back to the woman.

'No, by making us stay here, *you're* going to get us all killed,' came the reply. Nathaniel gritted his teeth as Cyrus tried again to get their attention.

'Everyone just stop, now,' he hissed through a whisper, purposely trying to dictate the volume. But it was completely in vain. A loud bang could be heard outside, the sound rumbling through the building. Dust blew in from the road through the doorway, and Rowley coughed as he got the bulk of it in his face.

'They're here,' the woman announced, firing an 'I told you so' glance towards Nathaniel. She pulled a proton pistol out of the back of her shorts and loaded it with a loud click.

'Since when did you get a gun? I thought Gabriel said two per team? Cyrus got one pistol and Mia had the other. You steal that off someone?' Nathaniel decided to deal with the situation by picking holes in his new found enemy.

'No, asshole. I was in Rowley's group, remember?' she responded. Nathaniel shook his head and looked to the ceiling.

'OK, that's enough,' Cyrus butted in. 'She's right, Nathaniel, we need to move now. Those mechs will be here any second. We need to be gone by the time they are.'

A piercing screech echoed through the building. Cyrus knew they had to move right now. He jumped to his feet as everyone looked on in search of some sort of inspired strategy from their designated leader.

'Here's how this is going to go,' Cyrus stated plainly. 'You move *now*, you survive. You don't, you die.' And with that he burst out of the building and out onto the street, adjusting the straps on the heavy backpack he'd hurriedly flung over his shoulder. Mia and the woman quickly followed, pistols drawn.

A moment went by as the rest of the group sat stunned, too afraid to join Cyrus in the open. Rowley knew they needed a push to snap out of it, and he took this thought quite literally, physically hauling them up onto their feet. One at a time he went round the room, picking each person up and shouting at them to get moving. And one by one they responded by bolting out of the door and in the direction of the three who had left moments earlier.

Eventually Rowley and Nathaniel found themselves the last two remaining in the building. Rowley offered a hand to help him up, but Nathaniel refused, batting it away like a tennis player returning a volley.

'I told you, I'm not going anywhere.'

Rowley's eyes widened as the terrifying boom of a mech's gun shattered part of a building nearby. He found himself torn between saving this man's life and saving his own. With every passing second, the odds of either happening were becoming increasingly slim.

'Come on, Nathaniel. We need you,' he pleaded. 'We need a strong head like yours.'

Nathaniel continued with his stubbornness, maintaining a haggard, bitter expression. Finally, he climbed to his feet and set off for the door.

'Fine. If it'll shut you up. But this changes nothing.'

Rowley breathed a sigh of relief and headed outside. But his respite was short-lived as the clunking mechanical sound of mech immediately preceded the sight of a golem marching with purpose down the street a few buildings away. Rowley stopped dead in his tracks, his feet skidding on the dusty ground, catching the golem's attention. Its head turned at an unnatural angle from its body and its tracking system spotted them instantly. The pair took off in the opposite direction as the mech's body spun around to follow its locked-on gaze.

The two panthers from earlier had now arrived at the scene, cutting off their route from the other end of the street. Nathaniel stopped in his tracks, transfixed on the beasts stalking their prey.

'Come on, this way!' Rowley yelled at him, pointing at a narrow alleyway between two apartment blocks. Nathaniel followed as best he could, hobbling along towards the alleyway while Rowley gave him cover with a few blasts from his rifle.

The mechs were closing in fast, and Rowley prayed there was a way through at the bottom of the alley. Every decision he made was split second and he didn't have time to think of the next step. The alleyway was the best option he could see for the pair to escape, although it may only have delayed the inevitable.

Rowley heard a cry from behind him just as he had turned into the alleyway. As he spun back around, he saw Nathaniel sprawled on the floor, his crutch on the ground a few feet away from him. His heart leapt into his mouth as he watched the terrified expression materialise on the poor man's face, looking up at him in desperation. Time seemed to freeze in the moment they locked eyes, and he went pale as his mind raced. Seeing the panthers and golem closing in from different directions, Rowley knew he didn't have time to help him. Nathaniel was as good as dead, and helping him would only lead to two deaths instead of one. With a heavy heart Rowley fired a few more shots at the panthers, all missing in his hastened aim, before leaving Nathaniel to rush down the alley.

'I'm sorry,' he said under his breath, a tear forming in the corner of his eye. 'I'm so sorry.'

**

Cyrus checked his watch as he paused to catch his breath. It had been exactly seven and a half minutes since they'd fled the building, and he hadn't seen Rowley or Nathaniel in that time. The rest of the group had caught up with him, and were now taking a short break inside another crumbling building.

'How much longer until we reach the supermarket?' someone asked. 'I can't take much more of this.'

Cyrus said nothing, as if he wasn't even listening. He posted himself by the door again, watching the road for signs of the missing pair.

It's been way too long. What are they doing?

Moments later a disheveled Rowley appeared from around the corner. As he got closer Cyrus could see he was white in the face, as if he had seen a ghost.

'Thank God,' Cyrus said as he greeted him with a hearty hug. 'I was starting to fear the worst.' He looked behind Rowley and back down the road he'd come from.

'Where's Nathaniel?'

Rowley said nothing. His eyes were red and slightly puffy. Cyrus closed his eyes and put a hand on his sweaty forehead in dismay. He suddenly felt the weight of the colony, the people he was supposed to protect, crash down on him like a piano from the sky. He was failing them. His other hand clenched into a fist as he struggled to remove his anger quietly. In a short burst of fury, he kicked up the dirt in front of him and grabbed Rowley by the arm, pulling him into the shelter of the house.

As the pair entered, Cyrus let go and headed off to another room to be by himself, leaving Rowley in the care of his fellow group members.

'Holy crap, you look like you've been to hell and back,' one said. Rowley was non-responsive. A woman interjected quickly, sensing something the others hadn't.

'He's in shock,' she announced, putting two soft hands around his shoulders and helping him over to a worn wooden chair. 'Now, sit there and drink this.' She handed him her near full water bottle.

'Jeez Marie, you've hardly had a sip yourself,' a man warned. 'You need to think of your own needs too, you know.'

'It's called being resourceful,' Marie retorted. 'I'm fine.'

'The sun's pretty hot today. You might want to have a sip before he chugs that whole bottle down.'

'The sun's hot every day,' Marie replied sarcastically. 'Let me make my own decisions, OK?'

Mia stepped in to help her. 'Marie knows what she's doing. She was a nurse. She's seen this a million times before.'

'Doctor, actually.' Marie smiled at Mia, who looked a little more sheepish now. But despite feeling the need to correct her, it was clear she appreciated the support.

Mia gave an apologetic half-smile back, before looking at Rowley. He was still pale and didn't appear to be taking in the conversation that had been going on around him. She put a hand on his shoulder and looked at him head-on.

'He'll be fine, he just needs some time,' said Marie. 'Why don't you go check on your boyfriend, he seems pretty worked up.

Mia hesitated for a moment. Talking to Cyrus wasn't particularly high on her agenda. In fact today she just wanted as much space from him as possible. Last night had been frightening to say the least, and she needed some time to process it all without him constantly checking in with her. She reflected on it for a moment, before deciding it best to just try and bite the bullet. There were a million and one things more important to worry about right now.

She got up from beside Rowley and walked into the next room. Cyrus was sitting against the wall with his rifle and backpack opposite him. She knocked faintly on the doorframe to catch his attention.

'Hey,' she began, offering one of her trademark beaming smiles that he loved so much.

'Hey,' he replied, with much less enthusiasm.

'Mind if I join you?'

Cyrus shrugged his shoulders. 'Sure.'

Mia sat down beside him and rested her head on his shoulder. She soon realised it was a step too soon, as he pulled away aggressively.

'What's wrong with you today?' Cyrus questioned harshly. 'One minute we're fine, the next you won't talk to me. And now you want to snuggle up like everything's hunky dory? People are dying, Mia. Nathaniel's dead. And it's all my fault.'

Mia's eyes widened at the news. A sickening feeling consumed her stomach and she looked to the floor as a mixture of sadness and fear swept over her like a rushing tide.

'Cyrus, it's not your f—'

'Not my fault? A man died because I couldn't keep my promise to him!' he snapped, staring at her dead in the eyes. Mia's heart pounded as a different kind of fear started to build up inside. This was a side of Cyrus she hadn't experienced before.

'Cyrus.'

Cyrus climbed to his feet and hastily retrieved his belongings, before marching back out to the rest of the group.

'OK, saddle up everyone,' Mia heard him say. 'The sooner we leave, the sooner this nightmare of a day can be over.' The sound of shuffling about quickly followed as the group readied themselves. It was clear the others had overheard Cyrus's outburst from the next room, and Marie touched his arm as he walked past.

'Can we wait a little longer? I'm not sure he's quite ready.' She motioned towards Rowley, who wasn't looking much better than before. She disguised her true concern well, but Cyrus ignored her, opting instead to try and rouse his friend back into the fray. He crouched in front of Rowley and took a long look at him.

'Rowley, come on buddy. We need you now more than ever,' he whispered. 'I can't lead this group by myself.'

Rowley opened his mouth, but nothing came out. Finally, he managed a few quiet words.

'Nathaniel. He died because of me.'

'No, Rowley. You did the best you could, don't blame yourself.'

Mia couldn't help but shudder at his blatant hypocrisy as she listened in from the doorway. She decided to hold her tongue as not to aggravate him.

'No, Cyrus. I left him. He fell, and I just—' he paused as a vacant stare took over him. 'Left.'

Someone piped up from the other side of the room. It seemed their whispering wasn't as private as they first thought.

'He was dead either way,' the man said coldly. 'If he stayed like he wanted to, they'd have found him for sure. You gave him a fighting chance.' The man looked at Cyrus. 'Both of you.'

The man's bedside manner left a lot to be desired, but his ruthless honesty seemed to serve its purpose here. After a couple of minutes the colour started to reappear in Rowley's cheeks and Cyrus managed to help him to his feet. A few of them whispered a small prayer for Nathaniel, before they set off into the wilderness once more.

**

The rest of the journey went relatively smoothly. There were a few close calls where they had to take cover to avoid the attention of more mechs wandered their path, but they managed to reach the supermarket without much further issue. Upon arrival Cyrus waved to the CCTV camera by the shutters at the front entrance. Seconds later there was a high pitched blip sound and the shutters began to open. Zion was the first to greet them as they made their way inside.

'What took you guys so long?'

Marie shook her head and took him to one side while the rest settled in. There were a few whoops of joy from some of the group once they saw first-hand the masses of food and water that awaited them.

CHAPTER SEVENTEEN

'They should be here by now. Why aren't they here? What's happened to them?'

Gabriel was pacing around the mall like a lion patrolling its border. He was wound tighter than a spring, and it was starting to unsettle the rest of the colony. It wasn't a great leadership trait by any stretch, but they could understand his concern for his friends' safety. Nevertheless, seeing the very person they relied on for guidance during this uncertain time adopting panic stations wasn't helpful.

'Cyrus said he'd come straight back, but he's not here. I should have gone with him. What was I thinking?'

'Hey, relax will ya?' Jane could sense the unease Gabriel was creating around the camp. But he didn't hear her; the sound of his inner voice pounding in his head drowned out everything around him. He felt like he was going mad. He was almost at the stage of arguing with himself.

'Hey! Big guy!' Jane tried again to get his attention, this time less subtly. Gabriel stopped pacing and turned his head to her. 'Everything's fine, don't worry,' she continued. But still it was in vain, as Gabriel immediately started pacing again, muttering to himself. Jane rolled her eyes and stormed after him, trying hard to keep up with his gigantic strides.

'Hey, listen to me.' She grabbed his bulky arm. The action seemed to catch him off guard, momentarily snapping him out of his daze. 'Listen to me,' she repeated, so it sunk in. 'I know you're stressed out, we all are. You're worried about them, we all are. But you're not helping anyone by stomping around here like a pissed off bull in a china shop.' She looked around at the group of people sat staring at them. 'These people need you to get yourself together, Gabriel. Hell, I need you to get yourself together. Think about the kind of message you're sending out. So Cyrus is taking a little longer than expected. You're acting like it's the damn apocalypse!'

Gabriel said nothing, but was at least looking at her to show he was listening. Jane softened her stance slightly, releasing her grip from his arm.

'You ever go flying?'

He looked confused by the question.

'You know, ever been on an ae-ro-plane?' She elongated the word condescendingly.

'Yeah, of course,' he replied, wondering where she was going with this.

'Well, you know when you hit a little turbulence, and the plane gets a little bumpy?'

He nodded his head, urging her to go on.

'What's the first thing you do?'

He paused for a moment, unsure of the answer, or at least the answer she was fishing for.

'Erm, grab the armrest?'

'OK, so you're a nervous flyer. What's the second thing you do?'

He thought about it for a moment. He suddenly realised how much clearer his mind was since he'd been talking with her. If she was just trying to distract him, it was working.

Then a spark came. Before he gave his reply, he already knew the point she was trying to make.

'Look at the flight attendants,' he replied.

'Exactly,' Jane responded with a pleased smile. 'And why do you do that?'

'To see if they're freaking out. Cause if they're not, you know there's nothing to worry about.'

'Precisely.'

Gabriel looked back at the people staring at him. Their eyes were wide, like rabbits in the headlights. He offered an enthusiastic smile and a wave, which may have been a little over the top as it was met with an exchange of confused glances.

'Why don't you go and talk to them, reassure them a little?' Jane suggested. 'Actually,' she hesitated, craning her neck to scout the area. 'Maybe start with them.' She motioned to a group on the other side of the room, before looking back at the group closest to them. 'I think you're freaking these guys out.' She gave him a friendly nudge and walked over to the nearby group herself.

**

The doors of the north-east entrance swung open with a bang. Cyrus, Rowley and Zion appeared shortly after from the darkness of the long corridor, much to the delight of Gabriel.

'They're back. Jane, they're back!' he yelled in delight, immediately dropping the conversation he was having to rush over to greet the trio. Jennifer and April followed, hugging them each in turn.

The three new arrivals stood there, completely motionless. They were partly stunned from the overly warm reception they'd received, particularly from Gabriel. But the weary looks on their faces said it all; they'd been to hell and back to get there, and that was only part one. The second part was about to begin.

'Was the road safe? Did everyone get there OK?' Gabriel quizzed. The three of them remained silent, slowly removing their backpacks and weapons. 'What happened? Tell me.' Gabriel continued to press, anxiety getting the better of him.

Cyrus looked at him with a stone cold stare. A lot of the people in the colony had mixed feelings towards Gabriel, but he had always been a supporter. But right now the man was really testing his patience.

'Give the guys some space,' Jennifer interjected, much to Cyrus's relief. 'April, can you go fetch us some water, please?' Her sister dutifully obliged.

'Boy am I glad to see you all back safe and sound,' Jennifer continued. 'Gabriel here was starting to get a little worried.'

Zion smiled as he slumped to the ground, laying back against his backpack. He spotted an opportunity and just couldn't help himself. 'Well that doesn't sound like the Gabriel I know. I hope you weren't too worried about us, buddy.'

Gabriel screwed his nose up as he tried to absorb Zion's sarcasm. He was never very good at being on the receiving end of his teasing.

April returned swiftly with the water. 'Here, take this.' She carefully placed the bottle into Zion's hands, holding onto them as she helped him lift it to his lips. The warmth of April's palms took him by surprise and caused the next joke he was brewing to slip right out of his mind. Whether intentional or not, she'd saved him from the wrath of Gabriel that would all but certainly follow had he delivered it. He took a large gulp and passed the bottle on to Rowley, who looked more exhausted than ever.

'Thanks, April.' He squeezed her hand to let her know his appreciation.

'Let's take five for the guys to catch their breath, OK?' Jennifer ushered Gabriel away as she glanced back over her shoulder with a wink. 'We can start preparing everyone for the move.'

**

As the rest of the colony gathering the last remaining belongings and readied themselves for the journey across the city, Cyrus, Rowley and Zion filled Gabriel in on the details of their last trip. The big man looked genuinely cut up about the news of Nathaniel. Despite their differences, he was still a human being; another survivor in this mad world, another terrified soul looking for peace.

He turned to Rowley and embraced him suddenly, which caught everyone off guard, not to mention the poor guy whose body was almost crushed from the weight of his humongous arms. But through his constricting grip, Rowley found a strange sense of peace, as if Gabriel had read his mind before he even knew what he was thinking. It felt oddly reassuring, like his friend knew what he was going through. He understood his pain.

'It's alright,' Gabriel said softly, the tone of his voice not quite in keeping with his usual deep grumble. He followed it up immediately with a long exhale; the kind a group would do together in unison at the end of a yoga session. 'You can't blame yourself, it's not your fault.'

The words resonated deep within Rowley. He took comfort in them as he relaxed into the embrace that seemed to be going on and on. There were a few awkward glances shared among the others, who stood watching the pair as they tried to make sense of this uncharacteristic behaviour. When Gabriel finally let go, he looked into Rowley's eyes and patted him on the shoulder. 'It'll get easier,' he said candidly. 'It'll make you stronger.'

Rowley nodded sheepishly in a mixture of confusion and appreciation. It was certainly an odd moment for everyone involved, but it showed a compassionate side of Gabriel that rarely escaped his tough exterior.

'OK then, why are we still standing here?' Gabriel addressed the rest of the group, snapping back into character. 'We've got a job to do.'

April rolled her eyes and turned away. 'That didn't last long,' she muttered under her breath.

The remaining members of the colony pulled together to make sure everything was packed up and ready to go. The people were split up into small groups of equal numbers, with a leader assigned to each one to guide them on their journey across the city, just as had been done before. Cyrus groaned as he lugged his backpack over his shoulder for the umpteenth time. He looked upon the nervous faces of his fellow companions, their complexions a little whiter than usual. He offered a few encouraging words to the young children, before regrouping with Rowley, Zion and Gabriel for a final briefing.

A young boy began to cry as the tension circulated around the room. The people were starting to regret voting for the supermarket, and the knowledge that their friends were safely on the other side was barely reassurance enough. They knew the dangers out there; they'd seen and heard it before.

'Hold on a second, guys.' Rowley cut from the briefing to try and console the poor kid, whose wailing was barely muffled as he buried his head into his mother's chest.

'Hey buddy, it's going to be alright. Your mom's here, she's not going anywhere.'

The kid sniffed as he listened to Rowley.

'Here, I know what. Take this.' He reached into his backpack and presented the boy with his favourite baseball card. 'You like baseball?'

The kid nodded as the tears kept flowing.

'Alright then, that's a good start,' Rowley continued. 'This here is a very special card.'

Cyrus listened in as he heard the same spiel his friend had given him time after time about that card. He smiled and appreciated the moment.

'I want you to hang onto this for me, OK? You can give it back when we get there.'

The boy took the card and studied it, before smiling widely. Rowley ruffled the boy's hair playfully and looked at his mother. 'If you need anything, just shout. We'll all be OK, I promise.' He walked back to the others and carried on with the briefing. Gabriel nodded to him in approval before giving them some quick instructions.

'Cyrus, you go first. You know the way better than me so it makes sense for you to lead. I'll wait a couple of minutes and head after you with my group. Rowley, you next, and Zion last. Try not to bunch up too much, but keep within eyesight of the next group. We want to keep a low profile, and we don't want to draw attention to ourselves. If we all go together those mechs will hear us for sure. Our footsteps are quieter in smaller groups.' He paused briefly to look each of them in the eye one by one, pointing his finger at them as he made his next point. 'If you get separated, try and keep your group together. Take shelter inside somewhere if you need to. Everyone got that?'

'You know we've done this before, right?' Zion quipped, one eyebrow raised.

Gabriel paused for a second, reeling at the comment.

'I get it, I'm scared too,' Rowley chipped in. 'In fact no, I'm terrified. We know what it's like out there, let's not sugar coat it. It's a nightmare, and…' he paused and took a deep breath as he looked to the ceiling. 'It'll be a miracle if we all make it there alive.'

A sombre atmosphere quickly developed between the four of them. Nobody spoke for a few moments as they reflected on the magnitude of the task ahead of them. Finally, Cyrus spoke up.

'It's now or never, gentlemen. The longer we wait, the weaker they're all going to be.' He looked back at the group of people whose lives would shortly be in their hands. They looked utterly lost. Gabriel followed his gaze.

'Then let's pray for a miracle.'

CHAPTER EIGHTEEN

An empty drinks can jangled about as it was blown across the road from the blizzard of sand that was brewing in the city. The still clear skies of that morning had quickly become a distant memory. Cyrus trudged on at the front of his group, but stopped for a moment to survey the changing weather. This day was starting to feel as long as the day before. He closed his eyes to shield them from the bits of dust that were being blown up from the ground, and longed to be somewhere else. A daydream quickly set in, and within moments he was transported to a paradisiacal beach. The blue sky and white sandy beach coloured his thoughts, with the leaves of the palm trees gently swaying in the cool breeze. He could almost taste the ice cold piña colada as the sounds of Rupert Holmes rang through his ears.

'Cyrus.' A stray old newspaper blew into his face as the call from another member of the group snapped him out of his daze. He reeled in his startled state to find a sea of concerned faces staring at him.

'This sandstorm's getting pretty bad,' a woman pointed out. 'How far is the supermarket from here?'

Cyrus pulled the map from his pocket and studied the path he'd drawn in thick red pen. He followed the line from the starting point and tapped when he located their position. He looked at his surroundings for confirmation.

'We're just about half-way,' he declared, slightly surprised that they had made such good progress. 'How's everyone doing?'

The woman looked at him cautiously. 'Well, there seems to be a sandstorm on the approach, but other than that we're just fine.' The irony in her voice was fool proof, and Cyrus took the hint.

'OK, good call,' he acknowledged. 'Let's find shelter while it passes.' He signalled to Gabriel's group, who had just about caught up with them, and pointed to the building across the street.

**

A short while later, all four groups had made it safely to the half-way point and were taking refuge from the storm inside a large, mostly intact building. Zion had identified it as the office of a well-known tech firm which specialised in virtual reality software.

'That's an awfully precise guess, Zion,' said Rowley. He often wondered how much of what Zion said was completely made up on the spot. 'What makes you say that?'

'Well…' Zion hesitated while he explored the large room they found themselves in. 'This was clearly an open plan office, but from the spacing of the desks not your everyday battery farm type. So that got me thinking, it had to be one of those companies that preaches about how their open spaces and freedom to roam facilitates their creativity, or words to that effect.'

Rowley raised his eyebrow, still unconvinced by the elaborate picture Zion was painting.

'It could just be a law firm,' Rowley suggested. 'Lawyers like having their own space, right?'

'Right!' Zion agreed enthusiastically. 'But lawyers like to have their own office. This here is a group of co-workers who like to talk to each other. I'm telling you, it's CyCorp.'

Rowley was gobsmacked. 'How can you possibly get that?' Zion shrugged and held his arms in the air apologetically. 'What can I say, I should have been a detective.'

'Or,' Gabriel intervened. 'The company logo gave him a clue.'

Rowley's eyes widened as he followed Gabriel's gesturing towards the corner of the room. Leaning against the wall were the red block capital letters *CC*. Zion winked at him to compound his embarrassment.

Cyrus returned from the stairwell, his cheeks red as he panted. 'OK, I've been to all the floors. Nothing there.'

Rowley looked at his friend with a bemused expression.

'Cyrus, I don't think there'd be any mechs in here.'

Cyrus responded harshly. 'No you idiot, I was looking for supplies. Y'know, food, water? We're still short on those.' He shook his head in disbelief and sat down to catch his breath.

Rowley's face fell, transforming his upbeat demeanour to one resembling a sulking child. He scuffed his feet on the floor and muttered something to himself.

'What did you say?' Cyrus challenged. Rowley lifted his head and stared wide into his eyes, taken aback. 'Come on, out with it,' Cyrus pressed, refusing to let it go. He was beginning to draw attention from the others, who looked equally as concerned as the startled Rowley. This was out of character, however as the days went on Cyrus was demonstrating this behaviour more and more. Rowley wondered how long it would be before this became his character.

'I, er,' Rowley bumbled for a moment. 'Nothing, Cyrus.'

'No, come on. What did you want to say? If you're going to say something, just say it. Say it to my face.'

Gabriel marched in between the pair and pushed Cyrus against the wall, defusing the situation instantly.

'Stop, now,' he hissed, keeping his voice sharp but quiet to avoid causing more of a scene. 'Whatever it is, just stop. You can be pissed at him when we get there, but for now I need you to get your shit together. You got that?'

Cyrus winced as Gabriel sprayed him with spit while he spoke. He was much too close for comfort. Gabriel specialised in invading people's personal space, but it seemed to get the point across that bit better. Cyrus held his hands up in submission. The two shared a nod of acknowledgement and Gabriel relaxed and backed away.

The next few minutes followed a sombre tone, everyone trying to ignore the elephant in the room. Cyrus and Rowley barely looked at each other, and it made things uncomfortable as they began to prepare for the next leg of their journey. Zion found a moment to have a quick word with Gabriel in one of the small offices off of the main area. Unlike some of his companions, he knew how to be discrete.

'Tell me I'm wrong, but things don't seem right, do they?'

Gabriel snorted and raised an eyebrow at him. 'You're kidding, right?' He was hoping Zion was just trying to be funny.

'No, not with them,' he clarified, looking back through to the awkward scene on the other side of the glass wall. 'I mean outside. Something's not right.'

'Well it's certainly different, that's for sure,' Gabriel agreed. 'We haven't run into any mechs, which is a godsend.'

'Precisely,' Zion agreed. 'When was the last time it was that quiet out there? It's never like that. It's like the city's completely deserted.'

Gabriel smiled and put an arm around him. 'It's the ideal situation. We've gotten lucky so far. If we have as uneventful a journey for the rest of today as we've had so far, we can count our lucky stars. Maybe someone's watching over us.'

'You believe in that stuff?' Zion asked, unconvinced.

'I haven't ruled it out. Times like this, a little faith might be just what we need. What else do we have?'

'Oh, I don't know, science, technology, a quick wit?'

'There's the Zion I know,' Gabriel remarked, before stepping back out to the main office space to gather the troops. Zion let out a loud sigh before following.

**

As they stepped out into the sun, the heat hit them like a punch in the face. Despite it being a common occurrence, they never got used to that feeling. It reminded Cyrus of the times he'd take Mia on a date to the cinema, and the sun would temporarily blind them as they walked back outside into normality. It was like stepping through a portal from the comfortable bubble of make-believe he'd created, back into the harsh reality of the world around him. The escape of the darkness brought a few brief hours of protection; a numbness to the troubles he faced in the exposed light of day. The moment brought with it feelings of dread and clarity simultaneously. It made Cyrus refocus on the task at hand,

and put into perspective the petty arguments he'd tried to create through his frustration.

The street was empty, the air still. The city's weather was certainly bipolar, and the calm mood was very much welcomed, making the absence of mechs that bit more obvious. It was unnerving for Zion, who had already aired his concerns about this strange activity, or lack thereof.

'OK, home stretch,' Gabriel encouraged. The group trudged on in the direction of the river.

**

The group finally arrived at the supermarket and were greeted to the usual warm welcome. They couldn't quite believe their luck; they'd gone the whole journey without a single hiccup. Gabriel joked with Zion that it could only have been a result of divine intervention. Zion rolled his eyes and gave a half smile.

'Alright alright, I won't rule it out, if it'll shut you up.'

Cyrus entered the supermarket and immediately looked for Mia. It didn't take long to find her as she was awaiting his return by the entrance, along with Jennifer and April.

She smiled as she saw him approach. 'I'm glad you're OK,' she said, before quickly moving on to help the other weary travellers with their bags. The awkward tension between them was worse than ever, which frustrated him. He wondered how long she'd be like this for, if not forever. It was in that moment that he realised how much he needed his friends, and how through his anger he'd successfully pushed them away. He took a deep breath and sighed, before heading over to Rowley, working up an apology in his head as he walked.

Rowley was busy helping everyone get settled into their new home. The little boy he'd spoken to back at the mall ran over to him and proudly presented his favourite baseball card to him.

'I took good care of it for you,' he beamed. Rowley studied the card, which was quite clearly in a worse state than when he'd given it to the boy. The boy shuffled about on the spot nervously. 'It got a bit crinkled in my pocket, but it's alright.'

Rowley beamed back at him and took back the card with another ruffle of the boy's hair.

'Thanks, buddy. I can count on you.' The boy's face lit up once more, his innocent smile emulating Rowley's. He then ran back over to his mother as Rowley spotted Cyrus approaching.

'Hey,' he said sheepishly. 'What's up?'

'Rowley, I'm sorry.' Cyrus came right out with it. 'I shouldn't have snapped at you earlier. I'm just so stressed with everything, y'know?'

Rowley laughed and shook his head. 'So that's it? You're sorry but it's OK because you're stressed?'

Cyrus was surprised by this reaction. Rowley continued. 'You know if you just stopped for one second to think about other people, you might see that maybe you're not the only one who's having a hard time adjusting to the end of the world.'

'Jeez Rowley, it's not like that.'

'Don't 'jeez Rowley' me. Don't do what you always do. Don't turn this around on me.' Cyrus saw a fire in Rowley's eyes that he'd never experienced before. 'You're having a hard time with Mia, I get it. But do you think you're the only one frustrated with your life right now? I was going to be somebody. Finally get a good job, maybe settle down, have a kid, live a normal life. You know, I even started writing about it, as if anyone would read it. But now that's all gone down the pan, and guess what?' Cyrus anxiously waited through what felt like the longest pause. He started to wonder if Rowley was expecting him to answer. 'We have to get on with it and make the best of what we have,' he continued at last, his eyes still ablaze. 'You're not the only one who has feelings, alright? So don't tell me you're stressed, like you're the only one having a hard time right now.'

'Jeez, Rowley. I—'

Rowley looked at him like he was about to throw a punch right onto his nose.

'Er, right, sorry. I'm just sorry.'

'That's fine, Cyrus. I'm glad you're sorry. Apology accepted. Just maybe you should spend a little less time daydreaming and a little more time helping out, OK? And when I do something you don't like too much, maybe try and look in the mirror before biting my head off about it.'

Cyrus got the feeling that he hadn't accepted his apology. It was at that moment that he sunk to the lowest point he'd ever remembered feeling. He felt alone and scared. Rowley had been his safety blanket, the friend he could always rely on when nobody else was there. He suddenly realised how much he had been taking advantage of that all these years, and how he had taken their friendship for granted. Rowley had always taken an interest, offered advice, shown encouragement when he really needed it. And he'd given barely a fraction of this in return. In fact, he'd actively shown the complete opposite on countless occasions. It was no wonder Rowley had snapped and finally drawn a very clear line in the sand. Frankly, the only question Cyrus took away from this was why the hell Rowley had put up with it this long? It was a level of compassion, of patience, that Cyrus could barely even comprehend, let alone demonstrate.

'Can I help you with these bags?' Cyrus asked, making his intention to make amends clear. Rowley continued to look at him, for a moment not saying a word. Cyrus watched as his arched eyebrows started to relax.

'Sure,' he replied, chucking the heaviest bag he had into Cyrus's midriff.

Across the other side of the supermarket, Gabriel was wandering around looking as anxious as ever. It seemed the relief of arriving there safely was fleeting to some. Moving from one aisle to the next, he tried to estimate how long the food would last before they needed to look elsewhere.

'Gabriel, my man. Do you ever rest? Or do your eyes take shifts at sleeping?' Zion quipped. Gabriel didn't acknowledge him, muttering some quick mental maths to himself.

'Hey,' Zion tried again, this time waving his arms at him from further down the aisle.

'I'm busy, Zion.'

'No you're not. You're just making yourself busy for the sake of it,' another voice chimed in. Jane strolled up to him and put her hand on his arm. 'I can read you like a book.'

Gabriel let out a deep sigh. 'Go on then.'

'It's Isaac,' Jane started.

'He's insane,' Zion interjected with a cheeky smile. Jane scowled at him.

'He's not insane, he's scared like the rest of us.' She turned back to Gabriel. 'He *is* acting a bit strange though. He keeps talking about some gang called *The Crimson Crows*. He says they're coming here to get him.'

'What do they want with him? Do you know why they're after him?'

Jane shook her head. 'Maybe you should talk to him.'

'What good will I do? You're the 'people person', you talk to him.'

'He's taken a bit of a shine to you,' Jane smiled. 'He probably feels a lot safer with you around.'

Gabriel rolled his eyes. Jane had a way of talking him into things, and they both knew she wouldn't quit until he did it.

'You're a real pain in the ass, Jane,' he grumbled.

'Right back at you, big guy.'

**

'How you holding up?' Aiden knelt by Cameron, who was sitting quietly in the office at the back of the building. He was swinging around on the desk chair, which made a slight creak and squeak as it pivoted.

'I'm alright,' he replied. 'I like it better here.'

Aiden smiled. 'They got cool chairs here, huh?'

'Yep.' Cameron smiled as he continued to spin himself around and around.

'Honey, don't make yourself dizzy.' Caitlin entered the room holding a blanket. 'Some nice people thought you might want this,' she said, placing it in the corner of the room. 'For when it gets cold in the evening.'

'That's nice,' Cameron replied. 'You want me to go say thank you?'

Aiden fired a glance at Caitlin, and the two of them shared a moment of warmth as their eyes locked.

'Good boy, that would be very nice,' she responded cheerily. Cameron gleefully shot out of the chair and went hurtling towards a nearby wall. Aiden managed to react quick enough to prevent him from hitting the wall head first, but

Cameron's momentum sent him bundling into him, knocking him clean over.

'Cameron, what did I just say?' Caitlin raised her voice.

'Sorry,' he replied as he gingerly got back to his feet, stepping all over Aiden as he did so.

'The nice ladies by the entrance. You remember their names?'

Cameron peeked out to the main shop floor and scanned the entrance. 'Oh yes I know!' he replied enthusiastically. 'That one's called April. She's pretty.' He ran off in the direction of the entrance, without a hint of a goodbye.

Aiden dusted himself down as he sat on the floor in a heap.

'I'm so sorry about that. Did you hurt yourself?' asked Caitlin.

'No, I'm OK,' he smiled. 'He's a good kid.'

'He's a handful sometimes. You're really good with him, though.'

Aiden blushed. 'He makes it easy for me,' he replied modestly.

'No, I mean it. Nobody's ever been so patient with him. He can be a bit full on sometimes.'

'Well just give it time, he might start getting fed up with me,' he joked.

Caitlin beamed, her eyes glistening as they fixed on his. She knelt down next to him, putting her hand out to help him up. As they grew closer, she noticed a spec of dirt on his cheek. She wiped it away with her thumb, caressing his face with it even after the dirt had gone. He looked back at her longingly as the electricity began to spark between them. She closed her eyes and slowly leaned in to kiss him.

'They said we're welcome!' Cameron burst through the doorway, his voice piercing the air and snapping the pair out of the moment. Caitlin pulled away, slightly startled as she whipped her hair back behind her ears.

'That's lovely, dear,' she replied. Cameron immediately plonked himself back down on the office chair and started to spin around once more.

'You were quick, buddy. You must have ran like a cheetah,' said Aiden. He tried to catch Caitlin's eye but she was facing away. The moment was gone.

**

'Hey, have you seen Isaac?'

'Yeah, he's outside with Rowley and Cyrus.'

Gabriel looked towards the entrance of the supermarket and noticed the back of Rowley's head through the glass doors.

'Brilliant, thanks April.'

He stepped out into the cool breeze that accompanied the evening. It was the best part of the day; the perfect middle ground between the sticky heat of day and the colder bite of night. He took a moment to soak it in while he admired the pinkish colours of the sunset on the horizon, hidden behind the torn skyscrapers. He rarely allowed himself moments like this, where he cleansed his mind of everything he'd been worrying about and just marvelled at the beauty of nature. This part of the city was slightly higher above sea level than the rest of Novasburgh, so the supermarket was positioned with an incredible view of the city centre. He stroked his beard and stood for a few moments longer. Finally, he turned his attention back to the trio who were immersed in conversation a few feet away.

'No, no, no, I will not have it,' Isaac insisted. He seemed to be really worked up about something. 'Sequels are never ever better. Name me *one* sequel that's better than the original.'

Cyrus and Rowley paused while they thought about it.

'*Star Wars*,' Rowley replied. '*Empire Strikes Back*, better than *A New Hope*.'

'No, no, no,' Isaac shook his head disapprovingly. 'You see, you're wrong again. *A New Hope* is so much better.'

'I have to agree with Isaac on this one,' Cyrus chirped. 'But *Return of the Jedi* is the best, right?'

The pair looked at Cyrus with raised eyebrows, as if what he'd just said was the most shocking thing they'd ever heard.

'I rest my case,' Isaac concluded.

'Gabriel, help us out here,' Rowley acknowledged Gabriel's arrival, immediately pulling him into the conversation. 'Sequels that are better than the original. Any ideas?'

'*Aliens*,' he replied almost instantly. 'Loved that film.'

The filmmaking industry started to go downhill years before the war, and soon very few new films were being produced; even less so good ones. Up until the end of the war, cinemas would churn out reruns of the best old films of each genre. Sci-fi was a popular category in this circle.

'The old ones are the best, I'll give you that,' Isaac agreed. 'But I have to say, the first one was better.'

Cyrus tutted to himself, but he wasn't as subtle as he intended and drew the attention of the others.

'I mean, it's all just subjective,' he pointed out.

'But it's fun to argue,' Isaac enthused.

There was a lull in conversation and Gabriel found his chance to bring up what Jane had sent him for.

'Isaac, Zion and Jane mentioned that you were concerned about a group of people that had threatened you.'

Isaac's face dropped and he suddenly looked very worried.

'They sometimes come here at night and bang on the security doors. I can hear them. They say my name and tell me they're going to get me.'

An uneasiness swept through the group like a cold chill, as if the change in tone of conversation had dropped the temperature ten degrees.

'Do you know why they're after you?' Gabriel asked. 'What do they want from you?'

'Hang on a second.' Cyrus interrupted Gabriel as he had just thought of something. 'You said they come here looking for you. We didn't have much trouble getting in here. Why haven't they managed to get in?'

Isaac sniggered. 'They're stupid. No other explanation. They saw the front door was locked, so they assumed the building was locked down.'

Cyrus frowned at his response. It wasn't a very likely story, which led him to wonder if he was telling the truth.

Gabriel tried his question again. 'Isaac, why do they want to—'

A loud boom erupted from the other side of the city. A large plume of smoke rose up from behind one of the skyscrapers. Another explosion followed soon after, and then another, and another. The ground rumbled from the shockwave. A flood of people streamed out of the supermarket to get a view of what was going on.

'The mall.' someone cried. 'That was the mall!'

CHAPTER NINETEEN

A flash of orangey-yellow light wrapped around the shopping mall in an inferno. Bits of rubble could be seen breaking away like dustings of flour falling off a loaf of bread. In a matter of moments, the entire building was blown to pieces, leaving an ominous black cloud of smoke in the sky directly above it. Screams rang out from the crowd of people that had gathered outside the supermarket entrance.

'What the hell just happened?' Rowley struggled to process what he'd just witnessed.

'They were coming for us,' Gabriel replied. His tone was intense, as though he'd just had an epiphany. His eyes were wide with fear as he looked on at the destruction before him. A wave of silence set in as Gabriel's words brought a sudden harrowing realisation.

'That man. The one with the woman who attacked us the other night.'

'Connor,' Caitlin interjected. 'His name was Connor. And the woman was Michelle.' Her involvement brought a few awkward glances from those around her. Caitlin suddenly felt very aware that she was the subject of attention from a large number of people.

'Yes,' Gabriel continued, turning around to nod to her in acknowledgement. 'He said they'd be back for us, and he wasn't lying. We can't underestimate these people, whoever they are. If we hadn't moved here as soon as we did, we'd be lying under that pile of rubble right now.' He pointed to the plumes of smoke in the distance.

'But we did move, and we're safe now,' April added. 'They don't know we're here. This is a good thing. They think we're dead, they think they've got their revenge, or whatever it is they wanted. Now they won't be looking for us anymore.' There were a few nods of agreement and mutterings from the crowd.

Zion piped up to give his two cents. 'I'm not convinced. You're right, they probably think we're dead. But they'll find us eventually. At some point they'll be coming here to ransack this place. It's a mystery nobody did it sooner.' He looked at Isaac with suspicion. 'Someone tell me it's not just me who thinks there's something fishy going on.'

Gabriel took this as his cue to continue his interrogation of Isaac. He knew this wasn't the right time or place, but his already thin patience was starting to become thread bare. He marched up to Isaac, his hulking frame doing half his job for him as Isaac crumbled at the sight of it.

'OK, OK, I'll tell you!' he spluttered, before Gabriel had even reached him. 'Just don't hurt me.'

Gabriel stopped dead in his tracks and wagged a finger at him. 'Tell us now, and tell us quick, Isaac. Why are *The Crimson Crows* after you? What did you do?'

Isaac paused for a moment, his eyes darting around as he looked helplessly at the rest of the colony. All he found were people staring back at him; some mirroring his panicked expression, others displaying a look of judgement as they expectantly awaited his story. Aiden got a sense of déjà vu, watching Isaac go through the same desperate and lonely feeling he had experienced in Michelle's group not that long ago.

'I...' Isaac started, his hand shaking. Aiden decided to step in and help the poor guy out. He stood by his side and faced the crowd, his body language giving Isaac a little respite as he absorbed some of the attention.

'Let's give him a minute, OK?'

Gabriel rolled his eyes. 'Aiden, we don't have time for this.'

'It's OK,' said Isaac, putting his shaky hand onto Aiden's arm in recognition of the gesture. 'I betrayed them. I abandoned them.' He breathed out deeply as he came to terms with the announcement, like an alcoholic finally admitting he had a problem. But again he was met with nothing but staring eyes, this time with slightly perplexed looks. 'Oh, right, right, yes. I need to start from the beginning.' He took in another deep breath and started.

'You see, these people, *The Crimson Crows*. I used to be one of them. We were just like any other soldiers, and we fought side by side. We were good people, but I betrayed them. I let them all down. Mechs are everywhere, bandits are everywhere. Nasty, horrible people. They exploit you and rob you and leave you for dead.'

'Sounds like we've crossed paths with the same people,' Zion interjected.

'Yes, yes!' Isaac was excited by their common interest, but it served only to create more unease. 'The war was over, that's what I said. I told them to stop the fighting, but they wouldn't listen. And then I abandoned them when they needed me most. Now they haunt me. They come back here to avenge their deaths.'

Everyone looked stunned from what they had just heard. Isaac had clearly gone mad. All this time he was afraid of nothing. A ghost, a fabrication of his own imagination. His fallen comrades were playing on his mind, haunting his dreams, his every thought. It seemed the war had hit him harder than anyone. Cyrus felt for the guy.

'It's OK, Isaac,' Cyrus tried to comfort him, or at least let him know he wasn't alone. Moments had gone by where nobody had said anything. The trembling Isaac stood there watching the sea of faces staring back at him. 'They're not coming to get you. It wasn't your fault, what happened to your friends,' Cyrus continued.

Isaac looked bleakly back at him. There was so much pain in his eyes.

'I can't forget,' he said. 'I'll never forget the look on their faces when I left them, right before they were killed.' A tear streamed down his face. 'I could have saved them.'

'No,' Cyrus challenged. 'No, you couldn't. There's nothing you could have done. They made their decision, and you made yours. If you stayed, you would have died with them.' Isaac winced at the prospect. 'You're here now, and you have a chance to save the people standing right in front of you today.'

These were all just words, but to Isaac it was a defibrillator to the chest. It was a kick-start to the rest of his life. It was as if he had been in an endless nightmare, and Cyrus had finally awoken him. Isaac's hands continued to shake as he wiped the tear stream from his face. He smiled and started to laugh. The same unnerving laugh that he'd expressed earlier. It was completely juxtaposed to the situation. Cyrus looked around at his friends for some kind of assistance, but was met only with a few shrugs of the shoulder.

'I will help you, Cyrus,' he said at last, pointing his shaky finger at him and smiling. 'I will help you and your friends.'

**

An hour had passed since the explosions at the mall, and the colony had moved back inside to stay out of sight of any mech activity. Isaac's story had been the cause of much discussion, and Gabriel was questioning his sanity. He didn't trust him, and declared that he was too unpredictable.

'We have to let him help us,' Cyrus argued. 'You can see how afraid he is. This whole situation has affected him more than anyone. He needs our support, and who knows, he could be the best thing that happened to this colony.'

'Let's face it,' Rowley chimed in. 'It can't get much worse. Bandits will always find us and try and rob us, or kill us. Mechs will always be out there tearing up the streets. We need to do something, we can't go on living like this, one day after another. It's not living, it's just surviving.'

Gabriel raised an eyebrow. 'So what do you propose we do?'

Rowley opened his mouth, but no words came out. He had nothing. Suddenly, a voice came from behind them.

'I think we should kick their ass.' Mia approached the group with an uncharacteristic swagger. The three of them paused, trying to register whether it was a joke or a serious suggestion. Mia helped them out. 'I'm serious. The city's a mess. There's no order, no rules, nothing. Everything we had has gone. Until these mechs are gone, we can't have a normal life. We certainly can't have a normal life while there are people out there robbing and murdering everyone they see. And what, there's some guy called 'The Jackal' kidnapping people and making them his slaves? We've got to find this guy and stop him.'

The three men stood in awe at the words that were coming out of her mouth. Cyrus realised that he was actually gawking at her, mouth wide open. He closed it quickly and rubbed his chin. Mia waited for their response. 'Well?'

'Well, what? It's madness.' Gabriel crossed his arms, unconvinced.

'Actually, it's genius,' Rowley countered.

'Come again?'

'This Jackal guy, whoever he is. He wants us to run. He wants us to go on living like this, so he can send his cronies after us. It's probably all just a sick game to him. If we take the fight to him, he'll be the one that needs to hide.'

'What else are we going to do?' Mia added. 'You agree right, Cyrus?' She fired a look at Cyrus that was the sort only girlfriends or wives could pull off. It was the sort of glance that added a deeper agenda behind the question. The kind that said 'I need you to agree with me, even if you don't, or I'm going to hold it against you for the rest of your life'. Everyone in the room knew exactly what it meant, except for Cyrus.

'I dunno, Mia,' he began. Mia started to screw up her forehead as she intensified the look she was giving him. Cyrus finally cottoned on and tried to backtrack. 'I mean, yeah, that would be exactly what he's expecting us not to do.'

Gabriel stepped in again. 'Mia, I'm sorry. I admire your courage, but what chance do we have again this guy? It seems like he owns the city as we speak. What makes you think we can take him down?'

Something caught Cyrus's eye as Mia and Gabriel began to discuss the situation. A soft red glow was coming from his chest.

'I don't know, but we can't just sit here and wait for him to kill us. I'm fed up being scared every day. This has to change,' Mia replied.

Cyrus looked down at the top of his t-shirt and pulled out the crystal from underneath it. It was glowing a warm red colour, fading away slightly and coming back again, like a lighthouse in the night.

'I know, I feel the same way too. But going up against him? We don't know how powerful this guy is,' Gabriel rebuffed.

'And he doesn't know how powerful we are,' Jennifer retorted, entering the debate firmly on Mia's side.

'It could be suicide.'

Cyrus thought about his family. His mother and sister who had disappeared without a trace. His father who had been MIA long ago. He had lost so much, and yet he had so much more to lose. He clasped the crystal in his hand and looked at Mia. She was right, this was no way to live. It had to stop sometime, and the only way for that was to fight back again the oppression. He felt a surge of courage rush through him as the crystal glowed brighter and brighter. His mouth opened before he knew the words that were going to come out.

'It *is* suicide,' he said bluntly. 'Or at least it probably is. Mia's right, we can't go on living like this. Do you want to spend the rest of your life in fear? Days, weeks, months, years? Who knows how long we'll last? The way things are now I don't imagine it'll be that long.' He paused for a moment before catching Mia's eye. She looked incredibly surprised at his sudden support, but the relief was clear to see in the small smile that was starting to etch across her face.

'My family are alive,' Cyrus continued. 'I can feel it.' He clutched the crystal once more and held it close to his chest. It began to glow a pale blue as he thought of his family with new found hope. 'We have to save them, and everyone else this monster has hurt.'

'I'm in,' said Mia.

Rowley threw his hands in the air. 'I'm in as well.'

Cyrus smiled at Mia and took his hand away from the crystal, revealing its pulsating glow. Mia titled her head in confusion, wondering what it meant.

'I guess that means you're feeling brave?' she suggested.

'Something like that.'

Gabriel cursed to himself. 'You're full of surprises.'

'So are you in? We can't do this without you.' Cyrus awaited the big man's response with bated breath.

Gabriel shuffled about on the spot, biting his lip as he thought. 'Screw it, I've been waiting to kick someone's ass for a while.'

Mia yelped in excitement and threw her arms around him, taking him by surprise. After the moment passed, she quickly took a step back and tucked her hair behind her ears, trying to compose herself once more. Avoiding eye contact with Cyrus, she headed off to Jennifer and April to spread the news.

'I hope you know what you're doing,' Gabriel said once she'd left.

Cyrus shrugged his shoulders casually. 'I honestly haven't got a clue.'

**

'We're not going anywhere!'

'We've only just arrived, why do we have to move again?'

'We're safe here, why should we give that up?'

Word was getting round the colony that Gabriel had decided everyone was going to leave. The people were pushing back, confused as to why they were being made to leave their new safe house when they had just arrived.

'Please tell me this isn't true, Gabriel,' a man protested. 'You can't be serious about this.'

'This is madness!' a woman shouted. 'This is the best home for us right now. We have food, water, shelter.'

Gabriel waved his arms in the air to get everyone's attention. One by one they piped down and awaited his response. He could sense that familiar feeling of uncertainty around the place, as he started to feel like he'd made no progress earning the people's trust. He let out a long deep breath and beckoned Cyrus over.

'We're not leaving, so relax,' he reassured, addressing the crowd. 'Not all of us, anyway.'

A few mumbles were heard and the air of uncertainty maintained. Gabriel nodded at Cyrus, who was now stood by his side.

'Cyrus will elaborate, it was his idea,' he finished, directing the attention of the colony onto him. Cyrus looked up at the man who towered at least a foot over him. This giant of a man was battle hardened and had experienced things Cyrus could barely imagine. Yet he couldn't face confronting a group of scared civilians. A true leader, he thought sarcastically.

The irony wasn't lost on Gabriel either, and it was at the point when he saw the wry smile appear under his bushy beard that Cyrus realised he was messing with him. He cleared his throat as he addressed the colony.

'Ahem, so, er, yeah.' He looked out into the crowd and started to feel hot under the collar. The cool hum of the freezer next to him emphasised the stupidity of the quest he was about to embark on. The people were right, they had everything here. They'd really lucked out and this place was the best place they could ever imagine at a time like this. There was enough food, good food, to last months, if they were careful and the power didn't cut out.

'Er, like Gabriel said, we're not all leaving. The world is a dangerous place, and—'

Gabriel made a gesture with his hands for him to get to the point. Cyrus reacted by raising his voice a little to make him sound more authoritative and serious.

'Well, you know. You've all seen it. It's hell out there, and there are people, bad people, who are exploiting the innocent.' He felt his confidence return as his courage began to rise up from his gut, into his throat and spill out through his words. 'I for one will not allow these people to get away with it any longer.' His voice was much louder now. 'I'm going to take the fight to them. With my friends by my side I know we'll have a chance, however slim that might be. It won't be easy, and we'll probably fail.' Cyrus started to sweat at this point, his courage wavering as his speech began to lose authority. He put his hand onto the nearby freezer to cool himself down. 'But we have to try. If we don't, we'll be living in fear for the rest of our lives. If you're able, you're welcome to come with us, but I can't guarantee you'll come back alive.'

Cyrus never was a good salesman.

There were another few moments of muttering among the crowd as he paused. Nobody was sure what was going to happen next, least of all Cyrus. Should he end it there? Should he wait for volunteers to come with them? The people seemed to be wondering the same thing as him. The atmosphere was awkward and a flickering light on the ceiling broke the tension for a brief moment.

Somewhere in the midst of the crowd, a sharp noise sounded. Zion stood there proudly, slowly clapping his hands together. Seconds went by, clap after clap, as he stood alone, the solitary sound of the palms of his hands coming together giving him the appearance of a sarcastic heckler. Eventually, another clap rang out to his right, a little out of sync with Zion's. And then another, and another. The tempo started quickening as more and more hands started clapping together. Jane and April let out a loud whoop as the colony fell into rapturous applause. Zion whistled and put a big thumbs up to Cyrus, who had gone completely red. Gabriel slapped him on the back with a big grin on his face. It took a little coaxing, but the colony were showing their gratitude to Cyrus and his friends for their courage thus far, and for keeping them safe up until now. Taking on The Jackal, the bandits of the city and the mechs would likely be an extremely dangerous task, and one that would likely end in their demise. But it was selfless, heroic even. Yes, Cyrus had an agenda outside of saving the colony; his own family, but nobody would question the altruism of this decision.

The applause died down and one by one everyone showed their appreciation to Cyrus and Gabriel with a shake of the hand, pat on the shoulder or a hug. It was then that Cyrus knew there was no turning back.

CHAPTER TWENTY

Cyrus decided that the sooner they left on their journey, the better. He couldn't hang around wasting time when he knew he wanted nothing more than to find his family. He thought about the last few months, since his mother and sister went missing. Why hadn't he gone after them sooner? Was he scared? Had he lost hope too soon? All he knew was that he didn't want to waste a single second more, and his anxious pacing was making this fact obvious to the rest of the group. His friends were still packing their bags and saying their farewells to the rest of the colony, and Cyrus was getting jittery waiting for them. Numerous people had asked him to stay just one more night, to regain his strength, but he wasn't interested. His friends could have done with an extra night's rest before they set off, but Cyrus had his heart set on making headway in the quiet of night. When his heart was set on something, it seemed like nothing, or no one else mattered. Through his compulsive nature, Cyrus had often thoughtlessly ignored the feelings and opinions of those around him. In this situation they had decided to let it go; this was too big a deal to start a petty argument about what time they left. Still, they would have liked to have spent a few last precious hours with their loved ones before setting off on a quest they may not come back from.

Aiden popped his head around the door to the office at the back of the supermarket. Caitlin's heart sank as she saw the backpack over his shoulder. The sorrow in his eyes said more than any number of words could, and quickly brought her to tears.

'No, no, no, you're not going!' she cried. 'You can't go, we need you here.' She paused to correct herself. '*I* need you here.'

Aiden stood in the doorway, struggling to find the right words to say. He opened his mouth but nothing came out. No words could have made things better. He inhaled deeply through his nose, looking to the ceiling as a tear formed in the corner of his eye. His chin began to tremble as he struggled to remain strong in her broken presence.

'You just can't,' Caitlin continued, with a look of desperation on her face. 'I won't let you.'

'I have to,' he replied. 'You know that.'

Cameron entered the room behind him, a puzzled look drawn on his face.

'Where are you going?' he asked. 'Are you going on an adventure? Like Cyrus?' Aiden wiped away the tear that had now run down his face and forced a smile for the boy.

'Yes, buddy. I'm going on an adventure.'

'Can I come?'

Caitlin covered her mouth with her shaking hand and looked away, stifling her crying.

'No, you have to stay here and look after your mom. OK, big guy?'

Cameron frowned in disappointment. 'OK, I guess.'

Aiden turned his attention back at Caitlin, who could no longer face looking at him. He asked Cameron to fetch him a specific can of soup, which bought him enough time to say a proper goodbye. He walked slowly up behind her and put his arms around her waist. She immediately turned and flung her arms around his neck, letting out a yelp of despair as she sobbed into his chest.

'Don't leave me,' she whispered. 'Promise me you'll come back.'

Aiden squeezed her a little tighter. 'I promise, I'll be back.' After a long embrace, he kissed her. The warm feeling of her soft lips set his heart alight, making his decision to leave all the more difficult. Caitlin pressed her lips firmly against his, and the electricity that sparked between the pair was almost visible in the air around them. The kiss was over all too soon and Aiden withdrew hesitantly, before setting off for the door. Cameron met him there with the soup and a smile on his face, which Aiden reciprocated with a tussle of his hair.

'Where's he going?' Cameron asked after he left.

'To be a hero,' his mother replied.

**

Cyrus and his group were almost ready to go, checking their maps and marking the route they'd take towards the southern part of the city to look for signs of The Jackal. They had no clue where the man and his bandit followers would be, but the map revealing the bandits' plan to seize the mall had been found south of the mall itself, suggesting they had been further south before then. Cyrus had a hunch that the bandits had met with The Jackal earlier that day, but Caitlin confirmed that most of that group had never met The Jackal. Only

Connor and a handful of close followers of Michelle had visited him to strike the deal in which weapons would be exchanged for slaves. Nevertheless, south of the city was where they were headed. It was as good a start as any.

Isaac suddenly came running over to the group, startling Rowley who had his back turned to him.

'Jeez, Isaac. What is it?' He reeled in surprise at the haste with which he'd come bounding over to them. Isaac had all but charged into him in his eagerness to speak with them.

'Don't go to The Jackal,' Isaac commanded. 'It's suicide.'

Gabriel raised an eyebrow at this new dishevelled friend of theirs. He believed Isaac to be unhinged, and this made him extremely wary of him. He always felt on guard in his presence.

'Isaac, we know it's going to be dangerous, but we need to confront him.'

Isaac shook his head franticly. There was clearly something he wasn't telling them, and he was desperate to get it out. 'No, no, no, you don't understand.' He put his hands on his face, peering out between the gaps in his fingers at the perplexed Rowley. He then put his hands on Rowley's face. Gabriel's eyebrow seemed to rise further up to his forehead, his eyes wide as he watched intently for the unpredictable Isaac's next move. Isaac stared deep into Rowley's now terrified eyes.

'I had a vision,' he whispered.

Gabriel couldn't contain himself any longer, and let out a hearty laugh. If he wasn't convinced before, he certainly was now. Isaac was a complete loony.

Isaac pulled his hands from Rowley's face and snapped his head round to Gabriel, leering at him as his eyes narrowed. 'I had a vision,' he repeated. 'I have seen The Jackal. A terrible man, with eyes like fire and scars on his face. A wicked man, indeed.'

Everyone was captivated now, including Gabriel, whose laughter was quickly cut short.

'Yes, the vision came to me in a dream. I did not realise what it meant, until you spoke of him and your quest to find him.' He turned to Cyrus and pointed to his crystal. 'You must not act on impulse, your emotions are too strong. If you want to stop him, you must first seek help.'

Cyrus clenched his fist around the crystal that dangled around his neck, as if to deter Isaac's attention away from it. He felt something strange here. It was the way Isaac looked at it.

'What do you mean?' Mia questioned. 'What kind of help are you talking about?'

'What a load of nonsense,' Gabriel interjected. 'Are we really supposed to believe this? He didn't even know who The Jackal was before we mentioned it. And now he's telling us he's seen him?'

'Yes,' Isaac nodded. 'The vision, it came to me in a dream, the night before you arrived in my home.'

'Bullshit,' Gabriel dismissed, waving his hand as he turned away.

'His name is Tobias.' Gabriel cocked his head back in Isaac's direction, failing to hide his interest that had piqued once again. 'I had not realised it until now. In my sorrow for my fallen comrades, my mind was lost in the sea of voices that shouted. I now recognise the name, *The Jackal*. It is not a name I have heard in a long time.'

Gabriel, like the others, was now firmly engrossed by what Issac had to say. His petty remarks had ceased as he listened intently.

'He was a soldier, like me. I met him in the academy as a young officer of the law. He was not the strongest man, but his mind was sharp. He was a tactical genius. His quick decision making allowed him to excel in the police force. Like all of us cops, we were some of the first to be enlisted into the war. He commanded his own unit and fought back against the rebellion. In the academy, a squad mate of mine once called him The Jackal, because of his cunning and opportunistic nature. A jackal feasts on smaller prey. He didn't take kindly to it then, and nobody mentioned it again.'

'So why would he call himself that now?' Cyrus asked. 'If he didn't like the name.'

'I don't know why,' he replied. 'But the war changed people, Cyrus. Tobias had reached the glass ceiling. The army had made it clear that he was not going to be given a higher role, they told him he was too hot tempered and undisciplined for that responsibility. He was hungry for power, and angry at his superiors. He betrayed his orders and killed his own men, joining MIRE. I wouldn't have thought he bought into their ethos either.'

'Vengeance?' asked Rowley. Isaac nodded.

As Isaac finished his last sentence, he took a sweeping look across the group of faces that were intently focused on him. 'I can't believe I didn't see it until now,' he admitted. 'But you should not confront him without first getting help.'

'What kind of help are you talking about?' Mia asked for a second time.

'You will need an army to face The Jackal,' Isaac declared.

Gabriel grunted impatiently. 'How the hell are we supposed to raise an army?'

'I don't know, but you must try if you are to defeat him.'

'Why do we need an army?' Cyrus quizzed. 'You have no idea how many people he has on his side.'

Isaac's expression drooped into a solemn look. 'This man is dangerous, Cyrus. You must believe me when I say he's not to be underestimated. The slavers, as you call them. In my dream I saw many of them, men and women. I saw them working people like prisoners of war, The Jackal sitting on his throne, laughing at them as they farm the land in the blistering heat. I saw fire and destruction, terror and despair. There is evil in him, Cyrus, stronger than I have ever seen.' Isaac's eyes were wide, his pupils dilated as he recalled the terror of the nightmare.

Cyrus stared intently into Isaac's piercing blue eyes. They were as light as the purest drops of the ocean. And the man's next words chilled him to the bone.

'I saw you, Cyrus. You too were in the vision.'

Cyrus's heart beat faster and faster, hammering away as though it was threatening to burst right out of his chest. He felt that same feeling he had when the two had first met the previous day. It was as if Isaac was staring right into his soul.

'You recognised me, the first time you met me,' Cyrus remembered.

'Yes,' Isaac replied. 'It had not become clear to me until now, but you are the key to everything, Cyrus.' He looked back at the jewel hanging from Cyrus's neck, which was glowing a bright amber colour. Cyrus broke his focus and looked down at the crystal, and the jewel faded back to its neutral pale state. Mia covered her mouth in shock, completely speechless by what had just happened.

Isaac reached for Cyrus's hand. As his fingertips grew near his own, Cyrus could feel a static shock between them. Isaac grabbed the hand suddenly and Cyrus felt a surge of energy penetrate his whole body. His vision flashed a brilliant bright white and for a moment he was completely stunned. At last it cleared and he saw the same vision, of the slavers and the poor souls who tirelessly farmed the land in the scorching heat, exactly as Isaac had described it. It felt so real Cyrus could almost feel the droplets of sweat run from his hair down his cheek. This time he could see his mother and sister among the slaves, overshadowed by the terrifying, demonic appearance of The Jackal sitting on his throne, laughing at them. He tried to call out to them but no sound came. Instead the scene changed to the streets of Novasburgh, a dust storm consuming his vision. Suddenly a panther broke through the cloud of dust, lunging at him with gaping jaws. He jolted in fright and was snapped out of the trance, the vision disappearing as quickly as it had arrived. The next thing he saw was Isaac looking eagerly at him.

'You saw it!' he exclaimed.

'Yes,' Cyrus replied, completely bemused.

What magic was this?

'How?' Cyrus found himself asking, not sure he would believe whatever answer would follow. None of this made sense. And yet, it had been so real.

'I cannot explain it,' Isaac replied solemnly. 'It is a gift and a curse.'

Silence fell upon the group as the seconds ticked by. Zion had remained quiet through the conversation. He looked deep in thought, taking in everything Isaac had said. He thought about Isaac's words. *You will need an army to face The Jackal.* The words bounced around his brain, repeating over and over again, as though they were haunting him. He squinted his eyes as he thought deep and hard at the conundrum. How would they be able to raise an army in such a torn city as this? The city was deserted, there would be nobody to help them. Suddenly a spark of an idea flooded his mind, like a lone beam of energy shooting up through his cerebral cortex, jolting him into life.

'The facility,' he breathed. 'That's it!'

All eyes fixed onto him, breaking everyone's concentration.

'The mech facility. They built weapons there. Vehicles too. I was there, I saw them with my own eyes. There must be some left over from when that place was sealed off. We could use them to fight The Jackal.' Zion's newly born enthusiasm bubbled up as he spoke, but was quickly quashed by Gabriel's dose of cruel realism.

'That place was destroyed by MIRE. Everyone knows that.'

'No, that's just a myth. A rumour spread by the rebels to fake another victory.'

'You can't confirm that,' Gabriel retorted.

'Confirmed or not, it's the best we have for now,' said Cyrus. They group fell silent for a few minutes, pondering their next steps. Gabriel began to pace up and down restlessly, his hand scratching his beard as he did so. The gentle hum of the refrigerators and the noise of the air being wafted around the room by the ceiling fans were all that was heard. It was a noise that he hadn't noticed before; it had always been blocked out in the background, but now it seemed to pound into Cyrus's head as he watched one of the fans spin around and around. The Jackal was one problem, but the mechs still roamed free, destroying everything in their path. Something had to be done about them.

He thought of Zion. Surely he must have known more about these mechs, about how the handlers controlled them.

He worked in the very place they were created. Had his shame placed a cover over his memory of it? He hoped he could get something out of him. This could be the key to unlocking the secret to ridding the city of them. He spoke with Jane and asked her to help him speak with Zion about it. He knew Jane would be the best person to ask, she had a way with words that got people to open up. Together they took Zion to one side and asked him about his time at the factory.

To Cyrus's surprise, he found Zion had softened up about his past and was much more willing to open up to them. He shared more stories of his time there as a guard, and how he longed to get involved with the research side to get to know more of the systems and technology used to power the mechs. He didn't have the answer Cyrus was looking for, but he knew that the technology they used was top secret, and only a few people knew about it. It was something that wasn't used in anything else, and was talked about with a tone of almost mystic proportions. Some people had even called it supernatural.

'I think we need to go to this facility,' said Cyrus. 'There's just something about it, it feels—'

'Yes, I feel the same way,' Zion agreed, without waiting for the end of that sentence.

'But how are we going to get in?' asked Jane. 'You said it was closed down, sealed off so nobody would be able to enter.'

Zion pondered the question a while, searching the deep recesses of his memory for a clue. Finally, another spark lit up his brain. He snapped his fingers as the brainwave hit him.

'The Oracle,' he said, with a big smile on his face.

Cyrus and Jane looked at Zion, and then at each other, completely perplexed. Had Zion gone mad?

'The what?' Cyrus asked.

'The Oracle,' Zion repeated plainly, as if they should both know what that meant.

'What is The Oracle?' Jane asked.

'You mean, *who* is The Oracle?' Zion corrected.

'Yes?'

'The Oracle was a friend of mine in the program I was studying in. He got accepted to work with the scientists on a project in the facility; the one I should have been on before I got kicked out.' For a second his hands clenched into a fist, before the smile returned to his face and his hands relaxed. 'We're talking about a real genius here. Quite a character too. I haven't seen him in years.'

'Do you know where he is now?' Cyrus asked. He felt a resurgence of hope in his gut.

'Last I knew he was working at the facility. But after it closed, I don't know.'

Cyrus frowned. Another dead end.

'He was always a mummy's boy,' Zion continued with a chuckle. 'My best guess, he went back home to Woodside. God knows if he's even alive though,' he backtracked, noticing Cyrus perk up again. 'There aren't many places with sustainable food supplies now. But if there's anyone who could survive, it's Kevin.'

'Kevin?'

'Kevin, The Oracle. It was his nickname in school, cause of, you know, his brains. Very smart guy.'

The hope that had rekindled in Cyrus's gut was now ablaze in his heart. His fingers tingled and all the weariness of the last few days seemed to fall right away, purged from his body like a reptile shedding skin.

After discussing with the group, and much convincing of Gabriel to trust Cyrus's gut instinct, they agreed to head for Woodside to look for Zion's friend. Cyrus prayed that he was alive, and that he could help them. Under the cover of darkness, with just a few day's supplies in their backpacks, the ten companions headed out. Cyrus had a spring in his step, and marched on ahead, his bag and rifle feeling almost weightless in his renewed optimism.

CHAPTER TWENTY-ONE

The streets of the city were deserted, which was nothing out of the ordinary. In fact, had they not been deserted it would have posed real concern for the companions. The sound of silence was expected, a far cry from the hustle and bustle of the city just a few years ago, before it all went to hell. A light breeze kicked up an old tin can, which jangled along the road in front of them as they walked. The sound grated on Cyrus, its metallic chiming as it skipped off the concrete amplified through the otherwise silent scene. The enthusiasm he'd set off with was already starting to waver, such was his ever changing mood recently.

He marched a little quicker to catch up with the can as it tumbled down the street, before trapping it with his foot to halt its progress. The can stopped with a sharp scrape under the weight of Cyrus's foot pressing down against it. He studied the worn label on its side carefully, taking note of the brand and variety of soup that was once contained within it. He licked his lips as he remembered how hungry he was.

'Oh man, I love pea and ham.' Rowley's voice came from behind him.

'Yeah, the supermarket only had tomato, vegetable and minestrone.'

'So much minestrone,' Rowley emphasised.

Cyrus lifted his foot back off the tin can and kicked it underneath a burnt out car nearby. It skimmed off the surface, bobbling along until finally hitting the rear bumper with a loud ping and stopping dead.

'Nice daisy cutter you've got there,' Zion joked. 'You need to lean back before you hit it, get a nice lift on it, right between the goalposts.' He demonstrated the action and then watched his imaginary ball sail through the sky.

Cyrus rolled his eyes and carried on down the street.

'It's alright,' Zion called after him. 'Even the best kickers have an off day. And what's wrong with minestrone?' He continued to tease Cyrus. Mia gave him a quick signal to tone it down. She knew that over the last few days Cyrus's fuse had been shortened considerably. She had been relieved to see a glimpse of the old Cyrus, the one she fell in love with, as he led the group out of the supermarket with vigour. However it was clear that his moods were coming and going with every passing hour, to the extent that any sort of ribbing from his friends could set him off again. It wasn't like him at all, but as the days went by she couldn't shake the feeling that something inside him had changed for good.

The group moved swiftly through the city, retracing their steps from their journey from the mall. Their route to Woodside would involve passing the shopping mall, and as they grew closer to it they became wary. They could see the smoke still billowing out of the top of the building, which was now concave in shape and had been completely torn to shreds on one side. Rubble lined the streets around it, and as they turned a corner to see the building in full view it suddenly dawned on them the magnitude of power the mechs could unleash. One thing was for sure, they wouldn't have survived the attack had they still been there.

To their relief there was no sign of mech activity. They would surely have heard their pounding footsteps, or even the screeching of one of the beasts on their way. The place was eerily quiet, almost too quiet for Cyrus's liking.

Gabriel split the group in two, with five walking on one side of the street and the other five, including himself, on the other. He ordered each group to walk single file as they passed the mall, hugging the wall of buildings to each side of the road as they did so. Cyrus's group on the other side of the road from Gabriel would walk closest to the mall. They took the path on the east side of the building, where the least damage had been inflicted. Slowly, with their weapons at the ready, they moved.

'Still no sign of anything,' Rowley whispered, staying close behind Cyrus.

Still they moved forward, each step placed slowly and carefully in front of the last. Mia trailed at the rear of the group, her poised proton pistol facing down to the ground as she moved. A shooting pain ran up her arm from her injured wrist, causing her to flinch. She squinted her eyes through the pain, trying hard not to yelp at the sudden sensation. She relaxed her grip on the pistol and took her injured hand away from it. From across the road April had noticed Mia's discomfort and caught her eye.

'You OK?' she mouthed. Mia nodded in reassurance, although her pained expression told otherwise. April decided to take action on this, nudging the man in front of her.

'Doug, we need to stop. Mia's struggling,' she whispered. Doug swivelled round to look in Mia's direction, quickly assessing the severity of her pain.

'Just a little further,' he whispered back. 'Just until we get to—'

A loud screeching sound pierced the air, cutting Doug off. The shrill sound reverberated through their bodies, stopping them in their tracks. The familiarity of it made their blood run cold and their stomachs jump into their mouths. They knew exactly what that meant.

Stomping footsteps could be heard heading in their direction from further up the street, just around the corner where the edge of the shopping mall met the start of the next block. The stomping grew louder and louder, and the footsteps were out of sync. Cyrus deduced that there were at least two of them coming their way.

Everybody looked to Gabriel; they needed a plan of action, fast. He answered them swiftly, pointing to a nearby alcove inside one of the buildings on his side of the street, opposite the mall. His team rushed over to the alcove and crouched down, disappearing into the darkness. Cyrus knew his group wouldn't make it there in time. The street was too wide and they would be spotted in the open before they made it to the other side. Instead he searched desperately for an alternative.

The pounding of footsteps were louder now, and another screech ran through Cyrus's ears, causing him to wince at the piercing sound. They would be on him in seconds. He needed to find a way out, fast.

'In here, Cyrus.' He wheeled around to find Rowley and the others taking cover in the pile of rubble that protruded from the outer wall of the mall. There was a small gap in the building, an empty space in which one, maybe two people could climb into. At best, two of the smaller members of the group would have been able to climb over the rubble, into the space and cover themselves with bits of brick and sheet metal; anything they could find. But even in the dark, the mechs would surely spot them; there were too many of them to hide.

Cyrus caught a glimpse of one of the mechs as it rounded the corner, just as he decided to dive behind one of the abandoned cars dispersed along the sides of the street. He didn't get a long look at it, but he was able to determine what it was. It was a golem, and luckily for him it hadn't been facing his way.

He crawled on his front underneath the vehicle. Luckily the car was a 4x4 and the space between the bottom of the car and the ground was slightly greater than average. This gave Cyrus more room as he wriggled, backpack still on, underneath the chassis. He bumped his head on the spare tyre protruding from the bottom of the vehicle and tried with all his might not to yelp out in pain. He looked to his left to see the terrified face of Rowley as he watched his friend struggle underneath the car. The look on his face said it all. This was a terrible decision.

Rowley sunk deeper, as far as he could go into the space behind him, squashing the others as he tried desperately to move his whole round body out of the moonlight and into the shade of the small alcove that had been fashioned from the partially destroyed wall. Cyrus saw his face disappear out of sight, and then he felt truly alone.

He had to remain as still as he could. A single sound could attract the mechs, and then they would surely find him. If anyone from the group, on either side of the street let out so much as a sneeze, the mechs would be on them in seconds. The darkness wouldn't hide them from the mechs for long. If they were alerted in any way, the mechs would engage their targeting systems and their night vision sensors would pick up Cyrus and his friends in an instant. He had to hope that they were just scouting the area and no suspicion had been aroused.

The mech trudged forward with slow thuds, and seconds later three panthers appeared. They raced around the corner, overtaking the golem and spreading out across the street ahead of it. They were like a pack of hungry lions, working together to scout out their next meal.

Cyrus's heart raced. Even if he stayed completely silent, they could still discover him should they get close enough. One of the panthers bolted from its position and ran past the car to search an upturned industrial sized bin. When it reached its target, it pushed the bin with its strong metallic frame and quickly discovered that it was empty. It screeched, drawing the attention of the other panthers. The metallic shrill of the panther was harrowing, especially given Cyrus had lost sight of them from his restricted view underneath the car. He half expected their giant terrifying faces to suddenly appear in front of him, like a jump scare from a horror film.

Cyrus was in shock at what he was witnessing. He had never seen the mechs act like this. It was almost as if it was screaming in frustration at the sight of the empty bin. It gave the mechs living qualities, like the very animals they resembled. The thought chilled him to the bone.

The golem trudged on down the street, getting nearer and nearer to the 4x4. The thud of each step as its robotic legs stomped along the road reverberated through the concrete, rippling through Cyrus's chest, which was pressed firmly against the ground. As the mech reached the vehicle it stopped suddenly, as though something had caught its attention. Its human-like frame swivelled on its axis, surveying its surroundings. The robotic arm fashioned into a heavy duty rifle remained poised, ready to fire at a moment's notice. Cyrus was a sitting duck where he lay.

The golem made a strange metallic noise, different to the screeching of the panthers. Its register was much lower. It walked about on the spot as Cyrus held his breath for its next move. If it grew suspicious and engaged its targeting system they were doomed.

Suddenly, the car above Cyrus's head shook with a loud bang. Cyrus jumped in surprise, cocking his head round to see what had happened. He saw the legs of a panther inches away from his legs, towards the back of the car. It had slammed its body against the vehicle clumsily as it raced over to the golem. It was as if the noise the golem made had alerted the panther, as though they were communicating. The panther stalked the perimeter of the car, its robotic paws slowly crumbling the smaller bits of rubble around it. Cyrus held his breath, praying it didn't move the car. It was certainly strong enough to upturn it if it wanted to, and it would take a mere instant for their prey to be revealed.

The panther reached the side of the car and was now in line with Cyrus's torso. It stopped and nudged the car with its head, peering into the window of the driver's seat. The windows had already been smashed in, but the remaining shards of glass in the frame shattered as the mech's head explored the interior. The moment seemed to last forever, and Cyrus felt a cold sweat run down the side of his face.

A stone kicked up off the floor a little way down the street, in the direction the group had come from. The panther immediately took his head out of the car and looked back in the direction of the noise. The golem too turned its attention down the road to the stone as it skipped along the surface. One of the panthers let out another deafening screech and all four mechs converged on its position, away from the car.

Cyrus breathed a sigh of relief and felt his body relax. He wasn't out of the woods yet, but he could afford this short moment of respite. The group remained silent for the next few minutes, as the mechs slowly made their way down the street, their footsteps getting quieter and quieter. Cyrus looked back, still from the underside of the car, and couldn't see any sign of them. Finally, he turned back to where Rowley and the others had been minutes before, and caught a glimpse of his friend's head sheepishly poking out from the darkness.

'I think they're gone,' a hushed voice came from his other side, taking him by surprise. It was Gabriel, who had come out of his hiding place. He knelt down beside the car and offered a strong hand to pull Cyrus out from under it. Cyrus's body scraped along the ground as Gabriel pulled, and soon he was back on his feet.

'Wow.' Zion was the first to greet him as the two groups reunited. 'You've got balls.'

'Err, thanks?' Cyrus replied.

'No time to stop and chat,' Gabriel interjected, keeping them focused. 'That was a lucky escape. Had Doug not distracted them, we could all be toast.' Doug smiled bashfully at what was as good a compliment as Gabriel usually gave.

'That was you?' Cyrus was surprised to hear this.

'Yes,' he replied, almost embarrassed. 'It was a bit risky, I know. It could have gone horribly wrong.'

'No, not at all,' Cyrus reassured. 'You saved my skin.' The two smiled at each other. Cyrus was always surprised by Doug. He was extremely quiet and kept himself to himself most of the time. But he came through when it counted, and was always the first to lend a helping hand. Shamefully, it was only really moments like that when Cyrus remembered he was around.

The group moved off after Gabriel, with the exception of Mia who was purposefully lagging behind. She walked over to Cyrus and wiped a blotch of dirt away from under his eye, before looking square into his pupils. Cyrus was instantly transfixed by her beautiful green eyes. Somehow, even in the darkness they seemed to glow big and bright. He suddenly noticed that his crystal was glowing a soft blue colour from beneath his shirt, illuminating Mia's beautiful features. Without warning, she grabbed his t-shirt with both hands, her face close to his.

'Don't ever do that to me again,' she said quietly, with a stern tone. And then her head rushed towards his as she kissed him softly on the lips. Her grip on his t-shirt intensified as she did so. The kiss lasted just a second, but that brief moment was savoured in Cyrus's mind. His heart began to pound once more, this time for a different reason. As she withdrew from him, she quickly reshuffled the bag on her back and headed off after the others, leaving Cyrus standing there, completely stunned.

CHAPTER TWENTY-TWO

The sun started to rise beyond the horizon, and light hit the streets with a pale orange tint. It had been several hours since their most recent close encounter with the mechs, but it was still fresh in their minds. The group moved cautiously from one block to the next, their weary bodies aching. They were reaching the outskirts of the western part of the city, and as they arrived at the slipway of the major road network leading out into the countryside, Gabriel signalled for them to stop.

Two paths were laid out in front of them; one heading left, and one to the right. The two paths ran up on slipways to the freeway which loomed overhead. The giant signpost in the middle of the two, protruding from the bridge the freeway ran across, pointed arrows in each direction, with directions to various destinations. Cyrus read the worn sign out loud.

'Woodside, to the right. Twelve miles.'

There was an audible groan from a few members of the group.

'That's a good four hour walk from here,' Jennifer estimated. 'We're exhausted.' She retrieved a bottle of water from her backpack and took a long thirsty gulp from it.

Gabriel took a good look at the sign, and then at the weary travellers behind him. It didn't take him long to make a decision. He pointed to a dilapidated bar just a few yards away.

'Who needs a drink?' he asked. The rest of the group stared at him in surprise. It was almost as though Gabriel had just made a joke.

'I hope they have scotch,' Aiden said, taking the opportunity instantly by heading over to the abandoned bar.

The inside was in as good condition as they could expect. The bar itself was still intact, however the same couldn't be said for the furnishings. What was refreshing was to see the building's exterior walls in one piece. Even the door worked.

As the group entered, Jane looked up at the sign embossed on the top of the door. It read *O'Callaghan's*.

'Huh, that's funny.'

'What's that?' Doug entered the bar after her.

'I've been here before. This used to be a nice Irish pub. Really friendly atmosphere.' She glanced around at what was left of the décor, trying to piece together her memory of the place. 'I met someone here once, on a first date.'

'Oh yeah? How did it go?'

Jane laughed heartily as she remembered. 'Awfully, actually.'

Doug smirked as he could feel an interesting story coming. He swivelled his cap around so that the peak faced behind. 'So I'm guessing he wasn't Mr Right?'

Jane scowled at the remark. '*She* was fine. But she wasn't what I was looking for.' Doug swallowed hard, his cheeks flushing in embarrassment of his presumption.

'Ah, I see. Sorry,' he offered feebly. Jane could see he was squirming, and threw him a bone.

'Don't be silly, it's alright.'

Doug gestured for her to continue with her story. 'So what happened? Why wasn't she what you wanted?'

'Well, ya know, on paper it was a perfect match. Our profiles got matched up and we both liked what we saw. And I'm not just talking about looks here, although she was real cute.' She smiled at the memory as she glanced around the room. The tired décor, or what was left of it, the position of the bar, the tripod bar stools. The whole evening came flooding back to her.

'Thing was, we were both of a similar age, both liked the same things; horse riding, travelling, adventure novels, long walks on the beach, all that. But when we met in person it became clear that we were just very different people, with the same resume. Ya'll know what I mean.'

Doug nodded in understanding, as did Jennifer who was now listening in. She was right, they knew exactly what she meant.

'I think she was a bit of a party gal, whereas I was more for settling down. She kept checking out the bartender too, which put me off.'

Jennifer snorted. 'I've been there.'

The clanging sound of bottles coming together caught their attention, and soon everyone was crowded around the bar to see what was going on. Aiden was perusing the selection of spirits on the shelf just above him. It was a strange sight, Aiden behind the bar and the rest of the group crowded around, propping it up. They were inadvertently recreating what a typical night at this place would have looked like. It was a strange scene, given the situation.

Aiden sifted through the bottles, most of which were empty or at least mostly empty. He selected two empty bottles and began throwing them into the air, twirling them around as he juggled with them. It was like an art form; Aiden's hands spinning the bottles into the air like juggling clubs, catching each one as it fell and throwing it back out into the air at a different angle. As one was in the air he spun the other behind his back and caught it. It mesmerised the rest of the group. At last he stopped the two bottles dead and slammed them cleanly onto the bar with a flourish.

'I used to be a bartender,' he said candidly. 'We used to do a lot of flair.'

The group watched him in awe, making him feel slightly uncomfortable.

'I guess we all have an interesting past,' Zion broke the silence at last. 'Pour me a drink, good sir.' He offered a glass to Aiden, who poured a shot of the first liquid he could find. Zion drank it with a bitter expression, his eyes closing and his face screwing up involuntarily. He gulped it down and let out a pained gasp as the liquid burned his throat.

'Not a fan of tequila, my good man?' Aiden joked. Zion pulled a dissatisfied face in response.

'You know,' he said, his voice strained after the burn of the alcohol. 'I've been thinking about this Jackal guy. It's quite a fitting name.'

'What, cause of the animal?' Cyrus replied.

'No, not just that. In ancient Egypt, Anubis was the jackal-headed God of the underworld. The way you described him in that vision you had, sounds just like our man.'

Cyrus thought about it. 'Actually, you're right, it's uncanny.'

'Although it would be weird if this guy had an actual jackal's head,' Zion quipped.

Meanwhile, Jane had discovered a pack of cigarettes behind the bar. There was one left.

'Damn, I could sure use a smoke right about now,' she said.

'You smoke?' April asked. 'Didn't anyone tell you that's not cool?'

'Well, used to,' Jane replied, a guilty smile appearing on her face. 'But what's the difference now?'

Doug retrieved a box of matches from his backpack.

'I was saving these for an emergency, but what the hell.' He beamed a cheeky smile at Jane.

'My hero,' she smiled back. Doug cocked his head, not quite sure how to take someone complimenting him for feeding a habit he'd never liked. Jane put the cigarette in her mouth in anticipation. He opened the slider and drew a matchstick, striking it against the side of the box to a satisfying scratch and fizz sound as the flame was lit. He brought the flame to the end of the cigarette and waited for the end to start burning. She took a deep inhale and he watched as she closed her eyes and recaptured a moment long forgotten.

**

Half an hour later, Gabriel called for everyone to get up and move out. They went through the same familiar routine of reluctantly throwing their backpacks over their shoulders, picking up their weapons and trudging slowly outside, taking care to focus on any signs of activity in the street.

The sun was shining brightly now, and Cyrus checked his watch. The hands were at half seven. He did a quick calculation in his head.

'All being well, I reckon we'll reach Woodside by lunch.'

He reached inside his bag and retrieved a chocolate bar. He had packed himself a good helping of snacks from the supermarket, and boy did he need them. Rowley shared in his enjoyment of the chocolate with his own bar, which was melting rapidly in his hands as he ate.

'These bars will turn to mush in our bags,' he said. Cyrus sighed in resignation, before licking his chocolate covered fingers and wiping the remnants of sticky food onto the sides of his beige cargo pants. They left a faint dark brown smear on one of the pockets.

'You certain about this?' he turned to Zion as he picked bits of honeycomb out of his teeth. Zion looked back at him with a perplexed expression.

'Woodside, I mean,' Cyrus clarified. 'You sure that's where your friend will be?'

'No,' Zion replied. 'I just thought it would be nice for everyone to go on a long walk together. You know, team building.'

Cyrus rolled his eyes. 'Great, thanks buddy.'

'You know I don't know for sure,' Zion switched to a more serious tone. 'We're taking a chance here, Cyrus, but I think it's the best option we have.'

The companions walked over to the slipway that took them onto the freeway. It would be the quickest route to Woodside, but they would be much more exposed should they come across any mechs. As he reached the top of the slipway, Cyrus took note of the path ahead of them. The road was intact, but was littered with abandoned cars and debris from various firefights that had played out during the war. He even spotted a helicopter that had crashed down on the other side of the road, making a large dent in the section of concrete immediately surrounding it. The chopper sat on its side, the rotor blades resting against the ground, where dark lines on the road indicated the point at which the blades had scraped the surface as it landed. Cyrus could only imagine the chaos that had ensued in the conflict here. It had all happened so fast, the fighting went from scattered pin-point attacks to all our warfare in the blink of an eye.

The journey to Woodside would feel long and arduous from here on in, as the landscape they passed would seem so repetitive. There was something about walking along the freeway, passing road signs at a snail's pace compared to driving that made the journey so much slower.

'What if he's not there?' Rowley asked him quietly.

Cyrus didn't respond and kept walking with his head up, looking in the distance at the road ahead. Rowley frowned, hurt by his friend's shun.

**

Cyrus looked at his watch. The time read ten forty. The road ahead wound on and on, twisting and turning this way and that in long smooth waves, like the concertina effect left behind by a snake as it slithers through sand.

The wind started to pick up and Cyrus feared a dust storm would start soon. Loose bits of newspaper whirled about in a mini twister a couple of feet from the ground and a few particles of dust swarmed at his face, forcing him to shield his eyes and pull the scarf from his bag to wrap around his face and cover his nose and mouth.

A signpost loomed high above the group, just far enough in the distance that they couldn't make out what it said. The group carried on walking until they were close enough to read it. By his estimation, Cyrus thought this should surely signal the turning off point from the freeway and into Woodside. He blinked his eyes repeatedly to clean them of dust, before peering at the sign with his hand cupped over his forehead, blocking out the sun which shone immediately down onto him. Walking a little further, he was able to align the sign directly between himself and the sun, and sure enough it became immediately visible. An arrow pointing to the right was displayed, along with the word *Woodside*.

Jennifer whooped for joy at the sight. Cyrus turned to his friends and smiled beneath his scarf.

Moment of truth.

Zion looked nervous. It was a lot of pressure he was taking on, and if he was wrong about this he wasn't sure he could forgive himself. But he tried to grip hold of the notion that they didn't have any other options at the time. His guess was as good as anyone's. Maybe, just maybe, it would work out the way it was supposed to for once.

The road wound around to the exit, and ten minutes later the group were on a small single track road that led straight into the town of Woodside. It would take another fifteen minutes or so to reach the town itself, which was situated across a river at the edge of a forest. The forest was built up of thousands upon thousands of tall cinnamon coloured trees. The giant redwoods that occupied the land stood taller than some buildings in the city, creating a landscape of greatness forged by nature. The sight of the forest beyond the small town before it left Cyrus speechless. In all his years he had ventured into the forest on just a few occasions, and every time he visited he was left dumbstruck by the majesty of the trees. So tall they were that standing underneath one and craning his neck upwards to see the top would make him feel dizzy. Even from a distance, on the other side of the river, they looked impressive.

The scenery of this unspoiled landscape was in stark contrast to the city itself, and seemed far removed from it. It was as if this small haven had been completely untouched by the war, and the conflict that spilled out from it. Cyrus wondered how this could be, given that as far as he was aware the fighting was widespread, not isolated to the city centre, or even one city for that matter. A war that ravaged a nation seemed to have completely passed Woodside by, and Cyrus couldn't have been happier for it. The sight of the lush forestry sparked old memories of what life was like before the fighting escalated, when civilisation was at a more normal state. Whatever normal was. To be taken back to a better time was a welcome reprieve, if only for a brief time as they passed through to continue their quest.

A wood pigeon cooed from a tree above as the group made their way along the road. Leaves from the trees littered the road, the yellowy-brown colours giving the path an autumnal feel. The leaves crunched beneath their feet as they walked. It was then that Cyrus felt as though something wasn't quite right about this place.

'What month is it again?' Cyrus had lost track of what year it was, let alone the month.

'September.' The reply came from Jennifer. 'Twenty third, in case you were wondering.'

'You remember the date too?' Cyrus was surprised at Jennifer's accuracy.

'Of course,' she replied. 'I never forget when my birthday is.'

Rowley reeled and looked despairingly at her. 'No way! I thought it was tomorrow? Sorry, I would have said something if I remembered right.' He frowned and looked to the ground.

Jennifer smiled and put a comforting hand around the back of his head as she looked deep into his eyes. 'You did remember right. What I meant is I never forget how far from my birthday I am. I've always counted the days until the next one, ever since I was little.'

Rowley breathed a sigh of relief. 'Just as well,' he smiled. 'I didn't get you a present.'

'Well you have the rest of today to find me a good one,' she teased.

'How old will you be tomorrow?' Cyrus asked.

Jennifer's smiled instantly fell into a frown. 'Don't you know it's rude to ask a girl that?' She folded her arms and raised her eyebrow at Cyrus, which caused him to squirm.

'Oh, sorry, I—'

'I'm just messing with you,' she laughed. 'You should have seen your face.' She then looked at Mia to bring her into the conversation. 'If you ever need me to teach you how to do that, let me know. It comes in handy sometimes.' She fired a wink for good measure. Mia giggled and winked back, then caught Cyrus's eye before sheepishly looking away and playing with her hands.

'For the record, I'll be twenty six,' Jennifer finished.

The group walked on in good spirits, and as the winding road straightened out the small town of Woodside was now in clear view. It was a quiet place, and on approach it seemed quieter than it once was. There was no sign of any activity whatsoever, and despite the houses seeming in pretty good condition, it was clear that the place had been deserted for some time. As they passed the first house, a light breeze took the exterior screen door, causing it to swing gently on its hinges and bang shut. It bounced off the beam it had closed onto and repeated the process the next time the wind took it. There was an old wooden rocking chair on the porch next to the door, squeaking as it rocked back and forth in the breeze. The daylight gave the scene a peaceful feel, but Cyrus imagined it would look much more sinister at night. He was secretly glad they had arrived so early in the day.

A hundred yards later, the group stood facing a signpost, which pointed to a few different options of street names they weren't familiar with. There was another sign with a tree symbol on it that pointed upward.

'Well, unless your friend lives in the wild, I don't think we'll be needing that one,' Doug acknowledged.

'Which way, Zion?' Gabriel prompted.

Zion's eyes flicked between each of the street names on the signpost. He didn't have a clue. The long pause before he said anything gave Gabriel the response he was dreading.

'Come on, Zion, there's got to be two hundred houses here, maybe more. Do we have to go and knock on every single one?'

Zion ignored him and concentrated on the street names, hoping something would spark his memory. He tried to remember back to the time he had worked with Kevin. He'd told Zion where he was from, where his mother still lived in their family home. But had he mentioned the street name? Zion thought hard. So hard in fact that he had jolted violently when a hand on his shoulder startled him and broke his concentration.

'Jeez, Zion, take it easy,' Doug took his hand away immediately. 'Is there something we can do to help?'

Zion looked around to see the whole group staring at him, waiting on him. His heart began to beat faster as anxiety started kicking in. He tried to come up with a funny retort to direct the attention elsewhere, but nothing came to mind.

Gabriel tutted and walked off down a pathway at random. 'We're wasting our time here.'

Zion ignored him once again and tried to concentrate. Memories of his time with Kevin came flooding back.

He remembered a conversation they'd had as they left the university program for Thanksgiving. He could see the shared dorm room as if it were there in front of him again. The small room, with a window on the far wall and a single bed squashed up against each side to the left and right. A thin neutral ground of carpet separated the two, however it was layered in odd bits of clothing that had neglected to be washed for days, maybe even weeks. Movie posters lined the wall on Kevin's side of the room, with figurines from numerous video games taking up the space on top of his bedside table. Zion's side was much less cluttered; a single poster of a basketball player leaping in the air mid-shot was the focal point, with a bulletin board to the side containing various torn bits of paper. Written on each piece was the name of a seminar or party Zion had attended that semester. He'd written them all on there at the start of term, serving as a reminder to not miss them.

Kevin was talking about a new software he was working on that allowed him to automate the cleaning in his mother's home.

'If I can find a way to get the vacuum cleaner to sense where it's dirty, I can program the machine to roam around the house looking for dirt. My mom will never pester me about doing chores again.'

'That's great, Kevin. If you figure it out, let me know. If your vacuum cleaner can navigate the stairs too, I'd pay good money for that.' Zion smiled at his friend and picked up his suitcase. 'What time are you leaving?'

'I told my mom I'd be home for dinner. It's just the two of us, so she said there's no rush, but I'd like to get started on my work before we eat. Plus, the buses are hell getting to Woodside. They only go once an hour, and then they stop at every town on the way out of the city.'

'Do you like it in Woodside?' Zion asked.

'Yeah, sure, I guess. It's all I've ever known. I was born and raised in that place.' He quickly changed the subject. 'You going to see Carina for Thanksgiving, Zion?'

Zion beamed and nodded. 'Yes I am.'

'God you're lucky,' said Kevin. 'If she's anything like the pictures you showed me.' He paused for a moment. 'She's like the hottest girl I've ever seen.'

'Easy tiger, that's my girlfriend you're talking about. I'll tell her The Oracle says hi.' He winked and then checked his suitcase, noticing a loose shirt that had been trapped half in, half out as a result of his rushed packing. He opened it back up to stuff the shirt inside. He thought briefly about the creases it would now inevitably have, but resigned himself to the fact that he'd gone a whole semester without ironing his clothes, he could manage another day.

'So you lived in Woodside your whole life? Aren't you sick of it by now?'

'Oh yeah, absolutely,' Kevin replied. 'But it's home, and it's nice, you know? We live right by the forest, which is kinda cool.'

'Sweet, sounds like a good place to take a girl on a date. Let nature do the romantic part for you.' Zion chuckled to himself.

'I don't know about that,' Kevin frowned. 'I've never gotten that far.'

'Well, I'll have to teach you when we get back,' Zion winked.

'Good luck with that. Most girls run away when they see me, let alone my house.'

Zion raised an eyebrow sceptically at his friend. 'Don't put yourself down, buddy. You're a catch. Who could resist a hot date in one of the most beautiful parts of the country with a guy who knows how to automate home cleaning?' The two let out a simultaneous laugh, which seemed to tickle Zion as much as Kevin, despite the fact he'd delivered the joke. A few moments went by before Kevin could speak again.

'That may be, but living in Woodside has its downsides. We're on the street closest to the forest, which is fine by me, but it gives girls that kind of creepy horror movie vibe, you know what I mean?'

Zion suddenly snapped out of his concentration and turned to shout after Gabriel, taking everyone by surprise.

'I know where it is!'

**

Sycamore Avenue was tucked away behind the mess of residential homes that built up Woodside, in a cul-de-sac that led to the start of the forest. A row of houses eight deep stretched down each side of the narrow road. About fifty yards to the side of the street was a parking lot that served as the basecamp for many an expedition into the woods for those who came from other parts of the city to visit.

Standing at the top of the street, Cyrus sensed a nervousness about Zion. There was something about all of this that didn't quite add up. Something Zion was leaving out. It had taken a lot for Zion to come clean about the work he used to do in the factory, and then his friendship with 'The Oracle'. But still something seemed to be bothering him, and Cyrus got the feeling there was more to this story than Zion had let on.

'So which house is it?' Cyrus asked.

Zion look down the street, casting his eye over each house in turn, looking for clues as to which looked most 'Kevin-like'. Nothing obvious sprung to mind, so he resorted to walking towards the nearest house and marching up the driveway.

'I have no idea, but there's only sixteen houses. We'll find the right one eventually.'

Gabriel shook his head in disbelief. This whole situation was really grating on him. They'd walked a long way to get here, and all on a hunch, which was looking more and more like a waste of time.

A wood pigeon cooed after a female, who was ignoring his advances from the roof of the first house, as Zion was striding up the last few yards of the driveway and towards the front door. He reached the porch and climbed the short steps to the front door. Clenching his hand into a fist, he poised himself, ready to knock on its wooden frame. But he hesitated slightly as the fear came rushing back through him. What if he was wrong? What if he wasn't here?

He looked back to his companions, who were watching him intently from the edge of the driveway. He caught April's eye and she smiled at him reassuringly. It was enough to encourage him, and he turned back to the door and began rapping on it with his knuckles.

Seconds went by, and nothing. Zion listened closely for any sound inside the house, for a sign of someone walking through the building to answer the door. More seconds ticked by, still nothing. Zion knocked again, this time louder and with more force. But there was still nothing. Nobody was home.

The group moved on to the next house while Gabriel walked over to the house on the opposite side of the street to save time.

One by one the group made their way through each house, knocking and waiting, knocking and waiting. A few times they even threw in a shout of 'Hello? Anyone home?' for good measure. Cyrus could see Zion beginning to panic as one by one the empty houses were crumbling his plan.

Cyrus was feeling the pressure too. They needed this to work, not just for Zion. If they couldn't find The Oracle, they would be back to square one and have nothing to go on. His hopes of finding his mother and sister would be dashed as quickly as they had been ignited. As the minutes went by, and the number of unchecked houses were diminishing, it looked like a lost cause. Jane, Doug, Aiden and Mia had joined Gabriel on the other side of the street to speed up checking those houses. Finally, there were two remaining, one on each side of the road. Cyrus took a deep breath before leading the way to the house on his side. Meanwhile, Doug was in front of his small group as they made their way over to the last house at the edge of the forest on the other side.

Cyrus took in the sight of the house before heading up the driveway. It was a typical cookie cutter house, an exact replica build-wise to the others on the street. The only difference was the basketball hoop that had been fixed just over the garage door. Cyrus immediately envied the kids that had lived there, and imagined the possibilities of growing up and playing in this neighbourhood. The forest made for a great canvas to paint some great adventures. Cyrus loved to play make-believe as a kid. He'd often pretend he was a spaceman lost on an unchartered planet, with his best friend Rowley there to help him fight off the alien attackers. They'd hold their arms out in a gun-like position and pretend to have all sorts of crazy weapons at their disposal. He shuffled the rifle about on his shoulder, feeling the heavy weight of it bear into his skin. It was a sobering sensation.

A loud scream from the other side of the street drew everyone's attention, and the source of the pained outburst was quickly discovered. Doug had slumped down in a heap on the edge of the driveway, a pile of leaves surrounding him. Aiden and Jane were the quickest to rush to his aid, and on brushing away the leaves revealed the bear trap that has ensnared his leg. Jane recoiled as she saw the trap bearing its way into his shin. Doug's face went white with shock as the pain seared through his leg. He looked up at Jane in desperation.

'AAARRGGHHH, GET IT OFF ME!' he screamed in agony.

Jane exchanged worried looks with Aiden, and they both crouched over Doug, unsure of how to help.

'Shit. Shit, shit, shit,' Aiden cursed under his breath.

'We gotta get this off him,' Jane snapped into action, reaching for Doug's leg.

'Wait!' Aiden was hesitant. 'We don't want to make it worse. What are we supposed to do in this situation?'

By this point the rest of the group had run over to help. Cyrus offered a helping hand. 'I'm sure they covered this in Scouts.' He tried to rack his brains to his Boy Scout days.

'I saw a documentary on this once,' Jennifer piped up. 'They said you need to pry it open with a stick. The group searched around frantically for a sturdy looking stick.

'Ah screw it.' Gabriel stepped forward and grabbed the two steel jaws that were digging into Doug's leg. With a hand on each side, he pulled them apart with all his strength. His muscles flexed and shook as he struggled with the vice grip of the trap, and after a moment the trap slammed open and Doug let out another loud yell as the pain intensified momentarily. Jane and Aiden pulled him away from the trap as Gabriel let go again. The trap closed shut instantly with a sharp metallic scraping sound. The jaws were red with Doug's blood.

'We gotta stop the bleeding,' Jane hurried into her backpack and retrieved the scarf she had used to protect her face from dust storms. She and Aiden wrapped it around Doug's leg and tightened it as best they could.

The door of the house they'd yet to check swung open and banged back against the side of the house. Out stepped a short rotund man with messy black hair and an unkempt beard that ran its way around his rounded face. His stubby fingers gripped the handle of a plasma shotgun, which clicked into action as he emerged from the house. He looked surprised to see the seemingly large group of people standing at the end of his driveway in what was an otherwise deserted town. The powerful looking shotgun in his hands was pointing out in front of him, towards the group, but his finger had not yet closed on the trigger. Cyrus had seen one of these shotguns before. They fired extremely high powered plasma rounds into a wide radius directly in front of it. It was a short range weapon, effectively useless against a moving target more than thirty yards away, but most of the group were stood well within range of its blast. He could see the curious look in the man's eyes as he scoured the group. They finally fell on Zion, and Cyrus could see his eyes grow wide with a glint of recognition. His aim dropped as he and Zion stared at each other for a few moments from either end of the driveway.

'Hello, Kevin,' Zion said at last.

The words were calm, which gave Cyrus a degree of reassurance, but the atmosphere remained tense as they awaited the man's response. The words lingered for what felt like far too long, and as the seconds ticked by Cyrus felt more and more uneasy. His concern that there was more to Zion's story than he was letting on was clearly true. The dynamic between the two made it obvious that there was some unresolved issue between them.

'You're a long way from home,' the reply came at last. Cyrus breathed a sigh of relief. The Oracle, or Kevin, hadn't felt the need to shoot them just yet.

'It's been a long time, friend,' Zion responded. 'I always promised I'd come visit The Oracle's home town one day.'

Kevin's eyes lit up at the sound of that. It was as if the name had sparked something in his memory that he had long forgotten. He let his grip on the shotgun relax completely and pointed it to the floor, holding the barrel in one hand.

'I guess we have some catching up to do.'

CHAPTER TWENTY-THREE

The inside of Kevin's house was drab and dirty. The décor looked old and reminded Cyrus of his Grandma's house. The curtains were torn and ragged and didn't look like they'd been washed since they were first hung up. Photos of Kevin and his mother lined the wall of the hallway. Some had been taken when he was a kid, and some looked more recent. Half the group were sitting in the living room, enjoying the relaxation of a sofa that was still intact. The other half were in the kitchen, where Doug was sitting in agony on a wooden chair while his leg was propped up on another. Jane, Mia, Aiden and April sat with him as Kevin boiled some water to clean the wound with.

As the kettle boiled, the sound of bubbling water suddenly made Cyrus aware that the house had electricity. The supermarket was the only other place that had electricity in all of the places he'd been to in the last few months. It surprised him that it hadn't clicked right away that this was odd.

'You have power?' Cyrus asked curiously.

'I have a generator in the basement,' Kevin replied, candidly. 'It's hooked up to the solar panels on top of the house, and I managed to re-route the panels of the rest of the street here too. Figured no one else was using them.'

'Ah,' Cyrus replied. He didn't know how to follow that up. He instead turned to Doug, and the pained expression still etched on his face almost allowed Cyrus to feel the effect of the wound himself.

'Don't worry, he'll be fine,' Kevin reassured. 'A wound like that'll take a while to heal, but he'll be OK.'

'Thank God,' Doug spluttered through the pain.

'You got any painkillers?' asked Jane.

Kevin thought for a moment, before rifling through the cabinets above his head. Cyrus caught a glimpse at the contents of the cabinets as he watched him rummage around. He didn't get a good look, but the cabinets were near on full.

Kevin retrieved a box of aspirin and chucked it across the room to Jane, who caught it with one hand.

'Thanks,' she said with a smile, before handing a couple of pills to Doug and lifting her bottle of water to his mouth. Doug took the pills and gulped them straight down, barely needing the water chaser. But he was grateful for the water all the same, and gulped that down too.

April turned to Kevin as she watched Doug chug it down a little too quickly and start to cough. 'We're running a bit low on water.'

Kevin nodded and disappeared out of the room. Cyrus could hear footsteps going downstairs, and a minute later Kevin returned with two large bottles of water. There must have been at least four litres there. April set about distributing the water between everyone's smaller bottles, taking care not to spill any.

'Thank you, we really appreciate this,' said Mia.

Zion entered the room just as Kevin poured the freshly boiled water into a large bowl and handed Jane a cloth to wipe the dirt away from Doug's wound.

'Wait for it to cool a bit first; that'll scold you both.' He then left with Zion to talk in the other room. Cyrus followed and sat himself down on the carpet next to four of his companions, who were each occupying a tiny space on what was clearly a three-seater sofa.

Kevin got straight to business. 'What are you doing here, Zion? After all these years.' He scratched his head as he thought for a moment. 'I mean, how long's it been anyway?'

Zion looked around at the faces staring at him, intently awaiting his answer. He felt like the audience was unnecessary, but times were desperate and the need for privacy was below the need for answers in order of priority.

'I dunno, like eight years maybe?'

'Eight years.' Kevin let it sink in. 'Has it really been that long?' He sat back in a single wicker seat and looked to the ceiling as he stroked his beard. 'How the time flies.' He scoured the room, taking in the faces sitting in his mother's living room, and laughed aloud. 'If my mom could see you all now—' he paused a second and his expression turned more serious. 'Well, she'd have one hell of a shock, that's for sure. I never used to have guests in this house. Never really had many friends over the years.'

'I'm here now,' Zion offered. But his words seemed to annoy Kevin.

'Don't do that,' he said, his tone harshening as he sat forward in his seat. 'Don't pretend like nothing's changed. You made your choice, I made mine. We both made mistakes and that's how life goes. But don't think you can just waltz back here after eight years and pretend like nothing's changed.'

'Come on, man,' Zion tried again. 'That wasn't my fault, or yours. They're the ones you should be mad at.' He pointed out the window as he spoke, and Cyrus was unsure who he was referring to. The government, perhaps?

Kevin began to reply, but stopped and hesitated a moment, as though he was working on his rebuttal. In the end he said nothing, but his posture had begun to loosen a bit.

'We're here because we need your help,' Zion continued. 'We're trying to get back at those sons of bitches who did all this.'

Kevin's ears pricked up at this, and he couldn't stop a smile from flickering on his face.

'You probably should have led with that,' Cyrus joked.

**

A few minutes later, Zion had caught Kevin up on the group's experiences of the past few months, and how they all found themselves together. It was obvious to see that he had been put at ease that these were people he could trust. He even seemed to be joking more with Zion, and Cyrus imagined they must have been close when they studied together. Eight years was a long time apart, but they seemed to pick up from where they left off. Kevin still showed the odd sign of remorse for the way they left things, but they found common ground in that there were other people to blame for that.

Kevin told of his story at the factory and how he had worked there for two more months after Zion left.

'They told me you tried to claim my research as yours. You always hated being a security guard, I just figured you were jealous.'

'That's why you reacted so coldly when we said goodbye,' Zion realised. 'You know that was just a cover up, right?'

Kevin nodded his head. 'You should never have been kicked off the course in the first place.' He rubbed his eye and blinked to get something out of it. 'How could I have been so stupid? You were never the jealous type.' He switched his attention back to Zion and the group. 'Once I found out they were using the technology to weaponise the mechs, I knew something was up.'

Cyrus leaned in closer, his body language beckoning Kevin to share more. But before he continued, a beeping emanated from the doorway, followed by a monotone voice.

'Greetings, friends of master,' the voice said. 'My master had not informed me of any visitors on September twenty third.' The voice was tinny and didn't seem to belong to a human. It changed tone slightly as it recalled the date, as if it was retrieving a sound bite from another part of its memory. It reminded Cyrus of the voice that used to make announcements on the train.

In came an object like nothing Cyrus had seen before; at least outside of a sci-fi movie. It was a small object, around three foot tall and roughly a foot wide, moving slowly into the room on small wheels that were tucked under its body. It had two long arms that drooped awkwardly down by its side, almost a little too big for its body, like those of an orangutan. Oddly, it also seemingly had no head. It was as if that part had been forgotten. The barrel-shaped robot wheeled its way into full view, before stopping and raising its arms out in front of it. A plastic tray was attached to the front of the machine, and its long arms extended to pluck it from its bodywork, holding it out in front of itself like a waiter at a cocktail party. At the ends of its two arms were three finger-like features, one of which acted like a thumb. The fingers wrapped around the tray, holding it steady from either side.

'Would anybody care for a drink?' the robot's metallic voice asked. Each word was slow, as if it was carefully considering each one as it came to say it.

Kevin rose from his chair and waved the small unit away. 'Not now, Gyro-3. We're in the middle of something.'

The robot paused a few seconds, as if trying to understand what Kevin had said to it. The top of its stocky body had a thin strip around it, through which a blue wave of light flickered. After a few moments it started to reverse slowly back out of the room, its hands still gripping the tray in the waiter-like pose. Cyrus could have sworn it was almost bowing as it left.

'Apologies, master, and friends of master,' the robot said as it removed itself from the room. The blue wave flickered more prominently as it spoke, similarly to the pattern of an audio file picking up frequencies of sound.

Cyrus leaped out of his seat and peered out of the door into the hallway, completely encapsulated by the little machine. He watched as the robot slowly wheeled its way down the hallway and into another room.

'What is that?' Cyrus spun around to Kevin. 'It's incredible! It's like something you see on TV.'

Kevin smiled at Cyrus's enthusiasm for one of his creations. 'I'm glad you like him. He's the third PRA I've built.'

'PRA?'

'Personal Robot Assistant. I designed them when I was a kid. I always wanted a robot friend.' He blushed as he spoke. 'I finished making the first prototype when I was in college.' He looked at Zion as he remembered a conversation they'd had years ago. 'He still can't do the hoovering for me.'

Zion let out a hearty laugh. 'He looks like he makes a decent waiter though.'

'The first one didn't even have arms. I focused on vocabulary and speech recognition first. He was just a box that you could talk to. This guy never leaves me alone now.'

'He's adorable,' Mia said with a grin on her face. She too was as encapsulated as Cyrus. 'His name is Gyro-3?'

'Well, he's the third of his kind, and I love Greek food,' Kevin replied with a shrug.

'I bet he's great to have around.'

'I have to say he's probably my best friend these days. And he's exactly the vision I had when I accepted the job at the research facility,' Kevin admitted. 'I wanted to design a PRA that could keep my mom company while I was away, and maybe help her out a bit around the house. But they had other ideas. The robots we were developing, they starting getting bigger and bigger, to the point where they wouldn't be functional inside a home. That's when I started getting suspicious.' His face turned angry as he remembered the experience. 'They started weaponising the machines, or 'mechs' as they called them. They justified it as self-defence, for elderly people and families who couldn't defend themselves from intruders. I pushed back, telling them that wasn't my vision for this project. I hadn't signed up for this. I was quickly pulled from the project and replaced by another team. It turns out they were using the mechs to raid small towns where they thought MIRE were holed up. They killed thousands of innocent people looking for them.'

He turned to Zion as the truth about the government was revealed to the group.

'When I found out, they forced me off the facility. They threatened to kill me if I told you,' said Zion.

'Those bastards,' Gabriel grunted.

'What then?' Cyrus was eager to know more. Like a child listening to a bedtime story, his impatience was a little too frank. He needed to know. Kevin dutifully obliged with a shrug of the shoulders.

'That's it. I quit. I told them I wanted nothing more to do with the project, and they showed me the door. But it was too late, I'd done too much. They had what they wanted from me. They had their mechs.'

Zion watched Rowley carefully, remembering the reaction he'd drawn after revealing his checkered past the other day. His face was still a little swollen from the punch. Rowley sat still, listening intently from the sofa. His expression was pensive, but stable. No sign of bubbling over, no build-up of rage for the crimes Kevin had unknowingly committed. Typical, he thought, he must have gotten it all out on him.

'That's it?' Cyrus was bemused. He wasn't satisfied with the ending to the story, and his outburst had surprised everyone else in the room. 'So you just left, and came back home?'

Kevin fidgeted on the spot, visibly annoyed at Cyrus's question. A question that felt more like an accusation, a challenge. Kevin heard the words differently to the others, as though Cyrus had accused him of running back home, hiding from the world. He'd heard it a thousand times before in the school playground. 'Go back to your mom and cry, mommy's boy!'

His mother was everything to him. The only person he could truly trust. His experience at the factory left him with nothing but guilt and hate in the very pit of his stomach. He knew then that he could trust no-one. No-one except her.

'Cyrus, buddy…' Zion recognised that Cyrus had inadvertently struck a nerve and fired a warning shot at his friend. Or an olive branch, depending on how you looked at it. At any rate, he didn't want Cyrus to fall victim to Kevin's wrath. That was a war nobody would knowingly want to start. He'd seen the aftermath.

One overconfident frat boy had once been the unfortunate recipient at a party on campus. A girl had been flirting with Kevin all night and they were really hitting it off. She was a classmate of Kevin's and they'd grown closer and closer over the semester. Then along came a shirtless bozo with more abs than brain cells, trying his luck to lean in to kiss the girl right off the bat. The girl's lips were locked with his before she had time to pull away. The guy slapped her on the butt and the other frat boys laughed and cheered as the girl blushed, awkwardly avoiding eye contact with Kevin.

Zion had never seen it until that very moment; that demon stare. The look that showed years of torment from more popular, more athletic, more attractive douchebags finally being unleashed through one cold stare. Kevin declared war in that very moment, unbeknown to the shirtless man chugging back a beer from a red plastic cup. Kevin was a stubborn man, and he could hold a grudge like nobody Zion had ever met. By the time Kevin was done with him, the frat boy was a humiliated wreck. Zion had to give it to him, Kevin was quite the practical joker, and an extremely creative one at that too. He thought the scorpion in the bathroom went a bit far though.

Cyrus seemed to get the hint, and cut short the barrage of questions his mind was thinking faster than he could ask them. What had Kevin been doing for the last few years? Living like a hermit in the woods by the looks of it.

'How is your mother?' Zion asked, distracting Kevin's attention away from Cyrus.

Kevin shuffled awkwardly in his seat, and shook his head. 'She's gone.'

Zion walked slowly over to his long lost friend and put a comforting arm around him. 'I'm so sorry.'

Kevin seemed to appreciate the sentiment. 'It will have been a year next Sunday. Shame you never got to try her meatloaf.' He forced a smile as he remembered her cooking in the kitchen while he sat eagerly at the dining table, knife and fork in hand.

'We're sorry for your loss, Kevin, um, Oracle,' Mia piped up, but stopping short as she tried to find the best way to address him. Kevin fired a glance at Zion, who did his best to avoid his eye contact. Mia continued. 'But we really need your help.'

'We need to learn more about these mechs,' Rowley chipped in. 'Cyrus had a vision. There's this guy called The Jackal. The tyrant has been kidnapping people and using them as slaves. Cyrus's mom and sister, they could be there. He's creating an empire of greed. We have to stop him.'

Kevin's attention was shifted around the room as someone else spoke up. This time it was Jennifer.

'While the mechs are running wild we have no chance of rebuilding a life, regardless of what happens to The Jackal. Do you have any connections at the facility? Where the mechs were made?'

Zion shook his head. 'Last I heard the facility was closed down, abandoned when MIRE took over it. They shut down the production of mechs and exposed the government for creating them. The place is likely locked down.'

'A lock just needs the right key,' Kevin smirked. 'You're telling me the great Zion can't hack his way into it?' He turned to the others. 'He's pretty handy, you know.'

'Oh yes, we know,' Cyrus smiled.

Zion shook his head. 'Hot-wiring the shutter doors of a supermarket is one thing. Breaking into one of the most secure research facilities in the country, well that's nigh on impossible.'

'Not if you used to work there,' Kevin's smirk travelled further up his face. 'If that place is still abandoned, all you need to do is unlock the doors. You can take your time, no need to worry about getting caught.'

'How tight is security?' Gabriel questioned.

'Key cards for the most part, and retinal and fingerprint scans as you get further in,' Zion found himself replying before having a sudden realisation. 'My access was revoked the day I was kicked out.' He looked at Kevin hopefully. 'Do you think yours would be the same?'

Kevin's smirk disappeared and he nodded slowly, dashing Zion's hopes in an instant.

'Damn.'

'But,' Kevin's eyes lit up again. 'I may have something that can help.' He rushed out of the room and could be heard banging about from somewhere else in the house. The group exchanged curious looks, anticipating what Kevin would return with. They didn't have to wait long as Kevin rushed back in as quickly as he'd left, holding a small device. It was a disc-shaped metal object, approximately an inch thick, sitting comfortably in the palm of his hand. He placed the device on the coffee table in the centre of the room and hit a button in the middle of the disc. A green light lit up from where he had pushed the button, pulsating periodically. Moments later a giant holographic display flashed into view, filling the room with the image it was projecting. Cyrus was taken aback by the sight. The image rose up out of the device into a huge sphere, illuminating the area with a blue-grey tinged map. Kevin pinched his fingers on an area of the hologram to zoom in. As he did so, the picture started to become clearer. The image changed from a sphere to the shape of a large network of buildings. There was a wire fence around the edge, giving the clue that this must have been the secure facility they were talking about. Kevin started drawing with his finger on the hologram, leaving behind a yellow trail as he pointed out a specific section of the scene they were looking at.

'This is the main research facility,' he highlighted the entrance to the large building in the middle. 'I smuggled these schematics out in this disc when I left. Wasn't sure why at first, but it's coming in handy now I suppose.' He drew a yellow ring around the building. 'You're not getting in here without a key card, retinal scan and fingerprint scan.'

He then pointed to the collection of smaller buildings surrounding it, zooming in on one to the left of the picture.

'This is your best bet for getting in. Security is a little lighter here, and if you can hot-wire your way in you might be able to bypass the key card zones.'

'That makes no sense,' Gabriel remarked. 'Why have a weakness on this side?'

'Security guards,' Kevin replied candidly. 'Zion knows all about it. This entrance was the service entrance, where they transported all the shipments of materials to the research labs. More guards meant less tech. Don't get me wrong, it'll still be tough to get in. But you'll save yourself some time taking this route.'

'What exactly are we supposed to find when we get into this place?' Jennifer was still unsure what the point of this was.

Zion smiled at her use of the word 'when'. Perhaps she hadn't considered her choice of words, but it was reassuring that subconsciously she had believed in their ability, or more specifically *his* ability, to break into the place.

'We're not sure,' Zion answered. 'We're hoping there will be something left over that will give us a clue as to how to shut down the mechs.'

A muffled thud rumbled through the living room, causing the place to fall silent. Seconds later, another one rumbled, this time making the floor vibrate under their feet.

Cyrus stood still, stunned at the sudden danger. The dynamic had changed in an instant.

Impossible. How did they find us?

It was as if by mentioning them, Zion had accidentally summoned them. Their timing cruelly poignant.

Another thud came and went, and Gabriel was the first to snap into action.

'They're here.'

Kevin seemed to know exactly who 'they' were and shot into life, grabbing the disc-shaped device from the table and hurrying everyone out of the living room. He bolted up the stairs as fast as his stumpy legs would carry him, followed closely by Cyrus, Mia and Gabriel. As they reached one of the bedrooms, Cyrus could see that the house could not have been better positioned for getting a good view of the Woodside residential landscape. The origin of the thuds was evidently clear. Off in the distance, at the point the group had entered the town, two gargantuans were plodding their way towards them. Their thick metal bodies were much larger than Cyrus remembered, and their enormous canons more menacing than ever. A number of golems and panthers were scouting around the sides of the giant mechs. A quick peak out the window was all they needed to get the message. They needed to move, fast.

Kevin rushed back out to the landing and down the stairs. As he reached the bottom he flung open a door to his right, revealing a set of stairs leading down into the earth. Cyrus remembered the water he had fetched for Doug; this basement must have been his storage room.

'Downstairs, now!' Kevin called. One-by-one, the group shuffled down the stairs into the dark basement. Gabriel and Rowley helped carry Doug down with them, who was still wincing in pain.

Cyrus made his way last, taking one last look at the sunlight streaming into the hallway, seconds before the loud piercing screech of the panthers sent a chill crawling down his spine. He slammed the door behind him and thrusted himself into darkness.

Walking gingerly down the steps, one-by-one in the pitch black, he ran his hand along the wall to keep his balance and steady himself. After the fourth step a light flicked on and the whole basement was illuminated. Cyrus could see a large generator in the corner of the room, humming loudly. There were a number of shelving units stacked full of tins of food and large bottles of water. He could see his friends gathered in the centre of the room, huddled around a wooden workbench.

'OK, OK, OK,' Kevin's voice was panicky and he was stuttering as his brain worked faster than his mouth. 'We don't have much time.' He was hurriedly searching for something in a set of drawers. Cyrus felt sorry for the poor guy. He'd chosen to stay hidden, live a quiet life in the place he felt safest; his family home. And now they'd come and ruined it all, dragging him into their mess with them.

Kevin's eyes lit up as he found what he was looking for. He presented a large rolled up piece of paper and began unravelling it. He used a coffee mug to hold down one corner, and twisted on the spot to find three more suitable paperweights. He reached under the workbench and retrieved a wrench, which sufficiently held down another corner. He then grabbed the nearest person to him, Jane, and placed her hands down on the table to hold down the other corners. She kept her hands still and he forced a half-hearted smile to show his appreciation at her willingness to help.

'OK, let's see here,' he muttered to himself. The rest of the group peered over the bench to see the crudely drawn map presented to them. The paper was a coffee stained brown, and the contents of the map were basic, with large red arrows sprawling across from various points. It looks like a child's drawing.

'This here is where we are,' he pointed to one of the arrows. There was a large green area shaded in just above it. 'And here is where the forest begins.'

'Where are you going with this?' Gabriel interjected.

'Just give me a second!' Kevin snapped. He rubbed his patchy beard with one hand while tapping his head with the other. He pointed to the bottom of the map, where the road met the entrance to the town. 'We don't have time to make it out this way, they're already too close. We can't stay here, they'll find us for sure.'

'Then where do we go?' Jennifer asked.

Kevin pointed to the large green section and tapped his finger on it. 'The forest, it's our only option. If we make it far enough we might be able to lose them in the trees.'

The group all seemed to agree with the plan; it was as good as they had and time was running out. Everyone checked their weapons and ensured the safeties were switched off, while Kevin fiddled with a switch on the wall. Somewhere in the distance there was a great explosion, which took the group by surprise.

'I was saving that for emergencies,' Kevin said as he marched back up the stairs to the house. 'That should distract them for a bit and buy us some time.'

'This guy is full of surprises,' Gabriel muttered as he lugged Doug back up the staircase.

CHAPTER TWENTY-FOUR

Cyrus rushed up the stairs to the first floor of the house, hoping to get another look at the mechs before leaving. He could see the plumes of smoke rising up from a ramshackle house a few streets away; the result of the detonation Kevin had triggered moments earlier. The mechs had flooded over to it; the towering figures of the gargantuan mech and the screeches of the panthers gave away the fact that the distraction had worked. However, it hadn't bought them much time.

He tightened the straps on his rucksack and took off back down to his companions, who were already making their way out the front door. As he followed them out, Kevin almost knocked him over as he came barrelling back into the building.

'Gyro-3! Gyro-3!' He went back for his robot companion, who was still in the other room. The small machine rolled up to the doorway and looked upon its master.

'Danger!' Kevin barked at the robot. 'Intruders incoming, we need to leave, now.'

The robot took a moment to register the words, and then the little blue wave of light running around the top of its frame turned red.

'Danger, danger,' it repeated, seemingly understanding the situation. The robot took off much faster than it had travelled before, racing out the door after Kevin. As it rolled quickly past Cyrus, the robot stopped and turned to him. 'Friend of master, please evacuate the house.' With that Cyrus took off after the rest of the group, followed in tow by Gyro-3.

**

The fresh air of the woodlands filled Cyrus's nostrils as he left the house. The crisp, earthy smell from the bark of the trees reminded him of his childhood, of adventures running through the forest on a hot summer's day. As the adrenaline built up inside him the memory was all too vivid, as though he was now reliving a real life version of the fantasies he once imagined as a child. He was the protagonist, running through the forest with his friends to escape the imaginary evil that pursued. However the reality was something different altogether. The scene was the same, but now he was not the protagonist. He was the prey, the insignificant pawn in a much larger tale. The excitement he'd felt as a child in this same scenario, hurdling logs and weaving between trees was replaced by a raw fear. The effect was the same; he was running as fast as his legs would carry him.

As he made it past the cover of the first few trees, he chanced a look back in the direction of the town. To his horror, he caught sight of the mechs swarming the street he had just vacated. The panthers were leading the way, spreading out around the houses, alerting the others of any sign of human activity like bloodhounds tracking the trail of a small animal.

Gyro-3 sped past Cyrus, finding it more difficult than the rest to navigate the harsh terrain with its small wheels. It seemed to be able to plot its path quickly as it moved from tree to tree, its navigation and special awareness calculations flowing smoothly from one to the other. However it had to take a wider path as it followed the smoothest route through the forest, zigzagging all over the place. The red waves of light were glowing from the thin strip at the top of its metal frame as it went on in search of its master.

'Danger, danger, danger,' it repeated as it whizzed by, the electric wheels humming loudly as they worked overtime to pull the small robot through the dirt.

Cyrus watched as the mechs grew closer, noticing one of the panthers take interest in Kevin's house. He couldn't help but watch as the mechs gathered around the bear trap that Doug had been ensnared in, unsure of what it was. Then something else caught his attention, in the corner of his eye. He turned to the right slightly to see one of the golems pointing its gun arm in the direction of the forest. In his direction. Before he could react a loud shot rang out and the tree next to Cyrus sizzled. He spun around to see a large hole in the middle of its trunk. The shot had gone right through, burning a hole through the middle and singeing the bark around it.

Cyrus ducked after he heard the shot, and upon seeing the aftermath took off like a startled rabbit, bounding his way deeper into the forest, using Gyro-3 as his guide.

The mechs were aware of their presence now and the chase had begun. Cyrus cursed under his breath that he hadn't kept his head down and ran from the beginning. He'd given away their position and lost precious seconds in the process.

Stupid, stupid, stupid!

He could hear the pounding of metal paws on the dirt behind him as the panthers gave chase into the forest. A screech from one of the robotic beasts made Cyrus instinctively cover his ears as he ran. He could see the rest of his friends further ahead turn when they heard the noise, and then run with a little more urgency as they saw the evil that pursued them. The plasma rifle on Cyrus's back became uncomfortable as he ran, hovering just above the backpack that seemed to have become a part of him, such were the tightness of the straps that dug into his shoulders. He realised the mechs would be on him before he caught up with his friends, and he needed to do something to buy himself some time. He could see Gabriel still carrying Doug in a fireman's lift over his shoulder and realised it wasn't just him who needed a few more seconds' distraction to get away. Gabriel was jogging with big strides, but the weight of Doug was taking its toll on his pace.

Without a second thought, Cyrus spun round and took up a crouching position at the top of a small hill, where he had a good view of the onrushing attackers. He drew his rifle and breathed deeply, wishing he had Rowley's keen aim in this moment. He pointed the gun at the panthers bounding towards him and squeezed the trigger. A burst of energy lit from the muzzle and the plasma round pinged off the side of one of the beasts, barely causing it to stumble as it raced on in his direction. Luckily the panthers were bunched up as they approached, giving Cyrus little choice of where to aim. He fired another round, and another, and another, pulling back on the trigger as fast as the tendons in his index finger would allow him. Sweat ran down from his head and dripped onto the rifle as he desperately pushed the gun closer to his face, squinting one eye to get a better aim at his targets. A round caught one of the panthers square in the eye, causing it to fall mid-sprint as it became lifeless for a second. Another panther smashed into the back of it, falling off course and flipping onto its back. Cyrus fired again, and again, hitting another panther which scratched at the floor as it tried hard to avoid colliding with a tree.

Another shot echoed through the forest as the dirt kicked up around Cyrus, causing him to fall back hard against the ground. Another tree to his side had been blasted clean through, and he took that as a sign to get back to running. He'd managed to buy Gabriel some time at any rate, which was something. Scrambling back to his feet, Cyrus pivoted on the spot and set off again, still clutching the rifle in his hands. Bark flew off another tree as a shot ripped through it, and more dirt was kicked up from the ground from the force of the blast. Again and again, debris and remnants of the once peaceful woodland were blown about from all sides. It was a miracle Cyrus hadn't been shot, especially given the usual dependable accuracy of the golems. He closed his eyes and dipped his head each time the shots rang out, shielding himself from the blasts.

As he started to gain some momentum in his sprint he looked ahead towards the rest of his party. They had created some good distance between them. He could spot Gabriel still lagging behind with Doug draped over his shoulder, but they were further from danger for the time being.

Onward Cyrus rushed, unsure of what his next move was. His plan was the furthest thing from long-term. He wasn't thinking more than a couple of seconds in advance. His mind set himself minuscule goals.

Just get past the next tree without being shot.

It looked like the plan was failing quickly. A large bow of a tall redwood clattered through the branches from above and landed in front of Cyrus with a thud. He didn't have enough time to react and barrelled straight into it, his knee clashing full force with the sturdy wood. He stumbled and rolled forward, losing both his rifle and backpack in the process. His cargo pants caught on a twig sticking out from the bow as he hurtled over it, and ripped at the hems. Cyrus hit the floor hard, kicking up dust and giving him an unwelcome mouthful of dirt. Shocked and winded, he lay still for a moment, sprawled across the ground. He gasped for breath as he spat the dirt from his mouth and tried to make sense of his new perspective. His chin was sore and his heartbeat pounded in his head. He fought for strength to get himself back onto his feet, and suddenly realising how long he'd been on the floor for, panicked. The mechs would be on him any second, their jaws snapping at the sight of his weak figure lying defeated on the ground.

As his senses began to return, the thunderous boom of tree exploding right beside him snapped him back into action. He sprung up onto his feet, but immediately his knee buckled from under him. He winced in pain, instinctively grabbing the leg to sooth the pain.

Then he saw it.

Its giant metal frame approaching him, the robotic eyes mad with the evil that had designed it. The panther slinked towards him, almost in slow motion, stalking its prey, teasing it. It was a killing machine, but it seemed to share the same wicked, torturous characteristics of the feline it was modelled after. It was toying with Cyrus, taunting him, beckoning him to try and fight for his life so there was more sport in the kill.

Cyrus took the initiative and searched desperately for his rifle. He caught sight of the barrel of the gun resting in a fern a few feet away. It was just out of reach, and the mech was too close to have any chance of retrieving it before it pounced. He took another look at the oncoming attacker, and then at the gun.

Screw it.

He scrambled his way over to the weapon as fast as his body could carry him, and the panther pounced just as quickly. The force of its body hitting its target would probably be enough to finish him off. Cyrus yelled out loud as he clutched at the rifle, swinging it around in the direction of the panther whilst desperately searching for the trigger with his finger.

The shot rang out loud as a flash illuminated the small gap between Cyrus and the mech. The burst of energy from the plasma round buried itself deep into the mech's jaw as it leaped head first. The round penetrated the gap between its metal teeth as its jaws opened wide, following through into the eye. The beast was flung away from Cyrus and into the fern.

Cyrus lay on his back, stunned at the fact that he was still alive. The rifle in his hands pointed out in front of him at where the mech had been, the butt of the rifle leaning on the ground for support. The blast had sent the mech sprawling away from him, but he noticed that the angle of his rifle did not match the trajectory of the panther, which now lay on its side, malfunctioning in the fern. Cyrus turned as a voice came.

'I told you never to do that to me again,' Mia said, lowering her proton pistol to the ground. 'What part of that don't you understand?' Her voice was firm but she couldn't help but crack a smile, relieved to see Cyrus in one piece.

Cyrus fell back against the ground and let out a low whistle. He picked himself up and looked at Mia with an expression of upmost gratitude. He wanted to say something to her, but the words didn't come. The sound of gunfire from behind reminded him that this wasn't the time, and they took off at breakneck speed back to the rest of the group.

It was a real sense of déjà vu for Cyrus as he ran through the forest. The dirt kicked up all around and bark flew off the nearby trees as the pair ran, and yet again they managed to come through unscathed.

**

Gabriel had been carrying Doug for a few hundred yards, and even with his herculean physique he was struggling to keep pace with the rest of his companions. Doug was still wincing in pain as his injured leg flopped about, unprotected as his foot bounced off Gabriel's torso. Gabriel was panting hard as he ran, each breath getting louder and louder, which only increased his bear-like resemblance. Gabriel had ditched his rifle near the start of the forest to shed weight, however as he looked over his shoulder he could see that it hadn't bought him much more time.

He could see Mia and Cyrus dashing towards him. Close behind were a couple of panthers that had re-joined the chase, overtaking the golems that were firing wildly at the pair of humans that were quickly gaining on Gabriel's position.

A quick calculation told him everything he needed to know. As things stood, he and Doug were about thirty seconds from being torn to shreds by the panthers, if a golem didn't get a lock on them first. The trees seemed to be providing sufficient cover from their targeting systems for now, but that wouldn't last forever.

'Cyrus!' Gabriel bellowed. His friend responded immediately by looking in his direction. Gabriel didn't need to say anything else, Cyrus seemed to get the message already. He saw him change course in an instant, drawing the panthers in an angle that moved away from Gabriel and Doug.

'Gabriel, it's not worth it,' Doug said, struggling to get the words out through the pain. 'You need to leave me behind.'

'That's not an option,' Gabriel replied instantly. He couldn't leave Doug. He wouldn't be able to live with himself if he let another person die under his watch. He had to find a way of getting them both through and away from the mechs, whatever it took.

Doug lifted his head just enough to see Cyrus divert the panthers away from them with a quick change of direction, taking a new diagonal path into another part of the forest. Mia followed his lead, firing off a few blind shots from her pistol to draw the attention of the mechs, if not to try and hit them.

'They're going to die because of me. You can't let that happen, Gabriel,' he pleaded again.

Gabriel refused to reply this time, focusing all of his energy on running.

With a quick glance over his shoulder, Gabriel saw two panthers chase Mia and Cyrus away into another part of the forest. A golem was also distracted by the wild firing of Mia's pistol and followed suit, unleashing sporadic rounds from his own gun arm after her. However something else caught his eye which made him pivot on the spot to face the direction they'd come from. Another panther was still heading in their direction, bounding at full speed! The second golem was also following, and as it spotted Gabriel it raised its gun arm and began firing. Gabriel instinctively leapt to the side, the shots missing him by inches. As he evaded the gunfire, he and Doug went tumbling to the floor. Doug wailed as he landed hard on his injured leg, and clutched it in his hands as he rolled about in the dirt. As Gabriel got to his feet, he searched desperately for Doug and saw that his friend had tumbled a few feet down a slope and had settled at the bottom. Doug lay in what was effectively a miniature valley, with steep inclines all around him. There was no way he'd be able to pull himself out in his condition.

Moments later, the panther entered the fray, spotting Doug instantly and setting off at him. Its jaws were gnashing open and shut as, almost hungrily, it launched itself towards him. Just a few feet away from the helpless Doug, the panther shaped up to pounce, but was thrown off balance as a strong weight slammed into it from the side. Gabriel had timed his jump to perfection, landing on top of the mech as it reached the bottom of the tiny valley. His plan was simple, to stop it from reaching Doug. That part had been successful, but there didn't seem to be any follow up plan and he now found himself on top of the stunned panther, which was clawing away at the ground beneath it. In a matter of seconds the beast would be up on its feet and sinking its sharp teeth into him. For all of Gabriel's strength, he wouldn't be able to overpower it. He needed to think, fast.

Gabriel moved away from the mech and back to Doug, shielding him with his massive frame. He noticed Doug was carrying a weapon that was strapped to his good leg. The proton pistol protruded from a makeshift holster, made from strips of leather cut away from a satchel Doug had found back in the mall. Gabriel snatched it and aimed at the panther that had now got back to its feet. With a buzzing sound the pistol fired a proton round right at its head, causing it to flail about on the spot as its circuits whirred and popped.

Gabriel marched over to the mech and fired another shot right into its eye, and another, and another, screaming at it as he squeezed the trigger repeatedly from point blank range. It seemed to make no difference, only stunning the mech for a short while longer.

'Gabriel!' Doug yelled. The voice broke his rage, and all of a sudden he stopped firing, freeing himself from his madness and regaining control of his trigger finger once more. He panted with long deep breaths as he looked at the malfunctioning mech in front of him. He then turned back to Doug, just in time to see a blast hit his friend clean in his stomach. Doug's eyes went wide as the shot rippled through him, creating a gaping hole in the middle of his torso, singeing from the heat of the blast that had hit him.

'Nooooo!' Gabriel roared as Doug's head fell back against the ground, his trucker hat falling beside him, and his body went limp.

The golem entered the small valley with a loud clunk as it jumped eight feet down from one of the slopes. No trees were in the way this time; Doug had been an easy target for it. The golem lifted his gun arm to Gabriel this time, its targeting system seeking a lock on him. Gabriel's rage returned in full force, the adrenaline giving him the guile to evade the first two shots, the third grazing the top of his shoulder as he rushed at the mech. The golem didn't get time to fire a fourth shot at its target, as a blast from Gabriel's pistol knocked the gun arm out of joint for a moment. The golem, still taller than the giant of a man that was rushing at him, was knocked over as Gabriel barrelled into it at full force, his teeth gritted in a crazed grimace. On hitting the ground, the golem immediately tried to right itself, swinging its arms wildly at Gabriel, who just managed to avoid taking a whack to the face. As the mech lay struggling on it back, its targeting system saw one last thing before cutting out altogether; the barrel of a pistol filling its vision.

CHAPTER TWENTY-FIVE

His legs getting heavier with each step, Cyrus wiped his brow as he twisted and turned through the dense woodland that surrounded him. Since heading off in a separate direction from the rest of the group, the foliage seemed to grow thicker in the part of the forest he'd found himself in. The ground was littered with shrubs, making it harder to see where he was stepping. Sure enough, Cyrus tripped on a root that protruded from the ground. It was the perfect size for his foot to get caught under; and as he stumbled his heart leapt into his mouth. He briefly thought about the irony of the moment; he had been chased by killing machines all this time, yet it was a tree that sent him sprawling to the deck. A natural trap for clumsy humans like himself. He managed to correct himself partially with his other leg, but he had picked up too much speed and was just delaying the inevitable. Suddenly a hand grabbed his back, pinching at his skin and held him upright just long enough for him to centre himself again.

'Thanks,' he called to Mia, who seemed to be saving his skin on a regular basis today.

Aside from Cyrus's clumsy footing, the thick foliage seemed to be working in their favour, as the bulky mechs were finding it more difficult to navigate the tighter spaces. The golems had stopped firing as their targeting systems had almost stopped picking up the pair altogether.

'I really hope our diversion worked,' said Cyrus, glancing back to estimate the number of pursuers they had.

'Well, I've felt those panthers breathing down our necks for the last five minutes, so it must have,' replied Mia.

'The forest is pretty dense here, we might start pulling away soon,' Cyrus said hopefully. He hadn't seen a mech for at least a minute and the intermittent screeches of the panthers seemed further away than before.

'Let's head for that waterfall up there,' Mia suggested, pointing up to a hill further ahead.

The light streamed in through the trees from a clearing a hundred yards or so ahead of them. The sound of gushing water was clear, and something of a novelty for the weary travellers who'd spent the last few months in the scorching heat of the city, void of any fresh water. No doubt the waterfall offered false hope too. The water would surely be contaminated like the river that flowed through the city. Still, the sound of the water pouring over the rocks was all too tempting. Cyrus longed for the refreshing taste of cool spring water.

He remembered the freshly filled bottle that had been sloshing about in his backpack. The backpack he'd lost in his encounter with the mechs. He hoped Mia had enough for them both.

The trees started to thin as the pair were suddenly faced with a sheer drop. They skidded to a halt as they peered out over the edge, down the forty foot drop to the pool at the bottom of the waterfall. The sight of the water cascading over the rocks at the top was majestic, with the light shimmering on the water as it tumbled gracefully down the face of the cliff. On another day this would have been the perfect romantic spot for the two of them to find themselves in. Cyrus made a mental note to come back here if they ever made it through this hell.

Part way up the waterfall, burrowed into the rock face was a small cave, hidden by the glistening water that flowed over it. Mia led Cyrus to it, where they waited, hoping their pursuers wouldn't find them. It was the perfect hideaway, and they'd managed to get enough of a head start on the mechs to take refuge without being spotted. Once they were in the cave it would have been impossible for the mechs to locate them. Lucky for them they weren't found, and another thirty minutes went by before they pondered leaving to search for the others.

The half-hour wait flew by for Cyrus, which surprised him as his last few conversations with Mia had been awkward. She seemed to be a lot more responsive to him, and as they sat waiting she had even leaned her head on his shoulder, something she used to do all the time. For the first time since being in the mall Cyrus had felt like he had the old Mia back, the one he knew and loved. He was glad for the short reprieve, and the odd smile from her beautiful face, her eyes lighting up like fireflies, reassured him that she was feeling the same way. She showed concern at Cyrus's cuts and bruises, paying him a lot of attention, and after a longing gaze into each other's eyes leaned in to kiss him. As her lips met his, Cyrus's heart raced and the jewel around his neck glowed a soft blue, illuminating Mia's radiant face in the dark of the cave. He wished he could capture that moment forever.

A quick check of his wristwatch let Cyrus know how long they'd waited, and he stepped out briefly to check if the coast was clear. The spray from the waterfall wet his t-shirt as he ventured out of the cave.

Squinting his eyes as they readjusted to the bright sunlight, Cyrus surveyed the land. The pool of water at the bottom of the waterfall looked even shinier from his vantage point. The foamy appearance where the water gushed into the pool quickly thinned out as it rippled towards a stream heading further away. Cyrus scanned the area surrounding the pool and then at the tree line of the forest, shielding his eyes with his hand. He breathed a sigh of relief. There were no mechs in the vicinity at least. Now he just needed to regroup with the rest of their friends. He hoped they'd made it safely away.

'All clear,' he said as he re-entered the cave. 'Looks like we managed to lose them.'

Mia looked positively relieved. 'I don't think I have the energy for any more running. Not in this heat.' She took a swig from her water bottle and exhaled audibly in satisfaction. Her grey tank top was dotted with patches of sweat, and she blew a moist strand of hair away from her face. She felt less than attractive, but Cyrus found her truly captivating. It might have been the way her hair seemed to look good no matter how it was arranged. Or her olive skin that seemed to become more radiant in the sunlight, the droplets of sweat glistening like the crystal waters of the pool outside. There was something about Mia that made it impossible for Cyrus to find her unattractive. And yet, beyond her beauty was this steely courage that Cyrus hadn't seen until recently. There was more to Mia than met the eye; a fierceness to her that was being unleashed as she dealt with the horrors of the world they were living in. She'd saved his life today, and risked hers in the process, just as he would do for her. She had run back to Cyrus, right in the face of the mechs to save his life and stick a middle finger up to the enemy.

This woman is badass.

He caught himself gawping at her for the umpteenth time, and unsuccessfully tried to look casual as she looked back at him inquisitively. Mia laughed and rolled her eyes.

'Cyrus,' she smiled. 'You never cease to amaze me.'

Cyrus was thinking the same thing.

**

Ten minutes later the pair had wandered back into the forest in search of the rest of their party. Cyrus gripped his rifle, making slow steps through the foliage around them. Mia emulated his movements, clutching her proton pistol in one hand. Her wrist had felt much better than the day before and it was healing nicely. She still had to swap the pistol between each hand every now and then, but she was functioning much better.

Retracing their steps back towards the town of Woodside, they grew more cautious in case of mech ambush. It was possible they were still scouting the area looking for them.

'I wonder which way they went,' he whispered. He took note of the location of the town in relation to where they'd come from and took an educated guess as to which direction they'd gone.

'My guess would be that way,' Mia responded, the direction of her pointing echoing the very thoughts he had. Cyrus nodded in agreement, and they changed course accordingly.

Mia stumbled across the remains of a brown backpack, the straps ragged and the bulk of the bag ripped in two. The teeth marks from the panther that had obviously been chewing it were clear to see.

'I think I found your pack,' she said, holding it up for Cyrus to see. Cyrus winced at the sight of the shredded material, knowing how easily that could have been him.

'Water bottle?' he asked.

Mia shook her head. 'Sorry, it's not here.'

A few moments later, Cyrus startled a squirrel that was crawling its way up a nearby tree trunk. The small animal scrambled further up with more intent, disturbing a bird nesting on a branch above. The bird shrieked and fluttered away, causing the branch to shake. Cyrus hit the floor, his chest bumping the dirt hard. This was the kind of unwanted attention he was trying to avoid. Any nearby mech would surely have noticed the sound, and would more than certainly be glaring in his direction now.

As his breathing grew sharper and his heart began to race, Cyrus lay in the dirt waiting. Nothing happened. He glanced to his right to see Mia, also prone. She was looking straight at him, her eyes wide, waiting for him to do something, anything.

OK, time to be brave.

The lack of a screech from a panther or the deep metallic sound of a golem should have comforted him. But the silence seemed to add to the uncertainty, and Cyrus couldn't shake the feeling that the second he stood up he'd find himself staring into the jaws of a panther. Just like in the vision Isaac had shown him. He always hated jump scares.

Taking each movement slowly and carefully, he got to his knees and pointed his plasma rifle out in front of him, looking down the sights as he concentrated. Nothing but trees, trees and more trees welcomed his vision. He stood up slowly, taking a wide circle as he surveyed the whole area around them. The forest had provided great cover to escape the mechs, but it also served as a great location to launch an ambush, with so many tall redwoods to hide behind.

He bent down again to pick up a rock around the size of his fist. He took a long backswing and launched it in an arc to a spot a few yards in front of them. The thudding sound as it hit the base of a tree would divert attention, buying them enough time to get a good head start as they scampered away. The rock collided with another stone with a loud clunk, and the pair readied themselves for a spring of action from one of the mechs. But still, nothing. Cyrus should have felt reassured by this, as it likely meant they were alone in this part of the forest. But there was an uneasy feeling he couldn't shake off, like they were still being watched.

'I've got a bad feeling about this,' Cyrus whispered.

'Me too,' replied Mia.

'Let's keep moving, we need to regroup with the rest.'

'I agree. The sooner the better, this place gives me the creeps.'

Mia was right, the forest did have a creepy quality to it, in spite of its beauty in the sunlight. It was a strange realisation though, as Woodside had seemed such a nice reprieve from the torn city they'd left behind. It seemed that everywhere they went, no matter how idyllic, turned to shit sooner or later. They brought trouble with them like a plague. He thought again of Kevin, and the quiet life they'd destroyed, simply by being here.

'So, are we going or not?' Mia was looking at him impatiently.

'Uh, yeah,' Cyrus said. 'You lead the way, I'll cover you.'

**

Half an hour passed and the pair still saw no sign of the others. Cyrus checked his watch as the afternoon seemed to be flying by. Mia was taking a swig of water from her backpack, quenching her thirst in the heat of the day. The giant redwoods gave the forest some cover from the sun, but it was still warm and the longer they went rationing one bottle of water between them, the less energy they had.

They were now deep in the forest and there were acres of trees scattered around in every direction. It was near impossible to know which way to go. Cyrus looked back at the direction they'd come from, and it looked exactly the same as the direction they were heading in. For all he knew they could be going in circles.

A rustling sound from the fern fifty yards in front of them caught their attention. Cyrus locked his plasma rifle onto the fern as Mia started to flank with her pistol drawn. The rustling continued, as though an animal, or worse, was getting ready to pounce as they approached. Cyrus waited for Mia to get in position, and from two sides of a triangle the pair slowly closed in. Fifty yards, forty yards, thirty yards. The fern rustled some more and just as Cyrus reached ten yards away the round figure of Rowley stepped out. He had mud on his face and was wearing some of the fern on his clothes and head. He beamed as he saw his friends.

'Cyrus, Mia!' he exclaimed. 'You made it!' He embraced Cyrus first in a bear hug and then treated Mia with the same gesture. She squeaked from the pressure of his brief, yet constricting embrace as it momentarily knocked the wind out of her.

'Rowley, what are you doing here? I nearly blew your head off.'

'Cyrus, you're a terrible shot. I was never in danger,' Rowley joked, much to Cyrus's displeasure. Mia fired a cheeky wink at him, reaffirming Rowley's comment.

'The others are waiting for you,' Rowley continued. 'They're not far from here, tucked away on the outskirts of the forest.'

'Oh, thank God,' said Mia. 'Everybody's OK.'

Rowley's face dropped suddenly. 'Almost everybody. Doug didn't make it.'

The words hit Cyrus like a freight train. First Nathaniel, now Doug. He had come so close to death himself, but it was becoming more and more real as those around him were being picked off by, one by one. Mia's eyes welled up and her lip trembled. Cyrus went to comfort her as she began to sob.

'Poor Doug,' she spluttered.

Cyrus tried to think back to the last thing he'd said to Doug, the last conversation they would ever have. Nothing immediately came to mind. Doug was a quiet guy and kept himself to himself most of the time. He wondered if he'd made enough of an effort to include him in the group, to make him feel welcome. He'd arrived with Gabriel and Jane, but they had both made their own mark on the group quite quickly. Doug had always been friendly, more than willing to help out. Yet he didn't really get involved in the banter between them all. Everybody dealt with the war their own way, he supposed. He thought again whether there was something he could have done to make him feel more a part of the group. It didn't matter now.

'We should go to the others,' Rowley said, hurrying them along. 'We lost the mechs, but who knows when they'll be back.'

He led them to the edge of the forest, although exactly which edge of the forest Cyrus could not say. He was so disorientated it could have been anywhere. An abandoned log cabin came into view as they left the maze of the trees into a clearing.

'They've been waiting for you. Figured you'd find us eventually. I wanted to make sure you did.'

'Thanks Rowley, we're lucky you caught us when you did,' replied Mia.

'Just a heads up,' he added. 'As you can imagine, everything's kind of tense in there. Gabriel's not doing too well, either. He was with Doug when it happened. Beats me how the hell he got out of there in one piece.'

Rowley knocked on the wooden door of the log cabin three times, and the cracking sound of a bolt being unlocked followed soon after. The old door creaked open and the trio went inside to reunite with their friends.

Sure enough, the atmosphere was exactly how Rowley had described it. Everybody was scattered around the hut, sitting or standing in various positions. Nobody was talking. Jane was crying in the corner of the room with Jennifer and April consoling her. Aiden, Zion and Kevin were stood dotted around what used to be the kitchen area, arms folded. Gyro-3 had powered down in the corner, probably a tactic used by Kevin to keep him out of the way. And then there was Gabriel, a stark contrast to the rest of the group. He paced back and forth like a frustrated lion patrolling the perimeter of its territory. He paused briefly at the sight of Rowley returning with Mia and Cyrus, and then immediately set off again, knocking over an unlit candle in a fury, which dropped to the floor, the wax stick snapping in two as it hit the ground.

'Goddamn it!' he boomed, making everybody else jump. Cyrus could see that his t-shirt had been torn in several places, revealing the dark skin of his chiselled body beneath. Dark red scratches could be seen across his chest and on his side. He must have been in one hell of a fight. He wondered how on earth he survived.

And then something unusual happened. Gabriel marched over to Jane, and was met with the protective glare of Jennifer. There was a moment of uncertainty, where Jennifer wasn't sure of his intention. The giant of a man was positively terrifying when angry, so they couldn't blame her. Finally the aggression that contorted his face relaxed and his eyes softened. A tear ran down his cheek and he reached out for Jane. She responded by hopping off the counter she was sat on and plunging herself into his arms. They cried together as they embraced.

'I'm so sorry,' Gabriel sobbed.

'No,' Jane replied. 'It's not your fault, you did everything you could. He knew that.'

Gabriel's heart warmed at her words, and in that instant something inside him changed. It was as if the burden of responsibility he'd had for Doug, for the group, for the whole colony back at the supermarket was lifted. He couldn't save Doug, but he had protected him far longer than any other person could have.

CHAPTER TWENTY-SIX

Cyrus woke with a start as the door to the cabin slammed shut. He was lying on the floor, curled up in a ball. After the events of the previous day, everyone was too tired, mentally and physically, to carry on. They'd camped in the log cabin, where for now at least it seemed to be safe. He figured he must have fallen asleep sometime after dusk, the sunset telling his body enough was enough, he needed to get some sleep. And sleep he did. One check of his watch wasn't enough, he needed a second glance to verify the time. It read ten fifteen. He'd been asleep for at least twelve hours, maybe longer.

He thought about how thirsty he was, and how he and Mia had been sharing the same small water bottle for the last few hours of the day before. She must have been feeling the same as him. He looked across the room to find her asleep in a similar position to him. It looked far from comfortable, but like him she would have been so exhausted she wouldn't have noticed. He overheard some muffled voices coming from outside the hut.

'Look, Kevin, we're sorry for what's happened here, but we still really need your help.'

'My help? You need *my* help? I got you out of this mess, I've done my part. I told you I'd help you against the ones that created the mechs. I'd tell you how to get into the factory, and that would be the end of it. Now I've been driven out of my house, a house that I can never go back to now!'

'Kevin, we said we're sorry. We didn't plan for this. But this is bigger than you, it's bigger than all of us. If we don't do something about The Jackal, he'll carry on tormenting the innocent. That's if the mechs don't get us first.' Cyrus recognised the voice as Zion's. It seemed he and Kevin were having quite the argument. As he listened on the other side of the door, which at this point felt redundant, Cyrus could perfectly understand Kevin's reasoning. They had ruined his life, his perfectly peaceful, self-sufficient life. And now they were asking him for more. They still needed him to help them get into the mech facility.

'We left behind the rest of our colony and walked across a mech-infested city to get here, because Zion told us our only hope was to find The Oracle.' Jennifer's voice this time. 'He said you were the only person who could help.'

There was a short pause as nobody seemed to be talking. Cyrus couldn't tell how the scene looked, but he assumed Kevin was thinking hard on what he'd heard. Finally he spoke.

'You had some nerve coming into my town, and leading *them* here.' His voice was stern. 'I had a future here. I had Gyro-3, I was doing OK. Even when mom—' he paused a moment. 'I was just fine, and now I have nothing. My house is probably burned to ashes because of you.'

'You weren't living,' Zion said. 'You were surviving, just like us. You, here, alone in this ghost town. That's not living, Kevin.'

'Don't you tell me what's living and what ain't!' Zion had pushed Kevin's buttons and he was lashing out. 'The point still stands. I was anonymous here. That's the way I wanted it.

And you come back after all these years and drive me out my own home. The home I've known my whole life.'

'And we're sorry, Kevin. God knows we wish it could have been different. We didn't know what trouble we'd bring by being here,' said Zion. 'I brought the group here, and I'll take responsibility for what happened. But the mechs, they weren't our fault. We're innocent in this, just like you. If we don't do something about it together they'll hunt us and every other living being down until there's no one left.'

'Kevin, we're desperate,' Jennifer added. 'We need you to help us.'

The voices went quiet again and Cyrus cupped his ear against the wooden door, straining to hear.

'OK,' Kevin breathed. 'I'll help you.'

'Thank you,' Jennifer said, with obvious relief in her voice.

A few moments later the door swung open, knocking the crouched Cyrus over. Kevin, who had entered the room first, looked down at him quizzically, before marching off to wake Gyro-3 from his sleep cycle. Jennifer and Zion also took interest in the huddled body of Cyrus on the floor, who was awkwardly nursing a bang to his head.

'Kevin's going to help us,' Zion said.

'Yeah, I heard,' Cyrus replied, dabbing his head with his hand, looking at it each time to check for blood.

Jennifer laughed and walked away. Cyrus swore he could hear her mutter 'moron' under her breath as she left.

Zion helped Cyrus to his feet and the pair followed Jennifer and the others into the centre of the cabin. Mia was now awake and sitting cross-legged on the floor, rubbing her eyes and yawning. Gabriel had resumed his leader-like stance, standing with his arms folded as he waited for the group to settle.

'Will you please accompany me outside?' he said. 'We'd like to say a few words for Doug.' He had Doug's hat in one hand. The group followed him outside, where Jane had finished erecting a makeshift cross from the ground. The two twigs, one longer than the other, were tied together with a shoelace and buried into the dirt so it stayed upright.

Gabriel looked around at the group as they surrounded the small memorial. He watched their sad, tired faces and took a deep breath. Just as he was about to speak, Kevin exited the cabin and stood at the back of the group, followed by the whirring wheels of Gyro-3. Gabriel exhaled deeply with a great sigh as he began.

'We've all lost a great friend,' he started. 'Doug was a good man. He showed what a kind hearted guy he was in his time in our colony, and likewise in his time with Jane and myself in our previous group.' He exchanged a smile with Jane, who obviously appreciated the eulogy. 'He never had a bad word to say about anybody, and he was selfless to the end. After he hurt his leg, he asked me to leave him behind so we could get away without his burden. Such was his nature; he never thought about himself, only how he could help his friends. We could all learn something from Doug, and we'll miss him deeply.' A tear ran down Gabriel's cheek and got lost in his thick beard.

Jane piped up. 'We'll miss you, Doug.'

Gabriel walked to the cross in the ground and placed Doug's hat on top of it, threading the top of the twig through the strap. It stayed put as a light breeze swept through the mesh of the cap.

**

Aiden was checking his backpack, ensuring he hadn't left anything behind before setting off back on the road. The morning had given everything a different outlook. Doug's death had taken its toll on the morale of the group, and the evening had been sombre. The morning light and the chirping of the birds had given things a fresh impetus, as though this day was the start of a new chapter. The memorial for Doug was touching and showed exactly the kind of nature humans should have, reaffirming for Aiden that this was exactly where he needed to be. The dynamic of the group was so much more genuine than when he had been following Michelle's lead. Those were dark days, where the only thing that kept people going was fear. Not the fear of mechs, or of slavers, but the fear of the very person you're blindly following. The fear that you might put a foot wrong and be chastised for it. Aiden didn't feel that here. Instead of being glossed over as an 'occupational hazard', as if it was accepted that people would die in this world, Doug's death was mourned in the same way it would have been before the war. And that's the way it should have been. Aiden felt like he was valued in this group, despite the fact he'd spent barely a few days with them. People like this were exactly the sort of people he could fight for. He thought of Caitlin and Cameron back at the supermarket. Everybody here was doing this for them, for everyone else they'd left in the city, and everyone that had been kidnapped by The Jackal, if the rumours were true. They were fighting for the good, innocent people of this world. And they were doing so together.

'Do you need a hand?' he asked, witnessing Rowley pack his bag with the worst technique he had ever seen. Rowley was practically stuffing his belongings into the backpack, which bulged and strained at the volume that was being shoved into it. 'Maybe you should start again,' he offered. 'There's way too much in there. Here, let me share the load.' He opened his bag up and gestured towards it. He was convinced that the two of them had packed roughly the same amount of food, water and other provisions. But the order, or lack thereof, with which Rowley had packed his seemed to create the illusion that he was carrying much more than he was.

'I don't get it,' Rowley said. 'It all fit in there before.' He pulled out all of the contents of the bag and started over. Aiden gave him a helpful tip as to which items should go in first, to maximise the space.

'I guess you were pretty good at Tetris,' Rowley remarked.

'Sorry?' Aiden pulled a confused look.

'Tetris,' Rowley replied, as plainly as he'd said it the first time. Still he was met with a confused stare. 'Oh right,' he continued. 'You don't know it. It's a really old video game, like *really* old. Sometimes I take for granted that other people haven't looked into this. You know, the history of gaming. It's fascinating, the journey the industry went on to get where it is now. Or where it was.'

'I'll take your word for it,' Aiden winked, and helped Rowley with the rest of the packing. 'So what is it, this game?' he asked.

'Oh it's a classic. Odd shaped blocks drop from the top of the screen and you have to organise them so that they make complete lines. When the lines are complete, they disappear and make way for new ones. It's all about utilising space.'

'Ah right,' Aiden chuckled. 'Sounds right up my alley.' He paused for a moment and thought. 'You said it was a video game?'

Rowley was anticipating this reaction. Everybody reacted this way. Video games were very different to what they used to be. What constituted a game in the twentieth century would barely be categorised in the same field now.

He was fascinated with the history of media. Movies, games, everything. His trivia knowledge on the matter was second-to-none, and he had a particular interest in the older games. Movies from past generations were commonly replayed in the cinemas, as there weren't a lot of new ones being filmed anymore. However video games had progressed quite considerably since the early years, when Tetris, Space Invader and Pac Man were in their prime. People got bored of movies, and there just wasn't a demand for them anymore. Video games became more and more immersive, capturing the viewers' attention and making them feel more a part of the story. This was why the video game industry carried on longer than movies. By the time they stopped being produced, the virtual reality that the games incorporated were so realistic it made the player feel like they were genuinely in the thick of the story. It was like living a movie in real life, but the player controlled the outcome.

Some shied away from the experience; it was simply too real. Others, like Rowley, thrived in it. He insisted that his ability to hold a rifle properly and shoot with surprising accuracy was all down to these games. He often thought the military should start using them as part of their training regime for new recruits. Hell, it had helped him ward off mechs for the last few months, it had to work to some degree. By the time Rowley was born, video games had stopped being produced, but that hadn't stopped him and Cyrus from buying a virtual reality kit and playing them through their youth. The space travel games blew Cyrus away, and had kick-started his love of astronomy. The sensation of drifting through space felt real and the vastness of it all was overwhelming. In the game you were able to travel to distant planets, even solar systems to discover new life. Cyrus had always wondered if there was more out there; if earth wasn't the only planet with intelligent life.

As Rowley zipped his bag closed and lifted it to his shoulder, something fell out of the top and fluttered down onto the floor. It was a thin piece of card and was lying face down. The card had obvious creases in the middle and had a picture of a baseball bat and glove on the back. He picked it up and handed it to Rowley, inspecting the front side as he did so. It was Rowley's prized Jackie Robinson baseball card. The black and white picture of the player on the front, with his name and stats was still visible.

'Looks like you dropped this,' Aiden smiled.

Rowley let out a low whistle as he realised how close he'd been to leaving behind his favourite personal possession. The card was given to him as part of a set by his dad, and had been in his family for years. How many years he didn't know, but he was sure it was long after Jackie Robinson actually played. The card actually had the year 2000 written in small font at the bottom, so it must have been sometime after then. It was probably part of a pack dedicated to legends of the game, or something to that effect. Cards for some of the more noteworthy individuals that graced the sport over a number of decades.

Rowley came from a long line of LA Dodgers fans, and Jackie Robinson made history by being the first black player to play for a Major League Baseball team when he played for the Brooklyn Dodgers, the team that was later moved to LA. It was his favourite card because for this very reason.

'I need to keep a closer eye on that,' he said, and proceeded to tuck the card into his back pocket. 'You know I bet this is worth a lot of money to the right buyer.'

Aiden raised an eyebrow. 'I think you're the only man in this city who'd be willing to buy that. Maybe ten years ago you'd have had a better chance.'

'Ha,' Rowley appreciated the irony. 'I suppose you're right. Besides, I'd never sell it anyway. Reminds me of my dad.'

'That's nice,' said Aiden.

'What is?'

'That you have something to remember your dad by.'

'You know, Jennifer said the same thing to me only last week,' said Rowley. 'She misses her dad a lot. He had to leave when they were quite young. I just hope I can be there for her the way he was.'

'You want to be her surrogate dad?' Aiden pulled a confused look.

'No, no, not like that. You don't get it.'

'I'm just teasing,' Aiden replied playfully. 'I get it, it makes total sense. You know she's independent and able to look after herself, but you know she needs someone to lean on sometimes, and you want to be that someone.'

'Actually, yes, exactly,' Rowley smiled. The pair left the cabin to get some fresh air and wait for the others. The warm sunlight shone down on them immediately, giving them a taste of the heat that was to come on their next journey, however long that would take.

'So what about Caitlin?' Rowley asked.

'What about her?' Aiden looked sheepish.

'You know what about her. What's the story? You together or something?'

Aiden fiddled with the strap on his bag. 'Ah you know, I haven't known her that long so we're not really 'together' per se. She's great though, and Cameron's great too—'

'You like her, it's pretty obvious,' Rowley pressed.

'I love her,' Aiden spluttered, the words coming out before he'd allowed his mouth to say them.

Rowley laughed. 'Well why didn't you just say so? She obviously feels the same way.'

'You think so?'

'Yes, absolutely. Never been surer of anything. You can see it in the way she looks at you. Like you're a superhero or something. Like the way Lois Lane looks at Superman.'

'Superman,' Aiden chuckled. 'I don't know about that.'

'Hey, don't get me wrong, you're a great guy but I don't see you with a cape on your back. But to her you're Superman, trust me.'

Aiden couldn't hide the wide smile that was starting to run from ear to ear. It lasted a moment and then he started to look more pensive as his doubts clouded over again.

'You know, I can't help shaking this feeling that maybe she only likes me because of the situation we're in.'

'How do you mean?'

'Well, I think she's the most amazing woman I've ever met. But what if I'm not the most amazing man she's ever met? What if to her I'm just the most amazing man she's met in the last few months, when everyone's lives changed. What if she just sees me as protection, like the best of a whole bunch of bad options?'

'I doubt that very much,' Rowley offered. 'But either way, that's something you'll figure out with time. But like I said, I've seen the way she looks at you, man. She's all gooey eyed for you.' He impersonated the eye bulge action of a wacky cartoon character, which made Aiden laugh. 'Plus,' he continued. 'You're the best damn father figure Cameron could ask for.'

'Thanks, man.'

The pair were distracted by the cabin door swinging open. Kevin stepped out, followed closely by Gyro-3.

'We're leaving,' he said abruptly. Both Aiden and Rowley could sense the frustration in his voice. Kevin trudged past them, with Gyro-3 hot on his heels, like a dog dutifully following its master. The rest of the group gathered at the entrance of the log cabin, ready to go with their gear. Cyrus was carrying Mia's backpack, while she carried his rifle. She wasn't comfortable with the man of their relationship carrying all the load; she thought it seemed a bit backward. She'd insisted on making a compromise to carry his rifle, swapping her proton pistol with him. Cyrus was grateful for it, he liked chivalry but boy did it hurt his back.

'Where are we going?' Rowley asked after Kevin, who had marched a good distance away already.

'To the factory,' he said bluntly, not bothering to look back. 'The sooner this is all over, the sooner I can go back to my peaceful life without you assholes ruining it.'

'O...K...' Rowley said quietly to himself, so only Aiden could hear. 'I'm not talking to him for a while in case he blows me to pieces.'

'You got that from *'asshole'*?' Aiden replied.

'Yeah, and the shotgun under his arm.'

**

Birds twittered from the trees and a squirrel scurried around with an acorn in its mouth as the group moved back through the forest. It had been twenty minutes since they'd left the log cabin and Cyrus sensed something different about the woods today. It seemed a lot calmer than the day before, which was expected with no mechs chasing them down, firing shots here, there and everywhere. It was as if, to the forest, it had never happened. As if it had no recollection of the death and destruction that had taken hold of it. Today was a new day.

Kevin was trudging on ahead, deliberately staying a good few paces ahead of the rest. Gyro-3 was in close pursuit, its wheels whirring as it worked against the dirt on the undulating path. He must have known where they were going, and seemed to be leading them purposefully in one direction, but Cyrus hadn't been filled in on the details. He assumed they were heading for the mech facility, as they had discussed back at Kevin's house. But he had no idea where that was, or how long it would take to get there on foot.

'Do you know where we're going?' Cyrus stopped to turn to Zion.

'The mech facility,' he replied bluntly.

'And is that within walking distance?' he followed up.

Zion shrugged and attempted to make light of the situation, much to Cyrus's annoyance. 'Everything's within walking distance, assuming you're willing to walk forever.'

Gabriel seemed to share the same annoyance, but had reservations of his own.

'So we walk all day, maybe for two or three days, and then what? What do we do when we get there and realise all of this is a big waste of time?'

'You said the same thing about Kevin, but we found him,' Zion replied.

'That was nothing more than luck and you know it,' Gabriel pointed his finger at Zion. It seemed he was in the mood for an argument. Jane moved in quickly to defuse it.

'Luck or no luck, Zion was right and we found someone who can help us learn more about the mechs. That's what we set out to do. We're all working towards the same goal.'

'Remember what Isaac said, about the vision he had?' Cyrus reminded Gabriel. 'I shared that same vision. I saw everything he saw. I know you have to trust something you don't understand, something you can't explain. But I need to ask you to have faith. We have to go with our gut now. What does it tell you?'

Gabriel grunted, a sound that showed his lack of confidence in this plan that to him was based on the hallucinations of a crazy man and the gullibility of another who desperately wished it to be true. Gabriel knew Cyrus hadn't given up trying to find his family, and as much as he wished they were alive and well he couldn't shake the feeling that he was chasing a lost cause. In his eyes, Cyrus was believing a false hope of what he wished was true and ignoring the reality that they were probably dead. Isaac's vision had ignited Cyrus's hope in finding his family. Who knows what crazy hallucinations Isaac had, but the vision Cyrus claimed to have seen could have been nothing more than remembering a dream he'd had of his family. Gabriel had always been a logical thinker, and struggled with the idea of anything that couldn't be explained, something otherworldly that was out of his control or understanding. This shared vision between Isaac and Cyrus seemed too farfetched to be true. It just didn't make sense.

'My gut tells me this is crazy,' he replied. 'But I'm out of alternatives.'

Up ahead, Kevin had stopped near an unusually large tree. The trunk stretched wider than the group had ever seen. The tree looked old, perhaps the oldest tree in the forest, and struck everyone with a sense of awe, as if its size was only a clue to its real significance.

Kevin paced back and forth, and then walked the full circumference of the tree, clearly looking for something. Finally he found it and started to feel the bark of the trunk, running smooth strokes of his hand across it.

'What's happening?' Rowley whispered, still intent on avoiding Kevin's attention. The shotgun was slung over his shoulder, but Rowley was keeping one eye on it at all times.

'The Oracle is working,' Zion replied with a smile, almost as if he knew what Kevin was doing.

Rowley decided to leave the ambiguous answer be and continued to watch Kevin's progress. After another moment, Kevin moved back from the tree and turned to Gyro-3, who was waiting patiently by his side. He touched a button on the little robot's front panel, and a blue light emanated from it, producing a holographic display. It looked just like the one they'd seen from the disc-shaped device in the house the previous day. Kevin finally spoke, the first time since leaving the cabin.

'The mech facility is another day's walk from here,' he said. Cyrus felt his heart sink as he mentally prepared himself for another day in the heat, another day further away from finding the answers he needed.

'So it's a good job we're not walking,' Kevin followed up with a wry smile. The hologram coming from Gyro-3 moved over to the tree trunk and revealed the map of the mech facility they'd seen before. It then zoomed out to a point where they could see the forest and the facility on the same screen, with the city also in view.

'It's in the middle of nowhere,' Rowley said.

'I think that was the point,' Jennifer commented. 'They didn't want anyone to know what was going on there.'

The hologram changed again as a dotted line from the edge of the forest to the facility was made, plotting their route across the desert-like terrain to the facility, which as Rowley had pointed out, really was in the middle of nowhere. The forest could be seen to the west of the city, however the facility was across the north-east, seemingly away from any civilisation.

'If we're not walking, how exactly are we going to get there?' Aiden asked, knowing full well Kevin was waiting for someone to ask that very question.

'I'm glad you asked,' Kevin said, almost with an air of grandeur starting to take hold, like he was waiting for some big reveal. Gabriel grunted again in impatience.

Kevin crouched down to the base of the tree trunk and broke off a loose bit of bark. Reaching his hands inside, he retrieved a heavy black box. It looked like a safe of some sort, but much smaller. He punched in a six digit number on the touch screen display and it opened with a click. He looked at the group staring at him incredulously and offered a quick explanation.

'I keep a spare set in this safe. It's heavy enough that the wildlife don't run off with it.'

'Run off with what?' Cyrus asked, just as Kevin produced a set of keys from the box.

'The keys to our ride.'

CHAPTER TWENTY-SEVEN

Kevin stood there, swinging the keys around his finger, the sound of the jingling drawing everyone's attention. It was a strange sight, and everybody was confused by it.

'Our ride?' April asked. 'You have a working car?'

It was a fair question to ask, and the confusion on everyone's faces was wholly justified. Ever since the Volt-Auto servers were destroyed in the war, all of the electric cars in the city had been inoperable. The strict safety procedures in place meant that even if a car broke down, the passengers were unable to drive it themselves. Automated driving had become the standard, and a human getting behind the wheel was deemed too dangerous, not to mention illegal.

'I don't understand,' Cyrus said. 'The driving grid was disabled two years ago. Nobody has been driven in a car since then.'

'Well, that's not technically true,' Kevin smirked. 'Gyro-3 has been driven around many times. Isn't that right, buddy?' He looked at his robot friend to affirm his claim. Gyro-3 retracted the hologram from the tree and turned to the group.

'My master is correct. He has driven me around in his vehicle on multiple occasions. My master drives a Toyota Tundra pickup—'

'That's enough, Gyro-3.' Kevin cut him off. He cursed under his breath. 'You always give the game away.'

The little robot didn't quite know how to process his master's annoyance, and just stayed still for a while.

'A Tundra? You have a Toyota Tundra?' Gabriel was in shock as he emphasised the car model like it was something truly remarkable. 'Anybody else think that's a little implausible?'

The rest of the group fell silent, confirming their ignorance of this particular make of car.

Gabriel decided to get them up to speed quickly. 'Toyota cars haven't been around for decades, ever since the government created Volt-Auto to become the only car brand in the country. When they made driving illegal and rolled out driverless cars, every other type of car was tracked down and destroyed. Don't you think it's a little strange that they missed one car?' He folded his arms and appraised Kevin with suspicion. 'And,' he continued. 'Those keys you're swinging around your finger, those are old style keys. Every electric car in the last fifty years has had solely remote locking. Which means this Toyota of yours must run on gasoline. There's no way an internal combustion engine car would run today.'

'But he has the keys,' said Cyrus. 'He's telling the truth.'

'Anyone could keep a spare set around. Doesn't mean they're useful for anything.'

Kevin was clearly getting agitated by Gabriel's accusations. He expected this to play out differently, for the group to at least be grateful for this remarkable realisation. He now felt silly for adding so much theatrics to his reveal.

'OK, OK. This was clearly a bad idea. Let me just show you the car, alright?' He gestured behind him into the forest, where a faint pathway could be seen leading through the trees.

It didn't take long for the group to navigate the path to the eastern edge of the forest. As they reached a clearing Kevin spun around to address them again.

'Maybe I should have just taken you straight here.'

Up ahead was a cluster of buildings. They were dilapidated beyond belief, but Cyrus could work out what they had originally been. It was an old gas station, and it had clearly been abandoned, made obsolete a number of decades ago. Beside it was an old garage.

Kevin led the group to the garage and used the smaller key on the set he was still jingling in his hands to unlock the padlock that held down the shutter doors.

'Retro security, man,' Rowley admired. It seemed his love for old technology extended even to padlocks.

Kevin ignored him and opened the shutters. Inside was dark and it took a while for the sunlight to fully illuminate the space as the shutter was slowly pushed upwards. Cyrus could make out shelves along the sides, with tools of various shapes and sizes scattered along them. But it was the centre of the garage that held everyone's attention. Right in the middle was a big lump, covered by tarpaulin.

'Here she is,' Kevin said.

As Cyrus continued to scour the space, he noticed a row of jerry cans on the floor by the shelves, which looked like they must have contained some kind of liquid.

Without further ado, and clearly still annoyed that his reveal of the vehicle had already been ruined, Kevin marched into the garage and ripped the tarpaulin off the lump, revealing the black outline of a car. A big car, bigger than

Cyrus had ever seen. Electric cars had been produced in much smaller forms, seating no more than four people. This machine in front of him had enough space for five, with room for more in the open cargo hold of the tailgate.

'Some of you will have to sit in the trunk, and hold on to something. I'm warning you now, I drive the way I drive, and that's that.'

Cyrus looked over to Gabriel, and wished he could document his expression. He hadn't said a word since the garage door had opened. His face was the perfect example of pure awe. It was clear he had never seen a vehicle like this before either, outside of images from the internet. Compared to the small electric cars that used to transport them around, this vehicle was an absolute beast. This was reaffirmed when Kevin inserted his key into the ignition and started it up. The engine roared into life, making everyone jump. The pickup truck had a menacing look to it, emphasised by the large grill at the front, grimacing with large teeth, almost mech-like. As far as pickup trucks from the twenty-first century went, it was fairly normal in size and appearance, but compared to the tiny electric driverless cars they were used to, it was absolutely monstrous.

As Kevin mashed the accelerator to the floor, the beast jolted on the spot, startling the group. Cyrus flung himself to the floor to get out of its way, before the sound of laughter made him realise it hadn't gone anywhere. Zion was pointing and sniggering to himself, much to Cyrus's embarrassment.

'How in the hell did you get this thing?' Gabriel finally managed. 'They tracked them all down, every last one of them.'

'Well they didn't get this one,' Kevin winked through the windshield. He stood up in the car, his short, stocky frame barely allowing his head to reach up through the sunroof. 'I actually found it a few years ago, right here in this garage. The keys were in the old kiosk of the gas station. How the government missed this place, I'll never know.'

'What I want to know is how it's still in such great shape,' Zion quipped. 'I wish I could age that well.'

'And the gasoline,' Jennifer added. 'Where did you find that?'

'There was quite a large stash in this garage, and some of the pumps there still had a little left.' He pointed to the gas station across the way.

'That's incredible,' said Jennifer.

'I've managed to ration it well, to be fair. I only drive for fun, and I wanted to keep having something to look forward to, so I only drive it twice a year. Been this way for nearly three years now. Reckon I've got enough gas for another six.'

'You're extremely disciplined,' Gabriel acknowledged, finally giving Kevin what was as close to a compliment as could be expected from him.

'And you'd be willing to drive us to the mech facility?' Cyrus jumped in, eager to get back to the point at hand.

'It'd be damn cruel if I wasn't, wouldn't it?' Kevin grimaced. 'What are you waiting for? Hop in. He opened the front passenger door and the group started to pile in. Half the group were treated to the luxury of comfortable seating in the five seats that were available, while the rest sat in the trunk and clung onto anything they could find. Gyro-3 rolled to the rear of the vehicle and used its long orangutan-like arms to lift itself very ungracefully over the tailgate. It whirred with delight at having successfully climbed aboard.

Kevin opened up the glove box and retrieved a pair of aviator sunglasses, putting them on and checking his appearance in the rear-view mirror.

'Badass,' muttered Rowley, amused by the whole thing.

The engine of the pickup truck rumbled and the whole group could feel the car vibrating. Kevin revved the engine a couple of times for effect, creating a little apprehension among his passengers. The vehicle snarled like a beast readying itself for a lunge towards its prey. As he shifted the stick into drive, the car took off, throwing the passengers back into their seats, and nearly causing those in the trunk to fall out the back. Kevin exited the garage in full throttle and lurched the vehicle around the corner onto the road that led away from the forest, the tyres squealing as he did so.

It took a few minutes for those in the trunk to fully relax, but the drive became a lot smoother after Kevin had got used to the feel of the car again. Kevin gave a small device to Mia, who found herself riding shotgun. It was the disc-shaped device from the house, and after fiddling around with it she was able to replicate the holographic map that Kevin had showed them earlier, plotting their progress towards the facility. Estimated journey time was two and a half hours, but at the speed Kevin was driving she supposed it would take much less than that.

She looked at Kevin as he drove. He looked completely in his element, a faint smile staying on his face as he gripped the wheel and tore up the road ahead. She was grateful that despite everything, there were still some small comforts to hold. Kevin's was driving, hers was spending time alone with Cyrus. She looked in the wing mirror to adjust her now windswept hair. She hadn't considered the breeze that would take hold of it with the windows down. Through the mirror, she caught a glimpse of Cyrus leaning on the side of the open cargo hold in the back, his arm trailing over the edge.

As the world rushed by at sixty miles an hour, Cyrus appreciated the breeze on his face. They weren't travelling much faster than any driverless electric car of the modern era, but the combination of being outside, the powerful engine rumbling through the vehicle and Kevin's reckless driving made it feel so much faster. He leaned across the side to get more of the cool air as it rushed by the truck. He caught sight of Mia playing with her hair in the front seat and after a moment her eyes met his through the wing mirror. They smiled at each other, sharing their enjoyment of this new experience. The distance between them over the last few days had well and truly disappeared now, much to Cyrus's relief. He hoped it would continue in this vein long into the future. He looked about the cargo hold at the rest of his companions, and then into those who had begun chatting away to each other inside the car. He was proud of each and every one of them, and infinitely glad for their company. He then patted Rowley on the shoulder, a small gesture of friendship which he showed all too rarely these days. He thought again of how he'd treated Rowley in recent times, of how judgemental and rude he'd been. Yet, despite all this, his faithful companion remained by his side, unwavering in his loyalty. Rowley was a special kind of person, the genuine best friend that didn't come around too often. Cyrus thought that it was about time he started returning the favour.

'Rowley.'

'Yeah, buddy?' Rowley's smiling face was the same as always when Cyrus spoke to him. Sometimes it bordered on creepy, but he knew that behind it was the best intentions of a sweet guy willing to do anything for his friend. Cyrus considered himself lucky to have him around. If he treated his significant other with as much kindness and gratitude as he showed him, then Jennifer was a lucky girl. Cyrus often thought Rowley was punching above his weight with her, but the more he saw them together the more he realised that looks weren't everything. Perhaps Jennifer wasn't as shallow as he was. As far as likeable personalities went, Rowley had it in spades, so it was easy to see why she was drawn to him.

Cyrus realised he'd been daydreaming once more and was staring at Rowley with a completely vacant look. Rowley was used to this, having grown up with Cyrus.

'Earth to Cyrus, you're zonking out again.'

Cyrus quickly snapped out of it. 'Sorry.'

'What was it you wanted?'

'Oh, right. I was going to ask you about your writing.'

'Oh, that.' Rowley looked uncomfortable at Cyrus bringing it up. 'It wasn't that serious, just a kind of journal I guess.'

'Like a diary?' Cyrus asked.

'No, a journal. It's different.'

'Oh, OK.' Cyrus sensed Rowley was being protective, like he didn't want Cyrus to know about it at all. This was surprising, since Rowley usually couldn't wait to tell him about literally anything that was going on in his life.

'What was the journal about?' Cyrus pressed.

Rowley still looked uncomfortable, but after a moment's hesitation he decided to tell him.

'It was about our life, our experience since the war ended.' Cyrus could sense the relief that he was finally comfortable telling him about it. 'If ever the world goes back to normal, I thought people might want to know what it was like.'

'That's a really cool idea,' Cyrus said, much to Rowley's surprise.

'Really? I thought you'd make fun of me for it,' he replied.

Cyrus suddenly felt cold inside. Cold and ashamed.

I'm such a jerk.

'I'm sorry I gave you that impression,' he said. 'I think you should keep doing it. When we fix this mess, you can tell our story.'

The pair exchanged a smile, and Cyrus could almost feel everything going back to normal already.

**

As the forest disappeared behind them, the terrain quickly became dusty, like the roads of the city. Clouds gathered above and the pickup truck drove onward into the wilderness. The outline of the city could be spotted to their right, but it would quickly disappear as they got closer to the facility.

The landscape was barren, almost desert-like in its appearance. The tyres chewed up the earth as the old vehicle pressed on. Kevin looked down at the dashboard, which indicated the fuel gauge. There was a blinking red light letting him know the fuel was low. They'd need to stop soon to empty one of the jerry cans he'd brought with him into the tank.

Mia looked across the dashboard at the light. 'Do we have enough gas to get there?'

'Yeah, we should have plenty. I mean, I can't judge how far it will take us. I never usually drive this far out.'

Dust started picking up around the car and the light faded slightly as the clouds covered the sun. They'd lived in the city long enough to know when a dust storm was brewing, and sure enough they were about to be in the epicentre of one.

'Let's stop before we hit the storm. It'll be easier to fill up if I can see what I'm doing. I don't want the tank to fill up with sand either.'

Kevin hit the brakes a little too vigorously, and the car juddered to a halt, throwing everyone forward and sending the people in the trunk flying into each other.

'Sorry,' Kevin muttered, barely audible enough for even Mia to hear. He climbed out of the car and traipsed over to the fuel tank.

'Can you pass me a gas can?' he called to the group in the trunk. The dust storm was picking up and Kevin found it difficult to hear their reply, if they'd even heard him.

'I said, can you pass me—'

Before he could finish, a jerry can was hurled out from the tailgate and onto the floor. As it hit the deck it unsettled the sand that was starting to collect on the ground, sending some of it flying into Kevin's face. He gritted his teeth as he blinked to get it out of his eyes. He cursed under his breath.

'Careful with that,' he called back to the group.

The storm was almost in full flow now and he needed to act quickly. No doubt the people in the trunk were getting peppered with dust and sand too. He opened the fuel cap and unscrewed the jerry can carefully. He then poured the contents into the tank as delicately as he could through his obscured vision. It seemed to work and after emptying the can he simply hurled it away into the wilderness. He couldn't see where it had gone, as his vision stretched no more than a few feet away through the storm.

As quick as he could, he scrambled back to the driver seat and slammed the door shut.

'Let's go!' he enthused, slammed down on the accelerator once more. But the car didn't move. The engine roared but it just jerked on the spot. Kevin looked down at the dashboard. The fuel gauge had lifted off empty; something else must have been wrong.

'Is it one of these things?' Mia pointed to the gear stick, which was set in the park position. Kevin slapped his head and put his aviators back on. Shifting the stick to drive, he stamped back on the accelerator and the vehicle roared to life, leaping away like a gazelle escaping a lion.

'Let's go, again!' he shouted as the truck ate up the road ahead of them.

In the trunk of the vehicle, Cyrus and his friends were struggling with the storm. The welcome breeze of before was now replaced by the harsh battering of sand and dust on their faces, forcing them to duck their heads and close their eyes. Cyrus fumbled around his bag for his scarf, and in doing so almost lost the entire backpack to the wind that swirled around the truck. Luckily he'd packed smart, leaving the scarf at the top, so he didn't need to rummage far before retrieving it. He zipped the bag back up and tucked it between his legs, then set to wrapping the scarf around his neck and pulling it over his nose and mouth.

The truck hit a pothole in the road, causing it to jolt suddenly. A great crunching sound as the truck jumped up and then hit the deck hard suggested that the suspension wasn't in as good condition as the rest of the vehicle. Rowley was flung on top of Cyrus, who was winded from the sudden unexpected weight. Rowley rolled over away from him and kept prone to avoid falling out of the car the next time it jolted. Cyrus lay on his back gasping for breath, the scarf still wrapped tightly around his neck and the lower half of his face. The sudden impact had shocked him into opening his eyes, and quickly the battering of dust and sand made him close them again. He grasped his arms around himself as he spluttered and coughed.

All around the car was the yellowy-brown tint of the storm. Up in the driver's seat, Kevin struggled to see more than a few feet in front of him, yet he insisted on continuing at high speed. Mia was terrified in the passenger seat as her field of vision was nothing but dust and sand hitting the windshield like hail in a blizzard. She still held the disc in her hands, with the blue hologram of the route showing they were nearing their destination. Kevin glanced over and asked for an update.

'Nearly there,' she shouted above the sound of the storm. She had wound up her window minutes earlier, but not quickly enough to prevent the inside of the car from becoming covered with dust. 'Any second now.'

'If this storm persists we might miss it altogether,' Kevin replied.

'Or drive right into it,' Zion added from the back seat.

'Maybe we should slow down,' April said. 'I don't like how fast we're going when we can't see where we are.'

'Don't worry, if we crash, this baby's fitted with airbags,' Kevin said candidly. 'We won't be harmed.'

'Erm, Kevin, I'm not sure that's right. You're not even wearing your seatbelt,' April replied. Sure enough, everyone had buckled themselves in, except for Kevin.

He hesitated a moment, and then started to lift his foot from the accelerator. Coincidentally, moments later the dust storm began to settle and the road ahead became a bit clearer. The truck passed a sign that read *Danger, Restricted Area*. They knew they must have been getting close to the facility. The storm finally lifted and the view on the horizon came into focus. Directly ahead, about a mile or so away was the mech facility, just as the hologram had shown. It looked bigger than they had imagined, but perhaps that was the illusion of the map, making it seem smaller than the reality.

The facility looked like a giant factory, with a large central building with white walls and a flat roof dominating the landscape. Other smaller buildings veered off the main one from each side. Cyrus recognised some of the buildings from Kevin's brief the previous day. As they drove nearer to the place, Cyrus was filled with a mixture of excitement and dread. He hoped more than anything that the answers he sought about the mechs would be found here. But at the same time he couldn't shake the feeling that there was something very wrong about this place. It was like the scene of a horror film, as if they were going to investigate the laboratory where Dr Frankenstein created his monster.

CHAPTER TWENTY-EIGHT

The truck pulled up to the carpark, just in front of the main entrance to the facility. The place looked deserted. If the rumours were true, this place had been abandoned for years. The last iteration of mechs had been produced a number of years ago, the ones roaming the city seemingly the last remaining ones from this region. Cyrus wondered what had happened to the rest. Surely if there had been more it meant that there was a way to destroy them. Unless they had been stationed in other parts of the country, which was likely as according to Kevin this was the main research and manufacturing facility of robotics in the country. Most, if not all of the country's mech defence robots came from this factory.

The carpark was open plan and spread out far and wide, like that of a theme park. Cyrus could see that there were numbers indicating the separations between each section of the lot, probably to help the employees remember where they had parked. The size of the place gave a clue as to the scale of the mech project. Hundreds, if not thousands of people must have worked there. Cyrus wondered how many of them knew exactly what terror they were contributing to.

As his friends stepped out of the car, Cyrus turned to the companions that had shared the horrendous journey in the trunk with him. Like him, they were covered in dust and were brushing themselves down before hopping over the side onto the ground. He was pleased to see that Gyro-3 had made it through the journey unscathed. Its heavy frame must have kept it low to the truck through all the bumps and jolts. Plus it seemed to be gripping the tailgate pretty firmly with its claw-like hands. Cyrus wasn't sure if the little robot was programmed to understand fear, but it seemed to be fine.

If that didn't scare it, nothing will.

Gabriel reminded everyone to give their weapons a quick clean to make sure no dust had got inside the mechanisms. The last thing they needed was to come face-to-face with yet another mech and have the guns let them down. Faulty rifles were already too common, as Mia had the misfortune of experiencing not that long ago. Gabriel's military background did come in handy quite often; Cyrus would never have thought to look after his rifle, or perhaps have been too lazy to do so. It was this attention to detail that would give them more of a fighting chance.

Cyrus dusted off his plasma rifle dutifully and started turning it over to check it from all sides. He wasn't sure what he was supposed to be looking at, but he thought he should at least be looking like he knew what he was doing to appease Gabriel. Truth be told, he didn't know a lot about guns, let alone how to dismantle them and clean them properly. The blue glow of the plasma container underneath the barrel was still as bright as before, which gave him enough confidence to believe there was nothing obviously wrong with it. He thought he should check with Gabriel just in case. He held the rifle up and pointed to the plasma container, which was met by an approving nod of the head.

Good enough.

Cyrus placed the rifle on the ground, along with his backpack, and took off his shoes to empty them of the sand that had somehow crept in there during the storm. The sand poured out like an hourglass, and he found the same to be true for the other shoe. Those who had shared the uncomfortable journey in the back with him all did the same. Kevin retrieved a rag from a pocket and started wiping down Gyro-3.

'This place is huge,' Rowley said, in awe of the facility ahead of them. 'The map didn't do it justice.'

'How long will it take to find what we're looking for?' April asked. 'Do we even know where to begin?'

'We don't even know what we're looking for,' Gabriel said. 'For all we know this could be a big waste of time. But I accept that we don't have any other options right now.'

'So we just walk around aimlessly until we find something?'

'Yes.'

'We won't be walking around aimlessly,' Zion piped up. 'Kevin knows this place like the back of his hand, and I remember it pretty well too. I wasn't authorised to access some parts of the facility, but I know enough to get around. Let's just get in and see what we can find.'

'OK, great plan,' Jennifer added, with a hint of sarcasm. 'Only one problem. How do we get in?'

The group stared at the giant building in front of them. There didn't seem to be any obvious doorway marked *Entrance*. Cyrus remembered what Kevin had said back at his house.

'Kevin, didn't you say we should go to the service entrance, where the deliveries used to go?'

'Correct,' Kevin replied, still attending to Gyro-3.

'OK, which way is that?'

He paused and shook off the dust from the rag, letting out a loud sigh. 'I'll take you there, just give me a minute.'

Cyrus exchanged a glance with Zion, looking for guidance on how to respond. Zion gave him a hand gesture that suggested he be patient. The smile etched on his face let him know that this was probably something he should get used to, and Zion had clearly seen it a hundred times before. Kevin didn't have the best people skills, but now wasn't really the time to be trying to change that. Besides, they needed him much more than he needed them. Cyrus decided to go with it and keep him sweet.

After what felt like an excessively long time, Kevin finally withdrew from his crouched position next to Gyro-3 and returned the old rag to his pocket.

'You've got to look after things if you want them to last long enough for you to enjoy them.' Kevin's words substantiated the attachment he had with his robot friend. He had been the first person Cyrus had ever known to successfully create a companion from scratch, and he'd done it exactly the way he wanted it. Gyro-3 was certainly a quirky little machine, and Cyrus was sure that it annoyed Kevin sometimes. But perhaps that was the part of it that made it seem almost human. There was a reason why Kevin had stopped designing the robot at the third iteration; he must have found the right balance to make his friend imperfectly perfect.

'Alright.' Kevin scratched his shaggy, patchy beard as he looked at the building, almost sizing it up. 'Let's do this.'

**

The service entrance was a short drive away from the carpark. The place they were planning to access was much smaller than the main building, but Kevin had promised slightly more lax security there. Cyrus could see that it connected to the main building through a corridor a few stories above ground level, so in theory they should be able to access the central building just fine.

A light breeze blew from the west, reminding him of the storm they had only just escaped. The ground was grainy with sand and other dirt, giving evidence to suggest that dust storms were common in this place.

The service entrance had a doorway that was plenty large enough for the pickup truck to enter. This was hardly surprising as it was probably used to receiving shipments of materials in much larger forms. Kevin switched the engine off and the rumbling of the truck stopped dead. Cyrus clambered over the tailgate and landed hard on the ground. Despite spending most of the last few hours in the pickup, his legs ached all over.

There was a spooky feel to the facility, but the prospect of walking around inside was more attractive than being out in the heat for longer. It was highly unlikely that the place would be air-conditioned, given the circumstances, but Cyrus enjoyed imagining it that way. The steel watch on his wrist had heated up in the sunlight and was hot to the touch. He tapped the face and watched the minute hand for movement. The face had been scratched from his recent encounters with mechs; probably the result of one of his many falls. His cargo pants were ripped at both knees now, the fabric torn away to reveal the cuts on his legs. The gash on his arm from his near-death experience with a panther the other day was still sore, but there seemed to be no lasting damage. He didn't mind if he was left with scarring, he considered himself lucky enough that he had escaped with his life, let alone with the arm still intact.

'How do we open the door? Do we need a key card?' Jennifer had left the group by the pickup truck and was now right in front of the door, waving her arms about as if the door would open if it detection motion.

'Yes, and we don't have one,' Kevin replied plainly.

'So what's the plan? Ya'll just knock and see if someone's in?' Jane's voice now.

Cyrus faced Zion, who looked a little uneasy. He wasn't sure if a confidence booster was what he needed, or whether he just wanted to hide away altogether. He went with the confidence booster.

'Zion's going to work his magic on it.' He fired a wink at Zion, who flipped him off in return. It was then that Cyrus realised how sarcastic it had sounded.

'Alright,' Zion groaned. 'Let's get this over with. Kevin, I might need your help.'

Kevin nodded and began rummaging around the footwell of the truck. He was head-first in there for a while, his legs sticking comically up in the air. Finally he found what he was looking for and, using the driver's seat as leverage to haul his stocky frame back up, returned to his feet. In his hand was a screwdriver and a pair of pliers.

'High-tech,' Rowley joked.

'If I told you I knew what I was doing, would you believe me?' Kevin asked.

'Not a chance,' Rowley replied with a smile, folding his arms expectantly. Kevin walked past him, and together with Zion headed for the door.

'The second that door opens,' Kevin called, facing away from Rowley. 'Prepare for an ass-whooping.'

Rowley let out a hearty chuckle. He was glad to finally get some banter out of Kevin.

'Looking forward to it,' he called after him. He watched as Kevin snapped his pliers together in a menacing fashion. Then a voice came from behind him.

'I thought you weren't talking to him for a while?' Aiden said.

'Yeah I know. But he left his shotgun in the truck, so I'm golden.'

Jennifer left the doorway and walked back to the truck, sitting inside one of the rear passenger seats to catch a moment of shade. She twisted the cap off her water bottle and took a few sips from it. She couldn't help but exhale loudly with satisfaction at how refreshing it felt.

'OK boys, show us what you've got,' she called to Kevin and Zion, who had now reached the door and were looking at a control panel to the side of the key card slot. The control panel was a flat metal box protruding from the wall. To the side of the key card slot was a black screen, around five inches wide and three tall. Kevin touched it with a stubby finger and the screen lit up, displaying a message that read *swipe card, await green light and tap screen to open door*. The instructions were simple enough. Zion bypassed the first two commands, tapping the screen to test if the door would unlock. The key card slot flashed an angry red and a loud noise sounded.

'Access denied.' The voice recording was that of a softly spoken, if not slightly robotic woman. Kevin looked at Zion with a raised eyebrow.

'Worth a try,' he replied.

The noise had caught the attention of the others, who were watching intently from the truck.

'Everything OK?' Jane called. The pair ignored her.

Zion instead turned his attention to the metal plate protruding from the wall, and used the screwdriver to twist out the many screws holding the panel in place. He let each one fall to the ground as he moved on to the next. There was no point replacing them afterwards. The panel came off easily, revealing an intricate set of wires, far more complex than the ones from the supermarket. Zion winced at the sight of it.

'That makes me feel sick,' he commented, peering into the web of colourful wires running this way and that, seemingly in no orderly fashion.

'You want to win some brownie points with your friends, now's your chance,' said Kevin.

'OK, OK,' Zion began to concentrate. 'Red wire running left to right, blue up and down. Green and yellow, hmm.' He paused for a moment and looked at Kevin. 'Something's odd about the way this thing is wired. Like someone came in here and messed around with it.'

'This whole facility is messed up,' said Kevin. 'Everything about it, every tiny detail, completely rushed.' He peered into the panel, observing the wires. 'Look at the circuitry here, it's a joke. They were in over their heads from the start.' Zion knew he wasn't just talking about the control panel.

'So how are we doing this? Cut the wires and hope for the best?' Zion asked.

'No, we don't want it to lock down,' Kevin replied. 'The system's still live, so if we cut the wire it will shut itself down and lock us out.'

'So they failsafe the door, but not the man-eating robots?' Zion took a step back and waved the screwdriver at the panel.

'OK, so we need to be smarter. How do we be smarter?' he ran his hand through his hair as he thought.

'You growing out that afro again?' Kevin asked.

'What?'

'Your hair. I haven't seen it that long since the first week of college.'

'What has that got to do with anything?' Zion asked, perplexed by the sudden tangent in conversation.

'Just asking,' Kevin replied. 'And I'm trying to distract you. Apparently it helps you think with a clearer head if you think about something else for a while.'

'Well now I'm just thinking about my hair.'

'OK, forget it.'

Zion went back to studying the panel of wires in front of him.

'Shall we just try turning it off and on again?' he joked. Suddenly, a brainwave hit him, almost a moment of eureka. He stared off into the distance as he pondered it. 'That's it!'

'That's being smarter?'

'Shut up and listen. You didn't by chance bring your old key card with you, did you?'

Kevin pulled a blank white card out of his back pocket and flipped it over, revealing the magnetic strip running down the back side. 'Of course.'

'Great!' Zion was starting to get excited. He hoped more than anything that his assumption was right. He pointed to the panel of wires with the screwdriver. 'You see that wire at the back, the blue one tucked away in the corner?'

Kevin followed the screwdriver, looking deep into the mess of colourful wiring. 'Uhuh.'

'Whatever simple chump wired this thing was clearly in a rush, but they were also forgetful. They couldn't remember which wire was which, so they labelled them.' He carefully used the screwdriver to move some of the closer wires aside so Kevin could get a better look. Sure enough, on the wall by the blue wire in the corner was a sticky label with the letters *CCD* on it. The wire was connected to a plug in the wall at the back of the panel.

'CCD?' Kevin asked.

'Clearance Code Database. That wire runs through to a computer that remotely accesses the central server. There's a database of access codes programmed into each key card, held on the server. Yours won't work because it's been disabled. Same as mine.'

'So what's the plan?'

'Try the card,' Zion said. 'Just to make sure.'

Kevin swiped the card through the slot. The familiar red light flashed and the touch screen read *access denied*. The softly spoken woman's voice came again.

'And now?' Kevin wasn't following Zion's thought process.

'Do you guys need a hand?' Aiden called from the truck. Kevin waved an irritated hand to discourage him.

'We're fine. Thanks though,' Zion called, before getting back to work. 'That disc of yours, the one with the schematics. Does it have access to the central server?'

'No, not a chance. Even if the server was accessible, we wouldn't be able to hack our way in. It's impenetrable.'

'Not if the connection is rebooted,' Zion smiled.

'I'm not following.'

'If the connection from this door to the server is lost, the door will lockdown, correct?'

'Correct.'

'And in theory, re-establishing that connection will force the computer to reboot its connection with the server.'

'Well…' Kevin thought on this. 'Well yes, in theory.' Then the penny dropped and he figured out what Zion was planning to do. Zion could see his eyes grow wide, reaffirming for him that the plan may actually be plausible.

'The server will only allow one terminal to access it from this door,' Kevin started to finish Zion's plan for him. 'If we use the disc to clone the terminal on the other side of this door, we can fake our way into the database and re-enable the card.'

'Bingo.'

The pair shared a smile and began to laugh. From Zion's point of view, it was good to see Kevin laugh again. It was a rare sight, and one he'd barely seen since college.

'Hey, remember when we hacked the Dean's social media account and posted all kinds of crazy shit on there?' Zion said.

Kevin laughed as he remembered the event. 'And when you rerouted the lights in the exam hall to flicker on and off in Morse code?'

'B, C, A, B,' Zion chuckled. 'I loved multiple choice.'

'You know I was in that exam.'

'Yeah, and thanks to me you got an A.'

The pair laughed again, this time for much longer. The others waiting by the truck thought they'd gone mad.

'Alright, buddy,' Zion said at last as he calmed down. 'Let's go break into Fort Knox.'

'More like Fort *Knots*,' Kevin gestured to the mess of wires once more, before dashing back to the truck to retrieve the disc.

As he reached the truck, Cyrus could see a glint in his eye; an eagerness with a hint of excitement. He could see that whatever they were doing, this was something they enjoyed. He had no idea about security systems, or electronics in general for that matter. His best effort would have been to try and ram the door with the pickup. Just as well there were a variety of skill sets in the group. Cyrus wondered what his skill set would be. What would be his superpower that differentiated himself from everyone else in the group, the one thing they'd depend on him for? He had absolutely no idea.

Kevin retrieved the disc Mia had been holding onto for the drive and raced back to the door where Zion was waiting. His short legs meant his strides were small and he had to work harder than most to cover the ground.

'Alright, let's fire this baby up,' he panted as he pressed a button on the disc. The hologram appeared instantaneously, displaying the map they had been using on the ride to the facility. Kevin held the disc in one hand and used the other to swipe frantically at the hologram, which twisted its shape in line with his hand movements. The map disappeared and was replaced by a blank space with nothing more than a command line. A small line blinked in the corner, a cursor awaiting Kevin's input.

Kevin set the disc on the ground and sat, crossed legged, facing it. He used a hand gesture to pull up a QWERTY keyboard from the bottom of the hologram, and proceeded to type away, punching in each letter with purpose. The blinking cursor underneath the first letter moved to the right each time a new letter was inputted. Kevin wrote *command* and hit enter. The cursor moved below the word and tucked back into the bottom left of the window. Next he wrote *establish connection* and then hit enter once more. The same result. He then inputted a series of further commands, and hit enter again.

Zion watched the console as it lingered for a while after the enter button had been touched. The blinking cursor did not move to the next line. It was as if it was lagging, as though it was processing something. The disc was trying to access the terminal to the server. The wait was excruciating as the pair stared at the hologram, waiting for something to happen. If it failed to find the server, it would be the end of plan A. There was no plan B.

The cursor moved down and to the left, and several lines under the last command were automatically generated. The disc had found the server, successfully mimicking the terminal on the other side of the door. Kevin clapped his hands together and rubbed them vigorously, pleased with his progress. Zion let out a loud exhale, suddenly aware he'd been holding his breath.

The last line on the console read *access*. It was awaiting a simple input of 'Y' before it tried to establish a connection with the server.

'OK,' Zion said. 'I'm going to cut the connection from the door to the terminal. When I put the cable back, be ready to go. The disc needs to access the server *before* the terminal on the other side of the door.'

Kevin typed in the letter *Y* and held his finger over the enter button, ready to go. Meanwhile Zion peered into the mess of wires and reached in with the pliers at the blue cable at the back. He gripped the head of the pliers around the plug that connected the wire to the wall and pulled it out. The display next to the key card slot went black. He looked at Kevin briefly to see if he was ready, before steadying himself to plug the wire back into the wall.

'OK, on my mark. We go on three.'

Kevin twitched his finger, like a cowboy in a standoff, ready to draw his six-shooter.

'One…'

Kevin stared intently at the enter button.

'Two…'

Zion felt a bead of sweat run down his forehead.

'Three.'

Zion plugged the wire back in as Kevin hit enter. The pair froze as they watched the console for a response. After another long wait, more lines appeared, one after another, with the message *server accessed*. The pair leaped in the air and shouted. The others at the truck watched the scene, completely unaware of what was going on. The pair were jumping up and down in joy, but the door was still firmly shut.

After a short celebration, Kevin got back to the task at hand. They were only half done. The next stage would be to hack their way into the database that contained the key card codes, and re-enable Kevin's access card.

Kevin made short work of the first few walls of security. He'd been doing this for years, and together with Zion they were an unstoppable hacking force. It took just a few minutes before Kevin was in, and before him on the hologram was a database with thousands of names, all assigned with an access code. Most were coloured in red; those that had been disabled. Those still in green were probably the people still working at the facility before it was abandoned. The names were listed alphabetically by surname. Kevin scrolled down to those beginning 'O', scanning the names for his. He stopped when he found 'Owen', but there were three with that name. His was the third, after 'A. Owen' and 'E. Owen'. He touched the name 'K. Owen', and it highlighted a soft white colour.

'I still think you have the most badass initials,' Zion quipped. 'You should have gone with that instead of 'The Oracle'.'

'What's wrong with 'The Oracle'?' Kevin asked.

'Nothing. It's just you already had… Never mind.'

Kevin tapped the name again and was taken to a new page, which detailed a list of his characteristics. Everything from his full name, height, weight and date of birth, right down to notes from his work at the facility. It was all there. Surrounding his staff photo was a red border, showing his access level. It was currently set to disabled. It took one password to change it to enabled, which Kevin decrypted in no time at all. The access level was re-enabled for all doors, retinal and fingerprint scanners. The photo changed to display a satisfying green border, and it was done. Kevin smiled at their success and backtracked out of the server. After Zion had cut the connection with the wire again, Kevin shut down the disc. On plugging in the wire again, the terminal on the other side of the door re-established connection with the server and the display to the side of the key card slot flashed on again. Kevin followed the instructions and swiped his card through the slot. The slot glowed green, much to his relief, and he touched the display to open the door.

There was a loud creaking noise as the bolts to the door started to move for what must have been the first time in a long while. The creaking grew louder as the door started to slide apart from the middle, moving into the wall on either side. The group cheered from the truck and rang out a round of applause for the pair's effort. One or two whistled for good measure. For that brief moment, Zion felt like a hero. Like he was finally doing something right, something useful. For so long he had lived with the guilt of his past, for his part in all of this. But now he had the chance to redeem himself, and he was taking it firmly with both hands.

Kevin slapped his friend on the back and gave him a wide smile.

'Just like old times,' he said, before heading back to the truck.

CHAPTER TWENTY-NINE

The inside of the service entrance was dark and cold. For all Cyrus knew, it could have been normal room temperature, but it was certainly an improvement on the heat outside. They found themselves in a small hangar of sorts, where a few heavy goods vehicles had been abandoned, no doubt redundant with the electric vehicle grid offline. The ceiling was high, and despite the dark it felt like there was a lot of space there. The pickup truck rolled through, the place illuminating more as it made its way further in. It was the combined result of Cyrus's eyes adjusting to the dark and the truck blocking the sunlight from the other side of the doorway less and less the further it went in. There was a conveyor belt moving through the middle of the place, presumably to transport materials from the shipments to the parts of the facility that needed them.

Kevin parked the pickup on the far side of the hangar and shut off the engine. The rumbling of the truck stopped and suddenly there was silence.

End of the line.

Cyrus hopped over the tailgate and watched as Gyro-3 pulled itself over, its long arms impressively holding its weight as it moved its frame from one side of the truck to the other. It seemed its arms could rotate almost the whole way round, anchoring itself while the body of the little robot moved up and over the tailgate. When it reached the other side, its arms let go and it hit the floor with an ungraceful bump. Cyrus was intrigued by the whole thing. He wondered how Gyro-3 coped with stairs. Probably very slowly.

The rest of the group had already left the truck and were gathered by a door in the corner of the hangar. Cyrus hurried over to catch up.

Kevin swiped his key card and the door opened, just as the last had done. Zion couldn't contain a smile at his good work. The doorway led to a stairwell which presumably led up to the walkway they'd spotted earlier, connecting the service entrance to the main facility. Everyone began to walk up the stairs as Zion found another excuse for a joke.

'What, no elevator?'

Cyrus found himself leading the way as he took the stairs two at a time, eager to explore the facility that awaited them. It was unclear what, if anything, they would find. But he could feel something deep in the pit of his stomach, telling him if they were going to find answers to the mech problem, it would be here. His backpack seemed to weigh a lot less than before, perhaps due to the adrenaline that was coursing through his body from the anticipation. Then someone called after him and he realised he'd been spilling the contents of his bag all down the stairs. He trudged back down, one flight at a time, picking up the tins of food that had escaped his possession. Mia stopped to help him to diffuse some of the embarrassment.

'Thanks,' he said.

'You're an idiot,' she replied, with that beaming smile that warmed his heart.

'Yeah, I know.'

The others had made it to the top of the stairwell and Cyrus could hear the door open. After double checking the zipper on his bag, Cyrus followed Mia back up the stairs and through the door that April had been keeping open for them.

The corridor they entered was dark, with no windows to let the natural light in. The group looked for a light switch but there were none in sight. Nonetheless, there was plenty of light coming from the building across the other side of the corridor.

The inside of the main building was lit in a dark blue glow. The group walked to the other side of the corridor and approached the next doorway. Again the key card worked first time, but a fingerprint scan was required too. Kevin smushed his stubby thumb against the reader and it scanned the print. After a second, there was a clicking sound as the door unlocked and Kevin pushed it open. April could see the smile on Zion's face and punched his arm playfully.

The group were now faced with an office-like environment. There were corridors going this way and that, illuminated in the faint blue glow of the lighting above. It seemed that the office was using its auxiliary power, because Cyrus couldn't imagine the people who worked here would thrive under such poor lighting.

On each wall were arrows pointing to various numbers. One wall had an arrow that read 358-398, while another read 260-270.

'The rooms must be numbered. We need to find a map,' Gabriel suggested.

'I remember this vaguely, but I can't recall where exactly everything is,' said Kevin. He reached into his pocket and retrieved the disc once more. After a few commands, he was able to pull up the schematics of the building. 'This ought to do it,' he said. 'I knew I stole this for a reason.'

He cycled through the areas of the facility, highlighting areas of interest. 'OK, there are a few areas we should look for. The chairman's office, the research labs and the manufacturing centre. I suggest we split up to make it quicker.'

'The chairman's office?' Gabriel asked, unsure of the logic.

'You'll be surprised what the big boss fails to cover up,' Kevin said. 'I met him once, total asshole. Seemed like the kind of narcissistic idiot that'd keep memoirs about his 'accomplishments'.' He used his fingers to simulate air quotes as he spoke. 'It might be nothing, but it's worth checking out.'

Gabriel took the initiative to delegate the tasks. 'I'll go to the research labs with Kevin and Jennifer. April, you, Zion and Rowley head to the chairman's office. Mia, Jane, Aiden and Cyrus, you've got the manufacturing centre. Everyone OK with that?'

Everyone nodded. It didn't seem like it mattered in the long-run.

Gabriel smiled at their compliance. He had half expected someone to complain. 'Alright then, let's go. Let's meet back at the truck in an hour and we can share what we found.'

The group started to disperse after Kevin gave them rough directions to each of their destinations. Rowley hugged Jennifer and kissed her on the cheek before she headed off towards the research labs. He then surprised Cyrus with a strong hug of his own.

'Be careful, OK?'

'Dude, I'll see you in an hour.'

'I know,' Rowley replied sheepishly. 'Just, you know, in case.'

'In case what?'

Rowley didn't reply and followed Zion and April towards the offices. Kevin stayed behind to escort Cyrus and his group to the manufacturing centre.

'You'll need me to open the door for you,' he said. 'You'll be able to get back fine, it's getting in that's the problem.'

As they walked through the maze of corridors towards the manufacturing labs, Jane caught up with Aiden.

'So, Mr Bartender, what's troubling you?'

Aiden looked confused. 'What do you mean?'

'You've been awful quiet since, well, since forever. You got somethin' on your mind?'

'Not really,' he replied. 'I'm just usually quite quiet I guess.'

'So it's nothin' to do with your lady friend back in the city?'

'What, Caitlin?' he asked. 'Is it that obvious?'

Jane nodded and nudged his shoulder with hers in a teasing manner.

'Well, I really like her,' he said. 'I think I'm in love with her.'

'That's great,' she replied. 'So why the long face?'

'Because I'm worried I'm not going to see her again.'

Jane frowned. 'Don't think like that. You need to believe that you will.'

'Yeah I know. That's what we're fighting for. But don't worry if I look miserable, I've been told I have an unfriendly resting face.'

'Oh y'all mean 'bitchy resting face',' she said as she started to laugh. As she did so, an unintentional snort came from her nose, which prompted Aiden to laugh along with her.

'You know she loves you too, right?'

'Caitlin?'

'No, the Easter bunny. Yes, Caitlin.'

Aiden felt stupid at the remark, but took heart from the fact that Jane was the second person to say that to him.

**

'This sector, along with the research labs, has the highest security clearance in the facility,' Kevin announced as they reached the entrance to the manufacturing centre. 'Hopefully you'll find something juicy.'

'We'll be sure to bring you back a souvenir,' Mia joked.

Kevin swiped his key card, stuck his thumbprint on the fingerprint panel and leaned into the retinal scanner to pass the third level of security. He blinked a couple of times and opened his eye wide as the green glow of the scanner lights surrounded it, moving left to right and up and down in fluid motions. The process took a couple of seconds, before the key card slot turned green and the door clicked open. Kevin pushed it open casually.

'Et voilà!' he said, bowing and gesturing his arm towards the door with an air of grandeur. Cyrus and his micro group entered through the door and watched it swing shut behind them. The lock engaged again and they could see Kevin shuffle back the way they'd come through the small porthole in the door frame. He noticed that despite the stiff security at each section of this facility, there was little secrecy as to what was behind each door. Many of the doors in the office area had simply been glass panes with handles, leaving extremely little to the imagination of what was behind each one. However the door to this new area was much thicker and seemed to be reinforced. There was no way of forcing your way through. The porthole was large enough to see what was on the other side, but all he was able to get was a view of more corridor. Nothing given away that would diminish the added security.

Cyrus watched Kevin pick up his pace a little as he made his way away from them, probably eager to get back to his group at the research labs. Cyrus wondered if they'd drawn the short straw in this treasure hunt. Surely the research labs were the best place to find out more about the mechs, and Gabriel had picked that for himself because he wanted to claim credit for anything he found. The manufacturing centre would likely be nothing more than the remnants of scrap piles and bits of mech they'd already seen a hundred times before. Even the prospect of snooping around a big wig's office felt more enticing than this.

Cyrus shook the thought from his mind as Kevin rounded the corner and out of sight. Short straw or not, he may as well see what he could find. The whole facility intrigued him, and he was curious to uncover anything he could about the mechs. Taking a look at the very place they were built would be fascinating, and it may even provide some clues as to the scale at which these things were produced. Cyrus had no idea how many mechs had been built in this facility. The few mechs that roamed the city couldn't have been all there was. Perhaps they weren't even all that was left. There may have been hundreds more scattered across the country. He wondered if there were other people experiencing the same problem as him in another city, like some kind of parallel universe.

I bet they don't have a psycho kidnapping people for slaves.

Turning to his own group, Cyrus realised he'd been left behind in his absentmindedness. The sudden feeling of being alone in this building spooked him and he took off down the corridor to catch up with his friends.

He didn't need to cover much ground, and he almost knocked into the back of Aiden as he rounded the corner at speed.

'Jeez, Cyrus, you scared the life out of me,' he said, surprised to hear the pounding of footsteps and the presence of another person suddenly right behind him.

'Sorry,' replied Cyrus, his heart beating fast. He caught Mia staring at him with a perplexed look on her face. Perplexed with a hint of annoyance; the kind of look a mother would give to a misbehaving child. Cyrus acknowledged it and sheepishly continued down the next corridor, taking care not to show any signs of erratic behaviour.

Smooth, Cyrus. Real smooth.

A few strides further, he noticed a sign for bathrooms. He hadn't had the luxury of working plumbing for longer than he could remember. He remembered the days of emptying buckets in the mall after the plumbing there failed. It was a messy job, but everybody took their turn. Luckily there were so many of them it didn't come around all that often. The feeling of a full bladder quickly hit him as he saw the sign, like some sort of cognitive response reminding his body that he needed to relieve himself.

'Guys, I'll catch you up, I need to use the bathroom,' he said.

As he moved towards the sign for the men's room, he heard Mia respond. 'Actually, I could do with a quick freshen up.'

Jane and Aiden decided it best to take their chance while they had it as well.

As he pushed open the door to the men's room, Cyrus cautiously checked his surroundings. In an unfamiliar place, he could never be sure if it was safe. It was highly unlikely that he would suddenly bump into a mech in here, but other humans? It wasn't totally implausible.

The coast was clear and Aiden went straight for the urinal. Cyrus stopped a moment to admire the place first. It was by far the cleanest bathroom he'd been in for a very long time. It was neglected, as could be expected in a facility that supposedly nobody had occupied for years. But it had a sterile kind of feel to it, as if it had remained the same way it was left, despite the years without occupancy. On closer inspection Cyrus could see that it wasn't actually clean, and layers of dust had built up around the sink. Still, the room was intact and the mirror on the wall completely whole, not a crack or scratch to be seen. Cyrus stared at his reflection, gazing upon the unkempt man staring back at him. It took him a moment to recognise himself through the shaggy hair that was forming on top of his head, threatening to cover his eyes if he let it grow any more. He noticed that his hair was getting slightly lighter in colour. It threw him back to a memory of his childhood. He had bleach blonde hair as a child, instantly distinguishable from the mass of brown haired friends he'd hang out with. It made picking him up from school that bit easier for his mother, as she could instantly pick him out in the playground and cut short his play time. Some of his friends would try and blend into the crowd of screaming kids, buying a few last minutes of running around before they went home. But for Cyrus this wasn't an option. During his teenage years his hair had gotten darker, matching his change in attitude as puberty brought the characteristic moods swings of adolescence.

He was largely considered mild tempered these days, or at least he was before the world turned sour. Now he was surprising himself with random outbursts and moments heated with anger. The unkempt, almost shabby representation of himself staring back at him in the mirror was one he hardly recognised. It drew a lot of similarities to the person he was becoming in this new world. He didn't like what he saw, and wished he could keep it locked inside that mirror. The blond streaks of hair that had started to reform on his head at least made him smile. It was as if an old part of him was coming back, a part he wanted to hold onto.

He noticed a cut that ran down the side of one cheek. He hadn't remembered any pain there. Perhaps he hadn't had time to. He twisted the taps in an attempt to wash his face. They squeaked as he opened them, a sign of neglect and rust starting to set in. No water came out. He sighed heavily and joined Aiden by the urinals.

'Don't tell the girls,' Aiden said with a smile. 'Apparently not washing your hands after you pee is a big turn off. Can't see why.' Cyrus laughed. It was a nice feeling and it felt good to keep in high spirits. It made him all the more grateful for the company he was in.

'Well as long as they can't wash theirs, they can't complain.'

**

Kevin blinked as the retinal scanner finished working its way over his eye. The key card slot turned a satisfying green and the door clicked unlocked. He pushed it open with one hand, the door stiff and creaky from underuse over recent years. The group moved through the door, Gabriel letting it shut behind them. The heavy door slammed shut and locked with a loud click. The sounds echoed around them, bouncing off the concrete walls and ceiling. The décor had changed drastically from the office, and it was disorientating at first.

The office, despite currently being bathed in the dim glow of emergency lighting had been fitted with soft colours on the walls and carpets on the floor in some places. It looked like a typical office space, and the group could imagine people dipping in and out of each room, a phone ringing constantly and the light tapping of keyboards being drowned out by people laughing by the water cooler. But taking a step beyond this door had brought them into a completely different environment. It looked extremely minimal, and had a grey feel to it. The lights here were different, the pale blue being replaced by a bright white that harshly illuminated the space immediately around them.

The corridor they were standing in seemed to stretch further in front of them, away from the doorway, but the lights hadn't come on there so it was difficult to ascertain how far it went. Jennifer took point and started walking along it, into the darkness. Sure enough the lights reacted to her movement and began flickering to life as she made her way down the corridor. Kevin and Gabriel followed closely behind, taking time to peer into the rooms leading off from each side. The glass panelled walls made it easy to work out what was in each room, and in keeping with the theme of this part of the facility didn't offer much inspiration. Each room was opened planned with various sketches and schematics hung up on the walls. Others were a little bigger and looked much more lab-like, with complex looking equipment lining workbenches inside.

'This could be interesting,' Kevin suggested, opening the door to one of the labs.

Another bright white light flicked on as he opened the door to one of the labs and stepped inside. Gabriel and Jennifer went on down the corridor.

Kevin studied the lab equipment, recognising most of it from his time at the facility. It seemed to be left relatively as he'd remembered it. He assumed testing procedures hadn't changed all that much from when he worked there. What had changed was the progress the scientists had made on the mech project, which was what he soon found himself staring at. As with the previous rooms, this lab had schematics and other sketches hung up on the walls, almost like kids paintings in a school art room. The researchers here took great pride in their work, and the progress they'd made constantly in eyesight offered motivation to continue the work, particularly after experiencing the setback of failed tests.

He saw some familiar schematics of some of the early robotics projects he had worked on. Numerous sketches of concept models for the early robots, with one in particular he remembered, which he later used in his design for Gyro-3. The sketch was a plain looking box, with a label on it that read *AI: Basic conversation.* He glanced at a few other sketches and saw the familiar arm design that Gyro-3 now sported. He looked at the sketch and then at his trusty robotic companion that had followed him into the lab. Gyro-3 was exactly what he'd envisioned when he started this project at the facility. Robotic companions with smart enough artificial intelligence to hold basic conversations and perform household tasks. It would have been a great success commercially. These robots would have made the ultimate companions for the elderly, who, like his mother, had struggled to look after themselves alone at home. Gyro-3 was not only better company than a dog, it was extremely useful around the house. He hadn't quite perfected the formula and Gyro-3 had limitations, but had he been able to continue his research at the lab he may have made great strides towards fixing this. However, the government had other plans and the project was taken in a new, twisted direction. The lab had an eerie feel to it, and the sight of it empty and desolate brought with it the feeling of shattered dreams. Kevin wondered if there would be a future for this place if the world went back to normal. He craved the opportunity to spend months working here with his own team, where he could continue where he left off.

As he looked at his robot companion, he wondered if it was able to recognise what was happening around it, or whether its reactions were based purely on his own actions. He'd built Gyro-3, but the little machine had continued to surprise him with its level of intelligence. It was almost as if it was learning, and remembering how to act in certain situations. True AI. It didn't seem to be aware of its surroundings in the context of what it meant, and it didn't seem to pick up on the irony of it being here.

More schematics were hung on the walls to the right of Kevin's old ones. He noticed some early models of mechs, much smaller than the ones that roamed the streets. He passed through into the next room and found more images scattered across a workbench. He picked one up and found himself looking at a Bengal tiger. Underneath the photo of the animal was a collection of roughly drawn sketches, again of the tiger, but with annotations on each part of its body. There was one sketch of a tiger with its body flat to the ground, ready to spring. More annotations were drawn, focusing on the legs and paws. Another sketch showed exactly the same image, but drawn in the form of an exoskeleton. It must have been the early designs of the panthers. Kevin raised an eyebrow at the work before him, before Jennifer's voice distracted him.

'Kevin, come in here,' she called from a room further down the corridor. Her voice sounded faint, but it was clear she was shouting so he could hear her. He took the sketches with him and followed her voice.

A few sheets of paper were swept off the counter in the swift movement and fluttered towards the floor in front of Gyro-3. The little robot stopped and picked them up with its long arms, holding a piece of paper delicately in each of its claw-like hands. It lifted the papers to the top of its frame, where its optic components started to analyse the drawings. It looked over them carefully, studying every element. It then followed its master out of the room, its wheels whirring as it rolled down the corridor.

Kevin found Jennifer and Gabriel in a lab towards the end of the corridor. They were staring at a set of photos on the wall. Above the photos read the title *Mech obedience test 42*. The photos were like nothing they'd ever seen. A row of golems stood in formation, facing a person who looked half their size. They were stationary, and from the photos didn't seem to move an inch. It was a very different sight from the golems they'd encountered in the city, which hunted down every human it saw.

Gyro-3 whirred its way into the room, and Kevin turned to see it was still carrying the sketches that had dropped to the floor. It presented them to its master dutifully, as if helping to clean up a mess. Kevin smiled and knelt in front of it like a father greeting his young son.

'What you got there for me?' he asked curiously. He looked at the drawings in each of its hands. In its left hand was a sketch of a box with arms. It looked remarkably similar to Gyro-3, minus the wheels and the flickering lights around the top of its frame where is head should be. The second drawing was of a golem, standing in a tall stance with one arm moulded into the shape of a gun. The little robot could distinguish between humans and golems, and had experienced both forms in recent days, however there was something it picked up about the two drawings, and Kevin could sense it. It was connecting them, and for a moment it seemed as though it was understanding the connection between itself and the golems. Kevin stared at the robot, and it stared back. It was in that moment that Kevin realised just how intelligent his robotic companion was.

'Master,' Gyro-3 said in its metallic voice. 'What is my purpose?'

Kevin put his hand over the sketches, covering the golem. 'You are not a mech,' he said firmly. 'You are my friend and you are one of the good guys.'

Gyro-3 continued to look at Kevin square in the face, reading his expression. After a short pause it replied. 'I understand. This knowledge pleases me. I do not wish to be a mech. Mechs harm master. I do not wish to harm master.'

Kevin smiled and took the papers, placing them on a nearby workbench. He turned his attention back to the images hung on the wall.

'This must be one of the handlers,' Jennifer said, pointing to the man standing in front of the line of mechs.

'Yes,' Kevin acknowledged. 'The mechs were assigned to handlers in small troop batches. It's unclear how many. Ten, twenty mechs?'

'And the mechs went rogue when the handlers died,' Jennifer added.

'So what did the handlers use to control them?' asked Gabriel.

'That's the million dollar question.'

They looked over some of the other images. There were action shots of the handler pointing towards a location with his arm stretched out. He was pointing at a cluster of mannequins at the far side of the testing area. The golems were turned in the direction of his point and were blasting away the mannequins with their gun arms.

Something caught Jennifer's eye in that image. The photo was taken in true action-shot style, and the handler seemed to have pivoted on the spot quickly, spinning around to point at the target he wanted the mechs to fire upon. The camera had caught something in the motion of his spin. Something hanging around his neck that looked like a bright light from the exposure of the image capture.

'What's that?' asked Jennifer, pointing to the image.

'What's what?' said Gabriel.

'That,' she motioned to the handler and the thing that seemed to be swinging around his neck as he spun on the spot. 'Doesn't that look familiar to you?'

CHAPTER THIRTY

Zion led the way towards the chairman's office. It had been a while since he had left this place for good, but the layout was still familiar in his mind and it didn't take him long to remember the way. April and Rowley were in close pursuit, the trio striding purposely through the winding office, turning this way and that. The chairman's office wasn't labelled as such on the walls; it was just another numbered office like the rest. But they knew it when they got there because it looked different to the rest of the rooms they passed.

The office was at least three times the size of a normal office in the building. The layout resembled that of the office of a head of state, and it gave a clue as to the sort of person that once worked there. A large flag was draped across the back wall, adding to the semblance. There was a large desk towards the back, with the flag providing a backdrop for visitors. It created a powerful setting for the man who had once worked there.

'From the one time I met him, I could tell this guy was patriotic,' Zion said. 'A little too patriotic if you ask me. Kinda racist too. Well, that and just plain xenophobic.'

'From the looks of it, he probably programmed the door to play the national anthem every time he walked through it,'

April joked, causing Rowley to snigger. 'Check out the furniture in here,' she said. 'And I bet that vase cost a few thousand too.'

'At least,' Rowley agreed. 'What do you think, will he mind if I smash it? How about we just tear this place apart and see what we find?' He winked at April, who also looked to be in the mood for some stress release.

'No, let's be smart about this,' Zion said, for once taking on the sensible parent role. 'Let's rifle through those cabinets and see what's there.'

'We definitely got the boring job,' Rowley frowned.

The trio split up around the room, pulling open drawers and rifling through papers to find anything that could help. They were busy for a few minutes before a loud smash stopped their progress. Zion turned around to find April standing over the remains of the large expensive-looking vase.

'Oops,' she said, before exchanging a smile with the others. They went back to searching the room.

'If I was the head of an evil government funded killer robot facility, what would I do in my office?' Rowley asked.

'Don't forget egotist,' April added.

'Oh yes. OK, if I was an egotistical head of an evil government funded killer robot facility, what would I—' He stopped talking as he struggled to open a drawer in the large desk. 'OK, everyone look for a key. This one's locked.'

'Just smash it open,' April suggested, tongue-in-cheek. 'Like the guys in the comics.'

'This thing's made of oak, but be my guest.'

April ran her foot over the ceramic fragments littered on the floor around her. Something caught her eye and she turned over a large piece to find a key.

'Well what do you know,' she said. 'Looks like Mr Ego didn't think someone would break his precious vase.' She handed it to Rowley, who used it to unlock the drawer with a click. The drawer opened, but there was nothing inside.

'Damn it,' he cursed under his breath. 'I thought we were onto something there.'

'Wait a second,' April said, an idea materialising. 'That drawer goes deeper than that. Look at it from the side.'

'Maybe a false bottom?' Zion suggested.

Rowley pried out the layer of wood, revealing the real contents of the drawer. Inside was a bound book and a small black device. He picked up the device and gave it a closer look. It had a triangle, a square and circle symbol, representing play, stop and record.

'Some kind of recording device,' he said, almost questioning if he had correctly identified the object.

'That doesn't surprise me one bit,' Zion said. 'He must have loved the sound of his own voice.'

'Let's hope his memoirs have something more interesting in them than his 'rise to the top of the food chain'.'

Rowley hit the play button and the voice of a middle aged man echoed out around the room.

'Good sound for a small device—'

'Shh,' April put her finger to her lips.

The voice introduced himself as Bert Miller, Chairman of the facility. The trio listened to it as it started its monologue.

'I'm recording this for my personal memoirs, as physical proof of my legacy once this place is inevitably burned to the ground by MIRE. I've been fighting for this country for my whole career, ever since I was a young recruit in the military.'

'Oh jeez,' Rowley said. 'I can see where this is going.' He found another button on the side to fast forward to a later recording. Before he hit play again, he noticed a photograph in a frame on the desk. It was of a busty twenty-something woman, with a beautiful face, blonde hair and slim figure. She was wearing a bikini, with a beach backdrop. The sand was white and the water a clear blue. He imagined it was somewhere exotic, possibly somewhere in the Caribbean.

'Is this his wife?' he asked 'She's hot.'

'Hey!' April said, snatching the picture from his hands. 'I'll tell my sister you said that.' Rowley responded by putting his hands up in surrender.

Zion took a look at the photo and laughed.

'I've seen his wife. She's his age. This isn't her.'

'His daughter then?' Rowley suggested.

'Why the hell would he have a picture of his daughter in a bikini on his desk, Rowley?' April arched an eyebrow.

Rowley frowned and returned his focus to the recording device.

'What a dog,' Zion murmured to himself. He pressed play once more and the next recording began.

'After playing golf with the ambassador, I was able to secure a meeting with the Treasury. Of course I invited representatives of the military to join, they were sure to find the agenda fascinating.'

Rowley simulated an exaggerated yawn to express his boredom at the man's voice.

'I told them of the work my facility was capable of, and of the scientists at my disposal.'

The word 'disposal' struck a nerve with Zion. He knew this man used it quite literally.

'It wasn't long before I had the full backing of the government. They agreed that my robotic guardians would cut crime in the country and provide more than adequate support for the country's defence. After we had the budget secured we advanced our recruitment and brought in more scientists. A certain Kevin Owen seemed promising, a very bright young man with some good ideas. He got us started with the mechanics, but once we advanced the process to larger, weaponised models he refused to cooperate. We let him go and we replaced him with someone more willing.'

Rowley glanced at Zion as they listened. He could see the pained expression on his face as he listened to the man's voice, and he realised how little Zion had been involved in all of this. The chairman had used him as a pawn in his game, just as he'd done to Kevin and everyone else who worked there.

The chairman's voice went off on a tangent, discussing more politics that didn't interest the trio.

'Zion, I'm sorry about the other day. I didn't know the full story.'

Zion smiled and put his hand to his cheek, remembering the altercation and the pain from Rowley's surprisingly strong punch. 'It's alright,' he said. 'I would have been angry too.'

The chairman eventually brought his ramblings back around to the mechs.

'Artificial intelligence was a risky game. We were building machines capable of killing a platoon of men without issue, so we couldn't leave space for them to think for themselves. They simply needed orders, and someone to give them. This is where the handlers came in. They were the modern day lion tamers.'

The trio were listening intently now.

'What we knew of the crystals was limited, but they provided the perfect element for this project. With much trial and error, we found a formula to create the mechs in a way that reacted with the energy of the crystals. The mechs responded to the handler that held the crystal flawlessly. Each handler was assigned a crystal, and each crystal was linked to a group of twenty mechs.'

'Crystals?' Rowley was completely bemused. 'What is he talking about?' April picked up the leather-bound book from the drawer and started leafing through it.

'At first the handlers had to show the mechs where to attack. But soon we were able to issue commands at large scale. We could send the mechs on complex missions, to search and destroy. The handlers didn't need to accompany them.'

The recording finished and Zion quickly played the next entry. It seemed time had passed since the last entry, indicated by the sudden change in the chairman's voice. It seemed much more hoarse, breathless and panicked.

'With every project there are setbacks, and MIRE had their input yet again.' He exhaled deeply before finding his next words. 'They infiltrated our ranks and killed our handlers. We didn't anticipate this at all, and now I know the full consequence of the project.' His words were heavy, his voice seeming almost remorseful. 'The mech project failed, and there is nothing we can do.' After this there was static coming through and the voice was gone. It came back again briefly.

'They can't be stopped. They will never stop.' Then more static and the recording finished.

Rowley and Zion looked at each other quizzically. The recording had been a goldmine of information, but it left them seeking more answers.

'What the hell was he going on about?' Rowley asked. 'Crystals, what is that all about?'

Zion shrugged. This was new to him too, and not even Kevin had mentioned anything about crystals before. Suddenly April piped up, her head buried in the book on the desk.

'It's here,' she said. 'It's all here. Well, all that they know.' There was an element of suspense as she read from the book, verifying what she was about to divulge. 'The crystal he's referring to is some kind of unidentified element, discovered somewhere in South America. It's not on the periodic table.' She read ahead once more as Zion raised an eyebrow.

Not on the periodic table?

'They called it kryodian, or something. His handwriting is appalling,' April continued. 'Apparently there was a cluster of it in crystallised form discovered on the border of Peru and Bolivia, in the Bahuaja-Sonene National Park.'

'Really? An unidentified element?' Zion asked, still bewildered by the concept.

'As farfetched as it sounds, that's what it says here,' April replied candidly. 'According to this journal it's like nothing anyone has ever seen.' She read an excerpt aloud for effect. 'It's like it has magical properties, as if it arrived here from outer space.' The trio burst out laughing. The whole thing was ludicrous.

'Outer space?' Rowley repeated. 'So they think some unknown element came from somewhere in the galaxy and landed in a park in South America?'

'It sounds too strange to be true, I know.'

'What it sounds like is the plot to a superhero film,' Rowley added. 'Back me up, Zion.'

Zion smiled. 'Dude, as long as I get superpowers out of all this, I'm golden.' Rowley laughed and slapped him on the shoulder.

'Guys, we need to start taking this seriously,' April said. 'Whatever these crystals are, I think they're real. Why would the head of the facility document them if they weren't?'

The guys didn't say anything. As ridiculous as it was, they knew she was right. They had to accept that there were just some things they couldn't explain or understand. Not yet at least.

'So what now?' Zion said. 'We go back to the others and tell them an unknown element from outer space is powering the mechs, and we don't know how to access it or control it?'

'What else can we do?' said Rowley. 'Gabriel said meet back at the truck in an hour. None of us are wearing a watch so that was an oversight on everyone's part. Let's just go back and wait for the others. We'll tell them about it when we get there.'

'I'll bring these,' April said, scooping up the book and recording device.

Zion paused as the other two started for the door. He thought about what the chairman had said. The mech technology reacting with the kryodian crystals, allowing them to animate based on the commands of the person who wielded the crystal. He knew the mechs utilised the technology he had come up with to convert solar power into energy in a compact, yet powerful form. The crystal seemed to be what activated and controlled them, but they needed the solar power to function. It was too complex to understand right now, but he knew one thing; it would be impossible to stop them from getting solar energy. If they wanted to beat these things, they needed to find the crystal form of an element they had never heard of.

**

The manufacturing centre was less than impressive. Or at least the part Cyrus found himself in seemed to be. There were loose sheets of metal and other materials littered on the floor, spilling out of buckets and barrels that had been knocked over or otherwise carelessly placed. Entering through the service entrance of the facility must have meant they were now walking through the storage areas, or by the looks of it the waste area. Cyrus remembered the conveyor belts from the garage that seemed to disappear into a wall like the baggage rail at an airport. They must now have been on the other side of that wall after snaking through the office.

'This place is a dump,' Mia remarked as she waded through the debris.

'At least we're not in the sewage system,' Aiden said. Mia looked at him, waiting for some sort of context, as if there was more to his comment. 'I mean, you know, it could be worse, right?'

'Yeah, you're right,' she conceded. 'Sewage would be worse.'

Cyrus was leading the way, but was struggling to navigate carefully through the area. The lighting had been so poor since leaving the last corridor that he couldn't tell how big this room was. He could barely see the floor around him and didn't want to trip over again for the millionth time.

'I see a light up ahead,' Jane said, pointing in the dark towards another blue light, similar to that lining the ceilings of the office. As they got closer they realised it was coming through the porthole of a door that sat at the top of a small staircase. Cyrus reached the staircase first and barely waited for his companions before climbing the steps. His feet banged against the metal one step at a time, each sound echoing around the place. The volume of the echoes led him to believe that this room must have been a lot bigger than he realised.

He peered through the porthole at the top of the stairs and surveyed the room inside. Despite the dim blue light on the ceiling, it was difficult to see what was inside. The door gave with a loud squeal as he pushed it open, the hinges rusted and worn. The moment he stepped inside a multitude of bright white lights flickered to life, illuminating the room around him. He found himself in some kind of control room, with a large pane of glass on one wall. There was a large computer system which took up the whole edges of the place, and an even more impressive one that stretched out into the room from the glass window. The area past the window was fairly dark and it was difficult to see what was outside it. The glare from the lighting was creating a hazy effect that seemed to be contained to just the room itself, and the window seemed to mostly reflect the light back at him.

'This place is cool,' Jane said. 'Like some sort of control room.'

'Do you think this is where they controlled the machinery to build the mechs?' Mia asked.

'Yeah, actually that would make sense,' Cyrus said. 'Maybe the factory floor is out there.' He pointed to the window, gesturing to the space beyond.

'I wonder if the computers are still on,' said Aiden.

'Yeah, look there,' Mia replied. 'There's a light blinking by that terminal. Maybe we can get it started.'

She moved quickly to the terminal and took a long look at the panel in front of her. It didn't look like a regular computer keyboard, or anything she'd seen. She moved her hand near to one of the buttons and a holographic display jumped out at her, causing her to recoil.

'Jeez, that scared me,' she said.

'Everything in this place gives me the creeps,' Aiden replied.

The hologram offered a much more user friendly interface, providing Mia with a host of options. She found an option for lighting and touched it, before receiving a number of further options. She touched a few more before the space outside and to the left of the room became illuminated. It looked like a walkway. She hit more buttons and more and more lights flickered to life. She hit a final one and a series of lights outside the window began to flicker on in a row moving away from them. The group were suddenly aware of what the space outside the window was. True to their assumptions it did look like a factory floor, with the control room sitting a few storeys above it. What they weren't aware of until now was the sheer size of it. It was absolutely massive.

It suddenly hit Cyrus just what they were dealing with. The size of the room was a huge reminder of the scale of the mech project. The government's rush to build these machines was one of the biggest errors they had made, and now the job of cleaning up this mess was so much more difficult. It wasn't just a handful of mechs, it was hundreds, if not thousands. Cyrus wondered how many they would have made had MIRE not been so successful in pegging them back.

As the lights slowly flickered to life one after another, something else was illuminated in what had been total darkness. Cyrus suddenly realised the darkness had created an air of blissful ignorance. Half of him wished it had stayed that way. One by one the lights revealed row after row of mech, stood in formation, completely still. The sight made the group dart away from the window so as not to be spotted. It took a few moments for them to realise that something was different about these mechs.

'They've been disabled,' Cyrus said.

'No,' Jane correcting him. 'They've never been enabled. Look at them, they're in perfect formation. They must have been the last batch that was built before the facility was shut down.'

Cyrus looked at the mechs and counted them. Twenty. They were arranged in order of height, and ultimately firepower. Ten panthers at the front, with eight golems behind them and two gargantuans behind them. The gargantuans were absolutely colossal, and even from his vantage point they were a towering spectacle. He had very little knowledge of these mechs as he'd come across them so infrequently. What he did know was that they were not to be messed with, as indicated by the humongous barrels resting on their tortoise-like backs. They had played a big part in the destruction of the city, acting like tanks as the government ploughed them through, looking for remnants of MIRE.

'It's so weird,' Aiden said. 'Being this close to them, yet not feeling the need to run.' His face was now pressed against the window.

The holographic display lit up, presenting a number of options for Mia as she went back to it and started pressing more buttons. Cyrus looked about the room, wondering if there was anything he could find that would tell him more about the mechs. If there was a way he could shut them down, disabling the ones roaming the city, this was the best place to figure out how. A long workbench with an array of buttons piqued his interest.

'I wonder what this is for,' he muttered.

'Don't go touching anything,' Mia warned. 'I know what you're like.' She turned from the hologram, on which she had been punching in commands without much thought, and gave him a cheeky smile. Cyrus rolled his eyes and went back to observing the buttons on his side of the room. Most of them didn't have labels or any clear way of knowing what they were for. He imagined there must have been a manual for it, but it was unlikely he'd find that here. One part of the workbench seemed more interesting than the rest, with a gap between two sets of buttons.

'What do you think this is for?' he asked, as he moved along the bench towards it. In that moment a sudden chill took over his body and he began to feel faint. He stumbled over onto the workbench and accidentally pressed a few buttons where his body slumped across it. His hearing went and white noise erupted in his eardrums.

'Cyrus,' Mia's voice was muffled through the noise, the sound reminiscent of a bad dream. Wide eyed, Cyrus looked at the gap between the two sets of buttons he had stumbled next to. The space was now illuminated in a bright blue colour, almost sparking with electricity as he stared into it. He thought he must have been hallucinating. The space looked like a wormhole, the energy pulling him closer into the abyss. The world around him looked washed out, all colour drawn from it and sucked into the wormhole that had been created. He fought hard against the pull of it and looked down at the crystal around his neck. The cord from which it hung tugged at the back of his neck as it hovered out in front of him. Like a magnet attracting a scrap of metal, the crystal hung in the air between Cyrus and the gap, as though it was desperate to leave him and embed itself in the workbench. The crystal glowed a brilliant white, the white noise building louder and louder in Cyrus's ears as he struggled against the unknown force pulling his head closer.

He heard more muffled voices cutting through intermittently.

'Is he OK?'

'What's going on?'

'Cyrus, can you hear me?'

The calls of his friends were futile, there was nothing Cyrus could do. He tried to answer them, tried to scream for help but the sound got lost in his throat. He closed his eyes and tensed, trying desperately to pull his head away. In that moment he saw the vision he'd shared with Isaac, the same one where he saw The Jackal, the mechs, his mother and sister. This time he saw himself, standing on a plain of sand. The vision was washed out, like the room around him had been. A pack of panthers raced out from behind, running past him and colliding with another pack. The mechanical beasts fought each other on the plain, dust kicking up all around.

Finally, the scene changed to a dust storm. It was so vivid he could almost feel it attacking his face, peppering it with dust and sand. Then came the voices again, louder and clearer this time.

'Cyrus. Cyrus!'

He snapped out of the vision in a moment and the room returned to him in full colour. His face was resting on the workbench, his fall causing him to inadvertently press multiple buttons, all of which were now lit up a dim red. Mia's face was the next thing he saw. She looked terrified.

'What—' Cyrus tried to get his bearings. 'What happened?'

'You just collapsed,' Mia replied, putting her hand to his head to check his temperature. 'And then it's like you were a million miles away. We couldn't get through to you. You looked in pain, are you alright?'

Cyrus thought about the question. 'I was. But I feel fine now.'

The others looked at him, still slumped against the workbench.

'The crystal,' he said. 'The bench did something to it. It was pulling me in.'

He stopped as he tried to lift his head. Something was still pulling at his neck. He placed his hands on the workbench and shuffled his weight about to see what he was caught on. Then he stopped still, his heart suddenly beating faster as he realised what had happened.

The crystal, still glowing a bright white, was locked into the space between the keys. The dark space that had seemed so bright, the energy that once burst from it was now just an empty space lit up by a blue LED. He face went pale as he tried to yank his head back and force the crystal free. Nothing gave. He felt like a character in the old fable of King Arthur and the sword in the stone. Except he wasn't King Arthur and the crystal wasn't budging.

'What the hell is going on?' Aiden said, staring at the sight before him. Then the group heard the noise. The single most terrifying noise they had ever heard. The sound of screeching panthers. It echoed around the vast factory floor, multiple mechs screeching in unison as they woke for the first time.

'Oh my God,' Mia gasped. The trio dashed to the window to see the animated mechs, moving their metallic frames for the first time. They were spotted straight away, and saw the panthers look right at them, screeching away.

'Shit!' Aiden shouted, a sudden wave of panic taking hold. 'They're coming right for us.'

CHAPTER THIRTY-ONE

Around the facility the others heard the screeches and jolted upright, like meerkats detecting an intruder. They had been so conditioned by it, the sound immediately bringing with it fear and an innate fight or flight response.

Kevin was the first to react, darting out the door of the lab and taking off down the corridor, back the way they had come. On entering the office, he bumped into April, Rowley and Zion.

'You heard it too?' he asked. They nodded.

'Sounded like it came from the manufacturing centre.'

'Cyrus,' Rowley gasped. 'We need to help them.'

Gabriel burst out of the door Kevin had just come from, eyes wide, gun locked and loaded. Rowley thought he looked just like a hero from a movie. The veins in his arms bulging in his ridiculously oversized muscles, threatening to burst right out of his clothing. There was one thought in his mind that overshadowed the fear. Whatever happened, he was going to stay as close to Gabriel as possible. The big man led the team swiftly through the office towards the manufacturing centre.

**

'We need to do something, guys,' Aiden was really panicking as he watched the mechs move to the nearest door out of the factory floor. Jane and Mia were helping Cyrus force his way away from the workbench that held him prisoner. The cord of his necklace had become tangled, meaning he couldn't shake it off and free his head.

The mechs made short work of the door, the combination of golem gunfire and brute force of the panthers blasting it open. The panthers then disappeared through it, and Aiden turned to the door they had accessed the control room through.

'Now, people!' he shouted. 'They'll cut us off soon.'

'We're trying,' Mia replied through gritted teeth as she tried to pull Cyrus away from the bench, without success. 'What the hell is this?'

'It's the crystal,' Cyrus said. 'It was attracted to the gap here. I had another vision. It was the crystal all along.'

'What do you mean?' Mia asked.

'The crystal, it's the missing piece of the puzzle. It must have activated the mechs. That's how the handlers controlled them. This console must have started the process.'

'Oh yeah? Those mechs didn't looked in our control to me,' said Mia. 'The process better get finished quick or we'll be dead.'

They heard the clattering of steel coming from somewhere else in the facility. The sound was a constant reminder of the mechs that were quickly hunting them down.

'How long until they're here?' Cyrus asked.

'How the hell do I know?' Aiden replied, still watching the last golems exit the floor below. The gargantuans stood still. It seemed they took a little longer to get going. He thought it best not to draw their attention and stepped away from the window.

'They're smart, they'll find a way here,' Jane said. 'Mia, maybe the computer can help us free Cyrus.'

'No,' Cyrus said. 'Freeing me won't help. The crystal activated them. We need to find a way for it to control them too.'

'Cyrus, I don't think there's a switch that says 'control mechs'', Mia replied, already back at the hologram.

A door sprang open some distance away, the familiar creaking sound alerting Aiden, who rushed to the doorway to play lookout. Now that the lights had been switched on, the cavernous space they'd walked through to get to the control centre was now fully illuminated. The floor was littered in loose sheets of metal and other materials, and Aiden could see a number of possible culprits for the origin of the sound. There were several doors leading into the area, and Aiden trained his rifle over each one in preparation for the oncoming attackers. He soon saw Gabriel bursting through the door they had entered not too long ago, followed by the rest of the group.

'Over here!' he shouted, his voice carrying through the place with an echo. The group spotted him at the top of the stairs and began making their way over to him.

Mia was still frantically scouring the navigation of the computer, swiping this way and that, punching the holographic buttons before letting out annoyed noises as she went from one dead end to another. Jane stood by her side, pointing out areas she hadn't tried yet.

'Cyrus, I'm getting nothing,' she said dejectedly. The sound of banging was heard, much closer now.

'Keep trying,' he replied. 'There must be something.'

Cyrus looked at the crystal, still stuck in the space by a force he couldn't describe. The whole crystal was clear in sight, close enough that if he wanted he could reach out and wrap his hand around it. Yet something was holding it in place, impossible to remove. It was like nothing he had ever seen. This place held more mysteries than he realised. He reached out to yank the crystal free, but a sharp electric shock stopped him from touching it as he got near. He recoiled and moved his hand away.

'Cyrus's crystal is locked into a console,' Aiden shouted to the approaching group. 'It's activated the mechs.'

Right on cue, the sound of banging came again. The mechs were very close now.

'I knew it!' Jennifer said as she raced alongside the others. 'Just like the one in the picture.'

'He should be able to control them. The crystal activates the mechs and then controls them. Is there not a command somewhere?' Zion called.

'We can't find anything,' Aiden replied.

In the control room, Mia was going in circles, checking menus she had already been through twice or three times before.

'Damn it!' she cried, becoming more and more desperate. Aiden abandoned his post to attend to Cyrus.

'Ya'll see anything over there?' Jane called across the room. Aiden and Cyrus both looked at the workbench, with the numerous buttons that made no sense. The ones Cyrus had accidentally pressed when he fell onto it were still glowing a dim red.

'It's got to be one of these,' Aiden said, his eyes darting from one button to the next.

A deafening boom erupted from outside the control room and a doorway was blown completely apart. A panther leapt through the cloud of smoke that had appeared. It surveyed its surroundings and didn't take long to identify the group, who were only halfway to the control room.

'Shoot it!' Rowley cried out, fumbling for his gun as the panther bounded towards them. Gabriel reacted quickly, firing two plasma rounds in its direction. Both cannoned off the mech's frame, failing to stop it. The others quickly fired their own weapons, the sound of plasma rounds echoing all around in a frenzy. The panther went down in a spasm, but more had already entered through the doorway and were converging on their position, flanking them from all sides in a surprisingly tactical manoeuvre.

Cyrus and Aiden heard the noise and started pressing buttons randomly on the workbench. They had little choice but to hope one of the buttons would halt the mechs' progress.

The mechs kept coming and the group stayed together, firing wildly into them. A few fell, but more kept appearing from the doorway. Another door blew open and the more panthers poured out, followed by a number of golems. Eventually the group were surrounded as the panthers circled them, toying with their prey. The golems aimed their gun arms at them, but didn't fire. Pure evil had been programmed into the machines. They weren't just going to kill them, they were going to drag it out, make them suffer.

The seconds dragged on as the panthers prowled around the edge of the group. They'd stopped firing, unsure of what to do next. They were certain this was the end, there was nothing to stop them.

Cyrus had been pressing buttons just as frantically as the gunshots were fired, but nothing seemed to be working. He looked back at the crystal, which still shone a bright white. An idea sparked in his mind. It wasn't a clever one, but he had nothing left to try, and nothing left to lose.

Here goes nothing.

He plunged his hand in and grasped the crystal tight. A sharp wave of energy sent a shockwave up his arm and into his body. He screamed in agony as he kept a grip tight on the jewel. The space around the crystal shone a bright blue colour again, and the whole control room lit up in a flash as Cyrus fought the urge to let go. Then the lights flickered and the pain subsided. Everything went quiet again and the sound of screeching from outside had stopped.

Cyrus fell back onto his backside and sat there staring at his hands, which were still holding the crystal. It had been released from the console at last, and was pulsating in colour. Mia rushed to his side.

'Cyrus, are you OK?'

'I think so,' his reply was quiet. He checked his arm where the energy had burned through him. No trace of anything, it left no mark whatsoever. He looked at Mia, his face a picture of awe and confusion.

'Did it work?'

'You better take a look for yourself,' Jane replied from the doorway.

**

What Cyrus saw was even more astounding than the event he had just experienced. The cavernous space was filled with mechs, all circled around the rest of his friends. They were completely stationary, like they'd been turned to stone. Also their demeanour had changed. The golems were no longer aiming their weapons towards the group in the middle of the circle, and the panthers were no longer prowling the edges, waiting for their moment to attack. They were stopped in identical positions, waiting.

'Holy cheeseballs,' Rowley exclaimed from the middle of the circle.

'You did it,' Mia smiled and wrapped her arms around Cyrus, who stood there completely bemused by what had just happened.

'What are they doing?' Cyrus asked.

'They're waiting for your command,' Kevin said.

'I suggest you don't command them to kill us,' April added.

He couldn't believe it. The crystal had been the key all along. He had carried it around his neck for years, unknowingly holding the secret to neutralising the evil of the city.

'How do I do it?' Cyrus asked, feeling a sudden amount of pressure. 'Do I just do this?' He waved a hand and pointed away to the other side of the room. Nothing happened.

'It's not working,' he said. The mechs stayed completely still, their presence still making the group nervous.

Cyrus thought about the crystal, the wave of energy he'd felt as he connected with it. He grasped it again in his right hand, and felt himself being transported into another realm. His senses suddenly dulled, yet he became acutely alert, as if he was more focused than he'd ever been.

The mechs animated instantly, making everyone jump. The great metal frames of robotic monstrosity then started moving away from the group in unison, marching toward the other side of the room.

Cyrus was completely still, his body remaining in the exact state he'd left it a moment ago. He channelled his thoughts onto a spot at the other end of the room, and the mechs fixated on the spot, moving in unison toward it.

'Unbelievable,' Zion whispered. He, like everyone else there, was completely mesmerised by what he was seeing. Everything they knew had been turned on its head.

Cyrus let go of the crystal and felt his senses come rushing back to him. First his hearing, and then the cool air making the hair on his arm stand up. Finally his sight returned, and he watched the mechs freeze in place on the other side of the room.

'Incredible,' he said.

'You're telling me,' said Aiden. 'They're following your every command.'

'Not just that,' Cyrus clarified. 'They're following the commands I make in my mind. It's like the crystal has fused itself into my brain. Like it knows my thoughts as soon as I touch it.'

'Like a mood stone,' Mia said. 'That's what we always thought it was. When it dangles from your neck, it changes colour depending on your mood. It must be because when it rests against your chest it knows how you're feeling.'

'And now it can read my mind deeper than that,' Cyrus added. When I touch the crystal, it sends me into this other place, like some kind of void. Everything seems grey and dulled, yet I feel like I've had a hundred energy drinks. It becomes completely in tune with my thoughts. Look, I'll show you,' he suddenly became very animated, excited about this strange and new discovery. 'Tell me what you want them to do.'

The group thought about it.

'Tell them to sit down,' April suggested. 'Can they do that?'

'Let's find out.' Cyrus grasped the crystal and felt himself being launched back into the void. A second later, the golems started to move, mimicking a human sitting motion, and sat in a prayer-like kneel. The panthers lay down in a way Cyrus would have expected a domestic cat to do. Lower than usual, but still ready to pounce at any given moment.

The group began to laugh at the sight of it, half through the strange comical value it provided, but also with a final release of tension. The relief they felt was overwhelming. They had come so close to death and it looked like nothing would be able to stop that. But by some miracle they were alive. How they had made it this far they didn't know.

'So what is it?' Mia asked, pointing at the jewel in his hand.

'It's all in here,' April said, bringing over the book she'd found in the chairman's office. 'Apparently it's a fragment of rock that came from outer space.'

'What? No way,' Mia said.

'Yes way, according to this.'

April caught everyone up on what they'd discovered from the chairman's recordings, while Zion investigated the control room.

This was a part of the facility he'd never seen before, and he couldn't pass up the chance to see it with his own eyes. The hologram from the computer was still displayed, and the workbench console Cyrus had been stuck to looked fairly innocuous now. Zion stood in front of the hologram and assessed his options. Numerous menu options were presented, allowing him to access the lighting in the manufacturing centre, progress reports on the latest batch of mechs, the locks to the doors around the area, amongst other things. The door locks seemed redundant now they knew the mechs could blow their way through them, unless they weren't built to contain the mechs.

He looked out of the window into the factory floor, which was now mostly empty, with the exception of the two gargantuans that were still stationary. He imagined they were now under Cyrus's control, along with the others.

Something started flashing on the computer hologram, catching his attention. A few taps and swipes of a hand later he realised what it was and immediately called in the others.

CHAPTER THIRTY-TWO

The whole group were now in the control room, gathered around the holographic screen that was displaying a map of the city and surrounding areas.

'What is it, Zion?' asked Cyrus.

'Look at this,' he said, pointing to a blinking dot on the hologram. 'We're not alone.'

'I'm not following.'

'We're not the only ones with control of mechs,' he said.

'What? How can you possibly know that?' Gabriel asked.

'The crystal around Cyrus's neck, it's emitting a signal. Whatever tracking system the government built is picking it up here.' He pointed again to the blinking dot on the hologram, which was located in the exact position of the facility. 'In the chairman's recordings he mentioned that one crystal was assigned to each mech handler, who controlled one group of twenty mechs. If someone has another crystal, and thus a mech army of twenty robot killing machines, their signal would be picked up here too.' He then pinched his thumb and index finger together to zoom out of the map on the hologram, revealing a second blinking dot.

'Son of a—' Gabriel muttered to himself.

'Impossible,' Cyrus breathed. 'All the mech handlers were killed, wiped out completely. Everyone knows that.'

'Not according to this,' Zion said plainly.

'It could just be the crystal, still emitting a signal where the handler died?' Gabriel suggested.

'I doubt it,' April countered, the book she had taken from the chairman's office still in her hands. 'It says here that there were loads of crystals assigned to handlers. Zion, zoom the map out again.' Zion obliged, pinching the hologram again to reveal more wasteland and the outline of the closest city to the north of Novasburgh.

'See?' she said.

'See what?' Cyrus asked.

April sighed. 'You boys are so slow. Doesn't it look strange to you that there was so much conflict in this part of the country, and yet there aren't any more dead handlers? If the crystal emitted a signal after the handler died, there would be loads of them blinking on this map.'

'Yeah, that does make sense,' Cyrus nodded. 'So there's really another mech handler still out there?' He fixated on the tiny blinking dot on the map. The point was located far outside of the city, further north and to the east of the facility.

'That's in the middle of nowhere. How have they survived this long?' Jennifer asked.

'If that is a mech handler, he could help us take down The Jackal,' Aiden added.

'Whoever that is, if Zion's right they have twenty mechs at their disposal. What if they're not friendly?' Rowley chipped in. 'I've had enough mechs chasing me down to last a lifetime.'

'We just evened up the odds,' April replied. 'So this handler, whoever they are, should have reason to listen to us. If they're at least a little human, they should care enough to want to stop slavery. They've got to help us.'

'April's right, we should at least try,' said Cyrus.

After more discussion, the group agreed that they would go to find the surviving mech handler, if not only to ask if they knew more about The Jackal's whereabouts. As they made their way back to the pickup, Gabriel hung back to talk to Zion.

'Thank you, for figuring this out,' he said almost reluctantly. Zion could see the pain in his voice as he said it. It was the ultimate apology. The 'I'm sorry, I was wrong.' He hadn't said it, but Zion could tell he'd meant it. It had been a long time coming, but he had finally proven himself to Gabriel.

'No problemo,' Zion smiled, as if he'd just thanked him for opening a door for him. 'Gabriel, as my gift to you, you can have dibs on pounding the life out of The Jackal when we eventually find him.'

**

The engine roared as the pickup truck tore through the dirt track road, heading north-east. The scorching sun, almost forgotten from the short time they'd spent in the mech facility was now out in full force, shining heavy rays onto Cyrus, who had resumed his position in the open air by the tailgate.

Before they had left the facility, a few of the companions had been getting agitated over how long their journey had been already. They wouldn't have enough food to last many more days. They agreed that if they didn't find The Jackal, or have any lead on his whereabouts in the next day, they'd head back to the supermarket to regroup and rethink. But Cyrus didn't want that to happen. This couldn't have all been for nothing.

With one hand grasped around his crystal he took a long look back through the dust kicked up by the vehicle. The spectacle he saw was one that no amount of time could get him used to. Bounding after the pickup truck were the mechs from the facility. Leading the charge were the panthers, almost keeping pace with the truck.

He was surprised by the sheer amount of concentration it took to command them. All it took was a focused thought pattern, a single concentrated burst of willing. But that was difficult to maintain over a long period of time, especially with the distractions brought on by Kevin's erratic driving. Cyrus found it intriguing how, if he focused hard on one mech, it was as if he could see through its eyes. Those terrifying eyes that he'd once looked right into, moments before a death-defying escape. It wasn't a clear sight, more a hazy blur of greys, like the dreams he'd had and the visions he'd experienced with Isaac and in the facility. He wondered what the mechs were thinking, if they thought at all, in those brief moments before they tried to tear him to pieces. Now he was on the other side, completely in control, and it was as if a new world had opened up before him. The feeling brought with it a raw sense of power, as though the odds had suddenly turned in his favour. It was then that he realised that it hadn't all been for nothing. If they never found The Jackal, at least they would be able to protect the colony from the feral mechs that terrorised the city.

Kevin navigated onto more tyre-friendly terrain, and the truck was now gripping much easier and began to tear away from the mechs. Cyrus could no longer see the golems behind the panthers, but once they arrived at their destination they'd wait for them to regroup. Interestingly without seeing the mechs with his own eyes it wasn't any more difficult to control them. The crystal was still glowing a bright white, reflecting the sun's rays like a diamond under a spotlight.

As the roar of the engine became a consistent rumble, Cyrus started to feel a sense of anxiety as they grew ever closer to their target. He felt a tight knot in his stomach, the adrenaline wearing off and being replaced with doubt. What if the surviving mech handler wasn't friendly, just as Rowley had feared? Was he prepared to fight them? Did he even know how?

'It's going to be OK, isn't it?' he said, breaking his concentration for a moment to look in Gabriel's direction. Gabriel watched as the panthers stopped dead in their tracks, the connection between them and Cyrus lost temporarily.

'Yes, it will,' he said, with a rare confidence that had been severely lacking in recent times. 'We made it this far with the odds stacked against us ten-fold. Now we have this,' he gestured to the frozen panthers that were quickly becoming smaller in their view. 'We're just going to talk to them, whoever they are. It's likely they have mechs too, but we should be even in numbers. We'll talk, and that's it. As long as they know we're friendly they have no reason to attack.'

Cyrus nodded and went back to focusing on the mechs, bringing them back in their direction.

Inside the truck, Mia had switched seats with Rowley, who had called 'shotgun' on the way to the vehicle. He held up his prized baseball card into the sunlight, studying its condition.

'Four generations,' he smiled. 'This card has been in my family for over a hundred years.'

The group sitting in the back seats weren't sure if he was talking to them, each one looking at the other for some guidance on whether to respond or not. Kevin had shut himself off in his own driving world, hurling the pickup truck around like it was a ride in an amusement park. A few potholes taken at speed had led to a few raised eyebrows. Growing up mostly in automated vehicles, the group didn't know how difficult it was to drive when you had no experience. But a few dodgy swerves of the wheel and a curse from Kevin's lips led them to believe that actually they might have been able to do a better job themselves.

Rowley sat back in his seat, still looking at the card. He must have looked at it a million times, but each time it was like he'd been presented with it for the first time. Cyrus had thought that it reminded him of a time when his father was alive. Perhaps the memory of his dad giving him the family heirloom was one he treasured, and liked to relive proudly. After the war ended and the world turned bad, Rowley seemed to retrieve the card from his pocket more frequently.

The car jolted over another pothole and the baseball card was launched out of Rowley's hands, which instinctively reached out to try and grab it again. A breeze moved through the driver's side window and out the other end, causing the card to dance in the air in a mini gust. Rowley yelped and swatted at it, desperately trying to catch it before it disappeared out of his window. His mind frantic, mirroring his motions, the card jumped higher and higher as he feebly attempted to halt its movements. The card moved dangerously close to the window, and another gust of air blew it under his arm and up over the other side. It was as if it was taunting him, a cruel twist of fate that he didn't deserve. Rowley reached for the button to close the window, but it wasn't working. Despite the miracle that had allowed the car to run after all these years, the electric windows hadn't aged as well. The window closed halfway before staggering and refusing to go any further.

Clawing at thin air, Rowley couldn't give up and kept swiping his hands close to, but yet so far away from the thin card that was blowing about around him. It was like trying to swat a fly; it looked so easy to do, yet the fly's reactions were so much faster than yours. The group in the back seats watched in silence. It looked comical, but they daren't laugh in case it hurt Rowley's feelings. Worst case scenario they knew they could just stop the car and go back for it, but Rowley's judgement had clearly been impaired. To him it was life or death, as if losing the card, even temporarily, would curse him forever.

It reminded Mia of the plant she'd bought Cyrus to put in his bedroom. It was a bonsai tree, notoriously difficult to maintain. He'd grown attached to it, so much so that the health of the plant meant everything to him. It was almost a symbol of their relationship. She'd bought him the plant, and if he let it die it meant the relationship would go with it. After taking a long trip away with her parents, the pair returned to Cyrus's house to find the plant brown and shrivelled. After a moment of held breath, Cyrus had erupted into laughter, and the curse was instantly lifted. However for Rowley it didn't seem to be that straightforward.

The card continued to dance and blow about freely, before Rowley took another lunge towards it, missing completely, and it got stuck under his armpit. A wave of relief swept over him as he closed his arm, trapping the card against his side. With his other free hand he plucked the card back out and sighed deeply. The group in the back started clapping and cheering, much to his embarrassment.

**

Cyrus took his hand momentarily away from the crystal and felt a sharpness return to his senses. Prolonged periods of concentration dulled his hearing slightly, as well as his vision as he focused on the mechs. Releasing his grip on the crystal was like the crystal releasing its grip on him.

He checked his watch briefly, just a flash of the wrist and a glance at the hands. Five fifteen. He tapped the watch face twice with his now free hand, and put it to his ear. In that moment he heard the faint tick sound of the minute hand moving along a notch.

Unbelievable, still working.

His hand went back to the crystal and he pushed himself back into the void.

'Up there!' someone shouted. Cyrus hadn't worked out who. He immediately lost concentration again and perked up at the outburst.

'I see it.' Kevin's voice.

The truck swerved violently and changed course, almost hurling Cyrus off the side. He dared to stand up for a brief moment, thought better of it and sat back down.

'Did you see anything?' Jane asked from behind him in the cargo hold.

'No, I couldn't see.'

He knocked on the back of the window into the interior of the car. The group in the back seats spun around.

'What's happening?' he asked, his voice muffled.

'Water,' Jennifer replied. 'I think we've found the river.'

She was right. Before long they were parked up on the bank of the river, the water flowing slowly from left to right. It looked murky, contaminated like in the city.

Kevin shut the engine off as he checked the holographic map he'd been using as his compass. They were getting close to the source of the signal they presumed the other crystal had been emitting. Now much more zoomed in, the map revealed the blinking dot near to the point where the river split off into two streams. It was difficult to see too far upstream from their position, with the land undulating more here.

They stopped for a snack and a dosing of water from their bottles. 'A hydrated mind is a sharp mind,' Gabriel said. It felt strange coming from his mouth. Gabriel wasn't the type for cheesy motivational sayings like that. Cyrus could sense that the man was in good spirits, apparently buoyed by the progress they had made in acquiring the mechs and tracking down the source of another handler.

Cyrus suddenly realised how hungry he was. Had they not eaten since they left the supermarket? No, that was two days ago now. Surely since then. The log cabin, perhaps? He couldn't remember. All he remembered was how good baked beans tasted cold. Something he'd become accustomed to now.

Sipping from a tin of soup like it was hot coffee, Kevin took a look at their progress on the navigation hologram. The source of the signal had stayed still; the handler probably camped up somewhere nearby. Another few minutes and they'd likely arrive at the source.

'How are you feeling?' he asked April, who was sat in the back seat, her legs up against the back of the passenger seat in front of her.

'How do you mean?' she asked, a little defensive.

'Just, you know, how are you?' he tried a smile this time.

'Oh,' she replied. 'I'm good, I guess.' She smiled back, purposely showing that she was grateful he asked. She was grateful, but the gesture was more to ensure that he didn't think she was rude. 'How are you?' she asked back.

Kevin grunted and knocked back the rest of his soup. 'About as good as I can be. This might be my last drive in this baby.' He placed his hands gently on the steering wheel, almost caressing it. The empty tin of soup fell from his lap into the footwell, splashing his leg with the few remaining orange droplets that had been left. He grunted a little louder, and April could tell the difference between that and the first one. The first had been resignation, the second pure annoyance.

'We're quickly running out of gas,' he said as he reached down for the tin can. He struggled as his stomach was wedged against the wheel. A quick pull of something on the side of the seat sent him shooting back, giving him room to clamber down into the footwell and retrieve it, but not before accidentally hitting the horn with his head. He duly tossed the can out the open door and it clanged as it hit a rock on the second bounce.

'Will we make it there?' she asked.

'Yes, easily,' he replied, looking back at the wheel again. 'But this could well be my last ride. I barely have enough juice to make it back to the city.'

April frowned, her forehead wrinkling as her face fell. She felt bad for him. He'd given them so much already without asking for a thing in return. He'd lost his home, and now he would lose another thing he cherished so dearly. All good things had to come to an end, but Kevin had lost it all in a day.

'We really appreciate it, you know,' she said, hoping it offered some consolation.

'I know,' he replied. 'Knowing the truth, about everything, I'd do it again. I actually wish Zion had found me sooner. Can't blame him though, we were both hiding from our past.'

He turned the attention back to April. 'You know it's very brave what you're doing, especially at your age.'

April tried hard to fight back against the obvious condescension, and her expression matched her thoughts exactly.

'Sorry, I didn't mean it like that,' Kevin backtracked. 'What I meant was you're very mature for your age. I didn't realise you were a teenager.'

Her face relaxed a little. 'I knew Jennifer would go with Cyrus, and I wasn't going to let her go without me,' she replied candidly. 'I'd have been a mess waiting for them to come back, knowing that they might not return.'

'You always were stubborn,' a voice came from outside the car. Jennifer's. She reached inside and put her arms around her sister's neck, kissing her on the side of her head.

'Just like Dad,' she said.

'Yeah,' Jennifer chuckled. 'Just like Dad.'

The rest of the group came back to the pickup truck together.

'We moving out?' Rowley asked.

'Huh?' Kevin realised all the eyes were on him in the driver's seat.

'The horn,' Rowley clarified. 'You were letting us know we need to move on.'

'No I... oh,' he realised. 'I was picking up something I dropped. I hit the horn by mistake.'

Rowley looked confused. 'Oh, so I guess we're good for a few more minutes?'

'We should probably get going anyway,' Gabriel interjected, reclaiming control.

'I kinda like it out here,' Rowley protested. 'The gentle current of water. It's nice.' He waited for the hint to sink in.

He wasn't ready to go on just yet. But after finding himself the subject of stares from the rest of the group, resigned himself to defeat and hopped in the truck.

CHAPTER THIRTY-THREE

Dust started to kick up off the ground around the truck as it powered through the desert-like wasteland. The river looked completely out of place in the scene, as though it had been placed there by man.

'Looks like another storm coming in,' Jane said, observing the change in weather.

'Let's hope it doesn't obscure our visibility,' said Zion. 'I'm not sure my stomach can take much more of this driving when we can actually *see* where we're going.' He caught Kevin's gaze in the rear-view mirror, and flashed a cheeky grin. On this occasion Kevin saw the funny side, much to the surprise of the rest of the car. He swung the steering wheel one way and then sharply the other, causing Zion to hit his head on the window next to him.

'Oops, sorry buddy, did I get you?' he apologised sarcastically. Zion cursed under his breath as he nursed the side of his head.

Kevin had changed noticeably in the short time they'd known him. It seemed the rekindling of his friendship with Zion had given him a more relaxed demeanour. Zion's jokey spirit was rubbing off on him, as it did with most people. The stern-face, dishevelled man that once pointed a shotgun at them was slowly disappearing, replaced by the child within who loved to drive fast.

Gabriel had been the most difficult to break down, but Zion would never give up on him. There were moments when he'd make a joke, which surprised everyone. He even seemed to surprise himself when he made them, evident by the way he quickly reverted back to his usual self; the firm and focused, yet soft-in-the-centre leader he was.

Dirt blew around the truck, peppering the bodywork as the storm began to worsen. The sky was a thin cloud of orange, the truck starting to be cocooned in that all too familiar feeling of dread that accompanied weather like this. This storm was more of an annoyance, an inconvenience that would set them back time as much as it was potentially dangerous. The road in front of the vehicle started to disappear, and as quickly as it had arrived it had clouded the car in dust and sand all around. Kevin was tempted to stop and hope it would pass, but decided against it. He pushed the truck to its limits, keeping the wheel steady as the giant beast of a machine bucked and jolted beneath him.

From the open cargo hold, Cyrus was cursing his luck at having to ride out his second dust storm from there. He closed his eyes, wishing he'd asked to switch seats with someone inside the car. Rowley, ever the gentleman, had stubbornly insisted on riding the whole journey in the back so others could sit in the relative comfort of the interior. Cyrus had felt obliged to do the same, even if his heart wasn't really in it.

Fortunately for him the storm was a short one and it passed as they sped through it. The road reappeared in front of the truck, the vehicle miraculously positioned dead centre, the remnants of a faded and worn dotted line flowing underneath. As the air around them cleared they could make out the river to their right, again a juxtaposition to the weather they were experiencing. It was a strange thing to see so much dust, with bits of sand flying around next to a bed of flowing water. It didn't make sense.

Shaking his head and fluffing his hair with his hand to get the dirt out of it, Cyrus gave a quick smile of relief to Rowley, who reciprocated with a thumbs up. Something caught the attention of the driver and there was suddenly a lot of talking from inside the car. Through the glass window the muffled noise was difficult to understand. Cyrus tapped on the glass to get in on the action.

'The river,' Mia mouthed back to him, before realising she may as well shout instead. 'It's joining with another stream.'

Cyrus cocked his head behind him and saw what she was referring to. There was a small waterfall ahead, about twenty feet high, the car high above it on the road alongside. Beyond that was a split in a larger river, with half the water trickling one way and half into the waterfall.

The ride was slower now, as even Kevin seemed to start feeling the nerves of the moment, displayed through his easing off the gas. Either that or the truck was running on fumes, Cyrus couldn't tell. They came to a ridge and parked the car at the top, admiring the view of the landscape below. They could see for miles. To the north and north-west, nothing but deserted space, much like the path across from the mech facility to the road by the river; dusty and desolate. To the right, the river, and beyond that more open space. The city of Cambrook was still a good number of miles further past the horizon. But directly below the ridge, in plain view was what looked like a shanty town.

Kevin checked the navigation on the hologram. They were exactly where the signal from the other crystal was coming from. If this was where the other handler was, it wasn't at all what they expected. For one thing, there didn't seem to be any mechs nearby.

'OK, this is it.' Gabriel didn't waste any time. 'You ready?'

The group stayed silent.

'Cyrus, how far away are our mechs?' he asked.

Cyrus thought for a moment. He had completely forgotten to keep them following the truck since they stopped for a break. His face said more than any apology could have, and Gabriel put a weary hand to his head, wiping away a bead of sweat. Cyrus knew it was best not to say anything after that. Just concentrate on fixing it. He ran his hands down the thread of his necklace and clutched the crystal, concentrating hard. The world around him quickly began to dull as his focus was turned to the mechs.

**

It took some time for the mechs to reach them, especially the gargantuans which were incredibly slow moving compared to the golems and panthers. By the time they had the mechs set up in a perimeter around the shanty town and were ready to move in, it was getting dark. Cyrus was mentally exhausted from the sheer concentration it took to bring the mechs this far.

The last glimpse of light headed beyond the horizon, the sun setting on what had been the strangest day of Cyrus's life. It seemed like each new day was more bizarre than the last. Gabriel had decided that waiting until dark was actually a smart idea, if unplanned. Leaving their backpacks in the truck, they closed in on the town, leaving the mechs in a wide perimeter behind them. The first sign of human or mech activity and they'd be ready. Cyrus would need to be quick on the draw with his focus.

'I'll wait with Gyro-3 in the truck, just in case,' Kevin said as the group started to move off. Gabriel nodded to him in approval. It was probably smart to have someone hang back.

Cyrus's hand was twitching like a cowboy waiting to draw his six-shooter. He felt strangely naked without his plasma rifle, his hand now hovering over the proton pistol he'd tucked into the makeshift holster he'd strapped to the leg of his cargo pants. His job was to utilise the mechs, not become distracted by any gun he carried. The crystal would be his weapon now.

'Let's split up,' Gabriel said, more a command than a suggestion. The group set off in different directions, using the same groups as in the mech facility for ease of dividing themselves up.

The houses here were no more than small huts, almost indigenous in their build, with a few modern elements splattered about. One had a small windmill on top of the roof, which was spinning around and around in the gentle breeze that was bringing the cold of night.

It suddenly occurred to Cyrus how small this shanty town was. It was much smaller than he had imagined it to be. What's more, it was deserted, like Woodside had been. Being in the tranquil setting of the forest had at least given Woodside the illusion that there could have been civilisation there. And that turned out to be true, if you classed Kevin as civilised. This place was in the middle of nowhere. Not exactly the best place to live. Nevertheless, the navigation system didn't lie, there was a crystal signal being emitted there.

'I've got a bad feeling about this,' he whispered to Aiden, who was closest to him. Aiden said nothing, concentrating on each decrepit shack they passed. 'Should we try and get their attention?' he said. 'Maybe they don't know we're here.' Again Aiden said nothing.

Cyrus cast a look to the sky and noticed how beautiful it was when it was clear. The stars were out in full, and he could see a variety of constellations. It reminded him of the night he'd been separated from his group and spent hours hiding from mechs in a hole beneath some rubble.

Focus, Cyrus.

He snapped back to game mode and realised Aiden had left him behind. He looked back to see Mia coming towards him, her rifle poised, the butt locked against her shoulder. Despite the way she was shuffling from one hut to another, her strides smaller than usual, she still managed to carry herself with a surprising amount of grace. He'd given her his plasma rifle, and in return he'd taken her pistol; a last resort option in case the mechs didn't get to them quick enough.

She looked at him and smiled. Even in the dark he could see those bright eyes twinkling in the moonlight, her smile showing her perfect teeth like a cheesy toothpaste commercial. But within a moment her smile suddenly faded and she raised her rifle up towards him. Cyrus felt a rush of adrenaline pour over him, the action changing the atmosphere in a heartbeat. Mia's eyes went wide as her aim on Cyrus fixed. Cyrus was bemused and terrified in equal measure as he watched the love of his life point a gun right at him, her face looking like she'd seen a ghost.

'Cyrus, behind you!' she screamed as she pulled the trigger. The gun backfired; the second time it had happened to her in recent times. As she was hurled backwards by the blast with a pained look on her face, Cyrus remembered the shoddy cleaning job he'd done on the rifle after the dust storm before the mech facility.

You useless idiot.

Mia hit the deck, the gun lying next to her, smoking away in its broken state. She pointed behind Cyrus and screamed again.

'Cyrus!'

Cyrus spun on the spot to where she was pointing, reaching for his crystal. He was just in time to see the flash of a figure rush at him through the darkness. Then nothing but blackness.

CHAPTER THIRTY-FOUR

Cyrus stirred as he began to wake from a bad dream. This time it was different to the dream sequence he'd had when he was in the mall. Darkness all around, Mia looking at him from the ground, pointing behind him, her eyes wide with terror. Something lurking in the night, preying on him.

He woke in an unfamiliar place, the sun streaming through the light through the barred windows. He twisted his head, suddenly aware he was awake and away from the dream. Then the pain came. A pounding headache worse than any he'd ever had shot through his skull. He clutched it with his hands, felt a bump on his forehead. He must have been hit pretty hard.

He tried to think back to the last thing he remembered. Darkness, the twinkling of the stars above him, the feel of dust kicking up from the ground as he walked. Mia, on the floor in front of him, yelling at him and pointing. It hadn't been a dream, what he was remembering was real.

Where am I?

His thumping head was having a hard time processing it all. He wondered where Mia was, and Rowley and the others.

The difference between dream and reality was becoming clearer, but he felt like he'd just woken up in a nightmare.

Sitting upright with a struggle and a gasp of breath, the room around him began to spin. He closed his eyes and sucked in the air. It was stale, the stuffy air in this cell-like place almost unwelcome as it entered his nose and mouth. A cell, that was exactly what he was in, he had suddenly realised. An empty room with barred windows where the air freely came and went. The sunlight shone through the small glass-less window, casting a shadow of the bars in the patch of light on the floor. Brick walls lined the space around him, with a door on the other side of the room. It looked pretty heavy duty; he wasn't bashing his way out any time soon. There was a slat towards the top of the door, a peep hole for the outside to keep an eye on their prisoner. Him.

He started to fit the pieces together in his fuzzy state. Mia screaming at him, the sudden blackness, the headache and the bump on his head. He'd been kidnapped. But who had taken him, and how had they done so without the others intervening? There must have been a lot of them, and they must have been fast. Whoever it was, they'd been expecting them in that shanty town.

He felt for the crystal, but couldn't find it. Panicking, he tugged at his t-shirt to feel for the cold jewel pressing against his torso. But still nothing. He groped at his neck, searching desperately for the woven cord the small crystal hung from, to find that it had gone.

Son of a—

A fury began to build up inside him, and he screamed out loud and banged his hands against the nearest wall.

The rage lasted a few moments, before his throbbing head ceased it and he lay flat on his back on the floor, spread eagled in resignation. He lay there for a few minutes, just staring up at the ceiling.

He began to wonder how long he had been out for. The blow to the head was substantial, and it was now daytime. He pulled his wrist close to his face and looked at the watch. The face was smashed, a crack running diagonally from the ten to the four. The hands were on nine and six, but he couldn't be sure they were accurate. He put the watch close to his ear and listened for the tick of the minute hand. Thirty seconds went by, nothing. Forty, still nothing. Fifty, then sixty, nothing. He listened for ages, calming his breathing to hear the faintest of ticks emanating from the watch. But it was no use, it was broken.

Cyrus suddenly felt completely helpless, all the power he'd felt before with the crystal around his neck and the mechs in tow vanished. Even the small pleasure of knowing the time had been taken from him.

He stood up slowly, wary of another dizzy spell. The barred window was set into the wall a couple of feet taller than him, offering him only a view of the sky and the blinding sun that seemed to be directing all its rays right onto his face. He strained through the brightness, jumped and reached up for the bars, grasping them with both hands. He hauled himself up, straining and cursing his lack of upper body strength. He never had been good at pull-ups, let alone when hungry and dehydrated.

He got a good look at the world around him, and what he saw came as a surprise. Before him was a peaceful looking little village. Well-built houses were erected in the middle, with farmyards beyond, leading out to the river. The houses looked modern, perhaps recently built, and the place had a sickeningly sweet vibe. It was in stark contrast to the city; no signs of bombings or conflict. Almost as if the war hadn't touched this part of the world at all.

The river to his right, trickling gracefully, gave Cyrus some clue as to where he was, but he couldn't be sure how much further up they were from the shanty town they'd stopped at. The air outside was clearer than in his cell, refreshing even. He took in a deep breath and enjoyed the cool air. His arms started to struggle under his weight and he had to let go. He stumbled as he hit the floor, the concrete arriving quicker than he'd anticipated, causing him to land on his backside. He sat there for a while, too drained to attempt to stand again.

There was a sound coming from outside the cell, of keys jangling and a door being unlocked. Cyrus was suddenly alert and on edge. Footsteps echoed from outside the cell, getting louder and louder. The steps were slow, and whoever they belonged to walked without care or urgency. The footsteps stopped as they reached the point directly outside Cyrus's cell, and a loud metallic scraping sound followed as the slat on the door opened. Cyrus watched intently as a pair of eyes were revealed, staring back at him on the floor. The slat closed again with another loud scrape, and Cyrus started to wonder who this person was. There was a long delay before anything else happened, which added to his apprehension. He knew they wouldn't be here to let him walk free. More likely come to give him a beating. At this point he wasn't sure he had the energy to fight back.

The door unlocked with a click, the sound sudden, cutting through the air and tension simultaneously. Cyrus waited anxiously as the door opened slowly with a creak. Light shone through from the hallway outside, blocked by the shadowy outline of a tall, stocky man.

'On your feet,' a gruff voice said. It was the kind of gravelly voice that didn't so much reflect the man's demeanour as allude to the number of cigarettes he smoked a day. Not likely a habit he could have kept up now, unless this community had a stockpile. He remembered the view of farmland outside his cell. It was a long shot that they were growing tobacco here. Not exactly the highest priority commodity, let alone the conditions required to grow it.

The man moved further into the doorway, his frame now completely visible as he entered the cell. He was looking at Cyrus with beady eyes, his bald head and rounded belly giving him a thuggish appearance. Cyrus instantly recognised the man as someone not to be messed with. The man kept staring at him, his head cocking to the side slightly as he appraised the person half his size sitting lazily on the floor.

'I said, on your *feet*.' He emphasised the last word to show he meant business. Cyrus gingerly picked himself up and waited for the next command. There was none. Instead the man shifted his weight to the side of the door, allowing a gap beside him. Was it a trick? Was he taunting him, showing how close he was to freedom, before blocking the way at the last minute? Cyrus hesitated, forcing the man to speak again.

'We haven't got all day. The Jackal has requested your presence.'

Cyrus's heart almost stopped beating in that moment, and his head started to spin again, a thousand thoughts swimming around it at once. The dumbfounded look on his face was impossible to hide.

The Jackal?

The reality of the situation suddenly hit Cyrus like a freight train, almost knocking him out as the pieces began to fit together. The other mech handler, it was The Jackal. The very person they were looking for, to confront and overthrow, had seen them coming. He'd anticipated them without them even knowing he knew they existed, and they'd fallen right into his trap. But how? It still didn't make sense.

Now Cyrus understood why Isaac had been so nervous when he spoke of The Jackal. Had he known about the crystals, the mechs under his control? There was something unsettling about the way he'd looked at it around Cyrus's neck.

He then thought of what the brute of a man in front of him had just said. The Jackal wanted to see him. But why? What good was he to him alive? Perhaps to rub in the fact that he'd outsmarted him, stolen his crystal and made him feel like an insignificant worm rotting away in prison?

The large brute, presumably one of The Jackal's guards, waved an arm at the space beside him, gesturing for Cyrus to exit the cell. He took a long look around the dingy cell and sheepishly walked towards him.

'I guess I might be back here in a few minutes anyway,' Cyrus said as he passed the man. The guard grunted in annoyance; he didn't seem like the type for small talk. Cyrus felt something grab his arm, and then the other, and before he knew what was going on the man was tying his hands together behind his back with a length of rope. The knots were tight and the rope chafed against his skin, digging into it with its rough feel.

On the other side of the doorway, Cyrus realised the sheer scale of the building he was in. Walkways lined the space above him, and on two levels were more empty cells that looked exactly like the one he had been in. He was literally inside a prison. The guard exited behind and grabbed Cyrus by the arm, pushing him to the left, dictating the direction he wanted him to go in.

'Alright, jeez, take it easy,' Cyrus said. The man said nothing in response and continued to push him in the back every few seconds. It was completely excessive, as Cyrus had already got a handle on where he was going. He figured the man was a perfect example of someone drunk on power. If he was this bad, he dreaded to think how The Jackal would be.

It suddenly dawned on him that in the next few minutes he would finally come face-to-face with the very man he'd been pursuing the last few days. So much had changed in that short time that it felt like this was something he'd been leading up to his whole life. It seemed like nothing else had mattered. If they wanted to survive, if they wanted to rebuild a future for this city, they'd need to re-establish society the way it was meant to be. And that meant that The Jackal had to be stopped, one way or another.

The man coughed violently from behind him, the noise sudden and startling. Cyrus listened as a phlegmy sound caught in the guard's throat, and he spat onto the floor beside him.

That'll be the cigarettes.

The guard gave him another push in the back, this time hard enough to knock Cyrus over. Having his hands bound behind his back was affecting his balance, and as he fell he'd instinctively tried to put them in front of him to protect himself, to no avail. Instead he'd managed to fall onto his knees, the concrete floor stinging his kneecaps with a sharp shock. He let out an annoyed groan as the pain came quickly.

'Alright,' he said. 'Had your fun now?' This guy was really getting on his nerves, and the helplessness of the situation was only adding to his anger. Again the man said nothing, and just hauled Cyrus up with one hand gripped on his shoulder, before pushing him forward once more.

The cell block had a few more corridors to navigate, these ones darker than before. The man continued to push and shove Cyrus, seemingly not yet bored of the sport, until they reached the door to the outside. Cyrus saw more people, who greeted the guard and stared at Cyrus with wary eyes, like he was some kind of criminal. It was like they were playing out a scene, but the characters were all wrong. Cyrus wasn't a criminal, and if they were The Jackal's people it was they who were breaking the law.

A pair, a man and a woman, both of average height and build, exchanged a few words with each other in hushed tones as Cyrus passed by, clearly talking about him.

'Wait,' the gravelly voice came from behind him. Cyrus stopped walking. The guard came around to the front of him and looked him dead in the eye. 'You run, you're dead. Understand?' The foul smell of the man's breath pierced Cyrus's nostrils. He nodded, his teeth gritted. At this point the anger that had built up inside him was overriding his fear of the man. He almost wanted the chance to take a swing at him, despite the consequence of what would surely follow.

The guard grimaced, revealing two rows of teeth that could only be described as a dentist's nightmare. Cyrus was sure one was dead in the corner of his mouth. He then turned and slowly walked over to the door at the end of the corridor. Nothing this man did was hurried.

As with the door to the cell, the twist of a key in the lock of this door was met with creaking and squealing, as though the lock was groaning at being used again. It opened noisily and light poured through in a blinding flash. Cyrus squinted his eyes as he waited for them to adjust, and noticed the familiar feeling of dust attacking his eyelids as a gust of wind blew into the prison. When he opened his eyes again, the guard was waving him over from a good ten yards away. He assessed his options, looking back the way he came. The man and woman were still whispering to each other, and paused to look back in his direction once more. Finally he resigned himself to being a prisoner a little longer and followed the guard outside.

**

The air was fresh, or at least fresher than inside the prison. It was hot outside, but less stuffy. Cyrus took in a deep breath and for once enjoyed the sun on his face. The novelty would wear off in no time, but he would take any small luxury he could to distract himself from what was happening. The thought made him wonder, what was really happening here? The sight before him was so different to what he had expected. Isaac's vision had shown him The Jackal, laughing maniacally while his men whipped slaves, who worked the land. The place had looked so much more sinister in the vision; a barren land where the hot sun beat down on the innocent and dried up the water supply. Instead, Cyrus saw what looked like the start of a new civilisation. Modern buildings being erected, the beginnings of farmland surrounding it. He could even hear the faint trickling of water somewhere in the distance. There was definitely a piece missing to this puzzle.

'So where is The Jackal?' Cyrus asked the guard. 'If he's so desperate to meet me, why didn't he come and visit me in the can?'

No response, yet again. The guard simply pushed him in the back to speed him up. Again Cyrus fell from the force of the shove, falling onto his side this time with a groan. The guard rolled his eyes and turned away to cough and spit once more. As he struggled on the ground, Cyrus felt something crumple underneath him. As he shuffled around he was astonished to find a dog eared baseball card with the name *Jackie Robinson* printed on it.

Rowley.

He wondered what Rowley's prized card was doing here. Either someone had taken it from him or he'd passed through here at one point. He prayed that his friend was OK. Cyrus glanced at the guard, who was busy coughing up his guts, and manoeuvred himself into a position where his bound hands could pick up the card and put it into his back pocket.

Minutes later they passed a house, which seemed to be empty inside. No furnishings, just a shell of a building.

'Where is everyone?' Cyrus asked, more curiously to himself than anything.

'Working,' the man grunted.

The building in the centre of the village was much larger and taller than the houses and huts dotted around it. The guard steered Cyrus towards it, and he figured this must have been the hub of the village. Part of the building was open, held together by makeshift scaffolding as workers hammered away. They were dressed in regular clothes like himself, and like his theirs were torn in places. Cargo pants becoming makeshift shorts, t-shirts becoming tank tops where the sleeves were ripped.

They approached a large door that seemed far too grand to be practical. It was as if the person who designed the building wanted to create a castle-like feel to the place. The door certainly gave off an intimidating vibe, giving the impression that it was made for something much bigger and much more powerful than him as he approached.

Two more guards stood either side of the door. Normal looking people again, unlike the hulking brute who was escorting him. They were holding plasma rifles and stood still like sentries. They too gave Cyrus a strange look as he approached, again making him feel like scum.

'The Jackal wants to see the prisoner,' the brute grunted from behind Cyrus.

Prisoner. He actually said prisoner.

The two sentries looked at each other briefly, one nodding to the other, who in turn unlocked the giant door. They each pulled one side open, grasping the rings that sat on the heavy wooden panels that together made an arc shape at the top. The inside of the building was revealed, a large open corridor with a high ceiling to match the height of the door. Despite being a new building, the place had the feel of an old Middle Eastern structure, like a sultan's palace. It was a spectacular sight, but Cyrus couldn't help feeling that it didn't really fit in with the rest of the village. The land in this part of the country was becoming more and more desert-like as the years went by, and on its own the building could have passed for some kind of crude rehashed interpretation of Arabian Nights.

The long corridor was dimly lit, and even more so as the heavy doors closed behind them with a loud bang. Cyrus could hear the sentry locking it again. Security was certainly tight.

The corridor snaked one way and then another as the guard continued to nudge Cyrus on at every turn. Rounding another corner, Cyrus could see the light from outside streaming through as a large opening appeared. He turned to the guard, who pointed ahead to the opening without saying a word. He didn't need to, Cyrus got the message; 'Go that way or I'll drag you that way.' He walked wearily and as he made it to the opening the sun hit him again, this time not so welcoming. He was suddenly aware of how thirsty he was, and couldn't remember the last time he'd had a drink.

The opening led to a circular courtyard, open to the heavens, with more building surrounding the entire circumference. It felt almost like a very large open air theatre. He squinted his eyes as the sun shone directly on them. Again the instinct was to use his hands to shield himself, this time to cup one on his forehead as a makeshift baseball cap. But again as he tried to move his hands chafed on the rope and it bore into his skin. He felt helpless, like a lamb being taken to slaughter. Was this where they'd kill him? Droplets of sweat dripped from his head, producing damp spots on the dusty ground.

And then he saw him. Lounging in a throne-like structure, too grand to simply be called a chair, yet too extravagant to be made purely for sitting. The throne was made from wicker and sharpened sticks, the back erected taller than it needed to be; designed to intimidate and allude to the power of the man sitting on it. And there he was, sitting there on his throne. The man he'd been waiting so long to find. The Jackal.

CHAPTER THIRTY-FIVE

Cyrus appraised the man before him, as he felt the man doing the same to him. The kidnapper of innocents, tormentor of slaves. The Jackal sat slumped in the throne-like chair sideways, his legs up over one armrest while his back lay against the other. It didn't look like a comfortable pose, but he imagined the relaxed nature of it was meant to create the illusion that he was completely at ease, holding all the power in any given scenario. The fact that the guards had locked the door immediately behind Cyrus led him to believe otherwise.

What struck Cyrus most from this first impression was how small the man was. He'd remembered Isaac talking about The Jackal as a cunning man, someone whose brilliant mind more than made up for anything he lacked physically. But in the vision he'd share with Isaac, he'd seen a different incarnation of him; a terrifying creature of at least seven feet tall, fangs for teeth and an evil tinge of red in his eyes. He had imagined someone so evil that their physical appearance had been warped into something akin to a demon from hell itself. But what he saw in front of him was nothing more than a below-average-sized man in his late thirties, with a receding hairline and slightly rounded belly. Beside his throne was a lazily placed plasma rifle, broken by the look of it.

'You know, Cyrus, you really ought to be more careful with guns. They're not toys you know.' The Jackal's voice broke the long silence that had developed between the pair, as he gestured to the rifle beside him. Like his demeanour, his voice was calmer, his words more collected than Cyrus had imagined. The demon-like interpretation of the man had brought an expectation of a harsher voice, every word spat with hatred. Cyrus looked at the gun and then to The Jackal, remembering back to the dream that hadn't really been a dream. The one where Mia had held the gun as it backfired, shooting her backwards onto the ground in a crumpled heap. Her scream echoed around his mind as the memory came flooding back to him. He tried to shake it off.

When The Jackal had spoken, he hadn't even glanced in Cyrus's direction. It was as though he was completely disinterested in him. Another power play, Cyrus assumed.

'You're a lot smaller in real life,' Cyrus said, trying to cut through the bull as quickly as possible. The Jackal laughed, a hearty laugh that seemed greatly exaggerated.

'Interesting you should say that. I recall many other people saying that before. Of course, they're all dead now.'

Cyrus tried hard to maintain some level of composure. The man was trying to scare him, and it was working. But he needed to show, even pretend, that he wasn't afraid. He had nothing to lose in riling him up. There was clearly something The Jackal wanted from him, and that was the reason he was still alive.

'I have to say, you're not what I imagined either,' The Jackal said, casually inspecting his fingernails. 'When my men told me about you and your friends, I was expecting someone a little more…' he stopped himself, searching for the right word. 'Intimidating,' he finished. 'You see, a leader of men needs to be just that. Someone who will guide his people in the right direction, where people will follow without question.'

Cyrus was confused. How did he know who he was? Had he been expecting him all along? And why had he assumed he was the leader of his group? Everyone knew Gabriel was the one who took up that role.

'That's not true at all. You don't lead through fear. That's not leading. That's dictating.'

'Oh but it is, Cyrus. The war took its toll on everyone. We are the last few people in this city, and who knows, maybe even the country. We are the innocent civilians left behind by the wicked cruelty of others, forced to forge a new path for ourselves.'

That was the second time he had called him by name.

How the hell does he know who I am?

'You're not innocent,' Cyrus could feel himself getting angry. 'You are half the reason we are in this mess. You and your sick desire to rule.' He marched forward towards The Jackal, but made it barely twenty feet away before a shot fired and the ground ahead of him lit up in a plasma explosion. Dust lifted from the floor and sprayed Cyrus's face.

The Jackal tutted and pointed to the roof above. 'That's close enough.' Cyrus looked to the sky, and saw that all around him were more guards aiming the barrels of their plasma rifles right at him.

'A leader must point the way and encourage others to follow,' The Jackal continued.

'I would hardly call this 'pointing the way',' Cyrus snapped. 'You're kidnapping people and working them like slaves to build *your* future, whatever twisted future that is. You don't give a crap about them, any of them.' He looked up to the rooftop of the surrounding building and raised his voice. 'He's brainwashing you! Can't you see?'

He recognised one or two of the people. They were some of the ones that had stormed the shopping mall with Michelle. They must have come here after they escaped. There was no reply from any of them, the men and women continuing to point their rifles right at him. The Jackal smiled and started to chuckle to himself.

'You don't see the bigger picture, Cyrus. I'm building a life for these people. They're not slaves, they're workers. They're doing their part to help build a better future for everyone.'

'Oh really? They're doing this of their own free will?' Cyrus challenged.

'You have this all wrong, my friend. Look around you. Look what I have created for these people. These refugees that were oppressed by the robotic monsters of the city. I've given them a new life.'

'You're the monster,' Cyrus replied.

'Am I? Tell me Cyrus, while I've been building a safe haven for the people, what have you been doing? Running around stealing food from supermarkets?'

Cyrus froze, the blood running from his face.

No, no, no, no, no.

'That's right, we know all about your little colony,' he continued, a grimace appearing on his face, akin to that of the brutish guard. 'You're so short-sighted. They couldn't survive in that place for long. You were sentencing them to death, leaving them while you went off gallivanting.'

'That's not how it was,' Cyrus protested, suddenly feeling like a man on trial. Here he was in the middle of a large open space, his hands tied behind his back and guns trained on him, pleading his innocence to a man sitting leisurely on a throne. It was all wrong.

Cyrus noticed something hanging around the man's neck. A crystal, just like the one he wore. Unlike Cyrus's, this one hung from a gold chain. As if the delusion of grandeur could get worse.

'So it's true,' Cyrus said with a sigh. 'You really are insane.'

The Jackal swivelled in his seat, sitting upright now with both hands on the armrests. That seemed to get his attention.

'I know the truth, all of it,' Cyrus continued. 'You're not saving people from mechs gone haywire. You're using them to hunt people down and make them fear them, so you can swoop in and offer them a 'better life'. Only when you 'save' them you bring them into a world far worse than before.'

'That's a wild accusation,' The Jackal replied, his grimace turning into an aggressive gritting of teeth. Cyrus saw this and pressed on.

'You hunted down my friends with those beasts.' He raised his voice deliberately so the guards nearby could hear. His fists clenched behind his back, the rope burning again his skin. That would leave one hell of a rash. 'How can you expect people to trust your lies after you kidnap them?'

'Who would believe this place existed? This town is everything everyone wished for after the war, it's almost too good to be true. They needed me to show them.' The Jackal's eyes widened as he pushed hard to regain control.

'It *is* too good to be true, asshole.'

The Jackal slammed his fists down onto the armrests and stood up. 'I have saved these people!'

A long pause followed as the pair looked at each other. A light breeze blew through the opening, creating a mini twister of dirt and dust a foot off the ground. The Jackal's eyes were wide and he was still staring at Cyrus, so deep it was as though he was trying to hypnotise him. Finally he regained a little composure and sat back down, shuffling about to get comfortable again as he shook off the anger.

'That's what you tell them, isn't it,' Cyrus said. 'That you'll save them from the mechs. That the crystal gives you the power to keep them away. Not entirely untruthful, but misleading all the same. You're smart, but your reign of tyranny is coming to an end.' He forced a smile that exuded much more confidence than he was feeling, moments before The Jackal raised an arm in the air. This was immediately followed by the simultaneous shift in balance of the guards on the roof, taking a closer aim at his prisoner.

Cyrus sweated more profusely now, feeling the barrels of the rifles bearing down onto him. Exposing The Jackal could have worked in his favour, should the guards believe him, but they were clearly already too brainwashed to believe the nonsense of their cherished leader's prisoner. Aggravating The Jackal had been a risky move and he'd been too cocky in his approach. He could order them to fire at any second.

The Jackal slowly lowered his arm, and the guards relaxed.

'I'm offering you a chance,' he said, his composure returning once more. 'Because I'm feeling generous today. I want you to buy into what we're doing here, I really do. I understand your concerns, but do you really believe the words that just came out of your mouth? I mean, how farfetched. Why would I put people in danger when I want to protect them?' He laughed heartily, prompting the guards above to laugh along with him, instantly keeping them on-side.

'Where are my friends?' Cyrus asked, ignoring his proposition. The Jackal frowned at this.

'Unlike you, they're grateful for what I've done. They're working on the farm as we speak.'

'Bullshit. You're forcing them to work. They're tough people, they won't give up. They'll fight back.'

'Oh really?' The Jackal shifted in his seat once more, leaning closer to Cyrus. 'Just like your little robot builder friend? Kevin, was it? He took off the second my men found you in that shanty town. Loyal friends you have there.'

A shiver went down Cyrus's spine. Was that true? Surely Kevin wouldn't have run away.

'I feel sorry for you, Cyrus, I really do,' The Jackal said. 'It's not nice to have your friends abandon you, is it? But I can tell you're a good man. You wouldn't abandon your companions, now would you?' A hint of a smile etched across his face. 'Oh, that's right, you did!' He clapped his hands together and stood up abruptly, the smile now running from ear to ear. 'In fact, if I have my facts right, and do let me know if I'm embellishing a little, but you left one of your men for dead.'

Cyrus frowned. What was he talking about? He thought back to the last few days. He couldn't have meant Doug. Gabriel risked his life for him. He thought harder, and suddenly a memory came back to him. Rowley's pale face after he'd lost one of his group to the mechs.

Nathaniel.

The Jackal could see the penny drop in Cyrus's eyes. 'Bingo!' he yelled. 'You see, Cyrus, you're not the superhero you thought you were. In fact, I would say that was quite an evil thing to do. Wouldn't you agree, Nathaniel?'

The sound of slow footsteps emanated from the other side of the courtyard. Cyrus spun around, The Jackal's words still bouncing around his mind. It was then that he saw the man on crutches hobbling towards him.

It can't be.

'Hello, Cyrus,' Nathaniel said.

Cyrus was gobsmacked. All this time he'd thought he was dead. It was like seeing a ghost.

'I know I never fit into your little clique,' Nathaniel said. 'But I didn't know you wanted me dead.'

'That's not how it was at all,' Cyrus protested. 'Rowley has been torn up inside because of what happened. He blamed himself. He mourned your death. We all did!'

'Nonsense, you wanted me out and you fed me to the mechs. If The Jackal's crystal hadn't disabled the mechs right before they tore me to pieces you'd have had your way.'

'Is that what he told you?' Cyrus laughed. 'That he "disabled the mechs" to save you? He's controlling them, Nathaniel. How can you not see?'

'Cyrus, you're embarrassing yourself,' The Jackal interjected. 'Nathaniel knows the truth, and he's lucky to be here. You need to start taking responsibility for your actions.'

Cyrus fell to his knees and cursed under his breath.

After a short pause, The Jackal waved over the brutish guard. 'As lovely as this reunion has been, I think we're done here.'

The guard marched over and grabbed Cyrus, hauling him up onto his feet. Cyrus took one last look at The Jackal and Nathaniel before being turned around and led back out the way he'd come.

**

As the guard poked and prodded him back towards the prison, Cyrus thought about the encounter he'd had with The Jackal. He was smart, a clear manipulator, evidenced by the kingdom he'd built for himself and the people who blindly followed him, acting as his puppets to enact his cruel work on the world. Seeing Nathaniel again had been surreal. He was glad he was alive, but seeing how brainwashed he was only added to his anger towards The Jackal.

There was something about the man sitting on the throne that hadn't sat right with him. It was clear that he could have killed Cyrus at any moment. Someone who was causing so much trouble to his reign should surely have been better dead. But for one reason or another, he'd kept him alive. That meant he needed something from him. He wasn't sure what, but The Jackal was trying to play his cards just right to get him to do exactly what he wanted. He needed to figure out what that was.

A few moments later they passed a house, smaller than the empty one he'd seen on the way in. This one was more hut-like. Cyrus could see a woman inside, stirring a giant vat of liquid in a cauldron-sized pot. The fire beneath was contained within a bed of straw. The woman looked at Cyrus, the pair making eye contact. She was an elderly lady, her appearance frail, nothing but skin and bone. Cyrus could see the fear in her eyes as she looked from him to the guard behind. There were some things that were better explained through actions and not words. In that moment Cyrus was assured that everything he'd feared about this place was true. The Jackal was lying, as he suspected. The people here, save for the guards, weren't buying into a new way of life. They were prisoners, and they were terrified.

In that moment a woman cried out in the distance, and Cyrus could hear the crack of a whip, followed by silence.

'What the hell was that?' he shot a glance back at the guard, who purposely ignored him. Instead he just pushed him onward, keeping him moving back towards his prison cell.

CHAPTER THIRTY-SIX

As he reached the entrance to the prison, Cyrus could hear voices coming from inside. The door opened and the darkness of the prison was revealed. The voices were louder now, and he started to recognise them. He squinted his eyes to see inside and could make out a number of figures, hands bound behind their backs the same way his were, walking in single file while a number of armed guards escorted them towards their cells. The first voice he heard was Jennifer's. 'Get your dirty hands off me, creep!' she called, struggling as one of the guards tried to hurry her progress.

He could make out other familiar voices too. Gabriel was at the front of the group, grunting at one of the guards, who seemed to be giving him a wide berth. At the back of the line, the last person to enter the prison turned around briefly, before emitting a wide smile when she saw him. Even from this distance Cyrus could see Mia's eyes light up in delight.

'Cyrus, you're OK!'

Cyrus smiled back at her, and enjoyed the moment when the rest of the group realised he was there with them, alive and well. It was a short moment of relief that he savoured.

Moments later, they were all locked inside their individual cells, the doors closed shut. Cyrus hadn't had a chance to embrace Mia in his arms, or high five Rowley. He would even have taken a sarcastic joke from Zion. All too soon the moment of being reunited with his friends had passed, and he was back in his cell, alone. The good news was that the cells weren't soundproof, and he could still communicate with them, even if he couldn't see them.

'What happened?' April asked, from the cell next to him. Cyrus decided to shout his answer so everyone could hear him, and proceeded to tell the group of his encounter with The Jackal, Nathaniel, the whole thing.

'And then they brought me back here,' he finished. 'Are you guys OK?'

'Oh yeah, we're fine,' April replied. 'We were worried about you though, we didn't know what happened to you after they brought us here. You must have been in that cell the whole time.'

'That crazy idiot is making everyone farm the land. He doesn't realise that it's not possible. The land is way too barren for anything to grow,' Rowley said, from the cell to his right.

'He's insane,' Cyrus added. 'He's telling everyone he saved them, but he's just trying to create a scenario where he rules the world. It's like he thinks he's some kind of God.'

'What are we going to do?' asked April.

'I don't know.'

'So Nathaniel is really alive?' Rowley's voice came through the wall again. Cyrus could sense his relief.

'Yes, he's alive. But he's pissed at us for leaving him behind. He's been brainwashed like the rest of them.'

'If I could just get my hands on that weasel,' Gabriel's deep voice came from the cell opposite.

'I think he took my crystal,' Cyrus said. 'I need to get it back if we're going to stop him.'

'What about Kevin?' Another voice asked. 'Anybody know where he is?'

'The Jackal said he took off after we were captured,' Cyrus replied. He remembered back to the shanty town, where Kevin had volunteered to stay in the truck, just in case.

'That traitor!' Gabriel banged on the door of his cell. 'He set us up!'

'He wouldn't do that,' Zion shouted from some distance away. 'I know him, he didn't have any part in this.'

'Oh sure, he just conveniently stayed behind while we were taken prisoner.'

'Gabriel, it's not like that.'

More banging could be heard from Gabriel's cell. Cyrus realised that the gentle giant he'd met only weeks ago had well and truly left, replaced by the aggressive, intolerant beast of a man that his appearance better suited. The banging soon stopped, and the group fell silent. There was nothing more to say, and nothing they could do until the guards came back for them.

**

Cyrus woke to a commotion outside his cell. The guards were rounding people up once more, to take them out to the plains to begin work for the day.

'We've told you already, it's pointless,' Aiden's voice came from directly outside the door. 'You can't grow anything here.'

'Shut up and get moving,' the familiar grunt of the gigantic guard from the previous day.

The cell door swung open with a loud squeak and the brute ducked his head to enter. Cyrus suddenly got the feeling of déjà vu.

'Out,' the guard spat. Cyrus obliged, putting his hands out in front of him in preparation for the rope. The guard frowned at him and ordered him to turn around and put his hands behind his back. He wasn't as stupid as he looked, after all. He bound Cyrus's hands tightly together and dragged him forcefully out of the cell and into a steady line of traffic.

There were at least thirty people in a line marching slowly out of the prison. Among his friends were more people, some he recognised from the colony at the mall and supermarket, and others he didn't recognise at all. He noticed a woman with a small boy walking close behind her, and identified them as Caitlin and Cameron. The Jackal wasn't lying about that, he had found the rest of the colony.

Aiden had spotted them as well and was calling to them. Cameron turned around and nudged his mother.

'Look mommy, Aiden's here!' he said with a broad smile on his face. Caitlin turned her head, her face a picture of surprise. Her heart skipped a beat when she saw him, and then she burst into tears. He looked dishevelled and his face was scratched to hell from the events of the last few days, but he was alive and she finally knew that.

'Don't worry, it'll be alright,' he called after them as they were pushed along to keep the traffic moving.

Cyrus was pushed into the line and found himself walking behind Jennifer.

'OK, we need a plan,' Cyrus whispered to her, low enough that the guards couldn't hear.

'Gabriel looks riled up,' she replied. 'If we can get him close to that brute over there, I think he can take him.' She nodded towards the gigantic guard that had dragged them both out of their cells.

Cyrus acknowledged the idea. It was perfectly feasible. 'How hot is security on the plains?'

'Too hot to rush them. They create a perimeter of four guards per group of twenty, each with rifles. They put some distance between us so it'll be difficult to rush them without being shot. They untie our hands when we get there.'

'Damn,' Cyrus said under his breath. 'We'll need to think of something.'

They were getting close to the exit now, and the brute stopped in front of Cyrus to halt the traffic. He let a few more people go towards the plains, and ordered the rest to follow him.

'You two,' he pointed at two guards. 'After you've fetched water from the river, come see me. I have more orders for you.' He then turned to another couple of guards. 'You two, with me. The Jackal wants to talk to these punks.'

As the guards began to funnel them away from the main line of foot traffic, Cyrus couldn't help but fixate on what the man had just said. There was something about it that didn't sit right, but he couldn't put his finger on why.

Cyrus turned to see who the guard had brought with him, and spotted Gabriel, Jane, Mia and Rowley. The rest of the group had been shepherded away to the plains to begin work for the day. He wondered what The Jackal wanted from him now.

**

The Jackal was sitting on his throne in the same lounging manner as the day before, and nonchalantly waved for the guards to bring his prisoners to him. They obliged by prodding and poking the group with the ends of their rifles until they were twenty feet away from him. The guards then kicked each of them in the backs of the knees, knocking them over. Cyrus gritted his teeth as he took in a mouthful of dust on hitting the deck. He slowly got onto his knees and looked up at The Jackal, who from their new vantage point was towering over them with a big grin on his face.

'Welcome back, Cyrus,' he said. 'And I see you've brought some friends with you.'

'Go to hell,' Cyrus replied, coughing from the dust.

'Alright, let's skip the pleasantries then, shall we?' The Jackal replied, seemingly disappointed with Cyrus's response. He checked his fingernails again casually, before fidgeting in his seat. He then clutched the crystal around his neck and Cyrus could see his eyes roll into the back of his head, his pupils replaced by nothing but whiteness. It looked incredibly creepy, like he'd suddenly become possessed. A sudden rumbling sound emanated from behind the group and a number of mechs poured into the large open space around them. Cyrus was suddenly aware that he must have looked the same way when controlling the mechs.

The Jackal closed his eyes and opened them again, his pupils returning, the mechs instantly freezing in place.

'Ingenious, isn't it, Cyrus?' he said. 'Technology we can use, yet can't truly understand. And the power it brings.'

Cyrus looked around him at the mechs that had entered the scene, and then at the guards stationed around the courtyard. Not one of them seemed phased by what was going on. Cyrus's pleas to them the previous day had been completely in vain. They all knew the truth, and yet still followed The Jackal like obedient dogs.

The Jackal dipped a hand into his pocket and retrieved Cyrus's necklace, broken at the cord, with the crystal dangling from it. It glistened in the light, and Cyrus couldn't help but stare at it.

'I can see the longing in your eyes,' he said. 'The desire to control them. It ails me too, you know. You and me, Cyrus, we're the same.'

Cyrus's trance was broken as he heard the words. He snapped his head to The Jackal and narrowed his eyes.

'We are NOTHING alike!' he yelled, surprising his friends with the rage with which he spoke.

The Jackal tutted. 'Temper, temper. Clearly the burden of possessing this crystal is too much for you. You can't keep control of it. I wanted your friends to witness the effect it has on you.'

'What is he talking about?' asked Mia.

'Your boyfriend is sick,' The Jackal replied. 'I'm trying to cure him by ridding him of the disease.' He held up the crystal, emphasising his point.

'Bullshit,' Gabriel grunted. 'You want it for yourself.'

'Now, Cyrus,' The Jackal continued, ignoring Gabriel. 'This little mech army of yours. The one you were planning on killing me with, I presume.' Cyrus glanced to his friends either side of him. 'Oh don't play coy with me,' The Jackal sighed. 'Your poker face is as poor as your military friend's tactical nous.'

Cyrus instinctively looked to Gabriel, whose face was displaying the picture of pure hatred towards the man sitting on the throne. 'Yes, that's the one. Muscular and formidable in close combat I'm sure, but rather too stupid to make it that close.'

Gabriel muttered something under his breath with a low tone, no doubt thinking aloud about what he wanted to do to the man when he got his hands on him. The Jackal merely smiled wider, before turning his attention back to Cyrus.

'Just think of how powerful you could be with a mech army twice the size. Your legion added to mine would be unstoppable. We could rule the country, one city at a time.'

'What?' Mia asked. 'You want Cyrus to join forces with you? You're out of your mind!'

Cyrus stared at the man in front of him, still trying to process what he had said. Was he really offering him a seat alongside him, to rule the country with him? He thought The Jackal wanted him dead. The crystal, his crystal, shimmered again in The Jackal's hand. He felt naked without it around his neck.

'This is absurd,' Mia continued. 'Cyrus, tell him you're not interested.'

Cyrus's vision started to get hazy. The more he stared at the crystal, the more his vision honed in on it and nothing else. Everything else faded to a dull grey colour.

'Cyrus.'

He heard nothing but white noise filling his ears, becoming louder and louder, drowning out the words Mia was speaking to him. He longed for the crystal, could feel its pull on him beckoning him to take it. There was a hunger inside him, a hunger for the power that the crystal brought. And what power it would give him. He would be invincible. He needed to feel the cold jewel against his skin, the security of the cord wrapped around his neck, keeping the crystal close to his chest. He would be able to clutch it at any time and let its power take hold of him, plunging him into a different world, seen through eyes more powerful than his. Now that he'd tasted it, it was agonising to see it in someone else's hands. He wanted it back. He needed it back.

'Cyrus!'

His senses came back like a rush of blood to the head and he snapped his gaze away from the crystal to see Mia looking at him with a concerned expression. This was worse than all the other times he'd been caught daydreaming. Worse than all of them rolled together.

'Cyrus,' she repeated. 'Tell him he's insane.'

Cyrus maintained eye contact with her, but said nothing. Seconds passed, and still he said nothing. Mia's expression turned slowly from one of concern and puzzlement to fear and sadness. Her eyes began to well up, but still Cyrus looked at her, his expression serious and emotionless.

'Give me the crystal,' he said at last. 'I accept your offer.'

**

The day was hot, as usual, and there was no let-up in the work the guards made them do. It was futile, just as they'd been pleading all day. This part of the country was a wasteland and farming would bring no reward, no matter how hard they worked. It was a strange part of the country, in stark contrast to the tranquil setting of Woodside, which felt like a different world from this one. They wondered how two such different places could exist less than a hundred miles apart.

'I'm telling you, it doesn't rain here. You'd need a comprehensive irrigation system to even consider the thought of growing crops,' Zion said.

'Shut up and keep digging,' the guard grumbled, taking his baseball cap off to wipe a bead of sweat from his own forehead.

'There's no point,' Zion replied.

'I'm warning you, don't test my patience,' the guard replied. Zion considered giving in. It would have been the smart thing to do. But as he watched the rest of his group dig away at the barren land a rage built up inside him that he couldn't contain. Something snapped, and he threw down the shovel he was working with.

'This is ridiculous. Look around you. Do you remember the last time it rained here?'

The sound of rifles clicking into action were heard all around him, causing him to pause briefly. The guard held his hand up.

'It's alright, fellas. No need to get twitchy. Our friend's got a point. It's hot out, I think he's earned a lie down. What do you think?' He grinned at the other guards around him, who began to snigger amongst themselves. Zion started to become uneasy. The rest of the group had stopped what they were doing at the sound of the commotion.

The guard sighed and started to walk forward in Zion's direction, his rifle swinging leisurely from side to side. The man walked with the lazy stagger of someone who's rest had been inconveniently disturbed, but Zion could see the perverse excitement in his eyes. He'd jumped at the chance to do this. Zion gulped as he knew what was coming. What concerned him wasn't that the man was going to attack him. The guard was tall but skinny, and Zion would have fancied his chances against him in a fair fight. But this wasn't a fair fight; one because the guard was armed with a plasma rifle, and two because if he fought back the other guards would shoot him dead.

The guard swung the rifle across his side, knocking Zion clean to the dirt. Before he had a chance to recover, the guard hit him square in the cheek, causing blood to spray out of his mouth. Aiden stood and watched in horror, trying with all his might not to jump to his aid. He too knew that if he intervened the guards would shoot them both.

'You see what happens when you back chat?' the guard yelled in Zion's face, before spitting on him and walking away.

From the dirt, Zion propped himself gingerly onto his side and felt a warm trail of blood run from the cut in his cheek. He made eye contact with Aiden, and they both knew that there was more to what the guard had done than fuel a simple power trip. Despite decades of progress, racism was still rife in this part of the country. Before the war, equality had been an expected, normal aspect of life. However the war changed everything, and in the aftermath they were now experiencing a backwards scenario that their ancestors may have lived through on a tobacco plantation in the late eighteenth century, possibly right in that very spot. The smug look on the guard's face indicated that he was enjoying the irony of the situation. The racial slur he'd uttered under his breath as he walked away confirmed it.

'Back to work,' another guard said. 'Unless anyone else wants a beating?'

The group slowly picked up their tools and began working once more. Aiden and Jennifer rushed to Zion to help him onto his feet. He seemed to be OK, save for the throbbing in the side of his mouth. He wiped the sweat and blood from his face with his arm, before picking up his shovel and taking a chunk out of the hard earth. Aiden patted him on the shoulder and whispered in his ear.

'The second we get the chance, we'll wipe that smug look off his face.'

'I said, back to work!' the second guard barked, pointing his finger in Aiden's direction. 'Don't make me—'

'Yeah, yeah, I got it,' Aiden dismissed, trudging back to his own patch of dry earth. For the next few minutes, nothing could be heard except the pounding and scraping of shovel on dirt.

After covering a seed with soil, convinced it would never see the light of day again, April whispered to her sister. 'I wonder where the others went.'

'I heard that huge guy say The Jackal wanted to talk to them. Can't imagine that's good news,' Jennifer replied.

April frowned as she thought of her absent friends. 'I hope they're alright.'

'They're tough as nails, just like us,' her sister reassured. 'As long as they stick together, they have a chance.'

CHAPTER THIRTY-SEVEN

Mia sobbed as the guard began to cut the rope that bound Cyrus's hands behind his back. The Jackal sat on his throne eagerly, one hand on the armrest, the other still clutching Cyrus's crystal.

'What the hell are you doing, Cyrus?' Gabriel couldn't believe what he was seeing. 'You're going to switch sides, just like that?'

Cyrus said nothing, his attention firmly back on the crystal. The Jackal allowed him to stand as he prepared to hand it over.

'Now remember, Cyrus. Don't try anything silly, or something unpleasant will happen to your friends.' He clicked his fingers and a guard marched over and grabbed Mia by the arm. Mia yelped as the guard picked her an inch or two off the ground, throwing her forward towards the throne. Cyrus flinched at the motion, but was not distracted enough to break his gaze from the crystal. It was as though he was hypnotised by its aura. He could feel his heartbeat pounding in his ears.

'No point in crying, my dear,' The Jackal said. 'Your boyfriend is gone. He took a little longer to convince than I first thought, I must admit. But no matter. He has made the first step to becoming invincible.'

'You monster!' Mia cried. 'Cyrus, listen to me, please!'

Cyrus ignored her plea and put his hands out in front of him, awaiting the crystal.

The Jackal rose from his throne, his figure looking even smaller as he stepped from it. Cyrus was a full head taller than him. Gabriel, still on his knees alongside Jane and Rowley, hands bound behind his back, didn't know what to do with himself. He wanted to lunge forward and take down the guard standing over Mia, but he knew he wouldn't get anywhere near before they executed her. He took a long look at the entranced Cyrus, completely bemused by his sudden change of allegiance. First Kevin had sold them out, leaving them in the hands of the enemy, and now Cyrus was turning his back on them.

Jane could sense his pain, but she knew there was nothing she could do or say that would be of any use. She really felt for Rowley and Mia; two of the most important people in Cyrus's life, suddenly cast aside in favour of the promise of greater power. She wondered how he could have made that decision. Cyrus was better than this, he was a good person. Perhaps the pull of the crystal was too strong, too powerful to understand.

The Jackal was now just a couple of feet away from Cyrus. He stretched out his arm, the cord the crystal dangled from spilling out the sides of his closed fist. He took one last look at Cyrus, before opening his hand and letting the crystal tumble down into Cyrus's grateful grasp.

Cyrus clutched the crystal with both hands and pulled it back to his chest, as though his heart had been aching for it ever since it left his company. The crystal glowed in a flurry of colours across the spectrum, and Cyrus wondered if the light show he was witnessing was seen by him alone. He was captivated by it.

'Now, Cyrus. Bring your army to me.' The Jackal spoke with authority.

Cyrus tied the cord of the necklace behind his neck, the comforting cold feel of the crystal bouncing against his chest once more. Without so much as a look back to his friends, he clutched the crystal and his mind was transported to another place.

**

April took a swig of water as she paused for a moment and let the bag of seeds she was carrying settle on the ground. She had started to feel a little dizzy from dehydration, the hot sun giving her an all too familiar headache.

'What I wouldn't give for some aspirin right now,' she said.

'I hear that,' Zion replied, as he gestured for her to pass the water bottle along. April passed the water to the woman next to her, who took a quick swig before handing it to Zion. As the woman turned to Zion, April did a double take and grabbed her by the arm. The woman turned to April in panic.

'Hey, what are you—'

The two shared a silent moment as they suddenly recognised each other. The woman was skinnier than she remembered, but it was definitely her. Cyrus's mother.

'Angela!' April's mouth stayed open in shock. The woman shared the same expression for a moment, before reaching out and hugging her.

'Oh my God. April, is that you?' she asked, dumbstruck. 'I almost didn't recognise you, you look so grown up.'

April smiled, too elated at realising Angela was still alive to think about anything else.

'Jennifer,' she called. 'It's Angela, Cyrus's mom!'

Jennifer dropped her tools instantly and rushed over to hug her. The three of them shared a moment of rare happiness, before the guards called for them to get back to work. They obliged, working half-heartedly from then on as they caught up. Angela called her daughter over, Cyrus's sister. At seventeen years old, April had got on really well with his sister, Isabella, or Izzy for short, for the brief time she'd known her. They'd gone to different schools, so despite being only two weeks apart in age, they'd not crossed paths until Jennifer started dating Rowley before the end of the war. Angela and Izzy had disappeared soon after.

'It's so good to see you both,' Jennifer said. 'What happened? We all feared the worst when you disappeared.'

Angela told them of their experience after the bombing raid. After MIRE attacked the city, they were trapped in a collapsed building for a day. They were pulled from the wreckage by a man claiming to be their saviour, who was building a new home for refugees to the north. They didn't know the truth until it was too late, and they'd been living in this nightmare of a place since.

'But how have you all survived here this long?' April asked. 'There's nothing growing here. It's not sustainable.'

'The Jackal has groups of followers that find food from other cities and bring it back here. He managed to build up a stockpile big enough to feed us, barely.'

'Like the ones that attacked us at the mall,' April was piecing it together.

'I'm not sure why he's making us farm here though, it doesn't make any sense.'

'He's insane, Angela. Nothing he does makes sense.'

'Yet he has all these people doing his bidding,' she said, pointing to the guards. 'They're either blind or just enjoy the power.'

'We all know which it is,' Jennifer gritted her teeth.

A rumbling sound came from beyond the hill to the south, a sound that became louder and louder each second. The group stopped to look, including the guards, intrigued by the noise. The ground began to shake as though an earth tremor was rippling through it, and small rocks bobbled down the hillside.

It was then that they saw it. An army of mechs, led by a cluster of panthers, poured over the hill and down into the valley where The Jackal's kingdom lay. The metallic monsters charging for the buildings ahead of them in unison were an impressive, yet terrifying sight. The guards leaped into action, readying their rifles in defence, but the mechs ignored them and simply ran by. First the panthers, then the golems, and lastly the gargantuans followed suit far behind, trudging slowly with powerful stomps. The gargantuans stopped still at the edge of the town, while the panthers and golems charged in.

'What the hell was that?' Aiden asked, as everyone stood in awe of the sight. Everyone but Zion, who had wasted no time in taking advantage of the distraction to rush over to the guard that had ruthlessly attacked him earlier. His eyes were raging as he grew nearer to his unsuspecting target.

Another sound then came from back over the other side of the hill; the faint rumbling of an engine. Zion stopped in his tracks as he realised what the sound must be.

It can't be.

The fender of the big black pickup truck appeared on the crest of the hill, launching over the top of it at speed. The guards were once again on edge as they tracked the vehicle with their rifles raised.

The pickup soared through the air, several feet off the ground as the front tilted back down towards the earth. The group could hear the whoops of the driver who still refused to take his foot off the gas.

With his aviators on, Kevin wished someone could have taken a photo at that exact moment. It was the coolest he'd ever felt. That was, until the truck hit the ground with a bump and he was almost launched right out of the driver's seat. The thick tyres blew dust up around the car as it chewed up the dirt in front of it. Kevin barely maintained control as it hurtled down the hillside and towards the farmland. The guards began firing, plasma rounds sailing past the pickup from all sides. One glanced off the radiator and Kevin heard a hissing sound emanate from under the hood. He cursed aloud and gritted his teeth as he focused his positioning at the people firing at him through the windshield.

Gyro-3 was perched precariously in the cargo hold, digging its claw-like hands into the hard metal of the tailgate with all its strength.

'This is it, Gyro-3,' Kevin called back to his little robot companion. 'This is our last ride. Let's go out with a bang!'

He mashed the accelerator as hard as he could, the engine roaring like a lion. With a loud yell, Kevin steered the truck toward the guards, who continued to fire at him wildly. A shot blasted the windshield, blowing a hole right through it on the passenger side. Unperturbed, Kevin continued to drive forward, slamming the car into one of the guards and colliding into a giant rock at the bottom of the hill. The car stopped with a loud crunch, and smoke fizzed up from the hood. One of the front wheels had come clean off and knocked over another guard on its way through to the rest of the group, who looked on in shock. Aiden jumped out of the way as the giant tyre threatened to roll right over him.

Kevin knocked his head on the steering wheel and was dazed. As he came to he saw the lifeless body of the guard that had been sandwiched between the truck and the rock, the man's torso lying across the smoking hood. He then looked down at the seatbelt that had stopped him from being thrown through the windshield after him. It seemed the one time he wore it was the most important.

The driver side door was pulled open suddenly, and an angry looking man wielding a plasma rifle glared at Kevin, before aiming and squeezing the trigger. Kevin had no time to react, and simply shut his eyes before—

A loud smack sounded and the guard was knocked to the ground. Kevin opened his eyes and squinted to regain his focus, before seeing the friendly face of Zion greeting him. A shovel lay on the floor next to the guard, who was stirring, seemingly confused by the sudden blow to the head.

'Nice save,' Kevin said, as he tried to exit the truck. He planted one foot on the floor before falling the rest of the way out.

'He had it coming,' Zion replied.

Chaos ensued as the guards were quickly becoming outnumbered. Aiden seized his chance and grappled with one guard as they fought for control of a rifle. Jennifer and April ambushed the next guard, who didn't have enough time to react. April hurled a rock at him, hitting him in the stomach. As he hunched over, winded, Jennifer sent a strong knee to the face, knocking him backwards and flat on his back. His plasma rifle fired harmlessly into the air as Jennifer got another punch in to knock him out cold.

The last remaining guard kicked a leg out, catching Aiden in the kneecap. He went sprawling to the ground, just as the guard regained his grip on the rifle. But before he could aim and fire, Caitlin appeared out of nowhere, grabbing the rifle and directing it away from Aiden. The rifle fired a plasma round into the floor next to him, the dirt sizzling from the heat of the blast. The guard kicked at Caitlin, but missed, and unbalanced by the motion he lost his footing and stumbled. Caitlin ripped the gun from his grasp and knocked him in the head with the rifle butt, sending him tumbling over.

'Don't get back up, unless you want a hole for a face,' she barked, eyes alight with rage as she pointed the barrel right at him. The guard covered his face with his hands, surrendering.

**

The sound of the mechs drawing near almost caused Cyrus to lose his concentration. His mind was looking at the world from the viewpoint of the mechs, however his real senses were crossing over and interfering. He hadn't had enough time to learn how to fully separate one from the other.

The Jackal had positioned his own army of mechs within the open space in which they stood, surrounding the group, just in case Cyrus tried to make a move against him. Cyrus was acutely aware of this while he concentrated on the progress of his own mechs.

Bursting through the open doorway came the first of his panthers, followed closely by the rest. The sentry guards at the doors stayed as still as possible, too afraid to move as the swarm of beast-like machines tore past them. The mechs then spilled out into the opening, circling The Jackal's own army. Cyrus left the gargantuans outside the building, as there simply wasn't room for them to get through. The Jackal's pair of gargantuans were also nowhere to be seen, assumedly in a similar position somewhere around the village. The mechs settled into position and froze as Cyrus took his hand away from his crystal.

'And so here we are,' The Jackal said, his arms spread wide with an air of grandeur.

Gabriel struggled with the rope tying his hands together. He was trying desperately to free himself, but the bonds were tight and he couldn't loosen them.

The Jackal waved to a guard by the doorway, who disappeared into the building. 'There is one more task I need you to do, Cyrus, before I can trust you.'

Cyrus, now fully away of his surroundings again, looked curiously at The Jackal, wondering what this task might be.

'Well you didn't expect me to just take your word, did you?' The Jackal smirked.

The guard returned to the opening with another prisoner, who was struggling and shouting abuse as the guard dragged him over to them. Cyrus swivelled on the spot as he recognised the voice, and saw the figure of Isaac being brought towards them.

'What is this?' Cyrus asked. 'Why is he here?'

The Jackal ignored his questions. 'I see you're already acquainted with Lieutenant Patel here?'

'He took us in, and you captured him just like the rest of us,' Rowley replied. 'Isaac's done nothing wrong.'

'Oh, is that right?' The Jackal said. The glint in his eye and lasting smirk told Rowley that he was priming them for that very statement.

'Lieutenant Isaac Patel was a good soldier. A Loyal soldier,' he continued as the guard forced Isaac on his knees next to

Mia, in front of the other three prisoners. 'Well, until the day he left his squad to die.'

'He told us everything,' Rowley protested. 'It wasn't his fault.'

'Is that what you told them, Isaac?' The Jackal pointed a finger at the group while addressing the new prisoner. 'Is that what you told them?' he repeated, louder this time, waiting for an answer.

Isaac whimpered. He was a man completely broken of body and spirit. His physique was even frailer than they remembered, his straggly beard unkempt and unclean. He spoke slowly through his sobbing.

'I'm sorry, I didn't know what else to do.' Cyrus found it odd that he was looking right at him when he said it, as though he was apologising to him, not The Jackal.

'You left them for dead, just like your friends here left my poor Nathaniel for dead.' The Jackal was ramming the point home. Nathaniel lurked nearby, listening in from the large open doorway.

'What does it matter to you?' Rowley asked, curious as to what this man's motivation was for punishing them. 'You betrayed the military to join MIRE!'

The Jackal sneered, not impressed by Rowley shining the light on him. 'MIRE was started years before the war. I was planted by them into the military to take down the mech program from the inside, and use it to our advantage.'

'To *your* advantage,' Rowley corrected. 'MIRE fought for peace, for a life without the mechs. You're using them to strike fear into people's hearts, to bend people to your will. You betrayed everyone. The military, MIRE. You're pure evil, and you're a fool if you think what you're doing here is going to last. You're not fooling anybody. Even your bodyguards know you're not bringing new life here. They just like the power trip it gives them.'

The Jackal remained silent for a moment, and then proceeded to laugh maniacally. It started out as a wheeze, before turning into a deep and exaggerated roar. Rowley wondered why he was laughing at this. He'd just exposed him for what he really was, and he didn't seem to care.

'Isaac didn't tell you the full story, did he?' The Jackal said at last. 'You see, Isaac has a very rare gift. A very special gift. He has the ability to see into the future, to show a vision of things to come. I met him in the military, and in fact I served with him for a while. When I found out about his gift, I was intrigued. I wondered what my future would hold.'

Rowley exchanged a concerned glance with Jane.

'I didn't like what I saw. It was boring, mundane. I didn't want to die following another man's ideologies. So I did what MIRE asked of me, and then I kept the prize for myself. Why shouldn't people follow *my* ideology? I'd start a legacy of my own.'

'You're crazy,' Rowley breathed.

'I'm a self-starter,' The Jackal countered. 'And I like to plan ahead. See, I knew Isaac would come in handy again, so after annihilating his platoon, thus rendering him the whimpering bag of bones you see before you, I continued with my mission and found some more leverage to bend his gift to my will.'

'What the hell are you talkin' about?' Jane asked, perplexed.

'He, he,' Isaac sobbed. 'He's got my family. You said you'd free them.'

The Jackal laughed again, this time slapping one of the guards on the back to add to the effect. 'Did I? I must have forgotten that.'

'Let them go!' Isaac pleaded.

The Jackal stopped laughing and wiped a tear from his eye. 'You see, Cyrus, this is why I brought him to you. Isaac has done nothing but deceive you from the moment he met you. A little while ago I used him to see into the future once more, and he showed me you. I knew that to become more powerful I needed a right-hand man, someone who could command an army of mechs like mine to rule by my side. You are that man, Cyrus, and I have allowed you to follow your destiny.'

Cyrus said nothing, but Rowley had put the pieces together.

'It was you. Isaac telling us to go to find Kevin; that was your plan all along. But it doesn't make sense. If you wanted him to realise the crystal's power, why did you attack us at Woodside?'

'You needed help to get to the facility,' he replied. 'I needed to make sure that geek friend of yours got off his lazy ass to help you. What does he call himself, The Oracle?' He sniggered to himself. 'He just needed a little push to get out there.'

'A little push? You killed Doug!' Gabriel grunted. 'You'll die for that.'

'I really don't think so,' The Jackal replied plainly. 'You're not exactly in a position to do anything about it, now are you?'

Gabriel said nothing and just kept looking at the man he hated like no other person he'd ever met.

'So, Cyrus, let's cut to the chase,' The Jackal moved things along. 'Isaac has wronged you. He lied to you, and now you have a chance to get revenge. He is of no use to anyone now, and his family will be dead soon anyway, so—' He turned to Isaac, who looked back at him with such innocence, and yet so much pain. 'Kill him,' he finished.

'That's my task?' Cyrus asked.

'Yes, is there a problem with that?' The Jackal replied. 'Killing him will prove to me that you can use the gift hanging around your neck to its full effect. Failing to do so will prove that you're too weak to handle such power.'

Cyrus turned to Isaac, kneeling next to Mia. The two of them looked back at him with dumbfounded expressions on their faces. Cyrus knew there was no going back from this when he made his choice.

'Cyrus,' Mia mouthed to him. 'Please.'

Cyrus ignored her and kept his gaze fixed on Isaac. Those piercing eyes of his locked with Cyrus's, and Cyrus could feel the man staring right into his soul once more. He walked over to them and stood right in front of the pair, between themselves and The Jackal. He took one last look at Isaac, and then locked eyes with Mia, whose gaze captured him in a totally different way. For what felt like the last time, he gazed upon the most beautiful person he'd ever known. And with that lasting memory he clutched the crystal in his right hand, his eyes rolling to the back of his head as he was transported into the eyes of the nearest golem.

While Cyrus stood completely still, the golem moved from its position behind another mech and walked forward, stopping finally alongside him, pointing its gun arm right at Isaac. The lost and hopeless man in front of Cyrus muttered a quiet prayer as he waited for the end.

A loud bang erupted through the area as the gun arm went off. From the moment it sounded, everything seemed to happen in slow motion. Cyrus let go of the crystal momentarily as he watched the guard behind the pair kneeling in front of him fall backwards, into the dirt, a massive hole torn through his torso. The Jackal's view of what had happened was obscured by Cyrus and the golem, and so hadn't realised who had been shot. The smile on his face was quickly wiped off as Cyrus turned and he saw Isaac still kneeling in place. As Gabriel, Jane and Rowley figured out what was going on, Cyrus shouted 'NOW!' and the trio were up on their feet, springing into action. Gabriel charged at the nearest guard, while Jane and Rowley urged Mia and Isaac to get up and run with them. Cyrus spun on his heel to face The Jackal and the two of them grasped their crystals simultaneously, launching themselves into void and into the eyes of the mechs around them.

CHAPTER THIRTY-EIGHT

After the forth guard had surrendered to Caitlin at point blank range, more of The Jackal's followers had left their post on other parts of the farmland to investigate the commotion. At the pickup truck, Zion was waving his hand in front of Kevin's face.

'How many fingers am I holding up?' he asked.

Kevin squinted as he concentrated on the blurry hand in front of him. He was still suffering from double vision, but could still make out the middle finger being pointed at him.

'You ass,' he said with a smile.

'What the hell were you thinking, coming in so hot? You're lucky to be alive.'

'You of all people know I don't drive any other way,' Kevin replied. 'When you've only got a gallon of gas left, you use every horse that baby's got.'

'Until you hit a boulder.'

'Until you hit a boulder,' he repeated. The two embraced and slapped each other on the back.

'It's good to see you,' Zion said. 'Where have you been?'

'One of those assholes that ambushed you in the shanty town got to me before I could warn you. Knocked me clean out. By the time I woke up it was morning. I've been looking for your trail ever since. Then just now I saw Cyrus's mechs heading this way, so I followed them here.'

'Cyrus,' Zion whispered to himself. 'They might be in trouble. We gotta help them.'

Just then a plasma round ricocheted off the pickup truck and the pair instinctively ducked. Another followed, pinning them down.

'Shit, more of them,' said Zion.

'More?' Kevin replied. 'How many of these guys are there? Are they with The Jackal?'

'Oh man, we need to catch you up,' his friend replied.

The gunfire continued as the truck was peppered with shots. It had tilted onto its side where the front driver's side wheel had fallen off, giving Zion and Kevin more cover on the passenger side. Zion peered sheepishly through the window, before ducking quickly to take cover once more.

'There's too many. Where are they coming from?'

Kevin was sat with his back against the still intact front wheel, using it for support as much as protection.

'I'm still a little dizzy,' he said. 'I'm not going to be much use with a rifle.'

The thought suddenly struck Zion. He needed a weapon, and fast. The second wave of guards were closing in on them, and with nothing more than a shovel to protect them, they were sitting ducks. The rifle of the guard he'd struck had been flung too far out of reach. Zion would need to break cover to retrieve it, and that was too risky.

At the sound of the gunfire from the second string of guards, the rest of the group had lay flat on the floor, with their hands over their heads, in an attempt to at least give the impression that they were surrendering. Jennifer caught Zion's eye and mouthed something to him. Her head flicked back and forth, from the incoming guards to back to him. She mouthed it again, and Zion could read her lips this time.

Three.

Zion nodded in understanding. Three guards. The firing stopped and Zion considered his next move. He looked at Kevin, and then at the truck. A brainwave hit him. Without a second thought, he stood up and reached his arm into the back seat of the truck, through the broken window. His hand groped around for a moment, before he found what he was looking for. Grasping the barrel, he pulled his arm back out to reveal Kevin's shotgun, just before another barrage of plasma rounds tore at the truck.

'I hate to say it,' Zion said. 'But I think your driving days are over.'

Kevin rolled his eyes. 'No, you think so?' he said sarcastically. 'I thought she'd be alright with a lick of paint.'

Zion handed the shotgun to his friend, but Kevin held his hands out to stop him.

'I told you, I can't see straight.'

'With this thing, you don't need to,' Zion quipped, before bundling it into his arms. 'Just aim it in that general direction.'

Kevin acknowledged what Zion was trying to achieve with a quick nod. He was just about to turn and fire, before something stopped him.

'Hang on,' he said. 'Shall we go on three, or after three?' he asked. Zion raised an eyebrow at him.

'*On* three. It's always been on three.'

'Right. OK. On three. One. Two—'

A plasma round ricocheted off the hood and fizzed right past them. They could hear the shouts of the guards getting closer.

'Three!' Kevin hissed and immediately swivelled round, plonking his shotgun onto the hood of the truck. Even through his hazy vision he could see the guards coming at him. They were too far apart to hit all at once, but he decided to fire blindly in their direction anyway.

The flash of his barrel sent out a deadly propulsion of concentrated plasma. The guards, startled by the sudden loud noise more than anything, stopped their forward progress and ducked for cover. One rolled to his side and found himself prone.

Meanwhile Zion used the sudden blast as a starting pistol and set off as fast as his legs would carry him to the vacant rifle a few feet away. He grabbed it on the move, but he didn't take it with him back to the truck. Instead he pushed it towards Jennifer, who was surprised to receive it.

The guards had started to regain their composure, just in time for another blast of Kevin's shotgun to send them scurrying again. He was buying Zion time, but that time was fast running out.

On the way back to the truck, Zion grabbed the shovel he'd used to take out the guard earlier. He arrived back at Kevin's side, who looked at him cautiously.

'I thought you were getting a gun,' he said. 'You risked your life for *that*?'

'I did get a gun, and now we've evened up the numbers,' he said, gesturing to Jennifer, who, still lying in the open, had not yet taken the rifle into her hands.

'I hope you know what you're doing,' said Kevin. Zion failed to reply, opting instead for a wink, before disappearing around the rear side of the pickup.

The shouts of the guards were extremely close now. Kevin inched his way closer to the corner of the vehicle to get a better look, and quickly found himself staring right down the barrel of a rifle. He recoiled, jolting back around the corner again just as the gun went off. He inhaled deeply as the blast rung in his ears, but he needed to act fast to avoid another shot.

On the other side of the truck, Zion had lowered his head far enough to see the feet of his attacker coming his way from under the vehicle. He waited for the opportune moment to spring out with a surprise attack. As the man drew closer, Gyro-3 became aware of his presence from the tailgate.

'Danger, danger,' the little robot chimed as the guard swivelled around at the sudden noise. Zion took his chance and rounded the corner of the truck, giving the man no time to react as he surprised him with a sweeping shovel swing to the legs. The man's feet were taken from under him and his scream alerted the other guards to the danger.

Kevin seized the chance from the other side of the pickup, as his attacker was briefly distracted. He swung around the corner once more and barrelled straight into the man, hitting him with a tackle square in the chest. The man's rifle between them, Kevin drove forward and pushed the man into the dirt.

They struggled for control of the gun and Kevin got a couple of punches to the man's side. It didn't seem to have much effect and Kevin had to go back to putting two hands on the rifle to attempt to pull it away.

The final guard had entered the fray, raising his rifle at the bundle of arms and legs attacking each other on the ground. He quickly distinguished friend from foe and aimed at Kevin, just before a searing hot blast slammed into him hard, knocking him off his feet and killing him instantly.

The barrel of the rifle Jennifer had fired was still smoking as she raced over to help Kevin. The rest of the group got up and did the same, charging to help the man that had sparked their breakout.

The guard relaxed his grip on the rifle with one hand as he reached into his pocket and withdrew a knife. With one swipe he caught Kevin in the shoulder, causing him to cry out in pain. Kevin instantly let go and grabbed where the knife had hit. The wound wasn't deep, but the pain was strong. The guard could feel he was getting the upper hand and grimaced as he clutched the rifle once more. He was about to point it in Kevin's direction when the barrel of another gun was pressed against his temple, followed by the words 'drop it.'

Led by Jennifer, the group surrounded the guard, and Kevin was able to wriggle out of the tangle in one piece. Zion helped him up and began tearing at the fabric of his own t-shirt to fashion a makeshift bandage for his shoulder. The guard was made to sit on his knees while the group muttered amongst themselves. Zion gave a quick introduction to everyone, explaining a brief account of the last few days; the mechs, Cyrus's crystal, Kevin and his ancient, now-in-a-crumpled-heap vehicle, everything.

The guard didn't take much interrogating to reveal everything they needed to know. He had come from his post watching another group of slaves on the farm, and didn't seem too remorseful about his part in The Jackal's delusional plan.

'It's dog eat dog out here,' he said. 'Why should I be working the land when someone else can do it for me? You'd do the same if you had the opportunity.'

Unsurprisingly, his comment wasn't met kindly, and by the time he would wake up he'd have a hell of a headache and a lump on his head.

The group headed towards the centre of the village, following the trail of the mechs. They seemed to have headed straight for the large building in the centre of the village, which looked much grander than the basic huts and half-built houses scattered around it. As they grew near they heard the ear-piercing screech of a panther, stopping them in their tracks and making their hearts thump in their chest. It was always a sobering moment; a feeling of absolute helplessness as the noise screamed danger in their minds.

They'd stopped off on the way to rescue the remaining workers from their oppressors, but it didn't take much effort and they were able to catch the guards by surprise. The patch of farmland nearest only had one person guarding twenty, as the other three had been accounted for earlier. It was a young guy, not older than eighteen, and he practically threw his gun aside at the first sight of them. April winced at the sight of him; someone roughly her age on the other side of these crimes against humanity. She couldn't fathom how these people had come to be like this. The war had really brought out the worst in some people. The greedy become greedier. Hungry, not for sustenance, but for power and authority. It made her sick to her stomach.

Izzy had been asking questions about her brother non-stop since she and Angela had been reunited with some friendly faces. She worried for his safety, puzzled as to why he was taken to see the cruel and tyrannical madman that ruled this place.

'What do they want with him?' she asked. 'What has he ever done to him?'

'I don't know,' April replied, shaking her head. 'It doesn't make any sense. Unless...' she paused. 'Yes, that's it! He must want his crystal. The one he wears around his neck.'

Izzy looked confused. 'What? You mean the mood stone? What would The Jackal want with that?' She turned to her mother, who avoided her eye contact. April could see that her lips were trembling.

'What is it?' she asked.

'It's not a mood stone, dear,' Angela said. 'Well, it is, but it's more than that. It was a gift to Cyrus from his father, before he left for his final deployment. He never explained what it was, just that he found it on mission he couldn't tell me about. Izzy, your father was in the Special Forces, and he wasn't allowed to talk about his work. He did his job, and I did mine. I didn't ask any questions, I understood our roles. He said it was too dangerous to tell me what he did, and he didn't want to put me or any of his family in danger. He gave Cyrus that crystal as a souvenir from one of his missions. Said he found it and wanted to bring it home for his son. He was very secretive about it though. He said even his army buddies didn't know about it. Just their little secret, he told him. Cyrus loved that, it made him feel special. I didn't think anything of it, until...' she trailed off as she remembered back.

'Until what?' Izzy asked, eager for her to continue.

'The crystal started to change colour, depending on Cyrus's mood. It would become bright blue, like the clearest sky when he was happy. And when he was angry it would turn a deep crimson. I'd never seen a mood stone like it, not one that reacted so dramatically, and so consistently. I knew there was something to this crystal, something his father never told him. After we were brought here, I saw The Jackal wearing one around his neck. It was just like Cyrus's.'

'Cyrus can control the mechs with it,' said April. 'We went to the place they built them on the way here. Something happened to him at that facility. It was like the crystal had suddenly activated. We found audio files from the man who ordered their creation, saying the crystals were some alien material that fell from space.'

A loud boom erupted from inside the large building and the ground shook, interrupting April. Part of the wall overlooking the opening in the middle of the building collapsed in a cloud of dust.

Everybody stopped and looked in horror at the scene, as the dust began to settle. Before they could see through the wall at what had caused the blast, a panther leapt out of the cloud of dust and appeared to sniff around, looking for its prey. It clocked them at a distance, and as soon as it did they knew it was too late. There was no escape.

**

Minutes earlier, Cyrus's plan had worked. It had actually worked! From the very first moment he met The Jackal, he knew the man needed something from him. When he had waved the crystal in his face, almost taunting him with it, Cyrus had wondered what else he could possibly want from him. But then it hit him, and since then The Jackal had confirmed it himself. Despite having the crystal in his possession, The Jackal couldn't actually use it. The crystal had been assigned to Cyrus the moment it got locked in the control panel at the mech facility. It became fused to Cyrus in a way that couldn't be undone; not physically, but in some other way that Cyrus didn't understand. The Jackal had said it himself; 'Technology we can use, yet can't truly understand.'

The Jackal understood enough to know that the only way he would be able to use Cyrus's crystal would be to use him as his puppet, to bend the mechs to his will. Cyrus played on the draw of the crystal, creating the illusion that he was under its spell, losing all ties he had to anything or anyone but the crystal itself as he agreed to do anything necessary to have it back in his hands. The Jackal was so hungry and so fixated on the possibility of having an army double the size, the illusion had been convincing. It was a long shot, and Cyrus didn't know how, but somehow he found himself one-on-one with The Jackal, and this time the odds had been evened. It was one mech army against another, until one handler was killed.

Cyrus had almost broken character twice before this moment. Once when Mia was forced to the ground in front of him, her tearful eyes searching for his, pleading him to listen to reason. The second time was after he learned that Isaac's family had been kidnapped by The Jackal. Cyrus could see it in Isaac's eyes, the way he stared right into his soul. He knew he was a good man, a kind man who was suffering without his family, at the thought of what The Jackal might do to them. When he had apologised in front of The Jackal, yet had been staring right at him, Cyrus could see the pain in his eyes for his betrayal of them. He hadn't wanted to do it, to play them right into The Jackal's hands, but he had no choice. He was doing what he needed to do to keep his family safe. Cyrus could forgive that. And as he clutched the crystal, plunging himself into the eyes of the nearest golem, which then planted a plasma round right into the guard behind Mia and Isaac, Cyrus was filled with fury at the man responsible for this. All of it. The fear of stepping outside, the desperate search for water after the river mysteriously became tainted. Doug's death, and who knew how many other atrocities.

As the guard dropped and Cyrus spun to face The Jackal, he let go of the crystal and his senses returned just long enough to note the surprise in his enemy's eyes. The crystal glowed a deep red, and he felt the raw power of it consuming him, urging him to take it in his hand once more, which he obliged.

Time to end this.

Cyrus was thrust back into the world he had only just discovered, yet felt an unnatural hunger to return to time and time again. His human senses were dulled as he saw the world through the eyes of the mechs, replaced by a single feeling that he could not describe. He couldn't feel the cold of the crystal or hear the shouts of his friends. He felt overwhelmingly focused, yet at the same time at peace. Every time he left this state and returned to his normal self he couldn't help but long to be back there, such was the draw of the crystal. It sucked him in, clinging onto him like a vice. He was starting to understand how The Jackal had become so lost and deluded. The crystal made you forget everything else. Everything but the pure power it gave you, and the feeling of invincibility it brought.

He saw through the eyes of the golem that had just dropped the guard and swung the mech around to face The Jackal. In the golem's peripheral vision he noticed Gabriel, Mia, Jane, Rowley and Isaac take off, their hands still bound behind their backs. They were running for freedom, but they would need help to reach it. He knew the guards scattered on the walls around the grand building would pick them off as they ran in the open. That was, unless The Jackal's mechs got to them first. Cyrus needed to draw their attention, distracting them long enough for them to get to safety.

He brought the golem's gun arm up, ready to fire at The Jackal. But just as he did so, the golem's vision was suddenly blacked out as a panther lunged at its torso, knocking it clean over. The Jackal had clutched his own crystal that hung from the gold chain around his neck. His reactions had been like that of a trained gunslinger in the Wild West, fingers twitching as the crystal pulled them to it like a magnet.

The panther was all over Cyrus's golem, its mouth full of metallic teeth snapping at its face while the golem tried to hold it back. Cyrus suddenly felt the presence of another close to him. This time not the golem, his actual human body. He switched focus to the panther nearest him just in time to see The Jackal's second panther rush towards his human form. It was strange seeing his own self from another pair of eyes. His figure looked so much smaller from this perspective. Cyrus's panther snapped into action, colliding with The Jackal's just before it could launch itself onto Cyrus.

The panthers scrapped on the floor, before The Jackal set more of his mechs in motion. Coming at him from all angles, Cyrus struggled to split his concentration between multiple mechs to fend them off. It was easy to direct the mechs to perform one unified goal, such as move from one point to another. But multitasking to cut off onrushing attackers from all sides was another thing entirely. The Jackal seemed well practiced at this and Cyrus had to break out from the void to dive to his right. The panther that had been charging straight for him, its head down as it rushed hard, missed narrowly. It skidded on the floor, dust kicking up in the same way ice does from the blades of a figure skater as they round a tight corner. It screeched loudly as it turned to its prey, and Cyrus quickly grasped his crystal once more. The panther rushed at him again, the dirt being eaten up where its metal claws scraped the earth. A blast hit the floor a couple of feet behind it, and then again to the left as the panther was almost on Cyrus. The third shot connected with the panther square in the face, and

Cyrus's golem stood in front of his human self as the panther malfunctioned in spams on the ground.

Cyrus brought a second golem to him, this time standing directly behind him, the two golems almost back-to-back, gun arms outstretched with Cyrus safely in the middle.

The Jackal stood close to his throne, the faintest hint of a smile breaking through his expression of concentration. His plan had failed, and for the first time he had been outsmarted, if only very briefly. But he was enjoying it, as though this was all a game to him. As though this was all a show for his amusement.

With a sudden switch in tactics, The Jackal focused on one of the gargantuans that waited outside the building. He fired a blast from the great cannon on its back towards a cluster of mechs, but the shot missed and part of the wall surrounding the opening in the centre of the building was destroyed. In an attempt to catch Cyrus off guard, he sent one of his panthers out through the newly formed gaping hole in the wall and set it on the people that had gathered at the outskirts of the village.

CHAPTER THIRTY-NINE

The panther emerged through the dust and debris of the collapsed wall and set its sights on the people gathered outside. They turned and ran as it began to charge.

Aiden sought out Caitlin and Cameron through the panicking crowd. Sure enough, he spotted Caitlin scoop up Cameron into her arms as she tried to hide behind a building. He caught up with them and she screamed at his arrival, half in fright and half with glee at being reunited.

'I'm not letting you leave my sight again,' she said, setting Cameron down briefly while she wrapped her arms around his neck.

'Good, I wasn't planning on making that mistake twice,' Aiden replied. He took Cameron in one arm and Caitlin's hand with the other and led them around the corner and deep into the village to find a safe place. He beckoned others over to follow them as they ran.

Meanwhile, April grabbed Izzy by the arm and pulled her with her towards a nearby hut. Angela followed and the three bolted for the safety of the small building. The small hut wouldn't provide much protection from mech attack, but it could be a good hiding spot, assuming the panther wasn't coming straight for them.

As they reached the hut, April spun to check if they were in the clear. What she saw horrified her and she put a hand over her mouth in shock. Where they'd been standing moments before were Zion, Kevin and her sister, Jennifer. They hadn't moved a muscle, still looking in the direction of the mech. Each of them were armed with a plasma gun of some kind; Zion and Jennifer carrying rifles, while Kevin had his shotgun pushed against his good shoulder. Stood like a firing squad, the trio were motionless, waiting for the mech to grow close.

April could see the panther gaining speed, eating up the ground beneath its metallic claws. She could hardly look as the robotic beast screeched as it approached its prey. The panther was fifty yards away now, but the three standing between it and the fleeing group didn't move. Their fingers barely twitched on the triggers.

'Now?' Kevin cocked his head to Zion. From a distance the trio must have looked fearless, standing in the face of death to protect their friends. But they were all terrified.

'Not yet,' he replied.

Still the panther came, closing in. When it came within twenty yards, Zion finally called for them to fire. A barrage of plasma rounds pummelled the mech. Zion's pinged off the shoulder, Jennifer's getting closer but missing the crucial soft spot by inches. Kevin waited just a moment longer as it got in range of his shotgun. Zion and Jennifer rolled to their sides to evade the rampaging mech, just as Kevin fired right at its face. The mech stumbled from the blast, but didn't collapse in its tracks. Kevin braced for the impact and was knocked aside as the panther steamed past on a collision course with the ground.

It skidded to a halt as it malfunctioned, giving Zion and Jennifer time to rush to Kevin's aid. The mech's shoulder had clipped him on its way through, sending him through the air and landing awkwardly in the dirt. Luckily the shotgun had taken the brunt of the impact from the mech and Kevin's limbs were still intact. The fall had caused him to twist his ankle, and he needed support from his friends to get back up and walking. It took some time, but Zion and Jennifer managed to carry Kevin, with an arm around each of their necks. April beckoned them over to the hut as they could hear fighting on the other side of the wall, in the courtyard of the grand central building.

'April,' Zion called. 'Get Kevin inside with the others. I'm going to find Cyrus.' April rushed out of the hut with Izzy to take Kevin. 'Stay out of sight,' Zion added.

'I can still help,' Kevin protested, but Zion stopped him.

'You've already saved our lives once today. I don't need you getting yourself killed to do it a second time.'

Kevin nodded in agreement. After the sure concussion he'd received from the car crash, and now a busted ankle, he wouldn't last long in another mech encounter.

'Just be careful, buddy,' he replied. The two shared a fist bump, before Zion rushed back into the open and toward the wall that exposed part of the courtyard.

'Don't worry, I'll watch his back,' Jennifer called back as she ran after him.

It had taken a while for them to escort Kevin to the hut, giving the mech enough time to recover from the malfunction. It got back to its feet and, after spotting Zion and Jennifer running toward the wall, took off once more in their direction. The pair could hear its stomping drawing near and ran as fast as their legs could carry them. If they could make it to the wall before it reached them they might have a chance of escaping. They were close now, and they were starting to believe they would make it.

Moments before reaching the gap where the wall had collapsed, another panther emerged from it, its giant metallic frame just a few feet from the pair. Its jaws opened wide as it climbed down the pile of rubble towards them. The hope quickly faded, and now they found themselves being charged at from both sides.

The pair stopped running and took stock of their options, which were quickly discovered to be zero. The panther by the wall would reach them quickly, and the one following behind would surely ravage whichever of them got away from the first.

But the panther didn't attack. Instead it leaped over them, the pair ducking as the robotic beast hurdled them. The mech then charged right into the pursuing panther behind them, and they watched in awe as the two mechs collided and began to fight. It suddenly dawned on them that it must have been Cyrus's mech, meaning he must still be alive. With that thought they climbed up the rubble with renewed vigour and entered the courtyard.

**

Cyrus was forced to come in and out of the void on multiple occasions as he struggled to evade the attacks of the onrushing mechs. Despite having the element of surprise in the beginning, The Jackal clearly had the upper hand now. His experience of using the power of the crystal was telling, and Cyrus was severely lacking in this regard.

'Give it up, boy!' The Jackal's voice ran through Cyrus like a freight train. This was another new experience; it seemed The Jackal could communicate with him through the void. His voice was different in this space, much harsher, almost demonic. It was the kind of voice Cyrus imagined The Jackal to have before he met him. It fit the name, and the persona depicted in Isaac's vision much more closely. Cyrus wondered if this was the result of the crystal. The power of the crystal had consumed The Jackal, twisting him into the snarling, sinister fiend that Cyrus could hear now through the void, almost as if he was in his head.

'You can't win, I'm too powerful,' the voice came again. 'You don't know the true power of the crystal. You are a fool to challenge me!'

Cyrus ignored The Jackal's words and concentrated hard on the mechs around him. He had just managed to get Zion and Jennifer to safety while simultaneously holding off mechs from himself. The multitasking was becoming a little easier, but it was wearing down his energy. He hoped that his companions would be able to distract The Jackal long enough to create an opening for him.

**

Gabriel and the rest of the group inside the courtyard had successfully escaped, and were now fleeing down a corridor inside the building. After Cyrus launched his surprise attack on The Jackal, Gabriel didn't need a second invitation to snap into action. His first priority was getting everyone safely out of the courtyard, away from the guards and mechs. The guards on top of the wall surrounding the courtyard had been too preoccupied with the mechs to worry about their escaping prisoners, and they were able to get away largely unnoticed. Gabriel had lunged at the nearest guard right from the off, knocking him over with brute force, while Jane and Rowley led Mia and Isaac away from danger. All of them still had their hands bound behind their back as they ran, stumbling over at points but eventually making it to the other side of the courtyard.

After knocking over the guard, Gabriel had seen the glint of metal on the floor next to him. It was the knife the guard had used to free Cyrus from his bonds. When the mech blasted the second guard dead, Gabriel hadn't given this one any chance to retaliate. His bear-like frame barrelling into him had sent him hurtling to the ground and the knife flew from his hands. Gabriel found it a mere foot from where he'd landed, and set about turning his body so his still bound hands could reach it. It took just seconds for him to work away at the rope that tied his hands together, until the last thin thread snapped and he was free. He kicked the guard once for good measure on his way out of there, taking the knife with him as he dodged in and out of the suddenly animated mechs.

Now the whole gang were free from their bonds and running for their lives down corridors leading who knows where. Priority number one had been achieved, they were all in one piece for now.

'Where are we going?' Rowley called from the back of the group. 'Cyrus needs our help!'

Gunshots rang out behind them and a plasma round seared the wall as they ran past. The group looked back the way they'd come to find a number of guards in pursuit. It seems they hadn't got away completely unnoticed after all.

'Cyrus needs to hold on for a bit longer, we've got company,' Jane replied as they rounded a corner.

Moments later another shot fired as the guards turned the corner after them. Rowley let out a yelp as the plasma round scorched the wall next to him, missing its mark narrowly.

'Keep moving,' Gabriel barked, leading them one way and then another. Sunlight was streaming into the corridor from the left side the whole way around, and they realised they must have been circling the grand building. If the guards were smart they'd have sent more the other way around to trap them. Through slits in the walls and the odd window they could see flashes of the battle raging in the courtyard, but not enough to see how it was developing. It was still going at any rate, which was enough to reassure them that Cyrus was OK.

A loud boom caused the ceiling to shake and crack. It began to open up and cave in ahead of them, so Gabriel led them into an alcove to their right. They packed themselves into it tightly so as not to be seen by the pursuing guards. They could hear shouting coming from down the corridor and soon the guards were there, looking and commenting on the pile of rubble that was once part of the corridor. The sunlight shone through from the sky, illuminating the place.

'Must have been one of those big mechs,' one of them said.

A woman's voice came next. 'The prisoners must have got through before the ceiling caved in. Climb over the rubble and get after them.' She then gestured to two of the guards behind her. 'You two, go back the way we came and flush them back this way.' The group could then hear footsteps scurrying away, getting fainter and fainter.

The female guard, along with her other two male companions, approached the rubble. But before they started to climb over something caught her attention in the corner of her eye. Before they had time to react Gabriel appeared from the alcove, towering above them like a yeti. Wielding the knife he'd taken from the guard in the courtyard, he lunged at one man, driving the blade into his hand and forcing him to drop his gun. The other guards reacted fast, bringing their guns up to retaliate. In the nick of time, Gabriel turned his guard around, using him as a human shield. The searing hot blasts from the weapons plunged into the man's chest. He was killed instantly, and the two guards paused in shock just long enough for the others to spring out of the alcove and overwhelm them.

Moments later they were stripping the unconscious guards of their weapons and anything else useful they could find in their pockets.

'Anything we can use?' Mia asked.

'No, just their guns,' Jane replied. 'Not even a spare cigarette going.' She exhaled deeply, failing to hide her disappointment. 'I know they have a stash somewhere, I could smell it on them.'

'Just as well,' Mia replied. 'Those things will kill you.'

In that moment, they could hear the voices of the guards coming close on the other side of the pile of rubble. Gabriel handed Mia a rifle. 'You get going. I'll buy you some time to get to Cyrus. He's still out there on his own, and we don't need more of The Jackal's thugs on our tail.

Mia ushered the rest of the group back down the corridor the way they came. As she started off, she did a mental headcount of her companions. There was one missing.

Where's Rowley?

Gabriel stayed behind, proton pistol in hand, awaiting the guards on the other side of the rubble. The voices came again, but he heard them head in a different direction. It sounded like they were climbing stairs. He assumed they must have been moving to higher ground to get a better vantage point, and he turned to follow his companions.

As he turned, something struck him on his back. Something hard and heavy, almost brick-like. Before he could turn back around, two giant arms wrapped around his neck, holding him in a chokehold. Gabriel's eyes went wide at the sudden attack, his pistol falling to the floor as his hands flailed around his head, trying to get hold of his assailant. It was the hulking brute that had escorted them to The Jackal; he recognised the foul smell of his breath.

As the man squeezed on his windpipe, Gabriel took desperate measures and tried something new. Fortunately the man had grappled him at the half turn, meaning Gabriel was now facing the wall. He was in close enough proximity to plant his feet up on it, and with one kick he pushed himself backwards, the weight of his own bear-like frame sending them both onto their backs.

Momentarily surprised by the move, the brute lost his grip on Gabriel's neck, giving him enough time to wriggle away. Coughing and spluttering and rubbing his throat in an attempt to catch his breath again, Gabriel brought himself up onto his feet. As he turned to face the brute, he was met with a fist that caught his cheek hard. Blood shot out of his mouth like a slow motion action shot of a boxer taking a sucker punch. He recoiled and was barely ready to defend himself for the next punch which came quickly after the first. The brute had got back to his feet surprisingly fast and was now unleashing a barrage of blows on him.

'I've been waiting for a chance to take a swing at you,' the man grunted.

Gabriel kept his fists up to block the onslaught. His guard was still at half-strength and another strong punch met its mark, almost knocking him off his feet. It was a rare occasion that Gabriel found himself on the losing side of a fistfight, but he knew that if he remained patient he would get a chance to fight back.

That chance came soon after, when the brute, confident of his dominance in this battle, let his guard down as he wound up a heavy uppercut. Gabriel quickly countered with a kick, planting the sole of his boot into the man's knee. It set the man off balance, and he cried out at the sudden pain.

'You and me both,' he retorted, before followed up with two lightning fast jabs to the nose. He wound up an uppercut of his own to finish the job, but before he could land it the brute blocked with his arm. The two exchanged a number of hits and blocks as they struggled against each other's sheer strength and determination.

'I'll make you suffer, and then I'll take your women as my prize,' the brute said, catching Gabriel's fist and countering with his own punch.

The words had the desired effect, and the anger on Gabriel's face showed it. He thought about the way the brute had treated the poor innocent people in this place, and of The Jackal and everything he'd done to the people of Novasburgh. The anger built up into a fury, which gave him enough strength to overpower the brute. He knocked the man's arms clear of his chest and rushed at him like a wild beast, head down. He tackled him with his shoulder, lifting the man up slightly off the ground as his momentum carried them towards the pile of rubble. The two went crashing into it, and the man was winded as his back fell onto the jagged surface.

The man coughed and wheezed as Gabriel climbed off him. He wiped the blood from his mouth and looked at the brute.

'That one was for my friends.' He then picked up the proton pistol and pointed it at the man's head. 'And this one's for me.' The pistol kicked back in his hand as the shot rang out.

**

The glints of light shining through the slits in the stone wall came and went, almost like strobe lighting as Rowley flew back down the corridor. He turned his head to the right as he neared a small window. As he passed he was able to make out Cyrus among the multitude of mechs clashing and firing on each other. It was absolute chaos, yet somehow the golems standing back to back, with Cyrus in the middle had managed to fend off The Jackal's onslaught.

He was armed with a proton pistol he'd nabbed from the belt of the unsuspecting guard he'd leaped on, moments before he charged back down the corridor and toward the doorway leading back out to the courtyard. The great wooden door was open just a crack, probably the result of the pursuing guards not wanting to encourage any mech to follow them inside, yet not having time to fully close it. Rowley reached for the handle and pulled, just before something hit him hard in the stomach, forcing him backwards. Another whack, this time to the back, sent him hurtling to the floor. He moaned and coughed, winded from the first blow as he looked up at the man standing over him.

'Not bad for an old man,' Nathaniel smirked, and he hit Rowley again with his crutch, stabbing it down onto his stomach once more. 'That's for leaving me for dead.'

'It wasn't like that,' Rowley protested, his voice straining through the pain.

'Whatever you say,' Nathaniel reached down and took the gun from beside Rowley, who was still clinging onto his stomach with both hands, struggling to get his breath back. Nathaniel looked at the weapon in his hands. 'You know, I haven't held one of these in a very long time. Since I had my other leg, actually. Funny thing about cripples, people think they're useless. You never let me carry a gun in your little colony. Why was that?' he cocked an eyebrow at Rowley, who was looked right back at him with fear in his eyes. 'Didn't you trust me?' Nathaniel asked, his face contorting into a grimace. 'Not so useless now, am I?'

He brought the gun down to Rowley's head, the barrel gaping. Rowley could see nothing but the dark steel crevice inside, waiting for the blinding flash as the shot was fired. He didn't close his eyes, but kept waiting, paralysed with fear.

'I never did like you,' Nathaniel said, shifting his weight on his crutch, before closing one eye as he aimed.

The heavy wooden doors to the courtyard were suddenly smashed open as a panther came bursting through. The gun in Nathaniel's hands flashed as it went off, his aim skewed by the mech as the metallic beast rammed into him, sending him flying against the far wall. The panther lay on the floor a brief moment, seemingly stunned as Rowley stared in shock from just a couple of feet away.

Moments later a second panther burst through the opening that was left where the double doors should have been. The wooden frames lay on the ground, having completely come off their hinges at the impact of the first panther falling through. It lunged at the panther before it could pick itself up, pinning it down. Rowley dragged himself backwards along the floor to get away from the brawl. How he was still alive was a mystery to him.

Footsteps echoed down the hall behind him and he turned to see Mia running his way, rifle in her hands. She reached him and helped him to his feet as they backed away from the panthers. She gasped at the sight of Nathaniel's limp body on the floor by the fall wall. His crutch had been left on the ground where he stood moments before, the force of the blow from the mech knocking him clean through the air, where he slammed against the hard wall. He was dead before his body reached the ground.

The second panther bit hard into the neck of the first, holding it down. It was looking right at the group, as though it was trying to tell them something. The first panther struggled underneath it, trying to force its way out with jerking motions and an ear-piercing screech.

'What's it doing?' Rowley asked, as the others joined them in the corridor, all staring at the scene in front of them.

'It's Cyrus!' Mia exclaimed. 'He wants us to help him.'

'How can you be sure that's Cyrus, and not The Jackal?' asked Rowley.

'Look,' Mia said, and without warning pushed the stock of her rifle to her shoulder and fired a plasma round right into the first panther's face, causing it to malfunction. The second panther let go of its prey, took another look at the group and then dashed back out the opening into the courtyard.

'That was too close,' Rowley breathed. 'Nice going, by the way.' He smiled at Mia.

'Well it's a lot easier when your gun doesn't backfire,' she said, the look of relief evident as she brushed a strand of hair from her face.

The group raced past the mech that was convulsing on the ground, and headed out into the courtyard. The light streamed in and they felt the hot sun hit them like a wave as they witnessed the battle raging on outside. A panther was charging at Cyrus, but was quickly taken down by the golems protecting him. Another attacked from a different side, but was intercepted by the lunge of Cyrus's panther, the two colliding, halting the first's progress.

'How can we help him?' Mia asked, assessing the limited options around them.

'We're dead if we take those things head on,' Gabriel replied. 'Let's try and create a distraction for him.'

CHAPTER FORTY

Jennifer picked off a man standing on the edge of the wall, who had been firing down at the melee in the courtyard. Plasma rounds peppered the golem standing between him and Cyrus, but the shots ricocheted off its metallic body. Jennifer and Zion had found a way up to the top of the wall through the rubble, and were making their way around its perimeter. The man Jennifer shot fell from the wall as the round hit his shoulder, and he tumbled a full thirty feet before hitting the dusty ground.

Jennifer wasn't the only one to have killed another human being for the first time today. With the exception of Gabriel and Isaac, none of the group had been in combat before, let alone thought about taking another person's life. The moment Jennifer realised she'd killed the man, the second one today, as the blast from her rifle sent him hurtling off the wall, a tight knot formed in her stomach. It was only the urgency of the situation and the adrenaline rushing through her that kept her from throwing up. She tried to make peace with herself with the knowledge that, like the first, the man had been trying to take the life of her friend, and she was merely protecting them.

Looking over the edge of the wall, she could see the man's body lying in a crumpled heap below, as the mechs clashed nearby. She saw Zion take another guard by surprise, who had been busy trying to get a clear shot at Cyrus. Approaching from his blindside, Zion threw his weight into the back of the man, knocking the rifle out of his hands. Jennifer didn't see what happened next as something else caught her eye.

A group of people were emerging from the doorway that one of the panthers had thrown the other through moments earlier. A huge wave of relief washed over her as she recognised who they were. She shouted down to them to make them aware of her presence.

'Look, it's Jennifer,' Mia pointed. She waved up to her, before the sudden cry of someone immediately above them distracted her. There was an audible thud sound as the noise stopped, and Zion appeared at the top of the wall right above them.

'We're sitting ducks out here. What's the plan?' said Rowley.

'Jennifer and Zion seem to be doing a good job of keeping those snipers busy,' Gabriel replied. 'The Jackal's had the upper hand because Cyrus has had multiple attacks to fend off. Let's give him something else to think about.'

'And how do we do that?'

'We need to get around those mechs to get a clean shot.'

'Impossible,' Isaac interjected. 'There's no way except through them, and that's suicide.'

'Well we need to try something,' Mia said impatiently. Watching Cyrus out there with all those mechs coming at him from different angles was heart-breaking. She was pumped up and raring to go.

Gabriel assessed his options. There was no obvious way up onto the wall, so there was only one way of getting close to The Jackal that didn't involve going back through the corridor they just came from. That would take much longer, but at least it was safer.

A screeching sound emanated from the doorway, and the panther that had been stunned by Mia's shot had now reanimated. It stormed out into the courtyard, blocking their path back inside. Gabriel cursed and made his decision.

He called up to Zion and Jennifer. 'Give us some covering fire. We're going through.'

They didn't need telling twice. Zion sprung into action, immediately racing off towards Jennifer to get a better vantage point overlooking the courtyard. The rest of the group formed into a tight bundle, Gabriel at the front and Mia at the rear. She watched the progress of the panther behind as they rushed through the melee of mechs ahead of them.

'It's charging right for us,' she informed the rest of the group, just as a loud boom erupted and the ground in front of the onrushing panther was blown to rubble, creating a crater that the panther stumbled into.

Gabriel led the team forward, stopping them suddenly as another panther rushed past, and leading them through the clearest path around the mess of robotic friend and foe that was quickly surrounding them. He instinctively ducked as a golem fired a shot in his direction, but realised soon after that it was meant for another mech behind them.

The whole time, Cyrus stood still between the two golems protecting him. His focus was well and truly cemented in the void as he used all his energy to deflect attack after attack. He was tiring and his concentration was breaking through the exhaustion. A golem took down one of his panthers, and a shot fired from one of The Jackal's gargantuans hit a cluster of his mechs simultaneously, allowing several panthers to break through his guard and come right for him.

Gabriel and the rest of the group pushed forward, but they got separated when a golem scooped up Mia on its way past. She kicked out at the mech but it was no use. It had her leant over its gun arm, the other arm pinning her close to it. She screamed out, causing Cyrus to lose focus for a second longer and for a brief moment he was dumped out of the void and into his human body. He saw Mia being carried toward The Jackal by the golem and concentrated hard, clutching his crystal ever so tightly as he launched himself back into the eyes of a nearby panther. Before he could race after the golem, another panther halted his progress, knocking his off balance. Through the eyes of the mech, which lay helpless on its side in the dirt, he watched the golem drop Mia by the feet of The Jackal, who subsequently reanimated in human form.

'It's over, Cyrus,' he said jovially. 'Oh what a pity.' He looked down at Mia, who lay on her back, staring into the jaws of a panther who had been frozen in place above her, the force of its metal paw pressing down on her enough to keep her pinned. 'You thought for a moment that you and your friends would beat me, didn't you? How foolish.'

Everyone was stunned, unsure of what to do. Gabriel made a quick decision to take aim at The Jackal from ten feet away, but The Jackal was quick to react.

'I wouldn't do that,' he said, grabbing the crystal around his neck, before tutting loudly. Gabriel had barely managed to get his gun up high enough to aim. 'Be a good boy and put your gun down,' The Jackal said. 'Or she dies.'

Everybody did so, throwing their guns to the floor with a clatter. The Jackal looked up to the roof, where his remaining guards had Zion and Jennifer at gunpoint.

'Now, that's better,' The Jackal grimaced. He clutched the crystal and thrust himself into the void, knowing that Cyrus was still there. The demonic voice that consumed him in this state spoke to Cyrus, the words bitter and piercing. 'Now I'll kill you all, starting with her.'

The panther above Mia reanimated, and screeched loudly in her face. She screamed, knowing full well what was to come next. Just as the panther was about to drive its jaws down onto her, something caught its eye. A flicker of movement made it stop and look up. Rowley was rushing right for The Jackal's human body at full speed. He was unarmed, but gaining ground and closing in on him quickly. The Jackal didn't have time to bring a mech around to protect him, and pushed himself out of the void to deal with it himself. On re-entering his human state he turned his head just in time to see Rowley coming for him a few yards away. With a sly grin, he reached behind him and drew a small blade from his back pocket. Rowley was screaming at him as he lunged, connecting with The Jackal just as he thrust the blade up and into Rowley's chest. Rowley's face went white and his eyes wide at the sudden, unexpected pain. He fell to the ground, revealing the bloodied blade still in The Jackal's hands.

Cyrus felt a searing heat rush through him as he watched his friend fall. Now back in his human body, he fell to his knees and cried out. 'NOOOOO!'

Rowley coughed and spluttered on the floor, wheezing as he struggled for breath. His face was contorted in pain. More pain than he had ever known. Cyrus could see the fear in his eyes as Rowley locked eyes with him. In that moment they both knew that this was the end. Rowley had always been the most faithful friend, and never asked for anything in return. And now he was going to die. It was unjust, unfair. He didn't deserve this. He was one of the good guys.

The Jackal sneered at Rowley. 'You stupid idiot. You thought you could outsmart me? Tell me, was it worth throwing your life away?'

Rowley's eyes were still fixed on Cyrus's, and for a moment Cyrus thought he could see the twinge of a smile begin to etch across his face. Rowley stretched out his hand and opened his fist. In it was the glistening white shape of a crystal. Cyrus suddenly noticed that it was the same crystal that was now missing from The Jackal's gold necklace.

The Jackal looked at the jewel in Rowley's hand with a look of pure confusion. He then reached down at his chest and clutched at nothing but gold chain. Looking down at the necklace, he realised his mistake, and his face quickly turned from confusion to panic.

'If it rids the world of your tyranny, yes,' Rowley replied finally, smiling fully through the pain. 'Not so stupid now, am I, asshole?'

The realisation of what had just happened was quickly setting in, and Cyrus wasted no time in acting. He took one last look at his best friend, before plunging himself into the void once more and into the eyes of a nearby panther.

Cyrus's panther snarled at The Jackal as it slowly approached the now helpless man before it. He shuddered at the sight of it and looked uneasy; a far cry from the overconfident king that had addressed Cyrus as a slave less than an hour ago. Cyrus thought it fitting that The Jackal be given a dose of his own medicine, and be faced with the very fear that he had unleashed on the city for so long.

The panther knocked him to the ground and stood over his quivering body, its metallic jaws wide as it screeched in his face. Cyrus could feel the power of the crystal taking over him. It was beckoning him to end it, to tear The Jackal's throat out and exert his dominance once and for all. It would be so easy, and with one move it could all be over and he could become invincible.

Cyrus stuttered and hesitated as he struggled against the crystal. He was suddenly aware that he had no idea if those were his thoughts, or those planted into his mind by the crystal itself. He watched the cowering man in front of him, and realised he was seeing the world from The Jackal's eyes for the first time. He was in danger of slipping beyond control, just as The Jackal had done. Cyrus froze the mech as he pulled himself from the void.

'You deserve to die,' he said. 'You're a murderer, a kidnapper, and you doomed an entire city for your own enjoyment. I know you poisoned the river, at the point it separates.' He remembered the conversation between the guards earlier, about fetching water from the river. He knew it sounded strange. The river in the city had been contaminated for some time, yet the guards here could take water from it to drink. Before the battle had commenced, he had realised what The Jackal had done.

'I'm not like you,' he shouted at The Jackal. 'You're a monster, and I'm not becoming that.' He rushed over to Rowley to try and aid him.

The Jackal laughed hysterically, relieved that he was still alive. 'Your grace is your downfall, Cyrus.' With that, he pulled himself to his feet and raced towards Mia, the bloodied blade he had used on Rowley still in his hands.

Cyrus reacted quickly, clutching his crystal and animating the mech that had been stood over him moments before. The panther turned to its side and lunged for The Jackal with its head. It grasped him firmly with its jaws, lifting him into the air and stopping his progress. His neck broke instantly, and

The Jackal's body fell limp, the bloodied knife in his hand dropping to the ground with a clatter.

Silence fell around the courtyard as the chilling moment sunk in. It had all happened so quickly and Cyrus hadn't had time to think, only act. The Jackal was insane, a man so consumed by the power of the crystal that he had lost his mind completely. The set-up of this village and his thirst for blood had confirmed that. He was hell bent on being the most powerful man around, and saw everyone as a potential threat to that, not least Cyrus.

As brutal and final an ending as it was, it was the only way to stop him. Cyrus hated violence, and the idea of killing another human being made him sick inside. But there was no reasoning with this man, no other way they could get him to stop the wicked things he was doing to mankind. In that moment, it was either him or Mia, and Cyrus acted to save the innocent woman he loved.

The clattering sound of weapons being dropped to the floor broke the silence. Jennifer and Zion turned around to find the guards that had been holding them at gunpoint now unarmed, standing there with panicked looks on their faces. They too had watched in shock as the events unfolded before them. They saw their leader turn from merciless killer to quivering coward, and back to merciless killer again in the space of seconds. It was as though the breaking of the crystal from the chain around his neck broke the spell he had over them. They suddenly saw their leader for what he really was. Looking down at their weapons they realised what a horrible mistake they had made.

Releasing himself from the pull of the void, Cyrus re-entered his human body and rushed to Rowley.

His friend lay on the floor, coughing and spluttering. Gabriel propped up his head as it rested on him. The dark red patch of blood covered his chest confirmed their worst fears.

'I'm—' Rowley coughed, struggling for breath. 'I'm not going to—'

'Don't say that,' Cyrus cut in, knowing what he would say next. 'You're going to make it just fine.' He said the words with meaning, as though trying to convince himself as much as his friend. 'We'll get you patched up, buddy.'

Jennifer had made it to the group and was now by Cyrus's side, tears streaming down her cheek.

'You silly fool,' she said. 'Look what you did.' Her expression suddenly softened. 'You saved us. You saved everyone.' She grasped his hand and felt him gently squeeze back.

'I did, didn't I,' Rowley smiled.

Cyrus looked at his friend, smiling in the face of death. It was incredible the strength he had. As he gazed upon those innocent and welcoming eyes he remembered their lives together, as though his pupils were a portal to the past. He remembered the moment they met, the silly games they played as kids, the times they'd saved each other's lives; or rather Rowley had saved his. Rowley had been the ultimate friend; giving everything and never asking for anything in return. And now he was dying, and there was nothing Cyrus could do to stop it. He wished more than anything that he could reverse time, do it all again and switch places with him. An overwhelming sadness poured over him as he watched the life slowly fade from the best friend he had ever known. All the while he watched that gleeful, childlike smile and that spark in his eyes, remaining right until the end.

'You're a hero, Rowley,' he whispered through the tears, as he watched him slip away.

CHAPTER FORTY ONE

Just before dawn the next morning, Mia walked along the dusty plains towards the hillside. Tyre tracks marked the steep gradient where the reckless Kevin had driven the pickup truck into the farmland and kick-started the fight for freedom. She looked to her side at the broken truck, and the lifeless body of the guard slumped over the hood. After The Jackal had died, it was like a spell was broken. The rest of the guards ran away, and the group had let them, on the condition that they never saw them again.

Through the darkness she saw a figure sitting on top of the hill, their legs dangling over the face of the small cliff as they looked to the horizon. She climbed up and minutes later found herself sitting alongside him. She nuzzled into his shoulder and felt his comforting arm close in around her.

'What are you looking at?' she asked.

'It's Rowley's old baseball card,' Cyrus replied. 'I still had it in my pocket. I hadn't had time to return it to him.'

The sun broke from the horizon, sparking an orangey yellow light that slowly flooded the plains below. The pair watched intently for a few moments as the sunrise enveloped the landscape, starting the new day. The first day without Rowley.

'I found his backpack in the truck,' said Cyrus. 'His notebook was inside. The one he was too afraid to show me because he was worried I'd laugh and make fun.'

Mia squeezed his arm reassuringly. 'Don't blame yourself for anything. Rowley knew you respected him.'

Cyrus forced a brief flicker of a smile. 'I really hope so.'

'What was in it?'

Cyrus opened the notepad and a pen dropped out from the last entry Rowley had written.

'It's an account of everything that happened after we moved to the shopping mall. Rowley was documenting what life was like.'

'Like a diary?'

'No, a journal,' Cyrus corrected. 'It's different.' He flicked through the pages and stopped on a collection of drawings.

'Wow,' Mia said. 'I didn't know he was such a good artist.'

'He usually drew pictures of robots, and, you know, nerdy stuff. Nothing like this.' Cyrus tilted the notepad into the growing sunlight as he held it out for Mia to see more clearly. 'Look at the annotations. He was drawing what he thought the world would look like after life went back to normal.'

'Do you think that's what it would look like?' Mia asked, admiring the shapes of the buildings. 'It's very green.' She pointed to the park full of trees, shaded in the light grey scratch of the pen.

'Yeah, I don't think that would fit in here,' Cyrus remarked, studying the desert-like plains around them. 'He must have been thinking about some other place when he drew that.'

'Woodside, maybe,' Mia offered.

'What do you think the rest of the country is like? Do you think there could be other colonies in the same position as us?'

'I doubt very much there are more people like The Jackal.'

'How do you know?'

'I don't,' Mia replied. 'I just hope that's the case.'

'It's so odd,' said Cyrus. 'Since the war ended, we haven't heard from a single other part of the country. It's like they just forgot about us.'

'Or maybe they have their own problems. They might not be able to contact us.'

'They'd send help.'

'Not if they couldn't.'

Cyrus sighed heavily and looked to the horizon once more. The sun was beginning its slow rise into the sky. Mia held his hand, her fingers interlocking with his.

'It's funny,' he said. 'I'm the one who's always daydreaming. But Rowley was the one with the real dreams.'

**

Rowley's ashes were scattered by the waterfall in Woodside. It was the most beautiful place Cyrus had ever been to, fitting of the final resting place of his best friend. There was a small ceremony where each of the group said a few words. They also said a few more words for Doug. With his final goodbye, Cyrus whispered a promise; a promise that Rowley's dream would come true, even if he wouldn't live to see it.

'Shine bright, buddy,' he whispered as he looked to the darkening sky. A wisp of cloud partially obscured his view of the moon, and the stars hadn't come out yet, but Cyrus held hope that somewhere out there Rowley would be looking down at him with a content smile.

Later that night he took a stroll through the woods. It had been days since the events at the village in the wilderness, and Cyrus was finally starting to fully appreciate the world around him again. The gentle trickling of the stream that undulated through the forest reflected the light from the bright moon above. The woods were a peaceful place to explore when you weren't being chased by one of your fellow man's most cruel creations. He felt thankful for finding his family again. Becoming reunited with his mother and sister was a bright spark of joy he clung onto in what was otherwise the worst day of his life. It was a bittersweet moment for him.

He had ventured deep into the woods to find a place to dispose of the crystals, somewhere nobody would find them. He thought about travelling to the coast and dumping them in the sea, but it would take him forever on foot. Mia had offered to go with him, but he assured her he'd be alright by himself; he'd only be gone a few minutes. As much as he craved her company, the task had given him an excuse to take a rare moment a solitude for himself. He would talk to himself as though he were talking to Rowley, up through the tall redwoods and into the sky, without feeling embarrassed.

Gabriel had tried brute force to break The Jackal's crystal into a thousand pieces, but no hammer or tool he could find in Kevin's basement could even mark the stone with a scratch. It was as hard as a diamond. So Cyrus decided the next best option would be to find somewhere to bury the crystals. Nobody would be needing them anymore.

Cyrus found himself back by the waterfall. He listened as the flow of water poured off the top, landing with a chorus of splashes in the pool below. As he stood close to the edge he could feel the cool spray against his face. Even in the cold of night the feeling was welcome and savoured. He followed the stream of water that trickled out of the pool, staying alongside it as it ran this way and that through the woods, growing wider and wider until it reached another pool half a mile away. He stumbled a couple of times as he struggled to see in the darkness. The LED torch Kevin had let him borrow was only getting him so far. The return journey to Kevin's house would be easy enough so long as he retraced his steps up the stream and remembered the way back from the waterfall.

Cyrus stood over the pool, taking note of the full frame of his reflection in the moonlight. He reached into the front pocket of his ripped cargo pants and retrieved The Jackal's crystal. It looked much duller once it had been stripped from its owner. Where once the crystal had shined a combination of colours, from blue to red to pure white, it was now a pale grey. Without a second thought, he tossed the crystal into the pool and watched it ripple the water with a plop, immediately lost into the darkness below.

For the first time since he could remember, he reached for the woven necklace around his neck and lifted it from his head. It was an act that felt strange for him; the only time he'd been separated from it was when The Jackal had taken it from him days ago. Now was the first time he had chosen to part with the one physical thing left that was connected to his father. The father that hadn't been around, but Cyrus had always known was there for him; thinking of him in every moment. This was his parting gift to him, and one that Cyrus was struggling to give up.

The crystal flashed brightly as he lifted it over his head, the woven necklace threaded through his fingers, the stone dangling playfully from it. It was as though it was calling to him, beckoning for him to reconsider.

It flashed again, a dark red colour this time. Cyrus's head throbbed suddenly as though a knife had been jabbed into his temple. There was evil in this crystal, a power that his father couldn't possibly have known was there. Cyrus hesitated. He was torn between the idea of giving up the last remaining link to his father in favour of ridding the world of the crystal's power, and ridding the world of the man he would become if he kept it. The truth was that nobody but Cyrus would be able to use the crystal, and thus the mech army it operated, but the longer the crystal was a part of him the more time it had to get inside his head. He didn't want to risk slipping into its grip the way The Jackal had done before him. Whilst Cyrus wasn't inherently evil, which couldn't be said about his nemesis, he could feel its hold on him, and the feeling of longing he had for it after using it. The more he slipped into the void, the more time the crystal had to taint his mind. It was a strong drug, and like most drugs it had dangerous side effects.

He placed the thread into his right palm, being careful not to clutch the bare crystal and send himself hurtling into the void once more. He leant back, lifting his knee and placing his weight onto his standing leg, just as a pitcher would. With a final lunge forward and a sharp exhale of breath, he thrust the crystal into the air and watched it soar into an arc over the pool, before the blackness of the water swallowed it up.

EPILOGUE

A cool breeze swept through the sticky summer air as the busy sounds of the city rang through Cyrus's ears. It was fifteen years in the making but New Novasburgh was finally feeling akin to the idealistic drawings that had been envisioned in Rowley's notebook. The war had devastated the country, but slowly humanity had managed to rebuild. Help eventually came, and little by little the city Cyrus had grown up with was reborn. After communications with the rest of the country had been restored, it was evident that they weren't the only city to be devastated by the war. They were however the only city to have been tormented by a twisted psychopath with a mech army. The mech project was made public and deemed a total disaster, and it was widely accepted that nothing of the sort would ever happen again. Cyrus and The Jackal were the last surviving mech handlers, and now Cyrus was the only one left.

The mechs were pulled apart for scrap metal years after the events at the village in the wilderness. The pull of the crystal and the idea of becoming the most powerful man around had not been enough to dissuade Cyrus from throwing away his crystal, and he had never looked back. Now fifteen years later the world seemed like a much better place.

The government reformed under new council, and Jennifer had been appointed a seat in office. She was given free rein to rebuild the city the way she saw fit, and unsurprisingly it closely resembled the drawings in Rowley's notebook.

Rowley's memory lived on, and the role he played in ridding the world of The Jackal was never forgotten. Cyrus found it fitting that the baseball field in the middle of the largest park in the city be named after him. The breeze blew through the trees as he headed through the park toward the field.

Dust and sandstorms frequently swept through the city, as it had always done, but they were finding new ways of lessening the impact when they hit. When rebuilding the city they took advice from architects in the Middle East who were used to this phenomenon, and the city felt much safer as a result. The storms were much weaker in the middle of the city now, and thus life could go on undisturbed day to day.

Cyrus walked towards the baseball field, passing the large trees with green leaves that had been brought from all kinds of places to be planted there. The place had become a little haven in this part of the country, just as Woodside had been. Cyrus imagined that in a parallel universe this was what someone like The Jackal might have wanted to create. In their universe it couldn't have been further from the truth.

As he sat in the bleachers he watched through aged eyes as the local kids' softball team pitched their first ball of the season. He cheered as his ten year old son stepped up to the plate, tapping it twice with the end of his bat; an involuntary habit that had been passed down from his father. The boy focused as the pitcher threw the ball, and the sweet sound of the bat connecting with it rang out, to more cheers.

A woman whooped with joy beside Cyrus as the boy hesitated for a moment, almost in shock, before composing himself and rushing to first base. Cyrus looked to his left at her, and even in the shade under the brim of her baseball cap, he could see that same beaming smile he'd loved since the moment he met her.

'He's getting better,' Mia said. 'He hit it this time.'

Cyrus laughed. 'Let's treat him to pizza and ice cream tonight. He's been working all week on his batting.'

A young girl, three years the boy's junior showed her appreciation for the suggestion.

'We're getting ice cream?' she asked.

Cyrus responded with a smile, picking up the cap that had fallen onto her lap and placing it back on her head.

'You betcha!' he exclaimed. 'But only if you keep your hat on. It's very warm out today.'

'OK,' the girl replied as she sat beaming in her seat. She was looking more and more like her mother every day.

**

Later that evening when the kids were tucked into bed, Mia stepped out onto the porch of their new family home in Woodside. Cyrus was sitting on a deck chair gazing up at the stars.

'They look beautiful tonight,' she remarked. Cyrus jolted, snapped out of his daydreaming and turned to face her.

'I could say the same about you,' he smiled. Mia's raw beauty seemed to be immortal; she hadn't aged a day since they first met. The same couldn't be said of himself, and he was starting to find grey hairs sprouting out of his head. Mia sat on his lap and wrapped her arms around his neck, kissing him softly on the cheek.

'Just to remind you, Gabriel's back from duty next weekend and I said we'd invite him round for dinner. Zion and Kevin will be there too.'

'Oh shoot, I forgot about that,' Cyrus said. 'Man, it will be good to see him again. I wonder how his first time back went.'

Gabriel had re-joined the military in the last year. Seemingly bored with menial labour jobs and working as an electric car mechanic, he had bit the bullet and gone back to the job he had once become disillusioned with. At least with the corrupt government gone, and the new reformed version working well, it gave him some motivation to reenlist.

Zion and Kevin had picked up where they left off, and ended up moving in together in Kevin's place. Gyro-3 was still rolling around and getting in the way, but they both enjoyed his company. Zion found love and got married a few years later, but they still lived in the same neighbourhood and saw each other every day.

'Don't forget to ask Kevin about his new girlfriend,' Mia said. 'He's very keen to show her off to everyone. I said they should come to the softball game next weekend.

'Good idea,' he replied. 'And April?'

'She's still in Rio with her fiancé. Cyrus, you really need to keep up with everyone. That's why we set up the group chat.'

Cyrus pulled out a small device from his pocket and saw the display flash up. Thirty three unread messages. Mia tutted and gave him a playful flick around the ear. He opened the latest message to see a photo of Cameron wearing a mortarboard and dark gown, with Caitlin and Aiden standing proudly at either side.

'Wow, they grow up so quick,' he said.

'Don't worry, I sent a graduation card to him,' said Mia.

Cyrus squeezed her arm. 'You're amazing.'

'I know,' she replied candidly.

Cyrus continued to scroll through the missed messages. Another photo of April and her boyfriend. April's bump was getting big, she must have been due any day now.

She'll make a great mom.

Scrolling further up he could see that Jane had shared some back and forth banter with Zion, who corrected 'ya'll' to 'you' every time she used it. She always took it in good humour. Last time he'd seen her, Cyrus remembered her talking about going back to school. She had mentioned a psychology program she was interested in.

'So,' Mia said, subtly bringing his attention away from the phone. 'You still wonder if there'll be commercial space travel in the future?'

Cyrus looked at the stars once more. It was something he'd dreamed of as a kid, and he and Rowley had always talked of the day they'd travel into space together. His eyes finally settled back onto Mia's. They twinkled in the soft moonlight, tingling with the pure and honest love she felt when she looked at him.

'Space travel can wait,' he replied. 'I've got my own world to worry about right now.'

Acknowledgements

Thank you for reading this novel, and I really hope you found it enjoyable. If you took a shine to any of the characters, found the journey they went on captivating, or if the action invoked tension and made your heart pump that bit faster until the scene was over, then the last two years spent writing this was totally worth it. Let me know who your favourite characters were too!

Feel free to write a review on Amazon, Goodreads or your book forum of choice, and please share the book with your friends. I love a good book recommendation, and if one day you were to recommend this to a friend I'll know I'll have truly made it.

I have so many people to thank, and there were so many of you who, knowingly or not, had a big impact on this book. Firstly to my family, thank you for all your support and encouragement, not only while I've been writing this, but over my whole life. It is because of the love and support you've given me that I had the confidence to even begin this.

To my colleagues, thanks for politely asking how the book's going every few weeks and for putting up with my same response to the question 'what did you get up to this weekend?' Hopefully I'll have some more interesting stories for you from now on.

To Kostas, I was honoured when you offered to design the cover art for the book, and I was blown away by how excited you were at the prospect of doing it. I hope you're proud of your work, you did an incredible job!

To my good friend Ruby, thanks for slogging your way through the first draft and giving me more constructive feedback than I could have ever hoped for. It makes me smile when you remind me that I should be proud of just finishing a book, no matter how well it does.

To my sister Hannah and my mum, Karen, thank you both for also slogging through the first draft and giving me such amazing feedback. Your attention to detail is phenomenal and it was amazing just how many typos alone you uncovered.

Lastly, and most importantly, thank you to my wonderful wife, Hollie. You have given up so much quality time together over the last couple of years while I shy away in the spare room tapping away on my keyboard. I am infinitely grateful for your patience, and you have no idea just how lucky I consider myself.

Printed in Great Britain
by Amazon